FORBIDDEN

Lisa Clark O'Neill

Copyright 2013

PROLOGUE

CAMP sucked.

That was the singular thought floating in twelve-year-old Tate Hennessey's head as she watched the empty Coke bottle spin on the cabin's plank floor. The tinted glass blurred, executing revolution after revolution, finally slowing to a drunken and uneasy rest.

Its open mouth pointed at her.

For one perilous moment the only sounds in the musty dark were the mechanical whirr of the ceiling fan and the rasp of her uneven breathing. Up to this point she'd been lucky, as for the past fifteen minutes of this dumb game no one had any reason to pay her any attention.

Looks like her luck had just run out.

"You know what that means, don't you Tate?"

The nasty, sing-song voice belonged to Lacy Chapman, a viciously perky blonde who'd already developed breasts. *Real* breasts, the kind that required an actual bra as opposed to one of those training jobs Tate's mother was always trying to push on her. Lacy's boobs apparently bypassed training entirely, heading straight to the Major Leagues. Rumor had it she'd let one of the boys from the other side of camp touch them. Tate wasn't sure if that was true, but she knew for a fact that Lacy was trouble. Her angelic looks belied a bully who liked nothing better than to make other people squirm.

And Tate was currently on the skewer.

Swallowing hard, she studiously avoided the five pairs of eyes which pinned her like an insect awaiting dissection. It was decision time, and she didn't much care for her choices. "Truth," she finally mumbled, not about to accept a dare. Since there were no boys around with whom to play spin-the-bottle the traditional way, they'd merged the two games to make it interesting.

"Okay." Lacy delighted in Tate's discomfort. She'd made it her mission over the past five days to make sure Tate was alternately ridiculed or excluded. The only reason she'd been invited to play the game tonight was that Lacy knew it would prove a goldmine of embarrassment potential. "What I want to know is… do you have a thing for Lifeguard John?"

Every bit of summer color drained from Tate's face as all eyes present snapped toward her. She'd been prepared to answer almost anything, but her mammoth crush on Lifeguard John – the hunky eighteen year old counselor – was her deepest, darkest secret. How had Lacy managed to figure it out?

Certain that she was stepping into a very carefully laid trap, Tate took the path of least resistance. She lied.

"N… No."

Several muffled giggles followed someone's curse of disbelief, causing Tate's green eyes to widen. If she'd said that word, right out loud, her mother would have cleaned her clock.

"Then how do you explain *this*?" Lacy held up the Polaroid of Lifeguard John that Tate had hidden in the bushes outside the counselors' cabin to take. Until that horrifying moment, it had been stashed beneath the mattress on her bunk.

"Give that back!" Tate lunged across the circle of snickering girls.

"Ah, ah, ah." Lacy's push sent Tate sprawling backwards onto her butt. A splinter lodged itself in the heel of her palm, but the sting of humiliation was more painful. "Would someone care to remind Tate what happens when you break the game rules?"

"She has to accept a dare," several voices rang out.

Lacy smiled as panic rearranged Tate's features. "And I know the perfect one for our little liar. Since Tate is the one who cost us the swimming trophy today, I *dare* her to go over to the boys' camp and get it back."

The ultimatum swung through the air like an executioner's axe. The best way to reach the boy's camp was by way of a walking trail through the forest.

The dark, creepy forest.

Not only was the dare cruel, it was also unfair. It really hadn't been her fault that they'd lost the competition. Beforehand, a boy named Timothy had told her stories about the monster of Lake Allatoona, and then swam underwater during the heat of the race to lay hold to her ankle. Panicking, Tate had floundered, causing Lifeguard John to dive to her rescue. But a little thing like the truth didn't matter to Lacy. Several girls snickered behind their fingers, and Tate knew she was sunk. It was either suck it up and walk through the dark, or spend the rest of her time here in misery.

Confronting the narrowed eyes staring back at her, Tate swallowed her rising fear. "No problem." But when she started toward her flashlight, Lacy's hand snaked around her ankle.

"No flashlight." Her tone was sweet, but her nails bit into Tate's skin. "If the boys see it, they might know that you're coming."

Jerking her ankle away from Lacy's grip, Tate stalked out the door.

Fluorescent light winked between the vents of the cinderblock bathhouse, but the shadowy path through the trees looked like the gaping maw of Hell. Shuddering, Tate picked her way a little deeper into the darkness, the ground mist swirling around her ankles reminding her of every monster movie she'd ever seen. Crickets sang their dirge to evening, woodland debris crackled beneath her sneakered feet, and something rustled in the underbrush beside the almost imperceptible path.

Tate jumped, a loud splash off to the right reminding her that the path followed the edge of the lake. Visions of the monster the scheming Timothy had tricked her with crowded her overactive imagination, but she valiantly told herself that there was nothing but fish in the lake.

Moonlight shimmered, giving the murky, brownish water an eerie glow, as fingers of that horror-movie mist stretched from the surface. Despite the "nothing but fish" chant running a continuous circuit in her head, she had no trouble believing that the lake was home to all manner of nasty creatures. Like the piranhas she'd seen on that TV movie. Or the Creature from the Black Lagoon.

Or Jason.

Oh. God. How could she have forgotten about Jason? She'd seen Friday the Thirteenth; she knew what happened to kids at summer camp. Any moment now, a hockey-masked, axe-wielding maniac was likely to break through the underbrush and do her in.

Frozen with the sudden onset of mindless fear, Tate sucked in tiny breaths of panic, until a sharp *crack* behind her propelled her willy-nilly down the moonlit path. Brambles scratched her bare legs, thorny vines tore at hair and clothing. But the blood trickling toward her socks seemed like no big deal compared to running for her life. Chest heaving with sobs, Tate broke through the trees, stumbling onto the pine straw at the edge of the clearing. She was cut, scraped, winded and terrified, but at least she was out of the darned woods.

Wait a minute.

She was *out* of the darned woods. A triumphant smile played across her tear-streaked face, but she put a little more distance between herself and the looming specter of the trees, just for good measure.

Creeping on silent feet toward the circle of the boys' cabins, Tate paused only to wipe the cold sweat that trickled into her eyes. The various trophies earned that day were kept on a special picnic table in the middle of the circle, and scanning the area for any sign of the enemy, Tate crept stealthily toward her quarry.

She grasped the coveted trophy – her own personal grail – until an unexpected noise coming from the direction of the boys' bathroom reminded her that she needed to clear out, quick. Being caught red-handed in the middle of the enemy camp would put quite a damper on the glow of success.

As she was creeping around the side of the building, the sound she'd heard began to distinguish itself into voices: one young, soft and worried, and a grown up voice, reassuring. She was almost sure that the younger voice belonged to the dreaded Timothy. She'd heard it in her ear enough that day to know. And though she couldn't be positive, she thought the older one belonged to the camp director, Mr. Logan. It seemed strange that he was up at this hour, in the bathroom with one of the campers. Maybe Timothy was sick.

Beside herself with curiosity, Tate couldn't stop herself from sneaking closer. But the voices inside had been replaced with other noises. Noises that made her uncomfortable.

Shivering, Tate felt the overwhelming urge to run away. But when she heard a quickly muffled cry, she peeked around the corner.

The swimming trophy slipped out of her hands as her scream rent the stillness of the night.

CHAPTER ONE

July 15, Present

JANIE Collier was hot, tired, and mad at the world.

Running away from home wasn't supposed to be so hard, but getting out of Charleston on foot in ninety degree heat proved to be more of an undertaking than she'd initially guessed. The asphalt was so hot that her sneakers sank into it, and about every fifth step one or the other of them threatened to come off. They were too damn big, anyway, because they were hand-me-downs from her sister.

Her stupid older sister who'd had to go and get herself knocked up.

Why the hell hadn't she listened when Daddy had told her that the Lawrence boy was no good? Hell, anybody with eyes could see Danny was only slumming when he'd asked her out. Her older sister had a body like one of them centerfolds Daddy was always looking at, and that's the only reason Danny Lawrence had shown the least bit of interest. Rich boys like him weren't in the habit of making girlfriends out of poor white trash. Danny didn't even come inside the trailer when he picked Joelle up. He just sat in his Mustang and beeped the horn, like he was too damn good to dirty his expensive sneakers by setting foot in their home.

And wouldn't you know it? Daddy's prophecy had come true.

Danny Lawrence had gotten in her sister's pants one time too many, but now that she was pregnant he was nowhere to be found. His parents had sent him off to visit some relative for the summer.

His daddy, a lawyer, had threatened to sue Janie and Joelle's daddy if he ever laid a finger on his boy. Since Janie and Joelle's daddy was a drunk, he hadn't had the good sense to listen: he'd attacked Mr. Lawrence at his high-falutin' home one night, demanding that Danny own up to his bastard.

Consequently, Danny had left the state, her daddy was in jail, and the child welfare people had been swarming over her and Joelle like flies.

Joelle, who was six months gone, was in a home for unwed mothers, and she – Janie – had just run away from her third foster home.

Not like those idiots were going to miss her. The wife had been okay, but her lard-ass husband looked at her in a way that made her feel like she'd come down with chiggers.

So she'd hightailed it out of there before Fat Hubby had decided to take those gropes-disguised-as-hugs to the next level. She was experienced enough to know exactly what the bastard wanted, and while she was no virgin, she preferred to choose her partners. Fat Hubby didn't make the list.

Janie shivered despite the heat.

Sweat trickled off the back of her neck, running down into her cotton panties, where little bumps of heat rash popped up like chicken skin. Looking at the road sign she'd just passed, Janie saw that she'd traveled approximately ten miles out of the city. At this rate, she'd turn fifteen before she made it to Florida.

Janie sighed, blowing out a breath that ruffled her sweat-damp bangs. She needed some shade, she needed some water, she needed somebody with *wheels.*

Coming upon a massive live oak, Janie dragged herself to the side of the road and sagged against the trunk. There was a fruit stand maybe a mile or two down the highway, and if she could just make it there she could buy herself an apple and a nice, cold drink out of the cooler. She'd love to have one of their cherry sodas, but she figured she'd better stick to water so she didn't get dehydrated. They'd studied that in health class last year, so she knew all about things like blood sugar and hydration. For the most part, school seemed like a huge waste of time, but she had to admit she liked learning about the body.

Maybe she'd go to college one day, become a nurse.

But first she had to get to Florida.

Janie pushed away from the tree and tried to convince her rubbery legs to move. She'd just about talked them into it when a car pulled alongside her. Warily, she looked it over – a dark-colored foreign job, one of those BMWs, she thought – as the man driving it lowered the window.

"Sugar you're not out here walking in this heat, are you?"

He looked to be about thirty, maybe a little older. She really wasn't the best judge of age. He was jacked and kind of handsome for an old guy, but that didn't mean she could trust him. After all, Danny Lawrence was handsome, and look what a crock of shit he turned out to be.

He turned in his seat to pull a soda bottle from a bag beside him, then extended it through the open window. "You look like you could use something cool to drink."

Janie hesitated, because she didn't know this guy from Adam. Just because he didn't look like a perv didn't mean he wasn't. She took in the expensive-looking watch on his wrist, the glint of gold on his ring finger.

He seemed okay, but still...

"Just take the soda, sugar. I promise I'm not going to bite." When she still didn't move, he held up his cell phone. "Is there somebody I can call to come pick you up? I bet your parents wouldn't be too happy about you walking down the highway all alone. I know I sure wouldn't."

"You have kids?" she asked, cautiously inching closer. He really did seem okay, and she was so thirsty.

"Just one," he admitted with a proud smile. "A little boy. And his mama would have my hide if she thought I passed you by without offering to help." He waved first the bottle, then the cell phone. "Would you like a drink, or would you like me to make a call?"

"There's no one to call." Janie accepted the beverage. "I'm on my way to visit my cousin in Florida, and I'm afraid if I call first, she won't let me come." Unscrewing the cap from the bottle, she upended and nearly drained it.

"Well Florida's a bit farther than I intended to go. But if you'd like, I can give you a ride down to Beaufort. Although if you ask me, I still think you should call your cousin."

"No." She shook her head, trying to decide what to do. She was hot and sweaty and exhausted, and the air conditioning seeping out his open window made her want to dive in. Hitching a ride to Beaufort might not be such a bad idea. Swaying a little, Janie thought the heat must really be getting to her, because when she looked down the deserted road the pavement seemed to move in waves.

Before she knew what was happening, the man was helping her into the backseat. "Easy, there. You look like you might be having a little trouble. Why don't you just lie down and rest, and I'll wake you when we get where we're going."

She was conscious of him tucking her feet into the car, tossing the small backpack she'd been carrying in beside her.

Then the door closed with a muffled thud, and she wasn't conscious of anything at all.

CHAPTER TWO

Two weeks later…

IT was just shy of eight a.m. when Clay Copeland arrived at his destination. The Isle of Palms was a little spit of beachfront off the Carolina coast, close enough to Charleston to be considered a kissing cousin. The island had been hit hard by Hurricane Hugo back in the late eighties, and with many of the original homes damaged beyond repair, the locals gathered up their insurance money and either rebuilt or cleared out. Consequently, McMansions had cropped up like so many mushrooms after a storm. Even after the housing bust, property values were at a premium, but Clay's good friend Justin Wellington had gotten a sweet deal because he happened to perform emergency gallbladder surgery on the little old lady who'd owned his home.

Clay parked his SUV beside Justin's classic 1940's pickup. The truck was all man, which made for an interesting contrast to the barren window boxes, shabby lace curtains and unruly flower beds on either side of the steps leading to the deep verandah. The lone rocking chair with its peeling paint was the punctuation on a sad, bachelor pad sentence. Chuckling to himself, Clay foresaw a long visit from Justin's mother coming up in the near future.

Having broken over the horizon a couple of hours ago, the sun now worked its watercolor beams through the tops of the palmettos and live oaks that shaded the small yard. Salt hung heavy in the air, and Clay sucked in a breath, savoring it like fine whiskey.

He'd grown up with the sea, and he'd missed it.

Not that his current home base of Quantico was totally landlocked, but as it stood he was only there half the month anyway. And even when he was there he was usually stuck inside, swimming in crime scene photos and autopsy reports instead of the surf.

Don't think like a federal agent.

The words his boss had uttered as he'd basically booted Clay's ass out the door were going to be Clay's own little incantation. This vacation was long overdue, and given the nightmares he still suffered after having his last case blow up in his face, Clay was forced to admit he needed the break. So for the next several days he was not Special Agent Clay Copeland, officer of the federal government. He was Clay Copeland, beach bum.

A worthy calling.

To that end, Clay locked his badge in the glove box of his 4Runner, tucking his gun and holster into the duffel bag that he dragged from the back seat. Eyes gritty from so many hours of staring at the road, he made his way down the oyster shell path toward what he presumed was the back door. Justin was a man of his word, and Clay found it unlocked.

Stepping quietly into the kitchen, Clay discovered it was pretty much more of what the house had offered from the front. At one time, a woman had lived here and left her mark.

Unfortunately, that mark was singularly ugly.

Taking in the lay of the land, Clay noted the slightly musty smell, the bumper crop of florals. He wandered into the living room, where the deep leather sofa, recliner and large screen plasma TV indicated the reassuring presence of a male.

Clay followed the open doorway off to the right in hopes that it led to a bed.

He encountered a linen closet, a room which housed some exercise equipment, a surprisingly updated bathroom – Justin had obviously gotten started on at least some of the home improvements – and a closed door which boasted a piece of paper attached to it with a strip of medical tape. A closer inspection revealed a scrawled message:

I'll eat the apple if you'll stay away.

It took Clay, in his sleep deprived state, a moment to make the connection. "An apple a day keeps the doctor away." He grinned, suppressing the urge to barge into Justin's room, just on principal. But he was too tired to mess with his friend. There'd be plenty of time for that later.

By process of elimination, Clay determined that the door which faced the opposite direction from Justin's must be the guest room. The wide plank floors had been refinished, the king bed attractively adorned with a simple blue quilt. Tasteful lamps topped washed pine nightstands, and white sailboats crossed a decorative pillow's calm sea.

Clearly, Mrs. Wellington had already paid a visit.

Exhausted, Clay tossed his bag in a chair, toed off his sneakers, and didn't even bother to pull the covers back before he collapsed on the bed.

The smell of coffee drew him from sleep like a penitent to a revival. From the level of daylight seeping through the wood blinds he guessed it was sometime around noon. A glance at his watch confirmed he'd slept for four and a half hours without moving.

And without dreaming of dead little boys.

Shaking off that thought along with sleep's vestiges, he swung his long legs over the edge of the bed. Despite the fact that he and caffeine had an uncertain relationship lately, he couldn't deny the allure. Seeing as this was now vacation coffee as opposed to work coffee, maybe he'd have better luck.

He shuffled toward the kitchen.

A skivvy-clad Justin was hovering over the coffee pot, dark head resting on the nearest cabinet. Clay thought of several cruel and immature ways to gain his attention, but hell, he was crashing at the man's house for the week, so common courtesy prevailed. "Hey," he drawled by way of greeting.

"Ah! Damn." Justin cracked his head against the cabinet before turning bleary gray eyes on his friend. "God, Clay, you scared the piss out of me. I didn't hear you come in."

"Obviously. Nice reflexes there, son. An efficient burglar could have waltzed in and out of here and you wouldn't have had a clue."

Justin's shrug was tired, or maybe just indifferent. "Other than the TV, I can't imagine what any self-respecting thief would want." Moving to take two chipped but functional mugs down from the cabinet, he proceeded to fill the first with coffee. "Aside from that, I'm six-three, one-ninety, and I grew up with four brothers. Self-defense wasn't a class in my house; it was how you survived until puberty."

Clay chuckled, accepting the steaming mug. He'd gone through Quantico with Justin's brother Jesse, so knew whereof the other man spoke. "You can rest assured that you won't be hearing any personal safety lectures from me this week." He took a sip of the rich dark brew while Justin poured his own. "I'm just here for sun, surf and loose women."

Justin grinned and motioned Clay toward the table, unconcerned about the fact that he was entertaining in his underwear. "I wish I could help you out there, but I've been pretty well out of circulation for the past… God." He scratched his head. "I don't even want to think about how long. My little black book probably has moths."

"Now that's just sad."

"Tell me about it." Justin took a bolstering sip of coffee. "What about you? I understand you've been pretty busy as well."

"An unfortunate guarantee that comes with the job." There never seemed to be a shortage of evil.

Despite all his talk, the pain of the past week was still fresh. As a member of the Bureau's Investigative Support Unit, he saw the very worst of human behavior, though for the most part, the victims he dealt with were beyond help. The best he could do was help overburdened law enforcement officials narrow in on the offender by understanding the behavior.

Until last week. When the suspect to which Clay helped lead Topeka officials took his own family hostage. Clay'd been thrown into the role of negotiator, and even as he'd tried to talk the desperate man down, the man turned the gun on his wife and his son.

A day hadn't gone by that Clay hadn't heard that little boy scream.

"I'm sorry about what happened," Justin said. "I know it's not easy."

"No, it's not." As a trauma surgeon, Justin had almost certainly learned that loss was an unavoidable part of his work. Funny that he, with all of his psychological training, was having such a hard time accepting that. "But anyway, that's the end of the shop talk. So what's on your agenda? I want to make sure to stay out of your way. Just direct me to the beach and a couple of restaurants and pretend I'm not here."

"Actually, barring an unforeseen emergency, I have the rest of the day off. We can slap a couple of sandwiches together, head to the beach if you want."

"Sounds good." Clay drained his coffee, felt the familiar kick. Things were starting to feel right with his world. "Let me grab my trunks, and I'll help you with the sandwiches."

After lunch they threw a couple of towels over their shoulders and waded through air thick and sweet as molasses. "God, I've missed this." Clay dropped down onto his towel, adjusting his shades as Justin stretched out beside him. Waves rolled in, a reassuring rhythm that dulled the senses and lulled the mind.

Casting his gaze down the crowded beach, Clay automatically noted the various activities going on around him. Numerous sandcastles were being alternately constructed or destroyed, a wicked Frisbee toss took center stage in the open area off to his left, and a large man in an inadvisably small swimsuit read a novel under cover of a striped umbrella. He tried not to survey the crowd in anything but the most casual manner, but given his occupation, his natural inclination was to look for signs of trouble or otherwise worrisome behavior. Those little unconscious quirks that gave people away.

Don't think like a federal agent.

As much as he disliked the notion of hearing voices, he didn't try to push his boss's advice out of his head. He wasn't here to profile the populace, or look for the socially deviant. He was Clay Copeland, beach bum, and he was here to have a good time.

He was perfectly content to just lie on his towel and do nothing. Maybe take a dip. There was nothing like fresh air and sunshine to…

"Joseph, Mary and all the saints."

Behind his sunglasses, Justin popped open one sleepy eye. "Problem?"

"None that I can see."

Justin leaned up on one elbow to follow the direction of Clay's gaze. "Nice," he agreed after a moment's observation.

The woman's black hair formed an artless jumble atop her head, putting the curve of neck and shoulders on tantalizing display. Shapely legs ran up to… well, damn near to her earlobes. And her elegant hands smoothed sunscreen over skin delicate as fresh cream. He could only wonder if the front view was as impressive as the back.

Both his and Justin's indrawn breaths when she turned seemed to lay that question to rest.

"She just undid the straps to her top," Clay felt the need to point out. Of course, unless Justin had recently gone blind, he'd already picked that up.

"Very nice," Justin amended his earlier observation. "Though with skin like that she should probably consider wearing a swimsuit with better coverage."

Clay turned, very slowly, to look at his friend with disbelief.

Justin blinked. "I can't believe that just came out of my mouth. I've been spending *way* too much time in the OR."

Clay's shoulders heaved with amusement. "We need to find you a woman, son, before you forget how to get one horizontal without the benefit of sedation."

Justin looked toward the woman in the yellow bikini, but was very abruptly cut off.

"Don't even think about it." Clay's words weren't harsh, but there was an edge to them all the same. He liked Justin, and he wouldn't want to have to hurt him. "That one's mine. I feel for your situation, man, but I'm not stupid."

Adjusting his sunglasses, he heaved himself off his towel.

TATE Hennessey rubbed sunscreen into her calves, wishing the faint dusting of freckles over her skin would just darken and run together. Better than looking like some kind of deep sea dweller that had just recently ventured out of its cave. She knew that baking herself on the beach like this was asking for trouble, but sometimes her milk maid coloring made her curse her Irish genes.

Loosening the thick ties to her bikini top, she stretched out on her stomach, wincing when something bit into her side. Reaching beneath the towel, she pulled out a small metal dump truck. "Max," she sighed, shaking her head as she pictured her imp of a five-year-old son. At least it hadn't been a Lego. She'd stepped on enough of those to have permanent nerve damage in her feet.

Not that she was complaining, Tate mused as she closed her eyes. Max was her world, even if being a single parent had its drawbacks. Sure, her family was always there for her, and bless them for it. But it just wasn't the same as having a mate to share the responsibility.

Someone to help her decide whether time-out or withholding privileges was the most effective strategy for dealing with tantrums. Someone to explain to Max why it really *is* important to aim his urine stream toward the toilet, instead of trying to write his name on the wall. Someone to whisper into her ear at night that she is raising a beautiful and well-adjusted child. Someone who would then whisper other things in her ear, and then rub…

"Oh!" The pressure on her back had Tate's eyes popping open. Either her always vivid imagination was really getting away from her, or there was a flesh and blood man with his hand on her back.

"What do you think you're doing?"

"You missed a spot."

The man's eyes were hidden behind dark shades, but the rest of him was clearly visible. From his short, streaky blond hair to his long, muscular legs. And just enough red tinting his broad shoulders to suggest that this was his first day at the beach. A tourist, she concluded. Looking to score.

And his hand was hovering dangerously close to her ass.

Whipping herself over, Tate swatted at the offending appendage. "Do I *look* that gullible, Mister …"

"Copeland." He smiled, to devastating effect. "Clay Copeland. And what you look like is a bad case of sunburn waiting to happen." Hoisting the bottle of sunscreen she'd tossed aside so recently, he waggled it around. "It's kind of tough to spread this stuff on your own back. I'd be happy to help you with it. With skin as beautiful as yours, I'd sure hate to see you get burned."

Tate could hear the gears of seduction working like a finely-tuned machine. Five years ago, she might have been impressed.

Come to think of it, five years ago she *had* been impressed, and that's how she'd ended up with Max.

She retrieved the bottle of sunscreen. "I'll just lie on my back, thank you, and that should take care of the problem."

"You lying on your back might take care of both of our problems," he murmured.

Tate's mouth formed a little "O" of surprise. "I don't know who you think you are –"

"Clay Copeland. I thought we'd already established that. However, I'm afraid I didn't catch your name. Ms…?"

"Hennessey," she contributed, before she could stop herself. "Tate Hennessey."

"Lovely name, Tate Hennessey." He tested it on his tongue, like fine wine. "It fits you."

Tate snorted and sat up, spreading one hand over the straps of her top and raising the other like a stop sign. "Are you here on vacation?"

"I am."

"Then let me save you some time. You'll have better luck with your spiel somewhere else."

Clay settled himself on the edge of her blanket, propping one leg to support his arm. "Why?"

Good lord. He looked like a page from a beefcake calendar. All that was missing was a tool belt, or perhaps a strategically placed fire hose…

Tate jerked her eyes up to meet his expectant expression. "Because while there are many things for tourists to do in Charleston, I'm afraid I'm not one of them."

He grinned, clearly more entertained than offended.

"I'll be sure to mention to my buddy that he better take you off the brochure." He motioned over his shoulder toward a very large dark-haired man who looked suspiciously like he'd passed out. They were probably a couple of drunks. She leaned a little closer to the man sitting beside her, detecting the salty sting of sweat, the unique muskiness that was man. But nothing that gave any indication that he'd been drinking.

He tucked his tongue in his cheek. "Do local men smell different?"

"What?"

"You'll have to forgive me; I was unaware of my pervasive 'tourist' B.O. If you'd like, I can head back, take a shower before I ask you out."

"That's not necessary," she demurred automatically, wondering how this conversation had gotten so far off track.

"Great, Tate Hennessey, since you're apparently" – he leaned in and sniffed – "a local, I'll let you choose the spot. I'd be happy to pick you up at let's say... seven." He consulted his watch. "Unless you'd be more comfortable meeting me. For a first date, that's really the best idea."

Tate blinked twice, not quite believing her own ears. Had she inadvertently agreed to go out with him?

She did a quick mental replay of the conversation, only to reaffirm that she'd made it perfectly clear she wasn't interested in accepting the offer which he hadn't actually put forth.

"Okay." She began to raise her hands in a gesture of dismissal, quickly aborted when her top started to slip. In a burst of impatience, she tied the straps together, leaving him looking disappointed. "I'll give you points for being persistent, but that doesn't change my answer. Now, why don't you go bother that woman over there?" She pointed to an attractive blonde in a ridiculously small bikini.

"Not interested."

Right. "You didn't even look –"

"Busty blonde, a little on the short side, almost wearing three black scraps of fabric. Looks like she's waiting for the sun to come down and personally gild her ass."

Tate smothered a burst of laughter. It was a very accurate depiction. "How did you know who I was talking about? You didn't turn around."

Clay shrugged. "I'm observant."

Her eyebrow arched in challenge. "Okay, Mr. Observant. Tell me about the sunbather lying next to her." She wanted to see if his powers of observation extended to anyone other than the attractive females littering the beach.

He rolled his shoulders, loosening himself up to meet the challenge. "Well now, Tate. I do believe you're trying to throw me off. Because calling that man under the umbrella a sunbather is something of a misnomer. Since his skin is the approximate color of a fish's underbelly, I doubt very seriously he's trying to catch some rays. Unlike you, he's probably comfortable with his complexion and doesn't want to ruin it."

Tate drew back, unsettled by his perception. "What makes you think I'm uncomfortable with my complexion?"

He gestured to her bottle of SPF 4. "You're out during the hottest part of the day, with insufficient protection. In this day and age, everybody knows about skin cancer and premature aging, and you strike me as an intelligent woman. So what is an intelligent, fair-skinned woman doing lying in the afternoon sun with a lotion that does little more than lessen the severity of the burn? She's asking for the burn, because she knows that with her coloring, it's the quickest way to achieve the sought-after tan. Of course, she'll probably just end up peeling anyway, but she's young, and that's a risk she's willing to take."

Tate gasped, finding that more than a little bit creepy. It was like he'd sucked the thoughts right out of her head. "What are you, some kind of mind reader?"

Clay smiled, looking rueful. "No, I'm actually… a psychologist. Behavior patterns and what they specify about the individual is sort of my specialty."

"So you're a therapist?"

"Not exactly," he hedged. "I have a PhD, yes, but I'm not in practice."

Tate tried to assimilate this new information. Okay, so the man wasn't a drunk, and he apparently had an education. But a couple of initials before or after his name didn't mean he was a swell guy. He was still forward, and blatantly suggestive, and more than a little cocky.

She narrowed her eyes. "So what's my behavioral pattern telling you now?"

"It's difficult to say. Maybe if you loosened the straps to your top again, I could get a better reading."

Despite herself, Tate laughed, because it was clear he didn't take himself too seriously. Shifting her weight back onto her hands, she studied the almost ridiculously sexy psychologist. He possessed the kind of humor and self-deprecation that transformed bravado into lethal charm. But since he was here for only a short while and she had more than her hormones to consider, she decided that she'd have to pass. "Although I can't say I'm not intrigued, I'm afraid I can't go out with you, Dr. Copeland."

"Clay," he corrected. "And why is that?"

"Well, for one thing, I have to work."

"Okay. Then how about I –"

"Mommy!"

Perfect timing, Tate thought. Then she raised a hand to greet the familiar duo heading toward them.

THE excited voice brought his head around, and Clay noticed a small, dark-haired boy running in his direction, followed at some distance by an attractive older woman possessed of silvery hair and a tired smile. He peered over his shoulder, gauging whether the pair was perhaps bearing down on someone behind them, but a quick glance at Tate Hennessey's wry smile put any doubts aside. And if that hadn't done it, the resemblance between mother and son was unmistakable.

The boy was beautiful. A beautiful, happy, *living* little boy.

Against his will, Clay felt himself shutting down, the ghost of his failure rising up to haunt him.

"Mommy, Grandma let me have *two* scoops of ice cream, instead of just one like you said." Flush with the excitement of his secret, he was too young to keep it to himself. "I had a scoop of 'nilla and a scoop of the pink one with all of those colored thingies in it."

"Cotton candy?" Tate suggested as she wiped her thumb across his chin, which still bore the evidence of his coup.

"Uh-huh. It was yummy, but I wish they wouldn't make it pink. Pink's a girl color. Who are you?" He turned his inquisitive green-eyed gaze on Clay.

"I'm Clay," he explained, hating his sudden stiffness. "Pink's not such a bad color, but you might not want to let any of your friends see you wearing it on your face."

The boy giggled as his mother wiped the sticky mess off his chin.

"Max, this is Dr. Copeland. Clay, this is my son, Max. The second and most important reason I can't meet you tonight," she informed him under her breath.

"It's nice to meet you, Max." Clay extended his hand, and the little boy eyed it for a second before slapping it with the traditional five.

"Ouch. That was more like ten." Max giggled and Clay felt something inside him breaking, a small fissure he wasn't quite sure how to repair.

The little boy in Topeka had had dark hair.

He opened his mouth to excuse himself, feeling panic begin to well through that fissure, but the arrival of the older woman stopped him.

"I take it the little heathen ratted me out."

"If he hadn't, the evidence on his chin would have done the job." Sending Clay an awkward glance, Tate made the introductions. "Mom, this is Clay Copeland. Clay, my mother, Maggie Hennessey."

Clay stood, extending his hand. "It's a pleasure to make your acquaintance, ma'am."

Mrs. Hennessey beamed approval. And catching the spark that lit her mother's eyes, he saw Tate roll her own.

"And how do you two know each other?"

"We don't," Tate informed her.

"Sunscreen," Clay said at the same time, trying not to notice the boy's undivided stare.

Seeing the confusion on her mother's face, Tate hurried to explain. "Dr. Copeland happened by when I was applying my sunscreen. He was kind enough to offer to assist me in rubbing some on my back."

Despite his discomfiture, Clay had to smile at that little bit of whitewashing.

"Oh. So you've just met," Maggie surmised. "Are you from around here, Dr. Copeland?" The spark in her eyes burned brighter.

"Clay. And no, I live in Virginia."

"Oh." The subtext of that single syllable reeked of frustrated maternal machinations.

"I think we've taken up enough of Clay's time," Tate said as she started to rise, and using her hand to block the sun from her eyes, turned to address him. "Thank you again for your… assistance."

Clay smirked at the blatant dismissal, but figured all things considered, it was for the best. "No problem." His shaded eyes drilled into hers one moment longer than was strictly polite, before turning toward her mother.

"Mrs. Hennessy, it was a pleasure. And Max." Somewhat reluctantly, he stuck out his hand again, but then jerked it away at the last second. "Oh. Too slow. You'll have to practice that with your mama."

The boy laughed and Clay barely repressed a flinch as he lifted his hand in farewell.

CHAPTER THREE

CLAY pulled on a white T-shirt over his freshly showered torso, wincing slightly as the fabric settled onto his shoulders. He'd overdone it a little today, staying out just long enough to make himself uncomfortable. After he and the lovely Tate Hennessey had parted company, sun awareness hadn't been at the forefront of his mind. Ironic, really, considering that had been a predominant part of their conversation.

As for ironic, how about the fact that he'd driven eight hours through the night to escape the recurring image of the dark-haired little boy he'd failed to save, only to have another one thrown virtually into his lap.

The psychological gods were obviously having a good laugh at his expense.

Winding a belt around his waist, he decided to put off analyzing the situation and his reaction to it for a couple more days.

After all, he was Clay Copeland, beach bum, and he was here to have a good time.

"Are you ready?" Justin inquired after a cursory rap on the bedroom door, dark hair glistening from his shower.

"As I'll ever be." Clay stuffed his wallet into his back pocket.

They headed toward a bar in nearby Charleston that Justin swore had the best happy hour in town. Pinks and vivid oranges had just begun to paint the sky with the colors of the approaching sunset, and as they fought their way through the tourist-laden streets, he cranked down his window to allow the heavy smell of history to permeate his senses. It was tough to remain melancholy about his own trials when surrounded by the indisputable evidence that no matter what he had or hadn't accomplished, time continued to march on.

Murphy's Irish Pub was nestled between an old-fashioned pharmacy and a private historic home cum bed and breakfast establishment, and Justin explained the arrangement was strategic: the folks at the bed and breakfast recommended Murphy's for dinner and liquid refreshments; the staff at Murphy's recommended the pharmacy for analgesics to ward off the next morning's hangover, and the pharmacist recommended that inebriated patrons book a night at the bed and breakfast to sleep it off.

The atmosphere inside the pub was festive, an interesting mix of traditional Irish camaraderie and southern hospitality. High tables clustered thick as barnacles along the scarred and stained wooden floor, which bore the marks of almost two hundred years of patrons. An angular staircase led to the dining room which occupied the historic building's second floor.

In one corner, a live band kept the crowd entertained with some rather bawdy Celtic music, and everyone of legal age had a pint or bottle tucked into their suntanned hands. The bar itself was shiny as a new penny from frequent passes of the polishing cloth, and behind it stood three strapping men doing their level best to keep up with the demands of the thirsty crowd.

Justin signaled to the oldest of the trio – Mr. Murphy himself – indicating that he and Clay were going to be taking over one of the tables toward the front of the bar. The man acknowledged him with a lifted chin, and turned to speak with one of the waitresses as he finished pulling a fresh pint. Within minutes a peppy brunette in a green Murphy's T- shirt and short black skirt appeared to take their order.

"I think it's been almost as long since I've been inside a bar as it has since I've been inside a woman," Justin remarked wryly, after she'd left.

Clay chuckled and slapped the other man on the shoulder. "The night's young, my friend, and ripe with opportunity." He cast his gaze around and noted the comfortably high female to male ratio. For the most part, the women were young, tan, and unencumbered by masculine companions, their body language suggesting that they were here to have a good time.

"If we can't drum up some female companionship in this crowd, we might as well hang it up."

Justin cocked an inquiring brow toward Clay. "Speaking of female companionship, you never did tell me what happened with the yellow bikini. I gather you struck out."

A glib retort trembled on the tip of his tongue, but the truth tasted bitter, so he spit it out instead. "It turned out she has a kid."

"So she was married?"

"I don't think so. She wasn't wearing a ring, and she didn't give off any matrimonial vibes."

Their drinks arrived, and after they'd thanked the waitress, Justin lifted his glass. "Okay, I'm sure you get sick of people asking how it is that you do what you do, but I have to know. What in the hell is a matrimonial vibe?"

Clay grinned, taking a pull on his beer. "Behavior is unspoken language," he explained. "You determine a person's baseline – or normal – behavior in a given situation. How they deviate from that baseline shows their instinctive reaction to the situation's stimuli. If she had been married, she most likely would have reacted in one of two ways when I approached her. She would have been dismissive – either politely or aggressively, depending on her personality and the kind of relationship she might have with her husband – or she would have been receptive in a… guiltily excited way. Kind of like a kid offered a second cookie that she knows she's not supposed to have." He shrugged. "She was cautious but not strongly dismissive, and she showed no signs of guilt when I finally managed to pique her interest. She acted very much like a single woman who was weighing her options about an unknown man. Eventually, she turned me down on the basis of her obligations to her son, but even if she hadn't, I probably would have begged off after I'd seen him. It sounds shallow, but I didn't come here to be around little boys."

"That's understandable. But I don't think you're going to have to worry about that tonight. Not a kid in sight."

Clay smiled, looked over the crowd, and homed in on a point of interest. "Now speaking of behavioral language, that pretty little blonde over there is practically oozing nonverbal leakage. She keeps trying to make eye contact with you, and she's playing with her hair, which is a definite sign of interest."

Justin looked at the woman, who almost immediately looked away. "You're full of shit, man."

"No, no." Clay took another swig of beer. "Trust me on this, Justin. It's what I do for a living. You see how she's laughing a little louder than the other women at the table?"

Justin rolled his eyes before cutting them toward the blonde. "Yeah. So what? Maybe she's just obnoxious."

"No. She's only become louder in the past few minutes. Ever since she looked over here and saw you. She's trying to draw your attention away from the others by making herself stand out. Sort of like a male peacock lifts his feathers to make himself appear larger when he's attempting to entice a mate."

Justin flicked his gaze at the table of girls. Flipping her hair when she caught him looking, the blonde offered up a smile. Justin turned and studied Clay.

"See? *Peacock.*"

"You're serious, aren't you?"

"Would I make something like that up?" When he saw Justin's raised brow he held up a hand. "Okay. I might. Yes, it's entirely possible that would be something I might do. But believe me when I say that I'm shitting you not. That lovely lady has shown numerous behavioral indications that she's hot for you. If you're looking to pull yourself out of your sexual rut, she's your best bet." Eying the dubious look on Justin's face, he grinned and pulled his wallet out of his back pocket. "Ten bucks says she comes over here within the next twenty minutes."

Justin looked at the money lying on the table with a great deal of skepticism, but put his own President Hamilton on top of Clay's. "You're on."

Eighteen minutes later, Clay left the table ten dollars richer. They'd no sooner polished off their shrimp and ordered a second round of Killian's when the blonde made her move. It turned out she was a pediatric nurse who worked at MUSC and had seen Justin around the hospital. Palming the money, shooting Justin a superior smirk, Clay excused himself to go mingle.

The crowd had grown thick as evening gave way to night, and he wound his way through it to find a spot closer to the band. Smoke rose in a thin blue cloud, dispelled occasionally by the salty breeze drifting in from the open windows. Patrons wandered in and out from the patio to the bar, and well-fed diners descended the worn stairs to mix with the crowd. Clay leaned against a rough-hewn support beam and watched them come and go, amazed, as always, at the way body language spoke volumes.

And his own body started screaming in his ear when a pair of long, tanned legs became visible as they descended from the second floor. The staircase was angled in such a way that he got an up close and personal view of those mile-long beauties before a torso or head came into view. Black sandals encased slim feet, a short black skirt hit deliciously at mid-thigh. The legs paused, one resting a step higher than the other, and Clay felt his body stir. If the rest of the package lived up to the preview, he was going to be on this particular woman like a flea on a junkyard dog. He had the overwhelming urge to just wade over and take a bite.

He took a sip of beer, instead, and waited for the follow through.

A green Murphy's shirt made an appearance, followed by a hand holding an empty tray.

Staff, Clay assessed. He wondered what time she got off.

Her other hand rubbed down a thigh as she seemed to be responding to a comment from someone on the stairs above her. The overwhelming jolt of lust he felt caused Clay to choke on his beer.

Wait for it, wait for it…

After another nail-biting moment, the legs made their final descent.

Clay blinked twice, to assure himself he wasn't seeing things. Then he began to curse the psychological gods again, for messing with his head.

"Nice tan," he murmured as Tate nearly passed him by.

It was loud so close to the band, but Tate heard him and wheeled around. "Clay," she said, his name falling naturally from her lips. Then she assimilated his comment, and blasted him with a frown. "Are you making fun of me?"

"Never," he assured her companionably. Her rich ebony hair hung thick and loose, making him want to wrap it around his fist while he plundered her mouth. Mother of a young boy or not, she stirred his juices in a way that no one had for quite a while. The green shirt brought out the intensity of her eyes, which right now were shooting irritated little darts right through him. "It's obviously important to you for some reason I can't quite fathom, so I thought I would acknowledge your rather dramatic change in coloration. How did you accomplish that, by the way? You were creamy and a little pink the last time I saw you. Like a double scoop of vanilla and cotton candy in a cone."

Tate bristled, tucking the empty tray under her arm. "Not that it's any of your business, but it came out of a bottle. I felt guilty after you so thoughtfully reminded me of the damage the sun can do." She took in his own red face. "I see that you obviously don't make it a habit of heeding your own advice, Dr. Copeland."

"Clay," he corrected, because he'd never been comfortable when addressed by his title. It made him feel like he should be wearing a sweater vest and an unfortunate tie. "And you caught me. We psychologists are notorious for doling out advice and then ignoring it. The profession is rife with hypocrisy."

"I'll be sure to keep that in mind. So what brings you here tonight?"

"My friend Justin's pickup." He grinned when she rolled her eyes. "Beer and shrimp," he amended, hoisting his glass into the air. "Along with half the city's population, it would seem. Busy place. How long have you worked here?"

"Since I was old enough to walk." She finally smiled when she saw his raised brow. "Patrick Murphy is my uncle," she explained. "My grandmother lived next door, and whenever we visited in the summertime, Uncle Patrick would put us to work. Now I just help out in the evenings during the high season, when I'm not helping my mom with guests."

Clay quickly did the math. "You run the bed and breakfast next door."

"Guilty. I keep the books and handle the business end of it; my mom cooks and charms the guests. We turned the house into a B and B after Grandma died, because it was the only way we could afford the taxes and the upkeep."

"It's quite an operation you have." Clay thought about what Justin had told him. "Do any of your family members by chance own the pharmacy next door?"

Tate blinked, and then added her lyrical laugh to the music dancing through the air. "My oldest cousin, Maureen, is the pharmacist," she admitted. "And that's Declan and Rogan, two more cousins, behind the bar with my uncle. I take it our fine reputation for business acumen precedes us?"

"You could say that. My friend spent a night with you all several years ago, when he was still a rube."

Tate turned to look where Clay indicated Justin was sitting. "Hmm. I can't say I remember him. But then I was either pregnant or dealing with a toddler at the time, so that's really not surprising." With that not-so-subtle reminder she offered him a stiff smile, and an even less flexible platitude. "Well, it was nice seeing you again, Clay. Enjoy the rest of your evening."

His hand shot out to grasp her wrist before she could move away. "The only way I'm going to enjoy the rest of my evening is if I spend it with you." It sounded like a line, but God, he hated the fact that it was true. Seeing Tate again made him wonder how he'd ever let her get away from him without securing another meeting. Whatever baggage she might have regarding her son, and whatever effect the boy might have on him, seemed suddenly insignificant.

"Be with me tonight."

TATE'S warning sonar went on red alert, screaming at her to *dive, dive, dive!* She was pretty sure Clay Copeland had a torpedo he was looking to use. And as attractive as she found him – and dear Lord, was he attractive, with those melted chocolate eyes – she'd already decided that was a bad idea. "I'm working."

He nodded to the sign over the bar. "That says the dining room closed at ten."

"Yes, well, I still need to close out."

"I'll wait."

Truly, his gall was amazing. "Look, I have responsibilities to attend to, and you've no claim on my time. If you're looking for a little vacation fling, you'll have to try someone else." She motioned expansively toward the crowd. "Take your pick."

"Well, since you offered…"

Clay left her gaping as he strode over to the bar.

She watched him carry on a brief but animated conversation with her uncle – which also consisted of several glances from both parties directed her way – concluded by Uncle Patrick writing something on a piece of paper. Then he clapped Clay on the back like a long lost friend. Pulling out his cell phone, Clay consulted the paper, tucking a finger into his free ear.

Moments later he was by her side again, retrieving the tray she still held under her arm.

"I pick you," he informed her casually, setting the tray aside. "Your uncle says you're good to go, and your mom says Max has been asleep for hours, since he wore himself out at the beach. She told me to tell you not to worry about anything, and to have a good time." He grinned wickedly and Tate felt the jolt of it all the way to her toes. "It just so happens that Good Time is my middle name."

Because he'd already drug her to his friend's table by the time she'd gathered her wits, Tate declined to cause an unnecessary scene. But for someone who was supposedly schooled in the workings of the human mind, he had an awfully strange way of winning friends and influencing people.

"Justin, Mandy – this is Tate. Tate, meet Justin and Mandy." Cursory introductions complete, Clay informed his friend that he was leaving. He said not to worry about the ride, he'd find his own way home.

Uncle Patrick waved at her as she was hauled out the front door.

"Where are you taking me?"

"I have no earthly idea."

"Great plan." She swam through the sticky night air in his wake. "Are you really so desperate that you have to kidnap a woman to get a date?"

"You're disparaging yourself when you say that, sugar. If I'm so desperate, then what does that say about you? What I am is selective. I could have made a move on any number of those women in there tonight, but I prefer to wait for the cream to rise to the top." He pulled their joined hands to his lips, and to her surprise, kissed her fingers.

Because her legs felt a little like Jello, her tone was purposefully bored. "You have a real obsession with cream, don't you? You must have been a cat in a former life."

Clay merely chuckled. "Given the other barnyard animals I've been compared to, I can hardly take offense."

"Barnyard animals?" Tate said as he gently propelled her forward again. "Let me guess. The last woman you abducted called you a –"

Alarm was a nasty surprise when he cut her off midstream, jerking her hard against him and covering her mouth with his big hand. Then he shoved her into an alcove. The bite of the doorknob he pressed her against had her struggling like a wild thing.

"Shhh." Breathing shallow and quick, every muscle in his body tensed, Clay molded his fingers against her lips, his attention focused behind him. Tate smelled the lingering traces of Old Bay and shellfish that clung to his skin, and tasted fear, acrid and bitter.

But when she jerked her head away from his hand she realized the threat didn't come from him.

The man who emerged from the nearby alley was all angles: jutting cheekbones, blades of dirty hair. He muttered to himself as he flipped through a wallet, pulling out the ready cash. Tate watched in horror as he tossed it aside, wiping something on the leg of his threadbare jeans. And couldn't stop the small squeal that emerged when she realized it was a bloody knife.

Hearing the noise, wild eyes whipping their way, the precariousness of the man's mental state became apparent. Instead of running, he chose to attack.

"Shit," Clay muttered.

Then in a series of rapid moves, he shoved Tate out of the way, blocked the assailant's forward momentum with his arm, and rammed two knuckles into the man's throat with enough force to send him staggering. But immune as he was to the realities of physical pain, the junkie regained his footing, charging Clay with renewed vigor.

"Run!" Clay ordered, and the moment's inattention caused him to catch an elbow in the gut. "Go back to the bar and call the police!"

Torn between not wanting to leave him alone with a knife-wielding maniac and knowing that he was right, Tate hesitated for only a second before shooting from the protective cover of the doorway. He'd dragged her out of the pub so fast that she didn't have either her purse or her cell phone. A scream for help clawed its way from her throat as she flew toward the safety of the crowd.

Glancing back over her shoulder, she saw Clay execute a well-placed kick that brought the junkie to his knees, just as she stumbled into the bar.

Her cousin Rogan was already at the door.

"What happened?"

"There was a man… with a knife." Terror had robbed her of breath. She sucked it in, pointing in the right direction. "Clay's fighting him. We need to call the police; I think the man killed someone."

By that time, a small crowd had gathered to hear what she had to say. Several people whipped out their cell phones to dial 911 while Rogan shot out the door. Clay's friend Justin, who'd heard the end of her statement, followed on Rogan's heels.

Shaking off the well-meaning hand of a concerned stranger, Tate chased after the men, pushing through the crowd that had formed on the sidewalk in order to head back toward Clay.

She could only pray that he was alright.

The rapid approach of sirens cleaved the thick night air, and by the time she made it back the first patrol car arrived on the scene. Relief mixed with concern as she saw Clay, battered and bloodied, but basically in one piece.

Glancing at Tate as she approached – a silent acknowledgement that all was well – he straddled the unconscious junkie's back until an officer stepped in to cuff the man.

From the bowels of the alley, Justin's voice rang out the cry for an ambulance. Apparently the man who'd fallen victim to the mugging was still alive.

Rogan stepped close enough to sling a supporting arm around her shoulders, and Tate leaned into his familiar warmth. Despite the heat, she found herself shivering.

More police cruisers arrived on the scene in a deluge of wailing sirens and blinking lights. An officer began to question Clay.

Somewhat reluctantly, Clay pulled a wallet from his pocket, offering his identification.

Surprise flickered over the cop's dark features, and then he handed the ID back to Clay.

"What do you know?" the cop called to his partner, tone bordering on irritation. "Our Good Samaritan here works for the FBI."

CHAPTER FOUR

Bentonville, South Carolina

"*WHAT* the hell are you looking at?"

JR Walker looked up from his plate in reaction to the question, which his companion obviously hadn't directed at him. An unruly trio of teenage boys huddled at the all-night diner's bar, snickering and casting furtive glances toward JR's table.

JR sighed over the all too familiar altercation. Unless disguised, his cousin's astounding size and stark albino coloring tended to draw attention.

And attention was something they didn't need.

"Simmer down, Billy Wayne," JR hissed between his teeth. "You start a fight, and it's going to draw heat. You know how small town cops operate – they've got nothing better to do, so a brawl at the local diner would be the high point of their evening. Unless you want to land your white ass in the county jail, ignore the snot-nosed brats and finish your food."

Billy Wayne's near colorless eyes slid back toward JR's, discharging hostility like a live electrical current.

"Don't look at me like that. If it weren't for you, we wouldn't be worrying about heat, now would we?" JR picked up his glass of sweet tea and stared over the rim, knowing that his cool rebuke annoyed the hell out of Billy Wayne. But it wasn't like the man didn't deserve it. He'd crossed the line back in Atlanta a few months ago, killing one of the girls they went to so much trouble to acquire.

"It wasn't that girl's fault you couldn't perform. I've been telling you for years that those 'roids were going to catch up with you one day."

Billy Wayne's thick fist closed around his fork as he stabbed a piece of sausage. "I don't need any of your lectures." He shoved the meat into his mouth, taking pains to be extra crude.

JR's chuckle had less to do with amusement than condescension. "Just try to keep yourself in check for a while. At least until we get the lay of the new land." Like their hometown of Atlanta, Charleston and its environs were undergoing a rapid population explosion, which meant that police departments and child welfare services were having a difficult time keeping up.

All the better for him and Billy Wayne to sweep up the sweet young things who fell through the societal cracks.

Human trafficking was a dirty business, but somebody had to do it.

Bored of poking at his cousin, he turned his own gaze toward the teenagers. Like overgrown sticks with hair, the lot of them. And they'd been just young enough, just stupid enough to disregard Billy Wayne's size.

He singled out the most obnoxious of the teens, and stared until the kid grew uncomfortable and turned back around.

Lucky for them he'd been there to talk sense into Billy Wayne.

The Inn at Calhoun, Charleston
"*OUCH!*"

Clay complained as Tate dabbed the antiseptic against his busted lip. He sat on the closed toilet lid in her bathroom – shirtless, bloody, and grumpy – while she straddled his legs and went about the tricky business of protecting his wounds from the threat of germs.

Tricky because every time she went near him with something medicinal, he snarled like a wounded animal. "Guess that barnyard comparison wasn't too far off."

"What?"

"You're growling."

"You'd growl too if someone poured liquid fire in your open wound."

Tate bit her own lip as she resisted the urge to laugh. Not that his injuries were amusing, but the fact that he'd so completely lost his unflappable arrogance pleased her greatly. He was acting like a petulant little boy, and that put them on more even footing. She was much more adept at warding off temper tantrums than slick seductions. "Hush. You'll wake up Max."

Clay merely scowled at her when she smiled.

Tate doubted that his various bumps and bruises hurt that badly. No, she suspected his bad mood was due more to the beating his plans for the night had taken.

It was tough to woo a woman when you were ignobly perched on her toilet.

"I thought Charleston was supposed to be a safe city," he complained, battered face giving him the look of a boxer who'd gone one too many rounds.

"You know, for an FBI agent, you're an awfully big whiner."

The glance he shot her was filled with chagrin. "I was wondering when you would get around to mentioning that. I hope you don't think I was yanking your chain earlier. I really am a psychologist. I just happen to be an agent, also."

Tate stopped dabbing the cotton swab against his lip and considered. He clearly hadn't wanted to divulge what he did for a living, and she couldn't help but wonder why. "Are you undercover or something?"

"Nothing that exciting." He leaned back, wincing as if his bruised ribs objected to the movement. "I'm just a guy on vacation trying to pretend that his real life doesn't exist."

Unsure whether the aggrieved tone of his voice was from embarrassment or discomfort, Tate furrowed her brow in concern. Maybe he was hurt worse than she thought. "Are you sure you don't want to go to the emergency room? I can handle a busted lip, but I don't know anything about bones. You might have cracked one of your ribs or something."

"I'm fine," he assured her. "Justin looked me over and said that nothing appeared to be broken. I'll just be sore for a couple of days." He shook his head, then turned a mocking look her way, voice lowered to a sexy murmur. "I know you had big plans, sugar, but the kinky stuff will just have to wait."

"And here I'd been looking forward to pitting your handcuffs against my whip."

She realized her miscalculation when his eyes turned hot, raking down her body with obvious intent. His gaze climbed slowly, leaving a trail of gooseflesh behind, and she crossed her arms over her chest.

"I was kidding."

"You sure?" He leaned back, cocky as hell again. "You'd look awfully good in my cuffs."

Tate pushed that image right out of her head. "Be that as it may, I think you've been beaten enough for one night."

Instead of putting him in his place, the words merely bounced off his ego. His eyes finished their lazy perusal, heavy-lidded as they met hers.

The walls of the bathroom suddenly seemed too close, or maybe he seemed too large. Too masculine. Too…

Hers to do what she wanted with for the night.

Irritated with herself, Tate tossed the used swab in the trash.

She could feel his gaze burning her skin, but was afraid to let her own get drawn back to his. Because the truth was she was sorely tempted. And that in itself was enough to make her wary. She didn't do one night stands, and she sure didn't do them with both her mother and her son just down the hall. So instead, she crossed her arms again, and after a few moments, heard him sigh.

"I appreciate the help, but I think I've taken up enough of your evening." He rose to his feet, closing some of the distance between them. The step Tate took back was instinctive, and Clay chuckled before leaning toward her ear. "You can relax now. I recognize a stop sign when I see it. Body language," he explained, when she raised a brow. "You're closed up tighter than a fifty-five gallon drum."

"I'm sorry," Tate began, feeling the need to explain. "But I can't –"

He waved her excuses away. "Probably for the best. I'll just call a cab to take me out to Justin's house. From the way things looked, he's going to be spending the night at the hospital."

Because, as she'd discovered, he was a doctor. Not a drunk. In retrospect, Tate guessed she'd misjudged both men pretty badly. But then, that was par for her particular course.

"We have a room available downstairs," she heard herself say, and cursed her tongue for having a mind of its own. She should simply let him call his cab. "A last minute cancellation," she continued anyway. "If you'd like, you're welcome to it."

He hesitated – just long enough to make her feel uncertain and foolish for having made the offer – but then a lopsided grin eased some of the tension from his face. "I'd appreciate it."

Tate opened the bathroom door. "Come on. I'll see if I can dig up a T-shirt big enough for you to wear, and show you where you'll be sleeping."

THE little boy called out to him for help. Clay could hear him crying in the background as he talked to the child's father over the phone.

"*Please don't shoot us, Daddy.*"

What kind of thing was that for a child to have to say?

And what kind of man could look into the terrified faces of his wife and son and pull the trigger?

Despite the fact that he was an expert on social deviants and their motivations, their sheer capacity for evil never ceased to disgust him.

"Carl." Clay called the man by his first name, establishing a rapport. "Why don't you just let Liz and Bradley walk out that door?" *Remind him of their names, remind him they were people, not possessions. This was the kind of man that if he was going down, would want to take everything he owned with him.*

"Because I'm not stupid. The second they're out that door, I'm as good as dead."

"No." Clay gave his word. "I'll see to it. My objective is to see that you get whatever it is that you need without anyone getting hurt. What do you need, Carl? Let me help you." *Keep it conversational, between you and Carl. If he's talking, he's not killing his family.*

The little boy cried out again, tears giving way to sobs. "What I need," Carl hissed through his teeth. "Is some goddamn quiet! Shut him up, Liz!"

Be quiet, Bradley, Clay silently pleaded with the child. Any threat to his father's control at this point could have devastating consequences. *Empathize,* Clay reminded himself. *Reassure.*

"Carl, I know it must be difficult to concentrate with Bradley crying. Why don't you send him out here? You can do that, because you're in control."

"Damn right I am! Liz, I told you to *shut him up!*"

From there it went downhill at a breakneck pace. Carl dropped the phone, and turned his gun on his family. Before Clay could even signal the sharpshooters, that little boy was dead.

His terrified voice still echoed in Clay's head. He wondered if he'd ever again be able to sleep without hearing him… *singing?*

Shooting up like a marionette on a string, Clay blinked his eyes at the dark-haired child sitting on the edge of his bed. He moved a bright yellow cement mixer back and forth as he sang in a charmingly off-key voice.

"Sally the camel has *tree* stumps, Sally the camel has *tree* stumps, so ride Sally ride. Boom, boom, boom."

For a moment, Clay thought he'd taken a high dive into shallow waters, but as dream faded into reality he found himself grinning. Max's off base lyrics were hysterical. He eyed his surprise visitor with a great deal of humor.

"You go riding tree stumps and you're bound to get splinters in your butt," he advised.

Max turned around to face Clay, covering his giggle behind a small hand. "You said butt," he pointed out with glee.

Well shit, Clay thought, scrubbing a hand through his mussed hair. What was the politically correct terminology these days? Bottom? Derriere? Hiney? "I meant to say 'in your behind'." He didn't want the kid to go rat him out to his mother.

"That's okay," Max said diplomatically, in that completely superior manner only the very young can pull off. "I know what a butt is. I know lots of things that Mommy doesn't like me to say. I hear 'em from Cousin Declan and Cousin Rogan. They're teaching me how to cuss."

"Are they now?"

"Uh-huh." Max pushed his cement mixer up Clay's leg and made the accompanying noises. His black hair was tousled, his face rosy from sleep. By the gray cast to the light diminishing the shadows in the room, Clay could only guess that it was just before dawn.

Max, apparently, was an early riser.

"They said that the boys at the big school next year will think I'm a sissy if I call my butt a bum-bum and my penis a doohickey," the little boy explained. "Mommy has funny names for things, but that's just 'cause she's a girl. Girls are kind of prissy 'bout stuff, Cousin Rogan says."

Clay wondered if Tate had any idea what her cousins were doing to her son. But Max's next comment pretty much answered that. "Cousin Rogan says that it's just a secret between us boys, and that I should never cuss in front of Mommy 'cause it wouldn't be 'spectful. I don't know what that means," he admitted philosophically, "but I think it means that it might make Mommy mad." He gave Clay a quick once over before returning his attention to his truck. "I figured it's okay to tell you, 'cause you have a penis."

In a bid to keep from cracking up, Clay bit his bottom lip, reopening his cut. Then he added to Max's education – or maybe corruption – by uttering a curse.

Max's eyes, so like his mama's, went wide with fledgling admiration. "Cousin Rogan said that word would make Mommy *real* mad if I ever repeated it. He said it the other day when he dropped a full bottle of whiskey on his pinkie toe."

Wiping fresh blood from his tender flesh, Clay nodded his head in commiseration. "I can understand why he did that."

"Did you cuss when the bad man hurt you in the face?" Max wanted to know.

"How did you know a bad man hurt me?" Clay wondered, hoping to turn the conversation away from its current uneasy course. He was floundering in a sea of anatomically correct names for body parts and inappropriate curse words.

"I woke up last night 'cause I had to pee, and I heard you and Mommy talking. That's how I knew you were sleeping in this room."

Clay had to admit to his own fledgling admiration, as well as a sincere and heartfelt concern for Tate's sanity when this kid hit fifteen. He was already showing signs of being both clever and sneaky – cute in a precocious five year old. Terrifying in a teenager.

"So your mom doesn't know you're in here?" he surmised.

Max shook his head. "I'm not s' posed to bother the guests. But you didn't lock your door," he said almost accusingly, just beginning to understand the benefits of reassigning blame. "So I wanted to come in and show you that I've been practicin'."

"Practicing what?" Clay asked warily. Lord knows what else Tate's cousins had taught him.

"Givin' five." Max huffed out an exasperated breath. "You said I needed to practice it with Mommy."

Something in Clay's gut twisted a little at the child's words. "I guess I did say that, didn't I?" Then he held his hand out and waited for Max to slap him.

"Ouch, you got me," Clay said when the small palm smacked against his own. He waved his hand back and forth to indicate the expected display of pain, and then ruffled Max's thick mop of hair before pushing back the covers. The beer he'd consumed last night was demanding to come out. He swung his legs over the edge of the bed, remembered rather suddenly that he was naked, and then made a grab for the shorts he'd dropped on the floor.

It was at that moment Tate unexpectedly appeared at the door, which was partially open due to the fact that Max had neglected to close it all the way.

Every bit of color draining from her face, she launched herself at Max, snatching him off the cherry four-poster before turning her maternal fury on Clay. "What the hell do you think you're doing?"

Clay, who was now very uncomfortably aware of the fact that he was without a stitch of clothing, slowly straightened and pulled the shorts over his naked lap. This was not exactly the way he'd hoped for Tate to see him in all his glory.

He blinked, a little surprised at her sudden ferocity. "Well, I was just about to put some clothes on so that your son didn't have to look at my bare *bum-bum* while I made a trip to the john. Waltzing around naked somehow just didn't seem appropriate." He took in her stark face and trembling limbs, knowing that there was something more than normal surprise or embarrassment at work here.

Max heard the angry timbre to his mother's voice and misinterpreted the cause. "I'm sorry, Mommy." He turned tearful eyes up toward her strained face. "I know I'm not s' posed to bother the guests, but I heard you talking to Mr. Clay last night and wanted to show him how I'd been practicin'. I got him really good, too, Mommy. Please don't be mad."

She cradled her son against her breast, stroking his hair while he wiped his runny nose on the soft fabric of her shirt. "You're mad at me, aren't you Mommy?"

Clay saw that Tate was too consumed with some deep and troubling emotion to answer. She'd simply gathered Max tightly in the circle of her arms, squeezing her eyes shut to fight back tears. "Your mama's not mad at you," he assured the worried Max. "She probably just got scared when she woke up and didn't find you in your bed." A glance at Tate confirmed that was indeed part of what had happened. "Sometimes when grownups get worried they seem angry. But really they're just happy that you're okay."

Max pondered that for a moment before pushing back to look at Tate. She put on the brightest of fake smiles. "Mr. Clay's right, sweetie. Mommy isn't mad at you. Now why don't you run along and go see Grandma down in the kitchen. She's making chocolate muffins this morning, and if you're lucky she might let you lick some batter."

The promised treat did the trick. Max scooted out of Tate's embrace and beamed a smile at Clay. "Just wait 'til you get up. Grandma makes the best chocolate muffins *ever*." With a quick kiss for his mother, he scampered out the door.

Tate watched him go, gazing at the door for several moments after he was gone. Clay could see her throat working, and the tracks of moisture that began to run down her face in helpless currents. She mustered her composure before brushing them away. He waited her out, knowing that she was working up the courage to offer an explanation.

When she finally turned her eyes on him the pain he saw behind them forced his heart into his throat.

"When I was twelve," she began in a harsh whisper, "I went away to my first and only sleep away camp. We lived in Georgia then, in a little town north of Atlanta. It was hot, the girls were mean, and I hated every minute of it. The only good parts were swimming in the lake and mooning over Lifeguard John." She offered Clay a rueful smile. "The first in a series of gorgeous blonds that I seem forever obliged to become besotted with."

Clay snagged the implication behind that comment and tucked it away for future examination.

"Anyway." She told him about a game, a dare. "When I finally made it through the woods and wound up on the boys' side of camp, I was about to abscond with the trophy when I heard… a noise. In the bathhouse."

Shit.

Clay felt pretty sure he knew the tenor of what was coming, but he made no move to cut her off. It was best to just let her say it out loud so that it lost some of its power. To avoid talking about it would make it seem shameful, make Tate herself feel as if she'd done something wrong.

She drew a deep breath, trembled slightly, and hugged her arms to herself. "I saw the camp coordinator, Mr. Logan. He was in there with one of the boys. He was molesting him."

Clay nodded in acknowledgement of what she had and hadn't said. "I understand."

"When I saw Max in here with you I…" she made a helpless gesture. "I guess I overreacted."

Clay grunted his disagreement. "You acted like any responsible parent trying to protect their child from a suspicious and potentially dangerous situation. I don't think you overreacted at all. Even if you hadn't had such a traumatic experience as a child, I believe it would still be perfectly normal for you to have questioned what you saw."

The breath she'd been holding came out in a rush. "I guess I'm lucky that it was you he busted in on and not some other unsuspecting guest. I'm sorry; he's usually not up before me. And there is a latch on the door to the third floor that is supposed to keep him from opening it. I'm not comfortable allowing him to mingle about unsupervised with any of the guests, for obvious reasons. I guess Mom forgot to engage the latch when she came downstairs this morning."

"It's a good idea to be cautious," Clay agreed, deciding that it took a lot of moxie for someone who'd experienced what she had as a child to run the kind of business she did. "You might want to consider having a motion sensor installed near the door to the stairwell. It would alert you to either someone trying to approach or Max attempting to leave."

TATE smiled, relieved that he understood her reaction so well, considering she'd stormed in like some wild-eyed harridan.

"I apologize if he woke you up this morning. He's going through this 'girls are dumb' phase and prefers the company of other 'guys.'"

"We had a very… enlightening discussion," Clay said with an amused grin. "He said it was okay for him to tell me things because I have a penis."

"Oh my God." He was naked. Tate had totally forgotten that critical fact.

Her eyes landed like heat seeking missiles on Clay's crotch, and he glanced wryly at his lap. Even through the thin fabric of the boxer shorts he'd covered himself with, she had no trouble discerning the appendage in question.

She hastily jerked her gaze away and covered her eyes with her fingers.

"I should just, uh…" her voice trailed off into a strangled noise of dismay. "I'll go now."

Eyes still covered, she backed herself into the door. But instead of exiting, she tripped over her feet and accidentally closed it, landing against the wood with a muffled thud. She cracked her head, dropped her hand from her eyes, and rubbed at the goose egg that was forming.

Then to her complete mortification, Clay came off the bed in order to assist her.

He was naked as the day he was born.

Lord have mercy, he looked like a cross between a Men's Fitness model and a porn star.

Heavy on the porn star.

"I'm okay." Tate held out her hand to ward off his impending approach.

Unfortunately for Clay, her hand shot out at groin level. It connected solidly with soft tissue and brought him groaning to his knees.

He landed, doubled up in pain, on top of her.

"Oh my God, Clay, I'm so sorry."

Then the gods of humiliation selected that moment for Max to lead her mother to Clay's door. He pushed it open in a flurry of innocent excitement, and then stood stock still when it bumped into the opposing weight of Tate's bottom, currently stuck in the air as she tried to wrench herself free of nearly two hundred pounds of wounded male.

Clay, hands cupped over his particulars, blinked at the new arrivals with the fatalistic acceptance of one who was caught in a thoroughly embarrassing situation and saw no discernible way out of it.

Then to her complete astonishment, he started to laugh.

Tate could feel her face running the entire spectrum of fiery shades from rose to scarlet, and her mother tucked her tongue in her cheek in a bid not to lose control.

She lost that particular battle when Max pointed at Clay and declared in triumph: "See, Grandma! I told you he has a penis!"

CHAPTER FIVE

Tate managed to maintain her composure as she and Max joined Clay for breakfast. Because really, it wasn't at all appropriate to cackle like a loon in front of the guests. But when Max crawled into Clay's lap, whispering something in his ear that had his laugh booming like happy thunder, she couldn't quite stop the little flutter in her chest.

They seemed... easy together, she thought. A far cry from yesterday's stiffness at the beach.

Chewing her lip because that flutter thing couldn't be good, Tate caught sight of her mother out of the corner of her eye. "Let me help you with those dishes, Mom." She pushed her chair away from the table and stood.

"Nonsense." Maggie dismissed her daughter with a wave of her free hand as she approached. The other hand was loaded with the delicate cups and saucers a couple of their elderly guests had used for their tea. "You're taking care of a guest."

The corner of Tate's mouth quirked into a wry little smile. "Given the circumstances both last night and this morning, I'm not charging him for the room, Mom."

Maggie straightened away from the table she was clearing and bristled indignantly at her daughter, a volatile combination of southern hospitality and Irish temper that had just been offended. "Paying or no, he's still a guest in our home."

She glanced over Tate's shoulder, and Tate followed her gaze. Max had dragged out one of his coloring books. He and Clay had their heads bent together, conversing sagely while putting their artistic stamps on Spider Man Versus the New Goblin. "Now, why don't you earn your keep by seeing if there's anything else he needs," Maggie suggested. Her green eyes twinkled over the stack of dishes in her arms. "Maybe you can try to compensate for some of the damage you inflicted earlier."

Tate felt the heat rush into her cheeks. As far as first dates went, she and Clay's had been a real doozy. She doubted many men had been put through quite as much in the pursuit of a little recreational romance.

Clay looked up from his rendering of Peter Parker as Tate returned to the table. "I haven't operated one of these in a couple decades." He held up the neon yellow crayon, studying it with a curious eye. "I think they've added a few colors since my time. All my early artwork consists of blue and red scribbles. Of course, that might say more about my lack of imagination as opposed to limited materials."

Tate grinned, bending over to admire their work. Clay seemed to show the same disposition toward grinding the point of the crayon into the paper that her son displayed. Probably something to do with inherent male aggressiveness.

"Very nice," she concluded diplomatically.

"I'll say."

Hearing the heat in the words, Tate glanced down, realizing she'd inadvertently flashed him. Her shirt gaped to frame the tops of her breasts, trapped in black lace.

"About those handcuffs..." he murmured.

Tate muffled a laugh, because that would only encourage him. And Lord knew the man encouraged himself enough as it was.

She pointedly ignored his disappointed look as she straightened, clasping a hand to the front of her shirt. "I'd be happy to give you a ride home."

At her offer, Max lifted his head and looked at her with innocent expectation. "Can Mr. Clay come to the carnival with us this afternoon, Mommy?"

Tate's gaze flew from her son's to meet Clay's with a nearly audible click.

"I'm sure Mr. Clay has other things to do today," she informed Max, trying to calm the rumpus taking place in her stomach. "You have to remember that he's here on vacation. His friend might not appreciate it if we monopolize any more of his time."

CLAY reclined in the chair, watching Tate unconsciously brush that long fall of dark hair away from her face. The delicate smattering of freckles across her nose stood out like sprinkles on a luscious expanse of cream.

He wanted to lick them.

God, maybe she was right. He was turning into a damn cat.

A hungry, predatory cat who could think of nothing he'd rather do than spend his day with the beautiful and highly entertaining Tate Hennessey.

His gaze shifted to her son. The kid was working out better than a paid accomplice. "What carnival?"

"Oh, it's nothing." Tate started to gather up the stray crayons they'd been using. Her voice was mild, but the jerky movement of her hands let him know how nervous he made her.

He probably shouldn't have enjoyed that so much.

"Just one of those traveling jobs that blew into town this weekend," she said. "You know – carnies and funnel cakes and tilt-o-whirls, oh my. We passed an advertisement for it on the way home from the beach yesterday, and my brain was so fried from the heat that I promised to take Max this afternoon." Shrugging, she tucked the crayons back into their carton. "I'm sure it's not your usual scene."

No. Clay's usual scene involved dead and dismembered bodies and humanity in its lowest forms.

"I'd love to go."

"You would?" Tate and Max asked at the same time.

"Why not?" His lazy smile expanded to include both mother and son. If someone had told him yesterday that he would willingly put himself in the company of a gorgeous single mother and her little boy, he'd have told them they were nuts. But maybe the repeated and prolonged exposure to stressful stimuli was more beneficial to his wellbeing than running the other way. Max had already done him the favor of superimposing the image of a child's laughter over another child's tears.

And besides that, he really wanted to get his hands on Max's mama.

"It's not every day one has the opportunity to ride a tilt-o-whirl."

TATE was surprised – and not a little alarmed – at how pleased she was that he'd agreed to come along. Other than her cousins, she never included men on any outings with Max, and she'd certainly never taken her son on a date. Partly due to her unavoidable wariness. But mostly because hanging out with a toddler wasn't a single guy's idea of fun.

It would be a mistake to read too much into what was merely a nice gesture, but it made her heart lift a little to see how Clay's easy acceptance made Max smile.

"How about you and your mama give me a ride to my friend's house," Clay suggested as he smiled at Max, "and then I'll come back here and pick you both up around noon." He looked at Tate for confirmation that the time was okay, and when she nodded, leaned his forearms on the table, bringing his head closer to Max. "Then I'll take you out to a big, greasy hamburger-and-French-fry lunch, and we can see which one of us can ride that spinning thing the longest before throwing up."

Max giggled and slapped the hand Clay extended for the now expected exchange. "I like you, Mr. Clay."

"You know something, Max? I like you, too."

Bentonville Fairgrounds

THE sweet, doughy smell of frying funnel cakes made Casey Rodriguez want to barf. Her mother ran the booth, and since Casey was off school and of an age that adults felt she needed to do something constructive so that she didn't wind up experimenting with alcohol, drugs and horny teenage boys, she'd been pressed into service.

Dropping the thick rope of dough into the vat of oil, Casey bit off a curse. Hot droplets leapt out to sizzle along her arm. She already had a whole armada of tiny red welts sailing around on her suntan, and she grimaced at the new additions. At the sound of her mother's laugh, she shot a nasty glance over her shoulder.

Lola leaned out the little sliding window, blocking whatever hopes Casey had for catching even a hint of a breeze. She was busy batting her heavily made-up eyes at some hulky looking guy in an Atlanta Braves cap.

Casey was forbidden to wear even a hint of lip gloss, but her mother looked like she'd been hit by a car driven by Mary Kay. Blues and pinks and thick applications of powder turned her pockmarked skin into a lumpy birthday cake disguised with too much frosting. And given the heat, it all ended up running off her sweat-bathed face in colorful rivers, anyway.

Bobo the clown, the official carnival mascot, had absolutely nothing on Lola Rodriguez.

Casey watched in disgust as her mother's frizzy, bleached hair blew around her face. It swallowed up the fresh air in a tornado of over-processed greed. The man outside didn't seem to notice how tacky she looked because he was entirely too fixated on the generous display of breasts that Lola's tank top did little to hide. And judging by the way her mother leaned over so that her soft, plump arms squeezed them up and out like ripe melons, she knew her outrageous figure was her best hope of snagging another man.

"Order up," Casey said dryly, stalking to the window beside her mother. It was hotter than blue blazes in the trailer, and the small amount of fresh air that made it past that puff of hair felt like a little slice of heaven.

Lola took the greasy plate from Casey without bothering to spare her a glance.

However, the man she'd been trying to seduce – about six foot, brown hair, brown eyes and enough muscles to indicate that he had a lot of time for weightlifting on his hands – appeared a lot more interested. His ball cap obscured his face, but from beneath its brim his gaze slid over Casey in a way that made her feel as if he'd just undressed her with his eyes.

At fourteen – or near enough, anyway, considering her birthday was next month – Casey was just beginning to show promise of the future beauty she was destined to become. She was lithe where her mother was voluptuous, dark where her mother was fair. Not to be stuck up about it, but genetically speaking, she'd hit the jackpot by taking after her slim, handsome Hispanic father.

As far as everything else was concerned, she'd drawn a bitch of a hand.

Her father had left her and her mother for parts unknown when Casey was still in diapers. Since then, Casey had watched a steady stream of losers parade in and out of her mother's life. About six years ago, one of those losers had convinced Lola to hit the road with him in this traveling flea-bag carnival, but he'd left her high, dry and pregnant when he met a sweet little thing in one of the towns they visited and decided to settle down.

Since then, Casey had been in and out of about ten different schools, lived primarily out of cheap hotels and campers, and acted as surrogate mother to her little sister while their real mother was at work.

Despite the unpredictability of their lifestyle, Lola was fanatic about guarding her daughters against the *wages of sin*, or whatever, and consequently Casey was sheltered in a way that most of the other girls in the carnival were not.

But she was still mortified when she found herself blushing.

She'd had plenty of invitations for experimentation from some of the boys they traveled with, but this was the first time a real *man* had bothered to look at her that way. Like she was more than just some kid. She glanced up from under the heavy fringe of her lashes…

He smiled.

Casey thought he was kind of handsome.

"Thanks, Casey," her mom said, in that absent way people talked when they were distracted. She handed the man his funnel cake and went about the business of making change. "Why don't you go grab your sister and take her on some rides?"

To Casey's slight disappointment, the man withdrew his attention. Probably because Lola offered another eye catching view of cleavage while counting out his fives and ones.

"Okay."

With a last glance toward the man she pulled open the door, welcoming the blast of fresh air as she strolled off to find her sister.

CHAPTER SIX

"*FIRST* I want to ride a roller coaster, and then I want to eat one of those frozen bananas on a stick, and then I want to go in the fun house but you might have to hold my hand because sometimes the fun houses aren't so fun and I get scared. I don't know why they call 'em fun houses when they make 'em all dark and spooky. Last time I went in one there was a gorilla in a cage and I almost peed my pants until Mommy showed me that he wasn't real. I don't know who would want to keep a fake gorilla in a cage when he's not going to get away because he isn't even real. And there was a funny mirror that made Mommy look real short and fat and she said that she didn't like it."

"He talks a lot when he gets excited." Tate's tone was rueful as they pulled into the grassy parking lot. So far her son hadn't managed to divulge any more than two or three of her more embarrassing secrets, but given the time he had at his disposal today, she figured he'd completely humiliate her before they made it back home.

She grimaced at Clay while the chatter from the back seat continued unabated.

"So I noticed." Clay's smile was easy as he turned the SUV into an empty spot. They'd just finished their greasy hamburger and French fry lunch and her son hadn't stopped babbling once during the entire ride.

Clay turned off the engine, came around to open Tate's door, taking her hand as he helped her alight. Then he opened the rear passenger door to unhook Max from his car seat. He studied the contraption in confusion, to which the chattering Max was oblivious, but finally managed to free her excited child from his restraint.

Tate's throat constricted as she watched him lift Max from the car.

She wasn't unused to a man with manners – southern men were famous for their chivalry, after all – but the unstudied ease of the action piqued her curiosity. "Do you have children, Clay?"

Clay startled at the question. "What? No. Why do you ask?"

She gestured toward the car seat and the small child standing in his shadow. "You don't seem the least bit uncomfortable."

"Ah. A by-product of training and experience." Tate took Max's hand and they started to move off in the direction of the action. "I studied under a renowned child psychologist, and my best friend – Justin's brother, actually – is the father of a three-year-old girl. Last time they visited, she refused to let anyone but 'Uncle Clay' do anything for her. I learned a lot in an awfully short period of time."

"I can relate," Tate said with amusement. She knew he'd never been married, as they'd discussed as much at lunch, but the possibility that he might have a child out there hadn't even been considered. "Being handed a helpless newborn is the ultimate on-the-job training. You learn fast out of sheer necessity."

"Watch your step," she advised Max as they crossed a small ditch to access the dirt path leading to the carnival grounds. The surrounding vegetation hung limp and lifeless, covered with a fine layer of dust. At almost two o'clock, the sun's rays were at their strongest, mercilessly beating recipients of their heat into submission. No larks or robins dared sing, and even the omnipresent mosquitoes – big enough to warrant the title of South Carolina's unofficial state bird – hung back in whatever shadows they could find while waiting for nightfall to begin their feeding. Sweat began to form at the nape of Tate's neck, making her glad she'd scraped the heavy mass of her hair back into a ponytail. She glanced over at Clay's short, spiky locks with envy, thinking that men had all of the advantages when it came to dealing with the heat. No one thought twice if they walked around shirtless, and they somehow managed to look both masculine and sexy while dripping wet.

In fact, she could see that Clay's white T-shirt was already beginning to cling, and she decided he was either crazy or a saint for volunteering to put himself through this when he could be relaxing on a raft in the ocean or taking a stroll through Waterfront Park.

CLAY was beginning to wonder if he'd taken leave of his senses.

He'd just consumed two cheeseburgers, it was an easy ninety degrees, and a rickety looking Ferris wheel loomed large in his immediate future. That off-hand comment he'd made to Max this morning didn't seem outside the realm of possibility. In fact, if he had to wager, he bet that he'd be sorely tempted to hurl chow before this little outing was over.

He must be insane to go through all this just to get a girl.

And hell, it wasn't like any of this was leading anywhere. He'd charm his way into Tate's affections, enjoy her for a few more days, and then it was back to the real world.

Romantic interlude forgotten.

Max reached up at that moment to tuck a small, trusting hand into his, and Clay felt like a total ass. He liked this mother and child too damn much to act like a typical schmuck. He felt his priorities rearrange as conscience began to overrule libido.

He'd treat them to an entertaining afternoon, drop them off safely, and then go about the business of pretending he never met them. Anything else was simply making suggestions of promises he couldn't keep.

How the hell he'd stumbled into this situation instead of a nice, uncomplicated vacation fling was beyond him.

He let go of Max's hand long enough to fish his wallet out of his pocket – he'd insisted on footing the bill in payback for his accommodations the night before – and garnered them three hand stamps signifying paid admission. It earned them a limited amount of rides, but games, food and additional ride tickets cost extra. All in all he figured these carnival folks had a pretty good thing going.

They made their way through the gate, and Max's mouth hung open for a full thirty seconds as he took in the bevy of available thrills. To a child, the carnival was a veritable wonderland of exciting possibilities.

To that child's male chaperone, it looked like precariously cobbled together hunks of scrap metal operated by a bunch of shifty-eyed and possibly criminal characters.

Tate's pained gaze met Clay's over Max's head, and he found his sentiments mirrored.

"This is the first time I've been to one of these in the daylight," she admitted, looking around. A leather-skinned vendor hawked enormous clouds of cotton candy as a mechanical dragon looped overhead, ferrying passengers squealing with glee. The specter of Port-O-Potties cast a malodorous pall over the far corner of the park, while the competing aromas of caramel corn and bratwurst vied for the upper hand in their assault on the olfactory senses. Harried parents shepherded hot, sweaty children. Ear-splitting screams erupted from the direction of the "Tornado," which spun unsuspecting folks in a vortex of centrifugal force while the ride's bottom dropped from beneath their feet. "It, uh, sort of loses something without all of the midway lights and, you know. Darkness."

The corner of Clay's mouth tugged into a commiserative grin. "I'd say the sanctity of Walt Disney's empire remains comfortably un-assailed."

"Can I ride the dragon, Mommy?" Max was clearly unfettered by the grown-ups' lack of enthusiasm.

"Sure you can," Clay responded, after catching an approving nod from Tate. Then he picked the child up, balanced him on his hip, and flicked his finger down the length of his nose. "How about we boys show your mama how real men handle vicious creatures."

They slew that beast, and many other mechanical monsters, over the course of the next few hours. Clay's stomach began to rebel at the thought of one more spin on any sort of rotating contraption. To appease Max and buy himself a few minutes on steady ground, he took one of the glib-talking carnies to task by attempting to level a milk bottle pyramid.

He'd been at it for a solid fifteen minutes despite the fact that he was pretty sure the bottles were bolted down, and wondered what the orthodontia-challenged man operating the booth would say if he whipped out his badge and demanded to inspect the set-up.

It was petty and immature of him, but he wanted to impress Tate by winning Max a ridiculous purple bear.

He tossed the ball in his hand, eyed the milk bottles like the enemy, and for good measure slid a menacing glare toward Bucky, the Keeper of the Bear. Max watched with eager anticipation, and Clay couldn't help but notice that Tate was biting the inside of her cheek. No doubt to keep from laughing.

He'd pitched a no-hitter at the last Bureau picnic-cum-softball game, and could nail a target with a knife from twenty feet.

Bruised ribs or no, he absolutely should not be having this much trouble taking out a few lousy little milk bottles.

He wound up, focused, and let fly.

The bottles wobbled.

But remained stubbornly upright.

"Ohh," the man called out in sympathy, slapping his chest and leaning back as if in pain. "You almost had it that time, Mister. Want to try your hand again?"

Clay heard snickering behind him, and turned to glare at the big, burly dude in the Atlanta Braves cap who was making the noise.

The man was muscle-bound to the point of looking unnatural. His slick, darkly tanned skin advertised that he was no stranger to the weightlifting scene. The hat shadowed his face, but Clay detected deep brown eyes laughing in his direction, and despite the heat the guy was wearing a long-sleeved shirt and a pair of jeans.

Something in the back of Clay's mind clicked, but Tate's hand on his shoulder distracted him into turning around.

"A frozen banana on a stick would be much more refreshing and entirely simpler to obtain," she suggested sweetly.

It was like salt in an open wound. Feeling his macho quotient shrivel, Clay wanted to punch somebody, drive a car real fast, and leap a tall building in a single bound.

He wanted to toss her over his shoulder and drag her off to his cave to make hard, hot love to her until his masculinity was safely restored.

He wanted to understand exactly when he'd degenerated from a civilized man into a baseball-throwing Neanderthal.

"Hey mister," the carnie said as he tossed the ball toward Clay. "This one's on me."

Clay caught the ball on the fly, flicked his eyes toward the milk bottles, and then returned his steely gaze to the carnie's face. Without sparing his target another glance, he sent the ball hurtling toward the bottles. It hit the bottom middle jug dead center, and the entire pyramid collapsed.

"You did it, Mr. Clay!" Max squealed as he jumped up and down.

"You were trying too hard before." The carnie grabbed a long hook and retrieved the fuzzy purple bear from its perch. "It happens all the time when a man's looking to impress his girl."

At that, Tate gave in to her stifled laughter.

"Thanks." Clay's tone was dry as he accepted his hard won prize. Wooing Tate was turning out to be more difficult than his last ten relationships put together. He'd been sunburned, attacked by a mugger, accused of perversion, incapacitated by a blow to the family jewels, forced to endure numerous rotations on various mechanical contraptions, and humiliated by a buck-toothed carnival worker with some suspicious milk bottles and a cheap purple bear.

All in all, it had been a painful twenty-four hours.

He figured it was a good thing that he'd decided to call his intentions in the wooing direction to a halt. Getting Tate Hennessey into bed might very well prove to be the death of him.

"Thank you," the woman in question whispered in his ear while dropping a quick kiss on his cheek.

All of his uncharitable thoughts flew out the window as she grasped his hand and squeezed.

Max – proudly clutching his tacky bear to his small chest – took hold of his other hand and looked up at him with adoration.

"Hell," Clay muttered to himself. No matter how hard he tried to convince himself otherwise, he was in full wooing mode, and saw no hope for relief in the immediate future.

They went in search of frozen bananas, and after Clay had procured three of the chocolate covered treats they retired to a wooden table that had been set up in the designated picnic area. The thick, twisted branches of a centuries-old live oak stretched above them like an old woman's petticoat. Fragments of hazy light stabbed through the limp and listless leaves, filtering toward the overheated idlers below until it lay scattered about them like dust.

Shadows grew long and languid as afternoon gave way to the welcome promise of dusk. A few intrepid crickets began calling lazily to one another from the shelter of the nearby woods. Families occupied the other picnic tables around them – hot, tired and lethargic from the excesses of their day. An old man in bib-overalls relaxed against the trunk of the tree. Clay recognized him as one of the handlers that managed the carnival's four tired-looking ponies.

A few teenagers had begun to gather in anticipation of the veil that nighttime promised to drop. They clumped together in small groups of quivering hormones, trying to look as bored as possible. The two sexes stood around, chatting and laughing, ostensibly paying no mind to the other while in reality gearing their every gesture, stance and mannerism to attract members of the opposite group.

When it came to sex, Clay thought, even the most sophisticated animal was reduced to the very basic and predictable rituals of mating.

"I haven't had one of these in years," Tate murmured around the banana, drawing Clay's attention away from the horny teens. Turning slightly, he started to make some inane comment, but the sight that greeted him froze his tongue to the roof of his mouth.

Sweet Jesus, Tate wasn't nibbling at the banana the way he and Max were doing.

She had her lush, delicate mouth closed over the damn thing and was actually *sucking.*

Then she closed her eyes, and licked the chocolate from her lips.

He quickly cut his gaze back toward the old man with the hairy armpits, hoping to substitute that decidedly un-stimulating image for the one that was wreaking havoc with his own hormones. He shifted uncomfortably on the bench. He was not going to give into the temptation to turn back around and watch.

This was a family environment, for God's sake, and he was in the company of this woman's son. Offering to replace her banana with his pertinent body parts was simply not an option.

"Mmm," he mumbled in reply because he didn't trust himself to speak. He took a vicious bite out of his own banana.

While taking out his frustration, Clay caught sight of the man in the Atlanta Braves hat he'd almost wrangled with earlier.

The man was lingering in the shade, sitting on top of a table in the far corner of the picnic area. Hat pulled low, his manner casual, he methodically consumed a plate of nachos and took long pulls from a bottle of water. He had another unopened bottle – this one soda – sitting on the table beside him.

He was minding his own business, paying no noticeable attention to anyone else, and seemed relatively average. He'd done nothing untoward that would in any way suggest ill intent, but something about the man sent Clay's radar on high alert.

What was a single male doing at a kiddie carnival in the middle of one of the hottest days of the year?

Waiting for his wife and child to finish a ride?

His left ring finger was bare, and he'd shown no interest in the younger children. In fact, when a mother walked a screaming baby past him, he glanced at them with disdain.

One of the male teens, cigarette dangling from his lips, walked toward the man and apparently asked him for a light. The burly dude shook his head, and then returned his attention to his plate. He seemed to be resisting any unnecessary attention.

Maybe he was a loner, and didn't like crowds. But if so, why bother hanging out where large groups of noisy people gathered?

Maybe the guy worked here, but from his basic good looks and well-kept appearance Clay sort of doubted it. He obviously devoted a lot of time to his body, and he didn't have that haggard look typical of so many carnival workers. Traveling the country in a trailer was no easy life, and that fact showed on most of the people who made their careers out of bringing their particular brand of pleasure to town after town. Nor did the lifestyle lend itself to regular, intense workouts. And this guy clearly worked out a lot.

In fact, it was the man's body that Clay found most disturbing.

Not the fact that he obviously lifted serious weights – there was nothing inherently suspicious about that – but it had been his experience that people who spent so much time turning their body into a veritable temple were inclined to show it off.

This man was pretty much covered from head to foot.

Why?

Clay took another bite of banana, and contemplated the probable reasons.

It was quirks like that, little oddities of behavior, that drew Clay like a moth to flame. Something about this guy just didn't add up. He wanted to know why that was.

"Mr. Clay?"

Max diverted his attention, making him realize he'd inadvertently slipped into professional mode. He was here to get away from that, damn it, so he put the puzzle of the burly dude out of his mind.

The little boy scooted closer, tugging at Clay's sleeve. He had streaks of chocolate from ear to ear and a hopeful look on his face. "Would you ride the Ferris wheel with me before we go home?"

"Max," Tate chastised lightly, reaching over Clay's lap to wipe the chocolate off her son's face. She wet the napkin with the tip of her tongue, causing Clay to shift uncomfortably.

He looked heavenward, studied the overhanging tree branch, and willed his body under control.

"I think that you've put Mr. Clay through quite enough for one day."

Oblivious to Clay's plight, Tate discarded the paper napkin in favor of her thumb, which she licked before rubbing Max's face. It was an innocent gesture – maternal, for heaven's sake – but that tongue sent his blood pressure through the roof.

And then she absently braced her hand on his thigh for balance as she leaned over.

Saints above, the woman was killing him.

"Are you okay?" Tate looked worried, and Clay realized he must have inadvertently made a noise of distress.

She glanced from Max back to him. "There's really no need for us to stay any longer."

Clay took in the slightly mutinous expression on Max's face, and gathered the kid thought otherwise.

"We can't leave without hitting the Ferris wheel on the way out." Which earned a beam of gratitude.

"Clay, you really don't have to –"

His raised hand stopped Tate's protest. "It would be like leaving Sea World without bothering to see Shamu."

Tate clearly thought that was a stretch, but the matching grins of masculine solidarity on the faces of her date and her son made the point inconsequential.

"Okay," she agreed. "One last ride on the Ferris wheel and then we'll call it a day."

CHAPTER SEVEN

BILLY Wayne Sparks tipped his cap down over his eyes, watching the growing number of teenage girls with interest. He'd known that he would have a veritable bumper crop of pretty young things to choose from as darkness began to stretch its tentacles around the day. Evening brought herds of fleet-footed little creatures gathering at the watering hole. But he had to be cautious, be patient, as he stealthily selected his prey.

One wrong move could send the whole lot of them scurrying.

The smart predator – the successful predator – waited for the weakest of the unsuspecting quarry to fall back, to separate themselves from the others.

The weak ones were the least likely to be noticed if they suddenly disappeared.

The girls draping themselves in provocative poses all over the picnic table to his right lacked a certain appeal. He and JR had discovered that most of their clients preferred an air of innocence in the stock. And bona-fide virgins fetched a hell of a price.

Of course, that meant that he himself was denied the pleasure of breaking them in.

But hey, there were plenty of girls in that not-quite-virgin, not-quite-slut category that afforded him the opportunity to show their consumers how the product performed. Although the current availability seemed considerably lacking.

It was unfortunate that the girls whose circumstances made it easiest for them to take were also the ones exposed to the realities of life at an earlier age. He'd like to grab one of the pony-tailed, Gap-clad young teens who traveled around in giggling packs like pretty gazelles. But the hue and cry that would result from taking a child of obvious means and protective parentage made such thoughts an extremely risky business.

Circumspection was the name of the game in this enterprise, thereby making the most babelicious of the little bubble-gum smackers off limits.

He returned his attention to the sluts.

One of the girls – a cute little brunette in a Hello Kitty T-shirt and a pair of booty hugging denim shorts – looked a little younger and less used than the others. Her legs were slim and nicely tanned, her breasts small but well rounded. He put her age at approximately thirteen or fourteen. As a rule, he and JR tried not to dip much below that end of their targeted age bracket, because in general people no longer viewed the girls as kids once they'd entered their teens.

It excluded them from some of the market, but it also helped to keep them off the biggest of law enforcement radars.

And besides that, Billy Wayne didn't enjoy having sex with kids.

Sweet young things, however, were a different story.

Watching the brunette casually from beneath the cover of his hat, he took another long drink of water. It was hot as a bitch today, and he rued the necessity of his cumbersome clothes. The tinted lenses and fake tan might enable him to blend in with the crowd, but it didn't protect his sensitive skin from sunburn.

The brunette laughed uproariously at something one of her compatriots said, tilting a bottle of Coke to her gloss-slicked lips. From the way she'd grown louder and more unsteady over the past half hour, he concluded there was something more than soda in the bottle.

Excellent.

It would be so easy to slip a little GSB in along with her vodka or rum, to watch her stumble off into the trees. Her friends would conclude that she'd passed out. He'd been watching, and most of the teens were well on their way to being drunk or high, showing little concern for anything but their own path to self-destruction. A friend who displayed signs of being dangerously wasted would be more of a cause for amusement than alarm.

He'd just about decided on his course when a movement off to the right caught his eye.

It was the girl from the funnel cake trailer.

She strolled into the perimeter of the picnic ground with a rumpled looking little blonde girl in tow – assumingly the younger sister. She made her way toward the big metal barrel where she threw the remnants of a half-eaten hot dog away. Her clothes – an apple green T-shirt and a pair of navy blue shorts – were a little ratty, mostly clean, and not in the least provocative.

Unless, of course, one had Billy Wayne's ability to envision what lay underneath.

She turned slightly, catching his eye.

It was tentative, but there could be no mistaking her smile.

Ho, ho, ho. What do you know? Most of the girls were too intimidated by his size to find him appealing, except for the ones who'd been had so many times that they knew what they were getting into. That wasn't the kind of target he wanted to attract.

But this little sweetheart had given him an endearingly flirtatious smile.

Senses sharpening, he became the predator – swift and sure – spotting its tantalizing prey in the tall grass.

This one.

Yes, this was the one he wanted. She might prove more challenging, for he had to take the little sister into consideration, but he would have her nonetheless.

Smiling, answering her unspoken flirtation, he delighted in her blush as she turned away.

He watched her head off toward the Ferris wheel. It rose above trees whose shadows fell longer and deeper as daylight disintegrated into night.

There was a path amongst the trees, he knew, leading to the rarely used dirt road. The road where he'd parked his van.

Plan formulated, Billy Wayne stood, indulging in a leisurely stretch. And then casually strolled toward the trash barrel to toss out his plate.

Just like any conscientious citizen.

THE hazy half-light of dusk had begun to settle by the time Clay and Max finally made their way to the Ferris wheel. Midway lights throughout the entire fairgrounds popped on in a symphony of rainbow hues.

"Look, Mommy." Max pointed toward the kaleidoscope of bright bulbs outlining the ride. Reds and greens winked against the pinks and indigos of the evening sky, creating a panorama of saturated color.

"It's beautiful, isn't it?" Tate scooped him into a hug, smiled over his head toward Clay. The first tentative breath of night sighed like relief through the trees.

"It certainly is." Blind to the lights, Clay looked at Tate, and thought he'd never seen anything more lovely. The fact that she'd seen both innocence and trust perverted, was raising a child without a father, and still managed to look at the world and see its wonder made Clay feel that he'd taken his first real breath of that air.

He'd been suffocating, Clay thought. In work. In routine. In the sheer, unrelenting misery he saw all too often. And here, here was goodness.

He wanted to drink it in.

TATE saw the change in his eyes – that flash of heat signifying intention. She touched the tip of her tongue to her lips, whether from nerves or anticipation she couldn't say. And watched desire slip like a living thing from the steel band of his restraint.

Oblivious to the press of the crowd around them, he brushed his thumb along the slope of her cheek.

"Max?" His normally smooth voice tumbled roughly, like a pebble skipping down a rocky slope.

"Yes, Mr. Clay?"

"You may," he suggested man to man, "want to turn around and look the other way."

"Why?" Max pulled his gaze from the lights, brows knit in a puzzled frown.

"Because if it's okay with you, I'm going to kiss your mama."

His lips on hers were undemanding, gentle as a summer rain. Tate felt herself begin the slide from reluctant interest to all-out attraction. If he'd pressured her, been the least bit aggressive, or hadn't taken her son's feelings into consideration, it would have been a heck of a lot easier for her to maintain some emotional distance.

But he'd asked her son's *permission*, for God's sake. And then proceeded to kiss her as sweetly as if they were both virgins on their first date.

It was that consideration that was her undoing.

She stretched an arm around his neck and found herself kissing him back.

"Excuse me," a syrupy voice drawled before the kiss could get really interesting. "The line's moving, and I think that y'all are next."

Embarrassment had her eyes popping open, her hands pushing against his chest. And turning, she apologized to the woman and three children waiting with varying degrees of patience behind them.

"That's okay," the woman chuckled. "If my husband looked like yours, I'd be all over him, too."

Tate's eyes went wide, but Clay's laugh rang out as he wrapped an arm around her to draw her forward. "Come on, sugar. You can watch me and the kid while we're on the ride, and I give you permission to be all over me later."

Shaking her head, Tate watched Clay get Max situated in the seatbelt.

And was struck, not quite easily, by what an amazing man he truly was.

How many men would voluntarily spend an entire day of their vacation entertaining the demanding five-year-old son of a woman they'd just met? A woman who'd made it clear that she had no intention of providing any diversionary physical entertainment?

Of course, if she were being honest, she would have to admit that a couple minutes ago she'd been on the verge of forgetting that she didn't engage in fleeting physical relationships with veritable strangers. Clay's tender kiss had rekindled long dormant fires that hadn't been lit since... well, she hesitated to actually recall how long. She'd been in such a sexual drought that she was like a little pile of dry kindling.

And Clay Copeland was quite a potent spark.

What would it hurt, she mused, to indulge herself with a little adult recreation? To allow whatever seemed to be igniting between her and Clay to develop naturally?

The Ferris wheel groaned suddenly, interrupting her thoughts, and she smiled and waved as Clay and Max began their backward ascent.

Clay winked, and then slid his arm around her son to help keep him from bouncing out of his seat with excitement. Max looked up at him with naked adoration.

It was then that Tate came to the sinking realization that she couldn't see Clay again.

Even if she *could* handle a brief affair in a mature and reasonable fashion – which, given her short and unimpressive history with affairs of any sort, was highly unlikely – she couldn't discount the effect such a relationship might have on Max. She'd always been very careful to keep her dating life, what there was of it, totally separate from her son. The look she'd just seen pass between Max and Clay reminded her of the wisdom of that decision.

For five years she'd done her best to shield Max from the rejection children inevitably feel growing up in single parent households.

Max was young still, but he'd already peppered her with questions about his absentee father. Where he was. *Who* he was.

Wondering why the other children he knew had daddies when he didn't.

It was no fault of his own that his bastard of a father hadn't been interested in making any significant contributions to his life other than donating his sperm.

As the Ferris wheel slid backward again, the little boy in question leaned over, waving an arm in enthusiastic greeting. Clay said something in his ear which had him erupting in a fit of giggles, and Tate winced even as she waved back.

No, she definitely shouldn't see Clay again. And especially not in the company of her son. Clay would be leaving in a few days, and if she allowed anything to develop, Max would be confused and possibly hurt when Clay waltzed easily out of their lives.

It would be best to thank Clay for a truly wonderful day, explain that she had nothing more than friendship to offer, and bid him farewell so that he could enjoy the remainder of his vacation.

Whether alone, or in the company of a more accommodating woman.

And it didn't matter, couldn't matter, which avenue he chose.

Drawing a fortifying breath, Tate pushed at an errant lock of hair and turned her attention to some of the other bystanders waiting for the ride to begin.

A happy set of plump grandparents waved enthusiastically to their grandsons, a father laden with camera equipment videotaped his wife and young daughter, and a pretty teen with dark eyes watched as a smaller girl climbed aboard and buckled herself in. From the child's competence and the teen's air of boredom they'd obviously gone through the routine before. A man in a ball cap strolled over and began chatting amicably with the teen.

When the cars were filled, the sound of groaning metal gave way to a blast of rock music that signified the carnival's shift into night.

Tate found herself regretting that their excursion was drawing to a close.

THE giant wheel circled, the cooler night air whispering against the accumulated heat at the back of Clay's neck. He smiled, watching the wind whip the layers of Max's hair into a froth of messy peaks. They reached the ride's pinnacle, the gaudily illuminated carnival grounds spread beneath them. Max tilted his face up in wonder, and Clay marveled at how completely privileged he felt.

"This must be what it feels like to be Superman," Max observed, hovering right at that border between fun and fear.

He clasped Clay's hand and snuggled in close. Clay felt something inside him swell, flow naturally as a wave into shore. "You're right." He gave Max's hand a squeeze. And felt pretty super himself. There was something… wonderful about having a young child look at you with such unaffected trust and affection.

And he quietly thanked whatever cosmic force that had decided to put this particular child in his path.

The day he'd spent with Max and Tate had done more for his shattered morale than any beach or booze or uncomplicated sex ever could have. It had restored his faith that there was goodness left in the world, and reminded him why he continued his disheartening fight. If his knowledge and skills could make the world a little safer for kids like Max, then every hour he put into that fight was worth it.

The wheel began to circle back around, and Clay caught sight of Tate's smiling face as she leaned over the metal railing. Something else began to swell in him, but it had little to do with altruism and a whole lot to do with physiology.

He was pretty damn sure he'd never wanted a woman this much in his life.

His eyes narrowed dangerously, easy smile turning feral as he watched her slide by.

That one little kiss had been just enough to learn the taste of her, and he had every intention of sampling some more of the delectable Ms. Hennessey by the end of the night.

The ride finally ground to a halt, but he and Max remained suspended in the air. Their car had come to rest near the top of the circle, and as such made them some of the last to disembark. Max's bright eyes bore the weight of sleepiness when Clay finally carried him down.

"Did you see me, Mommy?" He tried to stifle a yawn against Clay's neck. "Mr. Clay said that only the really cool people get to stop like that at the top."

"Did he now?" Tate thanked Clay with her eyes as he shifted the exhausted child into her arms.

"Uh-huh." Max blinked heavily, his lids reluctant to stay open. "Do you think we can come back again tomorrow?"

"Sorry, kiddo." Tate pressed a kiss to her son's temple. "But this has been a one day only kind of thing." They started to move off the ramp leading from the ride's exit, but a little blonde girl had them blocked. Like Max, she looked tired and overextended. Tears coursed in currents through the dust on her cheeks. "Sweetheart, is everything alright?"

The child looked at Tate out of wary blue eyes. Chin wobbling, she shook her head *no*.

Clay bent to the child's level. "Are you lost?"

Shaking her head rather quickly, she cautiously backed away. Sensing that she was intimidated by either his size or his gender, Clay straightened and motioned to Tate. The fact that she was a female – and moreover, a mother – might make the little girl feel more comfortable about confiding in a stranger.

Shifting Max from his position on her hip, she stooped toward the disheveled child. "Do you need help finding your mommy and daddy?"

Blonde curls tumbled as she shook her head again. But then the little girl lifted a chubby hand and pointed toward the crowd. "My mommy works over there."

Following the direction of the child's extended finger, Clay saw a conglomeration of metal trailers and blinking lights. "Your mommy works here at the carnival?"

"She makes funnel cakes."

He and Max had nearly made themselves sick gorging on funnel cakes earlier in the day, and Clay was pretty sure he remembered the trailer's location. He squatted down again to join the others.

"My name is Clay, and this is Tate and Max. If it's alright with you, we'd like to help you get back to your mama."

At the child's unhappy frown, Clay shifted so that he could get his fingers into his pocket. He pulled out his badge, flipped it open. "Do you know what this is?" he asked as the little girl studied the bright gold shield.

She shook her head again. "This badge says that I'm a policeman." Of sorts. "Did your mama explain to you that it's okay to trust a policeman if you're lost?"

"But I'm not the one who's lost."

At that, Clay frowned in confusion.

"Is your sister lost?" Max piped up from his position between Clay and his mom.

The little girl nodded and Clay turned his frown toward Max. "I saw them earlier," Max explained with a shrug. "She pointed at my bear and told her sister she wanted one. Her sister said 'get real'."

Impressed with Max's powers of observation, Clay's mouth moved in the hint of a smile before he returned his attention to the other child. "Where did you lose your sister?"

"Here," the little girl explained. "She always waits for me to do the Ferris wheel 'cause she's scared of heights. But when I got off this time she wasn't here."

"How old is your sister?"

"Thirteen," the child supplied. "But she'll be fourteen real soon. She wants an iPhone for her birthday, but Mommy told her she couldn't have one."

Clay relaxed a little as he catalogued the information. A disgruntled teen being pressed into babysitting duty had most likely simply wandered away. She was probably hanging out by the picnic tables where he'd seen the other teenagers gathering. He started to suggest that he and Tate walk the child back to her mother, and let the other woman deal with her misplaced teen, but Tate's next comment stopped him cold.

"I think I saw your sister talking to your daddy," she told the little girl.

"I don't have a daddy."

As Tate winced over her inadvertent blunder, Clay's instincts kicked into gear. "Why did you assume the man was her father?"

"I don't know." Tate shrugged. "He looked... older. I guess I just assumed he was her father. I should know better."

"Can you describe him?"

"Well, like I said, he was probably somewhere in his thirties, although I could be off because his face was partially hidden by the cap. He was big, though. Really bulky." She used her hands to guesstimate shoulder width. "Like maybe he lifted a lot of weights."

Clay cursed under his breath, just loud enough for Tate to hear. "Do you remember how he was dressed?"

Tate shrugged, clearly growing uneasy. She unconsciously pulled Max against her side. "To be honest, I didn't really notice. I just remember that he was wearing a cap."

"Anything on the cap? Any words or emblems?"

"Ah," she struggled to remember. "There might have been an 'A', like for the Braves."

With that, Clay returned his attention to the child. "Do you think you could tell me your name?"

The girl looked at the shield, which Clay had purposefully kept visible. Then she lifted her eyes toward his. "Amber."

"Okay, Amber." His smile was gentle. "Does your mommy have any friends that wear a cap with a letter 'A' sewn onto it?" There was always the chance the man was someone they knew.

Amber shook her head and frowned. "I don't think so. Old Tom wears a hat, but his is made out of straw."

Clay gathered that she was referring to the man in charge of the ponies. Not wanting to alarm her, he kept a smile in his voice when he spoke. "Amber, Miss Tate and I are going to take you back to your mama. And then you have my word, as a policeman, that I will help you find your sister."

He stood and offered his hand to Max. "Max, if it's okay with you, I think that Amber might be more comfortable if she held onto your mama's hand. Do you mind walking with me?"

Smiling up at Clay, Max tucked a hand into his. "I like walking with you."

The four of them made their way through the gathering throng until they arrived at the trailer peddling funnel cakes. The smell of fried dough and powdered sugar wafted out, and when the frizzy-haired blonde purveyor saw her younger daughter in the company of strangers, she frowned out the sliding window.

"Amber, where's Casey?"

Amber let go of Tate and raced toward her mother, who opened the door and caught the child in her arms. "What happened?" she demanded, dividing another frown between Tate and Clay.

"Ma'am, I don't want to alarm you, but we found your daughter alone near the Ferris wheel, and she claims to have lost her sister. Is there any chance your other daughter came by here?"

"No." Her worn face twisted into an angry mask. "She knows I'd tear a strip off her hide for leaving her sister alone. You sure she wasn't hanging around that ride and you just didn't see her?" she asked her daughter.

Amber shook her head and clung to her mother. "She wasn't there, Mommy, I promise."

"Ma'am, if you don't mind me asking, do you or your daughter happen to know any men who wear an Atlanta Braves hat? About six feet tall, dark hair and eyes, and very muscular – like a weightlifter?"

The woman opened her mouth, obviously wanting to deny any such knowledge, but seemed to change her mind. "A man like that bought a funnel cake from me today. I remember because he was a real hottie. I like a man that looks like he can handle himself, you know what I mean?"

She looked Clay up and down. "Why do you want to know?"

"Miss Hennessey" – he nodded toward Tate – "saw a man matching that description talking to your daughter while Amber was on the ride."

"And what, you think she went off somewhere with him?" She scoffed. "Casey knows better than to do something that stupid. She probably just went to the bathroom. Although I'm still going to lay into her for leaving her sister alone."

"I hope you're right," Clay said evenly. But he had a bad feeling, nonetheless. And after years of dealing with the worst kinds of offenders, he'd learned to trust his instincts. "Has she ever gone off like that before?"

She hesitated, growing suspicious. "Are you a cop or something?"

Clay pulled out his badge again, noting that this was the third time he'd done so on his vacation. "Special Agent Clay Copeland, FBI." He could tell he was making the woman nervous. "And I'm not interested in trying to persecute you for anything, ma'am. I'm merely concerned for the safety of your daughter." He handed her the identification so that she could study it, continuing in a friendly voice. "If you don't mind, I'd like to offer to help you locate her."

The first crystals of fear began to form in her eyes. "You think that man had something to do with her wandering off?"

Given the vibes he'd gotten from that man, he was afraid it was a possibility. "It would be premature to speculate at this point," he informed her. Freaking the mother out totally wouldn't do either of them a whole lot of good.

And there was always the chance he was wrong.

"Maybe you could just check the places you think she might have gone, and make both of us feel a whole lot better."

"You're right." Her smile came over-bright and false. "She's probably just back at our camper, or maybe hanging around those no-good teenagers over by the woods."

Clay turned toward Tate, skimming the back of his fingers along her cheek. "I know you and Max are both tired, but would you mind terribly if we stuck around?"

"Of course not." She shivered slightly. "And just for the record, I think it's awfully nice of you to want to help out."

Clay smiled, dropping a kiss on her brow before bending down to consult with Max. "I'm going to help Amber look for her sister, and I was wondering if you wouldn't mind taking care of your mama while I'm gone?"

Max's small chest deflated with disappointment. "Why can't I go with you? I could be your deputy agent."

Clay's heart swelled yet again, just like the damn Grinch on Christmas morning. But he didn't want Max tagging along, because he was afraid of what they might find. "You *are* my deputy agent, Max. And the assignment I'm giving you is to stay here and look after your mama. It's a really important assignment, because your mother is very special." And because he knew a little bit about child psychology, he pulled out the standard reverse. "But if you don't think you can handle it, I can give the job to someone else."

Max straightened his shoulders. "Nobody can take care of Mommy better than me."

"I'm counting on it," Clay said solemnly. And then he gave Tate's hand a final squeeze before heading off with the distraught mother.

CHAPTER EIGHT

TWENTY minutes later, Clay returned with a tearful Lola – that was the mother's name – after they'd dropped Amber off with some friends. Tate waited on the picnic table near the funnel cake trailer, Deputy Max asleep on her lap.

"No luck?" she asked as they approached.

Lola moved blindly toward the trailer, and Clay shook his head as he sat. "No one that we talked to had seen her. Normally, I wouldn't be all that worried because teenagers pull this kind of thing all the time, but I get the impression that this Casey is a pretty responsible kid. Responsible kids do stupid things, too, but factor in the vibes I got from that man earlier today and I don't like how it adds up. I convinced the mother to call in the local police, because I didn't want to waste any more time canvassing the area when there's a chance he took her out of here."

Tate drew in a shaky breath. "You think he abducted her."

It was a statement, not a question. Clay glanced toward the trailer to make sure Lola couldn't overhear. She was walking a fine line between holding it together and losing it, and he didn't want to push her over the edge. "I don't have enough information to make that call." He started to leave it at that. No need to upset Tate any more than he had to, either. But recalling the story she'd told him that morning, he realized that platitudes weren't enough. So he put aside professional circumspection, and said what he thought. "It's certainly plausible. There was something entirely wrong with the guy's behavior. I noticed him when we were in the picnic area earlier. I think he was selecting his quarry."

Tate flinched at the harsh analogy. But it was, he knew, how this type of perpetrator thought. "What happens next?" she asked carefully.

"We wait for the cops. You'll have to give them a statement. Luckily, the mother and I both got a good look at him earlier, so they won't have to rely totally on your description. But just to warn you, if she doesn't turn up in the next twenty-four hours, you may have to look through some mug-shots."

"Do you think she's going to turn up?"

Clay sighed and rubbed the tension from the back of his neck. "Unless she's simply off somewhere in a teenage pout, or went with that guy of her own free will, I'd say that possibility's unlikely. He allowed several people, including the girl, to get a good look at him. That means he's not concerned about being caught. If he's not concerned about being caught, he either wasn't contemplating committing any crime, or he feels sure he can't be tied to one." He reflected on the man's demeanor and suspected he'd been planning the abduction all day. "If he took that girl, you can almost bet she'll never be found."

Tate looked at the trailer, where the girl's mother was locking up, and clutched her own sleeping child. "Isn't there anything else that can be done?"

Clay felt the weight of that question settle like lead. "If the police ask me, I can offer them a personality assessment of the suspected offender. Combine that with eyewitness descriptions, put out some flyers, do some canvassing, and there's a chance someone will recognize him and turn him in. I can also suggest several techniques for drawing him out." He blew out a breath full of frustration. "But in cases like this, the first twenty-four hours are critical. If she's not located by then, there's less than a fifty percent chance of recovering her alive. The problem, of course, is that the local authorities are often reluctant to consider a person missing until twenty-four hours have passed. Children are a different story, but the fact that Casey is a teen doesn't weigh in her favor – they're notorious for exercising their own will."

"But you're here," Tate protested. "Can't you tell them that she didn't just run off?"

"I don't know that for sure," he reminded her gently. "I wasn't able to observe the girl personally, so I'm not really at liberty to offer an opinion about what she might be likely to do. I can only take her mother's word for that, and a mother's word isn't always reliable. However," he reached out and stroked her arm when he recognized her frustration, "I can offer an educated opinion that the man you saw her speaking with was not… on the up and up. Again, it's just an opinion, as we have no solid evidence of wrongdoing. Hopefully that opinion will hold enough water to prompt them into launching a full-fledged investigation. But that's their call to make, not mine."

Tate sank back against the picnic table. "It must be very difficult for you, doing what you do."

Clay looked at the sleeping child in her arms and thought of another little boy, now dead. "Sometimes more than others."

Two sheriff's deputies arrived, and Clay and Tate spent the next forty-five minutes giving statements and discussing what they'd seen. Then if the night hadn't already turned crappy, the arrival of a local news crew sent it right into the toilet. They'd been filming a human interest piece on the carnival and caught wind that something was going down. Lola, who was growing desperate to find her daughter, let it slip that Clay worked for the FBI. That particular piece of information had sent the ambitious reporter into a frenzy. But Clay calmly informed her that he was not at liberty to discuss anything because it wasn't his case, and that the FBI had no official role in the investigation. He suggested, quite equably, that she should direct any questions she might have toward the local sheriff. He wasn't inclined to have his face plastered all over the news.

"Are you ready?" he asked Tate softly, when they'd done all they could for the time being.

Tate nodded, and after offering a last word of support to Casey's mother, he shepherded his date and her sleeping child back to his car.

THE quiet ride home was a far cry from their trip out that afternoon.

Max had fallen asleep even before they'd left the parking lot, and the closed look on Clay's face kept Tate from peppering him with questions. She had a million, born of concern and frustration, but she knew they'd done all they could for now. And like he said, maybe he was wrong. Maybe Casey had gone off of her own free will. She wanted to ask what the statistics were for teenagers getting grounded until they reached adulthood for scaring their parents to death, but she thought it was better to leave it alone. Her cousin Kathleen was a homicide detective, and Tate understood that there were times when they just had to shut everything out.

Poor Clay.

Considering this was supposed to have been a no-stress trip to the beach, he'd spent more time embroiled in crises than lying on the sand.

"You know, for a man who's on vacation you sure haven't had much time to relax."

Clay's tone was rueful as he pulled into the inn's lot. "Well, I can't say our dates have been boring."

Tate studied him in the shadows. The gas street lamp cast flickering patterns of light across his face, which still bore the insult of last night's battle. The swelling in his lip was down but the bruise beneath his eye had bloomed a sickly violet. Added to that was the accumulated evidence of their day: His white T-shirt bled red from the grasp of ketchup-smeared little fingers, and his hair– stiff from sweat and dust – was more burnished now than golden.

There was a small piece of what looked to be a popcorn kernel caught between his two front teeth.

"Actually," she informed him to lighten the mood, and because she found his disarray ridiculously attractive. Perhaps because she'd learned that the shiniest things usually tarnished faster than most. "You can't really consider them dates. Last night you kidnapped me from my place of employment, and my son invited you along today. If anything they've been more like… random encounters."

"Random encounters?" One side of his mouth drew up in amusement.

"Uh-huh. Dates are when one person asks another to accompany them someplace. Usually involving a shared meal. Possibly some form of diversionary entertainment."

"I see." Clay leaned against the window. "Correct me if I'm wrong, but I do believe we shared an ungodly amount of food today, as well as hours of various forms of entertainment."

"True." The nod was acknowledgement. She was glad her teasing had drawn out his smile. "But you're forgetting that crucial 'date' component. You never actually asked me out."

"I see," he repeated, reaching out to stroke her fingers. She extended them to link with his. "Is this where you tell me that because I skipped a step I'm required to go back to the beginning? Do not pass go?" He kissed their joined fingers. "Do not collect two hundred dollars?"

"I'm afraid those are the rules."

"Well," he tightened his grip. "I've never been very good at following directions."

Dragging her over the console, Clay shot his other hand into her hair. Surprised, Tate could only blink as his mouth descended against hers. She'd been bantering with him, hoping to cheer him up… and possibly angling for another kiss like they'd shared beneath the Ferris wheel. A little sweetness to wash away the awful taste the last couple of hours had left in her mouth.

But this was no innocent sampling. He angled his head, parted her lips, and went after her with his tongue.

Some small, sane part of her brain whispered *this is a bad idea.* She'd lectured herself earlier about the dangers of playing with fire.

But her blood heated. Her skin went damp beneath the hand that slid under her T-shirt. The muscles in her stomach quivered when his fingers blazed a trail.

"God. You taste good."

As compliments went, it wasn't the most poetic. But when he nipped at her lip, traced the tip of his finger around the edge of her bra, she considered that sweet talk was overrated.

"That's just the chocolate from that banana."

He groaned against her throat, and the thick shoulders beneath her hands shuddered. "I have a confession."

The husky rasp of the words made her shiver.

"Oh?" She caught her breath. His finger dipped beneath the black lace.

The lace rasped against her nipple as he drew the cup down. "When I watched the way you were using your mouth on that tasty little frozen confection, I'm afraid it caused… an involuntary reaction."

Tate was pretty sure he was reacting now.

And as much as she wanted to be put off by that, the fact was her blood was sizzling. His fingers skimmed, then cupped her breast as if to weigh it. Circled her nipple, drawing a whimper from Tate's throat. And when he pinched, ever so slightly at first, then just short of actual pain, it short-circuited whatever protests her brain might make.

She tugged his hair to get his mouth back on hers.

CLAY had hoped to throw her off guard with that first kiss, shake her up a little. Not allow her the time to think it through. But since she wasn't the only one who'd been shaken, he fought to wrestle his desire under control.

Tate was sweet, so devoid of artifice, and she'd gone utterly willing under his hands.

Not that he wasn't delighted about that. But she deserved the time and space to do this right. If he wasn't careful, he'd end up taking her in the back seat.

Shit.

The back seat.

Opening one heavy lid Clay caught sight of the sleeping Max, still clutching that purple bear to his chest. They definitely needed to move this inside. The boy could wake up any minute, and Clay didn't want to invite any more observations about his penis.

"Tate," he said against her mouth. Her arms twined around his neck. One hand slipped down to stroke his chest and he had to force the words out through his teeth. "We need... to go... in the house."

"What?" She squirmed a little closer, all but climbing onto his lap. He felt her breasts crush against his chest and beat his fist on the dash.

"For God's sake, Tate." His voice was raw with desperation. One more minute of this and he was going to burst through his fly. "Let's get Max put to bed and we can finish this inside."

The words were like a slap in the face. Tate shot back, looked guiltily toward her son, and then blinked at Clay in horror.

"Oh, my God. You must think I'm awful."

"I can assure you," Clay said on a pained laugh. "Thinking you're awful never entered my mind."

The look she shot him was incredulous. "I just jumped you in front of my son."

"He's sleeping."

Tate apparently failed to find that reassuring. "Well. As you were kind enough to remind me before I tossed myself bodily into your lap, I believe it's time to put my son in bed."

"I'll help you carry him up."

Clay slid out of the car with no grace whatsoever and hobbled around to open Tate's door. And when he lifted Max from his car seat, barely controlled a wince.

Tate's eyes flew to his crotch. Recognizing the cause of his discomfort had heat creeping back into her cheeks. "I'm sorry," she said helplessly as she attempted to open the back door. She fumbled the key, dropping it before finally wrestling the door open with a squeal of hinges.

They entered a large and cozy kitchen, gleaming with commercial grade appliances. The two coloring book pages attached to the huge Sub-zero refrigerator gave Clay a jolt that faded into pleasure.

The picture of Peter Parker was his.

Mossy green walls formed a quiet well of shadows, the light over the range guiding their passage. Tate moved past its thin yellow glow and showed Clay toward the back stairs.

He'd been doctored in her bathroom the previous night, so he was familiar with the third floor layout. He turned left at the head of the stairs and walked to Max's door. Tate rushed ahead of him to push it open, brushing a small army of toys from her son's bed. When she turned down the Thomas the Tank Engine sheets, Clay laid Max between them.

Max rolled over, clutching his bear.

Tate pulled off Max's shoes before covering him up, grimacing at his dusty feet. The kid would need a bath first thing in the morning. Then she straightened, offering Clay a grateful smile as he reached out to shut off the light. He put a finger to her lips, grasping her hand.

And then drew her toward her bedroom.

PULSE pounding an erratic beat, Tate recalled her earlier conversation with herself, which had focused on why sleeping with Clay was a Bad Idea. She just didn't do that sort of thing.

And besides, he would be leaving in a few days. There were simply too many factors to consider. And after weighing them – again – she knew what she had to do.

"Clay." She pulled back on his hand to stop him from crossing the threshold. He lingered there, arching a brow. He looked so handsome, even in his disheveled state, and so utterly capable of fulfilling her every fantasy, that telling him "no" seemed like shooting herself in the foot.

She didn't want to do it.

"I…" God, now he was going to think she was a tease. "I'm sorry, but I don't think we can do this."

"Sure we can," he said in a low voice, cognizant of the nearby presence of her mother and her son. "Tab 'A' goes into slot 'B'. Trust me; people do it all the time."

Tate knew he was trying to make her relax, but this was one time humor wasn't going to work. "It's not that simple for me, Clay. I'm not the type of woman who thinks purely in terms of the physical."

Clay cupped his hand under her chin. "Is that what you think this is?"

Tate shrugged, a gesture of futility. "How can it be anything else?"

She had him there, but Clay didn't like it. "It can be whatever we make it."

Tate hesitated a moment, wanting desperately to believe, but it didn't change the fact that he was leaving. She already cared enough that she would feel his loss when he was gone.

How much more significant that loss if she made love with him?

She cupped her own hand over his, which had moved to stroke her cheek. "I'm sorry." And she was, truly. "I can't. Even if I understand why you have to leave, I'm not sure that Max would, and I don't want to set us both up for disappointment."

THAT statement hit Clay like a blow. He hadn't even considered Max. And it both pleased and horrified him to realize he could have that kind of impact on the child's feelings.

And Tate was a conscientious mother to keep that at the forefront of her mind, because he had absolutely no doubt that she wanted him.

And God, he wanted her.

So he purposely stepped back, allowing her some distance. "It's okay." Although it wasn't. "In the grand scheme of things, I respect your decision. I might not like it." His smile was wry. "But I respect it."

Because there was nothing left to say, because if he didn't get out of there he'd forget his good intentions, he leaned forward, dropping a regretful kiss on her cheek. "Good night, Tate Hennessy. Tell Max that I said goodbye."

Clay cursed himself on the way to Justin's for making a royal mess of his vacation. How the hell, in two days, mind you, had he managed to form – what the hell was this? An attachment? An obsession? God help him, an actual *relationship?* – with a woman he met on the beach? And not just any woman, either.

A woman with a kid.

A really super-terrific kid, whose smile was almost as appealing as his mother's.

It was one hell of a package deal.

Whoa, Nellie. He put a rein on those horses before he found himself flattened by the pitter-patter of little hooves. There were absolutely, positively no deals to be made here, because he had nothing to bring to the table. He lived in another state. And his job kept him on the road nearly four days out of seven.

Not to mention the fact that he was a confirmed… well, womanizer wasn't exactly the word. That indicated that he lacked respect for women, which he didn't. He genuinely admired and liked women. He liked *a lot* of women. And in general the feeling was reciprocal.

There was absolutely no room in his life for any type of commitment.

"Shit!" Clay almost drove his truck off the Cooper River Bridge when that traitorous thought entered his head. Not that he was afraid of commitment. Exactly. Hell, he'd had relationships before, hadn't he?

But not after a few days' acquaintance. And not with a woman who came as part of a set.

Cringing, he vividly recalled busting Justin's brother Jordan's chops quite recently for pretty much the same thing.

"Christ, Copeland." Clay scrubbed his hand over his face and tried to think. What had he consumed today that had turned his mind to mush? It must have been that last, high-intensity spin on the Tilt-O-Whirl, combined with a boatload of sugar and saturated fat that had managed to pickle his brain.

Of course, it hadn't impaired his *second* most highly functioning organ, which even now was protesting the fact that he'd done the decent thing and tried to make love to Tate *inside.* If he'd kept his big mouth shut, he probably could have opened his fly, adjusted her position by a couple inches, and had this whole little dilemma taken care of.

Right now he'd be driving home physically sated, thinking clearly, and... feeling like a total jerk.

Tate was simply too special to be treated like a piece of... hell, he couldn't even think it. Putting her name and *ass* in the same sentence made him want to punch his own face.

There was an edge here, and he was walking dangerously close to it. And whatever lay on the other side was scary as hell.

Deciding that he really, *really* needed to get some sleep, he pulled his vehicle in beside Justin's, a little cheered that his friend was home. If he didn't have to work tomorrow night, they'd go out and paint the town red.

Clay opened the back door, which Justin had thoughtfully left unlatched, and wandered in to find his friend sprawled on the leather sofa. He was stripped down to his underwear again – boxer shorts, this time, at least – and watching the evening news. He looked dazed and a little groggy.

Justin looked him over skeptically. "What the hell happened to you? You look like you came out on the losing end of a food fight."

Until then, Clay honestly hadn't noticed how much crap his clothes had accumulated. He was smeared with ketchup, chocolate, dust, grease and God knew what else. Plus he had the strange and sudden certainty that there was something lodged between his front teeth.

Shit. Had that been there when he'd been kissing Tate? No wonder she'd told him to get out.

"Carnival food," Clay explained, as he crashed into the recliner. He noticed there was gum stuck to the toe of his left shoe.

Justin raised one dark brow. "Was it worth it?"

If you called a bad case of indigestion, a fortune spent to win a stupid purple bear, a nice foray into the complexities of trying to seduce a woman while in the presence of her young son, not to mention a brief stopover into everyone's favorite nightmare – child abduction – worthwhile, he guessed he hadn't come away empty handed.

Then he thought about the feel of Tate's soft lips as they raced over his, and the look on Max's face when he'd called him his deputy.

And the way his stupid frickin' heart had swelled all out of proportion when he'd walked – just walked – holding both of their hands.

He'd gotten more out of the day then he'd bargained.

"It was fun," he told Justin with a shrug.

Being a guy, Justin considered the subject dropped and pushed the volume button up on the remote.

Just before the sports could be recapped, an aggressively groomed brunette with a microphone filled the screen. A large Ferris wheel dominated the background, spinning gaily amidst a blinking array of lights. Clay sat mesmerized, a sinking feeling beginning to pull at his already abused stomach. He did a little mental cataloguing, filing this under Things That Did Not Bode Well.

He just *knew* that woman was going to find a way to drag him into this.

He sat rigidly as the reporter began talking.

"Traveling carnivals are as ubiquitous to the American landscape as baseball and apple pie. But tonight, this slice of Americana set the stage for tragedy, as thirteen-year-old Casey Rodriguez disappeared from the area surrounding this Ferris wheel right behind me, where she'd been waiting for a family member to finish the ride. Law enforcement officials on the scene – which included local sheriff's deputies and an FBI agent – have declined comment, explaining that their investigation into the girl's disappearance is still pending. However, sources close to the investigation have indicated that there is suspicion of foul play. Volunteer search teams have fanned out tonight in the woods and fields surrounding the fairgrounds, hoping to find some clue that might lead to the discovery of the lost teen's whereabouts."

Here, the camera panned to show several policemen and volunteers on the scene, and then cut to some earlier footage that included Casey Rodriguez's mother. The reporter kept babbling, but Clay focused in – as did the camera – on an interesting tableau in the background. Clay, with his arm around Max and Tate, was deep in discussion with one of the deputies who'd been among the first responders. The cameraman had the perfect angle to all but zoom in on the badge on Clay's hip.

Shit, Clay thought again. Wasn't that just dandy? They'd made it seem like he was a participant in the investigation. So when that little girl's body turned up in a ditch they could point fingers at the feds.

Then Justin finally woke up to what was happening and cranked up the volume even more.

"Hey man. You're on TV." His tired voice was mystified.

As Justin – and the rest of the Channel Five viewing audience – watched with interest, Clay dropped a kiss on the little boy's head before turning his mouth toward the child's mother. Then he put his arm around her and squeezed. Possessively.

Justin's brow raised as the camera panned back to the reporter, who wrapped up the segment with a grim smile. "This is Paige Lowell reporting for Action Five News."

He turned around and smirked at Clay.

"Fun. Yeah."

Clay sat there, numb, not because he'd been pretty much name-dropped – those three little initials were like fairy dust sprinkled magically to increase the case's sensationalism and thus the channel's ratings – but because he'd just watched his behavior with his own eyes.

And the verdict wasn't pretty.

He could circle around, backtrack and bluster all he wanted, but he'd just seen the irrefutable evidence.

"Shit."

It had become his favorite word.

With the sound of Justin's laughter as an exit score, Clay heaved himself out of the chair and hauled his commitment-phobic, way-too-busy-for-a-relationship, down-for-the-count ass off to bed.

CHAPTER NINE

"*WHAT* the hell were you thinking?"

Billy Wayne popped the second contact from his gritty eyes, blinking several times before sliding his gaze toward JR. The smaller man was standing across the room, clutching the remote in his fist. If Billy Wayne hadn't already shaved his hair, the heat of his cousin's glare would have singed it.

JR rarely lost his temper – he was colder than an Eskimo's tit – and to see him so close to boiling was something of a novelty.

Billy Wayne tossed the disposable lens into the trash can next to the sofa, crossing his booted feet on the cheap oak coffee table. The place they were using was a dump, and he missed the luxury of his condo in Atlanta. It had been a long time since he'd lived out in the boondocks like this, and the memories the dingy little house brought back set his teeth on edge.

He didn't need JR's attitude to send his own temper simmering.

"I got the girl – a virgin, I might add – and no one made me or followed. Even if some people saw me talking to her, they're going to describe me as a dark-skinned, brown-eyed man with a full head of hair." He pointed to his bald head, from which he'd recently removed his wig. "It's not like they had hidden cameras and facial recognition technology at that damn carnival. Who's going to recognize me like this?"

Despite the fact that he had an extremely distinct appearance, Billy Wayne was decent with disguises – not as good as JR, who could be old, young, dark, fair and everything in between – but decent. The only thing that really tripped him up was his overabundance of muscles, which he stubbornly refused to do anything about.

It was the one legacy from his piece-of-shit father that he didn't actually hate the man for. Norman Sparks had beaten and ridiculed him as often as not, but the steroids and weightlifting he'd pushed Billy Wayne into had given him the means to get even.

In fact, he'd taken the first body building trophy he'd won and beat his old man half to death.

Vaguely aware that JR was still glowering, he glanced at the TV. The news anchor had just titillated the audience by dropping hints about the girl's disappearance, with the full story coming up at eleven.

True, having their newest piece of merchandise bandied about on the evening news wasn't exactly standard operating procedure, but all in all Billy Wayne thought that JR was overreacting. They already had a buyer lined up to take her off their hands, so it wasn't like they even had to advertise the girl in their usual circles. They'd simply complete the transaction, the case would grow cold, and that would be the end of the sordid little story.

He said as much, and amused himself by watching steam practically rise from his cousin's blond head.

Man, he'd charmed a sweet little girl and pushed JR over the edge, while he himself maintained a firm hold on his temper.

Was this a banner night or what?

JR pinched the bridge of his nose and brought himself under control. This was the second inexcusable miscalculation Billy Wayne had made – the first being beating one of the girls to death because he couldn't get it up for the camera, then selling the footage as a snuff film behind JR's back.

He was beginning to think his cousin had gotten careless.

Carelessness and a life of crime were two things that didn't mix.

Yes, this girl was a good find, and yes, they likely already had a buyer. But snatching a kid who would be missed right away was not only risky, it was unbelievably arrogant.

Combine arrogance with carelessness and you have a recipe for disaster. That particular combination brought even the cleverest of criminals down.

And if Billy Wayne went down, he'd try to take JR with him. That was one thing he positively could not allow.

JR watched Billy Wayne watching him, and visibly shook off his rage. Angry confrontations were not his style, as they were usually counterproductive.

Two pairs of blue eyes held each other's gaze until the newscast began in earnest. When a reporter came onto the screen with a Ferris wheel looming large behind her, JR cranked the volume and then stood, hands on hips, waiting to assess the damage. They might have to cut their losses, get rid of the girl, and pull out of Charleston if this thing attracted too much attention.

The brunette started mouthing off about baseball and apple pie. And about thirty seconds into the newscast, dropped an unexpected bomb.

There was an FBI agent involved in the investigation.

Now, what the hell were the Feebs doing sticking their noses into a missing persons case that wasn't even three hours old? They had jurisdiction over kidnappings, but there should have been no indication that the girl had left the fairgrounds under anything but her own free will.

Behind him, Billy Wayne began to make angry noises of protest, but JR stopped him with a quelling look.

Then the camera panned out, showing a blond man and what looked to be his family. JR noted the badge on his hip. He was dressed casually – not standard government issue – and was holding onto a dark-haired woman and a sleeping child.

From that JR surmised that the man probably had been off duty. Simply a matter of being at the wrong place at the wrong time. Which meant the FBI wasn't hot on their trail.

Lucky thing for Billy Wayne.

Then, just as JR was about to lose interest – after all, the locals would never be able to catch them – the off duty FBI agent kissed his wife on the mouth. As she turned, JR caught a glimpse of her face.

Memories long buried erupted to the surface.

He tilted his head. Squinted his eyes. He couldn't be certain.

The last time he'd seen her in person had been outside a crowded courthouse. She hadn't seen him, of course – he hadn't wanted anyone to see him, to know that he'd been drawn as helplessly as a fish on a line – so he'd dressed as a homeless bum. It had been his first attempt at disguise.

And he'd kept up with what you could call the *main players* for a number of years afterward.

Until...

Well. Until there hadn't been any reason to keep up with them any longer.

Anger crept slowly back in, an unwelcome visitor with muddy feet, messing up the inner rooms he'd swept clean.

The woman turned more fully toward the camera, and doubt fled out the door so recently opened by his intrusive guest. It was her.

Then his gaze slid toward the sleeping child.

A boy.

Tate Hennessey had a son.

An emotion even more foreign than anger caused the remote he held to tremble.

CHAPTER TEN

SHIT.

It was Clay's very first thought of the morning. Before he'd showered, before he'd had coffee, before he'd even taken a leak, he had his cell phone in his hand.

And what, he asked himself, was he planning to do with it?

Call Tate?

Saying what, exactly?

Hi Sugar, it's me. You know that man you kicked out of your life last night? The one who has so far managed to drag you into an almost-mugging, give a peep show to your mother and your kid, disabuse any wide-eyed notions you might have about my big, bad FBI abilities to locate a missing teenager, and who all but forced himself upon you in my car's front seat?

The one who is in town for no more than a few more days and has absolutely nothing to offer other than a couple of dates and some hair-raising sex, and will leave you and your little boy with some nice memories and a stupid purple bear?

Yeah. That's the one. So do you want to have dinner tonight?

Double shit. He'd lost his ever-loving mind.

Clay wondered exactly when he'd gone from being Clay Copeland, expert on human behavior, easygoing bachelor and master of the fine art of Avoiding Entanglements With Women, to Clay Copeland – total head case.

Maybe he could find a way to engrave those new credentials on his badge.

Forget Fidelity, Bravery and Integrity. FBI – as pertaining to himself – now stood for Full Blown Idiot.

As he lay there in Justin's guest room watching the morning light dance through the blinds, he realized that somehow, in the past few days, he'd succumbed to what countless hours of putting himself in the mindset of some of the country's most evil and diabolical killers hadn't managed to do. He'd gone off the deep end, blown a fuse, gone postal or whatever you want to call it.

Because the first thought he'd had this morning, the last notion in his head before he'd succumbed to fatigue – hell, the *dreams* that had plagued him all night – had all revolved around how exactly he was going to get his hands on Tate.

Not that he'd stop with his hands.

Oh no.

He wanted his mouth, and his tongue, and his... everything to suddenly fuse themselves to her like some kind of parasitic growth.

He wanted to taste her, to consume her, to frickin' *devour* her. And then start the entire process again. He wanted... Hell, he didn't know what he wanted.

Liar. He did, too.

He wanted to have Max crawl into bed with him in the morning, and for it to be perfectly okay for him to be there.

Because Tate would be there.

On a regular basis.

Really regular.

Like every day.

He felt himself freefalling into complete and utter mental chaos. "Shit, shit, *shit.*"

When the phone in his hand started ringing, Clay nearly did that in his pants. "Copeland," he sighed into the phone, trying to keep the tone-of-a-man-who-has-lost-it out of his voice.

He sort of hoped it was his boss. Cutting his vacation short. Getting him out of this rabbit hole he'd fallen into so that the world could start making sense again.

"Agent Copeland? This is Deputy Jones with the Bentonville sheriff's department. We spoke to each other last night?"

Well thank God. Law enforcement. He felt familiar ground begin to grow under his feet. "Yes, this is Agent Copeland. How can I help you, Deputy Jones?"

"Well, Agent Copeland, I understand that you're on vacation, but I was hoping you might be able to carve out some time today to come down to the station and help us out. We put out some feelers last night to some of the other law enforcement agencies in the area, and, well… we're beginning to think that we might have a situation that could benefit from your expertise."

Ask and ye shall receive, Clay thought. It was his job to be on hand to assist the locals if they should need it. And concentrating on work should help keep his mind off Tate. "Absolutely," Clay answered, sitting up in the bed and glancing toward the alarm clock on the nightstand. Eight a.m. There were still almost twelve hours left in that critical twenty-four hour period. He didn't hold out a lot of hope that they'd find Casey Rodriguez within that time, but he was thankful that the Sheriff was proactive enough to want to bring him into it.

"Give me thirty minutes to shower and get changed and I'll head out. Give me the station address."

The man rattled it off and Clay snagged a pen from a holder on the nightstand and jotted it down on the handy little notepad.

"Got it," Clay said. His blood juiced at the thought of getting back to work, and that worried him even more. He'd come here to get away from work and now he was going to work to get away from here.

Somewhere along the line he'd gotten completely messed up.

He was just about to end the call when the deputy cleared his throat. "Uh, I don't mean to sound indelicate, Agent Copeland, but… is Ms. Hennessey with you, by any chance?"

Clay knew what the deputy was going to ask. He wanted Tate to come down to the station house and look through some mug shots. Maybe help a police artist work up a sketch. This is where he should tell the man that Tate was *not* here, and that he should try to reach Tate at her home. They could arrange an appointment on their own time, and it didn't have anything whatsoever to do with Clay.

Tate had made it clear that she had no intention of continuing to see him, and as a gentleman, he should respect that.

As a commitment-phobe, he should applaud that, running as fast and far in the opposite direction as he possibly could.

As an agent of the federal government, he really shouldn't lie.

"Ms. Hennessey is… unavailable at the moment." Hey, it was an accurate piece of information. The fact that she was across town and not merely in the shower was simply a matter of semantics. "But I'm assuming you'd like her to come in as well?"

"Yes, if it wouldn't be too much trouble."

"Not at all." Clay did some rapid thinking. "But it may take us a little while to get there. We'll need to make some arrangements for her son."

Man oh man, he was so full of it. Not to mention being a scheming, calculating *idiot* who didn't know enough to get out when the getting was good.

He said his goodbyes to the deputy, stared at the rotating ceiling fan.

The last part of his sanity crumbled.

He opened his phone again to call Tate.

TATE frowned at her reflection in the hall mirror as she stabbed an earring through her left lobe. Even with an application of concealer, the skin beneath her eyes was a particularly unappealing shade of lavender. Visible proof of her restless night. After Clay left, she'd lain awake for what seemed like hours. Her body felt tight and achy, and her mind… her mind bounced from contemplating how differently the time would have passed if she'd let him stay with her to imagining – all too vividly – what could happen to a young girl in the clutches of a twisted, narcissistic adult. Sick, feeling guilty for even beginning to think of her own physical needs at such a time, Tate felt tears roll down her cheeks and soak her pillow. The day had brought too many bad memories to the surface. Her experience at camp. Her mother, so distraught and overprotective and very, very angry. The nightmares. The subsequent trial, during which whatever scraps of innocence she'd maintained had been tattered and torn to bits.

When she finally managed to fall asleep, her dreams had been full of muscle-bound men with leering faces painted like clowns, of the Ferris wheel lights – no longer lovely, but gaudy and bright and sinister – spinning faster and faster until she'd awakened with a scream clawing its way out of her throat.

She'd practically fallen out of bed, and raced to Max's room, to find him sleeping soundly. Her baby. She'd spent the rest of the night curled up on the floor beside his bed.

Tate couldn't fathom what Casey's mother was going through right now.

Hell, she thought, and stabbed the other silver hoop through her right lobe. Sheer hell.

When Clay had called earlier, she'd been hopeful that it was with good news. Instead, here she was, getting dressed to go down to the police station to look at mug shots. She felt… not dirty, exactly. But stained. As if the filth that had altered her life so drastically that long ago summer had never quite washed off.

When the knock sounded at the back door, Tate smoothed her damp palms over the skirt of her sundress. She was nervous, she realized. Though whether it was due to her upcoming task or to seeing Clay again, she couldn't say.

She pasted a smile on her face and opened the door.

To a very well-dressed and armed federal agent.

"Good morning." Clay's brow quirked over his sunglasses when she just stood there. No doubt with her mouth agape.

"Oh. Right. Good morning." God, she sounded like an idiot. She'd known he worked for the FBI, of course. But for some reason, the sight of him in that dark suit, weapon holstered beneath his jacket... he looked so unbelievably responsible. It was a strange thing to get flustered over, but then everybody had their buttons. Considering the negligent ass who'd fathered her son, Tate guessed that upstandingness was one of hers.

She gestured him in, the cool, dim interior of the back hall a welcome relief from the morning's heat.

"Let me just get my purse." She started to turn, but Clay whipped his glasses off and shifted to block her path.

"Are you alright?"

"I'm fine," she hedged, feeling uncomfortable under his scrutiny.

In a gesture that was becoming familiar, he brushed his thumb over her cheek. "These shadows say otherwise."

"Another curse of the fair-skinned. And how kind of you to point them out."

"Your skin is lovely." He tapped her nose in a light reprimand. "I'm sorry. Given what happened, I should have realized you'd have a rough night."

"It's nothing. Really," she said when he gave her a dubious look. "I'm okay."

"Mr. Clay!"

Tate closed her eyes at the sound of her son's voice, because she'd been hoping to avoid this particular scene. But Max was running down the hall, small bare feet slapping against the wood floor, an excited expression on his elfin face.

And a familiar purple bear tucked beneath his arm.

Clay's frown melted into a warm grin as he held out his hand for Max to slap.

But Max pulled up short when he caught sight of Clay's gun. Eyes huge, he looked first at Clay and then at Tate. "Are you and Mommy going to *shoot* the bad guy who took Amber's sister?"

"Max," Tate began, but Clay held up his hand to show that it was okay. Then he hunkered down to Max's level.

"Your mama and I are going to try to help the policemen find the bad guy we think took Amber's sister. And if they find him, *they'll* take the man to jail. I'm not going to shoot anybody, and nobody's going to shoot at me. When I'm working, like I am today, I'm required to carry my sidearm." He patted the weapon. "But that doesn't mean we'll be in danger. Your mama will be perfectly safe."

A mixture of both relief and disappointment flickered across Max's face. Clearly he'd been envisioning something akin to the OK Corral. Clay smiled, ruffling her little boy's hair, and Tate's heart squeezed. "So what lucky lady gets to stay with you while your mama's gone?"

"That would be me," came a deep voice from the end of the hall.

CLAY looked up to see Rogan Murphy leaning indolently against the doorway. His thick, brown hair waved almost to the top of his broad shoulders, which were bare as the rest of the torso that rose out of a snug pair of jeans. The lazy expression in his blue eyes didn't fool Clay for a minute. The man was clever and quick – he'd made the scene of the mugging with an impressive display of speed – and apparently a favorite with Max.

And he looked like a walking ad for Calvin Klein.

If it wasn't for the fact that he was Tate's blood relative, Clay would have hated him immensely.

As it was, he still felt inordinately... jealous.

Stupid and immature, but there it was.

Rogan raised a glass of amber liquid in Clay's direction. "It's nice to see you again, Agent Copeland."

"Same here," Clay lied, gaze narrowing at the glass. My God, was the man drinking *beer* at nine o'clock in the morning? What was Tate thinking, leaving him alone with Max?

And then, to Clay's horror, Mr. I'm Too Sexy For My Shirt passed off the drink to the child, who took a huge gulp before smacking his lips together.

Apparently, Tate's cousin was teaching Max to do more than cuss.

"There's nothing like a refreshing glass of apple juice to wet your whistle, is there Max?"

Clay looked up, and sure enough Murphy was smiling at him as if completely aware of what he'd been thinking. Okay, so add *perceptive* to the list of reasons to dislike the man.

Then he chastised himself for behaving like a Full Blown Idiot.

If this was how he handled a completely innocuous situation with another male, imagine what he'd do if the man hadn't been related. He'd probably have strolled across the room and tossed the guy on his perceptive ass.

Just chalk it up to his complete and total mental breakdown.

He turned to Tate, still not liking the bruised look of her eyes. And looking at mug shots all day wasn't likely to make things better. "We should probably be leaving."

"Okay." Tate grabbed her purse off the console table, then glanced at her cousin. "Are you sure you don't mind watching Max until Mom gets home?"

Rogan passed it off with a wave of his hand. "Max and I are cool."

"Okay, well…" she bent down to hug her son. "Be a good boy, and listen to Rogan."

Recalling what Max had told him about cussing and bottles of whiskey, Clay silently wondered if that was such a good idea. But he swallowed that thought and his ridiculous bout of jealousy, because acting like a possessive asshole wasn't going to win him any points with Tate.

He said goodbye to Max, nodded to Rogan and shepherded Tate out the door.

THE Bentonville sheriff's office wasn't much to look at, with its speckled gray linoleum and cinderblock walls in that hideous shade of green Clay thought of as institutional. Why bureaucrats insisted on painting civic buildings a color that was sure to drive a bunch of armed people to depression was completely beyond his ken. The frigid blast of air-conditioning that greeted them was welcome, though, as it had to be reaching toward ninety outside. Just the walk from the parking lot to the station had caused his shirt to plaster itself to his back. Tate's hair – piled atop her head with some kind of clip – had loose, damp tendrils trailing down. It was unbelievably sexy.

Clay peeled his eyes away and looked for Deputy Jones.

There was a small grouping of desks in the center of the room, separated into cubicles by a freestanding partition. They stepped up to the reception desk, and when Clay flashed his badge, the woman pointed toward an office in the rear. Through the glass on the closed door he could see Deputies Jones and Harding, whom they'd met last night, standing near the desk of an older man that Clay took to be the sheriff. All three men looked up as he rapped on the door.

Deputy Jones motioned for them to come inside.

The sheriff rose to his feet as his deputy made the introductions. Sheriff Nolan Callahan was a big man, balding and ebony-skinned, with a paunch that even the world's best posture couldn't disguise. And while he looked like he'd be more at home kicked back in his Barcalounger with a beer and a ballgame than behind a badge, Clay knew that looks were deceiving. He'd run a check, and Callahan had a solid reputation in the county. It might not seem like much, considering the county was little more than a backwater, but Clay well knew that even backwaters can harbor dangerous microbes. It was therefore with respect that Clay shook the man's hand.

"Agent Copeland," Callahan said with a nod, cool dark eyes radiating intelligence. "I appreciate you coming in."

"It was fortunate that I happened to be in town."

Sheriff Callahan's eyes darted toward Tate. "Yes, well, we're sorry to have interrupted your vacation, but I do thank you. As Deputy Jones told you this morning, I believe we might have a situation." With that, he turned to the second deputy – the one named Harding – and asked him to escort Tate to the interview room, where she would begin the process of looking through the mug shots.

For a moment, nobody moved.

Then Harding – who with his mussed hair and too-pretty face had a boy band sort of thing going on – blushed to the roots of that artfully arranged coiffure when he realized that the sheriff was talking to him. He hadn't heard him, apparently.

Because he'd been staring at Tate's legs.

"Oh, uh, yes sir." Harding snapped out of it and stepped from behind the desk. He smiled at Tate, flushed again, and steered her toward the door.

Clay forced himself not to bristle.

What the hell was a metro-sexual male doing working as a sheriff's deputy in East Jibip? Something just wasn't right.

Like your malfunctioning brainwaves, Copeland. Stop thinking about the girl and start acting like you know what you're doing.

"Okay, Sheriff." He stepped closer to the desk. "What kind of situation are we discussing?"

CHAPTER ELEVEN

TATE took a sip of the lukewarm bottle of water Deputy Harding had brought her almost an hour ago, but it did little to settle her stomach as she slid her finger across the screen of the digital mugbook. They'd started off by showing her shots of all the registered sex offenders in the area – which had pretty much stolen her breath when she realized there were so many – and then expanded her personal little cesspool to wade through by expanding the search to almost any and all apprehended felons who fit the physical criteria.

She'd taken her time, trying to give each face due consideration as opposed to just a cursory glance, even when they all started to look alike. It had been dark when she'd seen the man, and he'd been wearing a hat with the brim pulled low, and on top of that he'd been backlit by a barrage of blinking lights. Not exactly the best scenario for identification purposes. Aside from the fact that he'd been dark – dark hair, dark skin, dark eyes – she wasn't absolutely sure that she would recognize his face.

His body, however, was a different matter.

The man had been huge, with bulging muscles evident despite the covering of clothes. There had been a few large men in the mug shots she'd examined, a few that she would describe as burly and a few that might qualify as jacked. But so far none of them had shown quite the size or well-sculpted delineation that she remembered.

She kept searching, all the while hoping that Casey had simply run away from home or gone off somewhere with a boy, and not fallen prey to the man she'd seen talking to her.

A small, vulnerable girl didn't stand a chance against a man like that.

Shuddering, she sat the bottle back down and studied the screen.

The door opened with a squeak of hinges, and Tate looked up to see Deputy Harding entering with a sketch pad and a laptop computer.

He scraped in just a little shy of six feet, had the sort of lean, muscular build she associated with runners, and was the most inherently... stylish man she'd ever met. Even in his police uniform, he possessed an air of elegance that was quite at odds with his surroundings. Taking in his trendily styled dark hair, laser beam blue eyes and charmingly lopsided smile, Tate had no doubt that Deputy Harding brought all the teenyboppers in town to their knees.

"Hi." He sat the laptop down on the table. "Still no luck identifying anyone?"

Tate shook her head. "Lots of scary-looking people, but no one that I recognize."

"Well, thank God for that."

Surprised, Tate looked up.

"I mean, it's too bad that you can't ID the guy we're looking for, but a relief that you didn't see your next door neighbor in there and have to be like 'Oh my God! Bob's a sex offender!' That kind of thing's always a bummer."

Tate grinned. The guy was all kinds of adorable. And he was, she suspected, trying to make this easier for her by keeping things light. She motioned toward the sketch pad. "Is this the part where you bring in the artist and I have to describe a man that I only vaguely got a glimpse of, and she ends up doing a sketch that looks like Sponge Bob wearing a baseball cap?"

His smile was wry as he flipped open the pad. "I'm not sure whether to take that as disparagement of your observational skills or an insult to my artistic abilities."

"Oh my goodness. You're the... uh, artist?"

"Guilty."

Tate decided she didn't like the taste of having her foot in her mouth. "I'm sorry. I didn't mean to imply –"

Deputy Harding waved her apology away as he sat down. He smelled good, like quality bath products and a light dash of cologne. "Don't worry about it. My dad – who was sheriff until about three years ago, when they practically had to pry his behind out of that chair in there to get him to retire – had a similar reaction to the idea of me becoming an artist. So we compromised. I got to do a few years at the Savannah College of Art and Design on his dime, and I then had to put in my time as a sheriff's deputy." He smiled at her, showing a row of perfectly aligned teeth, and then tapped his pencil on the sketch pad. "It came as a surprise to both of us to learn that I could find a way to combine the two. In a couple weeks I'll be starting with the Charleston PD, doing this kind of thing on a regular basis. So when you see the wanted posters of Sponge Bob hanging around, you'll know who did them."

Tate laughed, charmed and chagrinned, and the deputy smiled back.

CLAY heard the burst of mingled laughter that erupted from the interview room, and turned away from the report he was studying to see what the hubbub was about. Through the open blinds he could see Deputy Harding leaning close to Tate as they consulted. They'd been at it for about thirty minutes, and this was the second time they'd broken out in giggles. Clay had no idea why trying to put together the sketch of a suspected child abductor should be so amusing, and frankly, it was beginning to piss him off.

Blocking out the sound of that thrice damned laughter, he returned his attention to the report.

It was a missing persons from a county just west of Charleston, involving a fourteen-year-old girl who'd run away from her third foster home just last month. The story was pretty unremarkable – kids ran away from bad home situations all the time, and an unfortunately high number of them were never heard from again. In this case, the girl had an older sister – pregnant and living in a state-run home – who told the police that her sister was trying to make it to their cousin in Florida.

She never arrived.

And the case would have gone very cold, very fast, if it weren't for the fact that an on-the-ball service station attendant had noticed a girl matching the teen's description sleeping in the back seat of a late model BMW. Apparently the car had blown a tire and pulled into the station's lot to change the spare. The driver of the BMW – a large, muscular blond man between approximately thirty and forty years of age – had politely refused offers of help, explaining that he was trying to get the whole thing taken care of as quietly as possible so as not to disturb his sleeping daughter.

The attendant bought the story and didn't give the matter a second thought.

Days later, when the local authorities had gotten around to making some inquiries about the missing girl, the attendant put two and two together and gave them the lead. No BMW matching the description had surfaced, but it at least gave the authorities a place to start.

And Sheriff Callahan, smart man that he was, remembered that case after Casey was reported missing. He'd gotten a copy of the report, as well as any others involving missing girls in the Charleston area, after Clay told the deputies that he believed that they were dealing with an experienced offender. Clay now had a stack of files about six inches thick, entailing over twenty young women who'd gone missing over the past six months.

Clay was sure a couple of the cases involved family abductions, and a few more were simply disgruntled teens running off with the boyfriend of the month, but there were several that struck him as warranting further attention.

There was no proof of foul play involving any of the girls, and without a body or a crime scene it was difficult for Clay to learn much about an offender's behavior. But by studying the victimology – supposing the missing young teens *were* victims – he was beginning to glean an overall pattern.

And the pattern reminded him of a conversation he'd had the previous week.

On a hunch, he retrieved his cell phone from his pocket and put in a call to Kim O'Connell. Kim was an agent with the Atlanta field office, as well as one of Clay's best friends. She'd been struggling with a nasty case involving young girls who disappeared, reappearing on some very bad porn sites on the web, or in one case as a murdered truck stop prostitute. But it was the snuff film her team had gotten their hands on that came to Clay's mind. She'd called him to pick his brain about some of the behavioral idiosyncrasies, and a couple of the points they'd discussed sounded disturbingly familiar.

The phone rang four times before it was answered by an out of breath woman.

"O'Connell."

"Did I catch you in the middle of something?"

"Ha!" Kim exclaimed when she recognized Clay's voice. "You caught me running to catch the elevator, but I failed to make it there in time. And of course the team of defense lawyers who just piled onto it weren't about to hold it for me, considering I gave the testimony that drove the final nail into their client's coffin. But enough about us lowly working stiffs. How's life treating you in the Big Easy?"

"I'm in Charleston, Red. The Big Easy is New Orleans."

Kim snorted. "Honey, anyplace that's not here is the Big Easy in my book. So are you gloriously drunk and half naked on some lounge chair? Hold the phone up so I can hear the sound of the waves. A little vicarious relaxation is better than none."

Clay chuckled mirthlessly, cursing the headache he had brewing. "Actually, I'm sitting in the Bentonville, South Carolina sheriff's office, entangled in the search for a missing girl."

"*What?* How on earth did you get involved in something like that? You're supposed to be sipping drinks that come with little umbrellas and ogling hordes of bikini-clad babes."

Clay indulged himself in that image for a moment or two, but the only bikini-clad babe he could envision was Tate.

"It's a long story," he summed up, knowing that if he mentioned Tate and Max and the carnival he'd be answering Kim's questions for an hour. "But anyway, I was wondering if you could do me a favor. I'd like to get a look at the film we discussed last week."

After a couple beats of silence, Kim said "You think there's a connection between my snuff film and your missing girl?"

"I don't know. I started thinking about our conversation, and the perp in this case seems to be a mid-thirties male with a body builder's physique –"

"And my perp was also a mid-thirties male with a body builder's physique."

"Yes, well, you know that putting two and two together doesn't necessarily make four. But I got a look at him last night, and I want to compare what I saw to your footage. It's likely nothing, but I'd still like to check it out for myself. Do you think you could e-mail it to me?"

"You got a *look* at him? Where?"

"At a carnival. But anyway –"

"You went to a *carnival* last night?"

Clay sighed, rubbing the tension that had shifted to the back of his neck. "As I said, it's a long story. How long do you think it will be before you can get me that footage?"

"Tomorrow morning," she answered after only a moment of hesitation.

Clay's shoulders slumped, disappointment running a brief course through his veins. "Is that the best you can do?" Kim was busy, he understood, and this case wasn't her priority, but he'd hoped to get this taken care of today. He either wanted to rule out a possible connection so that he could rethink the emerging pattern, or make the connection and offer both the Bureau and the sheriff's department a promising lead.

"I'm afraid so. I have to wrap things up here, and it will take me at least six hours to get there. That would put me in Charleston too late to do any good today. But I'll be raring and ready to go first thing in the morning."

"Wait a minute." Clay shook his head, trying to figure out where they'd gone off course. "I asked you to *e-mail* the footage, not hand-deliver it."

"I realize that. But I'm all finished with this trial, and if there's a break, I want to be in on it. I'll bring the disc and the autopsy report from our dead vic, and my notes pertaining to the case."

"Kim, that's really not necessary. I don't want you to come all this way based on what's little more than a hunch."

"My ass," Kim disagreed. "Your hunches are usually better than someone else's smoking gun. Is this sheriff that you're working with territorial?"

"No," Clay assured her. "That's why he asked me to come in on this so early."

"Good. Then he won't have any problem with my participation in the investigation. That way you can back out and get on with the drinking and lying on the beach. This case isn't really ISU fodder anyway. These guys do what they do for the almighty dollar. That's more my area of expertise than yours."

It was true, Clay silently acknowledged, although he felt there was more to the man he'd seen last night than just your run-of-the-mill felon.

"Okay," he finally agreed. "I'll spend the rest of the afternoon weeding things out and trying to make sense of this from my end, and when you get here tomorrow morning give me a call. We'll compare notes, watch the footage, and if there's a connection, I'll gladly dump this thing in your capable hands."

JOSH Harding angled the sketch toward Tate, and watched as she chewed the inside of her cheek. "The jaw line," she said hesitantly. "I think it should be a little more… square." Josh deftly wielded the pencil, a new face emerging from the strokes.

She sat back in her chair.

"You're really very good. I had no idea that I'd noticed that much detail. And for you to be able to put it on paper…" her voice trailed off, and she lifted her gaze to his. "That's amazing."

Josh felt his cheeks suffuse with color. He wasn't sure what it was about this particular woman that made him regress to seventh grade, but his palms began to sweat. "Thanks." It was a rather uninspired comeback. What he really wanted to say was *you're amazing, too. Would you consider bearing my children?*

Needless to say, that didn't come out. He wasn't entirely certain what the deal was between her and Agent Copeland, and quite frankly, he didn't want to piss the guy off. He came across as all amiable and polite, but Josh had seen him glancing over in his and Tate's direction a time or two with murder in his eyes.

While Josh was no wimp, and could well take care of himself, he didn't want FBI, spelled out in bullet holes, decorating his ass.

So he'd bide his time, and wait until the guy cleared out.

As if thinking of the devil could conjure him, Copeland chose that moment to open the door. He leaned in, smiling warmly at Tate.

"It's after one, and I was thinking you must be hungry."

"Oh." Tate looked at her watch. "Now that you mention it, I guess I am."

"Sheriff Callahan says there's a sandwich shop next door. What do you say we grab a bite?"

"Sounds great," Tate agreed, and then shifted her gaze toward Josh. "Would you like to come along, Deputy Harding?"

Josh, who understood the male psyche far better than Tate, weighed the pleasure of dining with the lovely woman against the pain of having his face ground into the dirt. For despite the pleasant smile, Copeland's eyes said *join us and die*.

Being fond of his life, and having no great desire to eat dirt, Josh wisely opted to bow out. And gathering his sketchpad and laptop, excused himself from the room.

THE S&K Sandwich Shop was a throwback to simpler times, the wares advertised on a backlit plastic board in black removable letters. The selection was pretty basic southern fare and the air so redolent of oil from the deep fryer that they decided to dine al fresco. The patio was dwarfed by a large live oak whose graceful limbs cast welcome shade, and compared to the heat and grease of the restaurant's interior, felt almost balmy by comparison.

Clay nodded toward a picnic table on the far side of the oak, brushing aside an errant piece of Spanish moss before offering Tate a seat. As he unwrapped his sandwich from the wax paper casing, Tate eyed him across their trays.

"Do you think you'll be able to help them find Casey?"

He took a bite of barbeque. Tate knew there was a lot of stuff happening that he wasn't at liberty to discuss, and he was clearly considering his response.

"Finding Casey, while obviously urgent, isn't the reason they asked me to come in. My role as a 'profiler' isn't to locate missing persons or apprehend perpetrators, but to try and help the police understand the *whys* of the situation. Why was Casey selected? Why does the man who took her feel the need to do what he does? And by understanding both the victim and the victimizer, they will have a better chance of locating their man by predicting his behavioral pattern and thereby preventing him from striking again. I'm trying to help lead them to their man, which, in a perfect world, will also lead them to Casey. But I want you to be prepared for the fact that they may not find her in time."

Tate chewed on a piece of Texas toast while she considered Clay's grim prediction. He had to have an iron will to be able to separate the fact that a young girl's life was at stake, and concentrate on the task of studying her abductor. That cool professionalism, so different from the warm and engaging man she'd come to know, intrigued her on an entirely different level. It took tremendous strength of character to do what he did, and she found her admiration deepening.

Whatever came – or didn't come – out of her acquaintanceship with Clay Copeland, she'd walk away from this whole thing with a lot of respect for him as a person.

And she also remembered that just two nights ago he'd claimed to be a guy on vacation, trying to pretend like his real life didn't exist.

And yet here he was, working.

Because he'd been nice enough to take her and Max to that carnival and got sucked into what he'd come to Charleston to avoid.

"I'm sorry," she said suddenly, and he looked up at her, surprised. "I just realized that if it weren't for me, you wouldn't be stuck working on your vacation."

Clay ripped one of the paper towels off the roll in the middle of the table so that he could wipe barbeque sauce from his mouth. "Don't be ridiculous. If it weren't for you, it might have been hours before anyone knew Casey was missing, and the sheriff almost certainly wouldn't have given her disappearance the high priority it has right now. Doing your part to help that little girl last night, and to help ID Casey's possible abductor today… that's nothing for which you need to feel regret. Trust me, when I signed on with the ISU, I realized that interruptions and inconveniences to the regularly scheduled program were part and parcel of the life."

When he put it that way, Tate realized how insignificant a missed day of vacation was when compared with a young girl's life. But still, everyone was entitled to a break now and then, and there was something about Clay's demeanor over the past couple of days that suggested the break was sorely needed. She remembered how he'd shied away from Max that first day on the beach.

"I don't mean to pry, and I know it's none of my business, but…" Tate hesitated, wondering how to best phrase the question. "Did something bad happen on one of your cases before you came here?"

"Something bad has happened on every one of my cases. People generally don't call me in when a guy sends his girlfriend flowers."

Tate frowned at the flippant remark. "That's not what I meant. It's just that you seemed… I don't know, a little gun shy when you first met Max. Like you'd had a bad experience or something. At first I thought you simply didn't like kids, but that's obviously not the case. You're really, really great with Max. He adores you."

Clay took a sip of iced tea. Cleared his throat. "I, uh… Don't know what to say to that. Thank you. Max makes it pretty easy to be, you know, great."

Tate smiled, dredging a fry through ketchup. "You know, you didn't really answer the question."

"No?"

She shook her head.

A bead of sweat rolled off Clay's temple and he wiped it with the back of his hand. "It's really hot out here. Do you want to finish our lunch at the station?"

"If it's something you can't or don't want to talk about, I didn't mean to make you uncomfortable."

"The *heat's* making me uncomfortable."

Her bland look had him sighing in acknowledgement. "Okay. You're right." He pushed his tray to the side and leaned back. "A few weeks ago, I was in Kansas working a case. The specifics aren't important, but my profile helped lead the locals to the right man. The guy had a wife, a kid – five-year-old boy, cute as a button – that he used as target practice when he wasn't out assaulting his victims. When the police cornered him, he took his family hostage. Anyway, long story short, I got pressed into trying to negotiate. I failed. Completely. The guy blew himself and his family away before I could even say *boo*."

"Oh, Clay." Tate reached for his hand across the table. "And yet you volunteered to spend the entire day yesterday with Max. How difficult that must have been."

"Actually," he squeezed her hand. "It was remarkably easy. Yet another reason to knock the guilt block off your shoulder. Being at that carnival with Max was good for me. I'd been avoiding the issue ever since it happened, first throwing myself back into work, then throwing myself into vacation. Because I was… afraid. Afraid of admitting that I felt like a failure. That if

I'd been a little bit smarter, a little bit better, a little bit faster, that child might still be alive. But last night I realized that I'd done the best I could.

"And besides, if I hadn't been there, I wouldn't have gotten a look at the perp, and you and I probably wouldn't be sitting here enjoying our daily dose of indigestion."

Tate smiled, although she suspected he was changing the subject on purpose. Humor was obviously his default coping mechanism, as he'd managed to find the comedic side of almost every lousy situation they'd found themselves in.

"So how'd the sketch turn out?" he inquired, clearly wanting to close the door on the previous topic. "I meant to look it over to compare it against my own observations, but Deputy Harding hotfooted it out of the interview room before I had a chance to ask."

"The sketch looks great. I might not have described the guy exactly, but it seems to be much closer than I would have thought possible. Josh is really a fantastic artist."

Clay muttered something under his breath.

Tate's head popped up. "What?"

"I said Deputy Harding seems like a nice guy."

"He is nice," she agreed, although she was sure that was not what he'd muttered. "Actually, it's kind of surprising. Given my experience, men who look like that can't see past their own reflection."

When he was quiet, Tate looked up to find his warm brown eyes sharp with comprehension. "Max's dad?"

She didn't want to talk about... the jerk... not ever, but after the way Clay had bared himself, she didn't feel it was fair to shut him out.

"Yes." It was a simple answer to his question, but she could tell by the look on his face that he was waiting for the story. Maybe it would help him to understand why she'd called a halt to their physical relationship, as well as to remind *herself* why she didn't do casual flings.

There were simply too many repercussions.

"It's nothing dramatic," she warned, pushing a stray lock of hair behind her ear. "Just your typical love-struck girl falls for ego-centric guy who dumps her the moment he finds out she's pregnant."

"You don't have to say any more if you don't want to."

But Tate suddenly felt the need to get it out. "Final semester of my senior year in college, I did an internship at the Regency in Atlanta. I was a glorified gopher, but I loved it." Had loved it more, she recalled, for a certain recurring guest. "Anyway… there's a spa there that's absolutely to die for, and some of the suites offer complementary services with return visits, which is a really nice lure for drawing people back. I was working the spa rotation – helping at the desk – when I first met Max's dad."

"One of those repeat guests?"

"Um-hmm," she agreed. "He was a sales rep, traveled a lot. And as you can probably guess, he was gorgeous and charming. I was naïve and smitten – young and stupid enough to mistake sophistication for class. As you said, long story short, we had a raging affair that ended in condom failure. When he found out I was pregnant, he…" she swallowed, lingering shame rising like bile in her throat. "Well, that's when he suddenly remembered that he was married. Separated, but legally married, with no interest in complicating the situation with a child. Ba-da-bing, ba-da-boom. Not a very original punch line."

"He's an asshole."

Tate couldn't help but smile at his quick assessment. "I'm inclined to agree. He's the kind of man who puts his interests above all others, just recklessly crashing through life not really caring what he might break. But if he hadn't been an asshole, I wouldn't have my son."

AND suddenly, Clay felt like an asshole, because he realized that on some level, he was no better than Max's dad. Of course, no way in hell would he ever cheat on his wife, nor would he abandon Tate if she were pregnant. However, he *was* putting his own interests first, because Tate had given him some very valid reasons as to why she couldn't take their acquaintanceship to an intimate level.

And here *he* was, disregarding that, trying to find a way to finagle himself into Tate's bed.

Shit.

He'd already been through all that this morning. He had nothing to offer this woman other than a temporary good time. A long distance relationship was impractical if not impossible, and did he really want to put either of them through that?

God. Was he actually considering a relationship?

This was further proof that he'd blown some kind of gasket.

Relationships were difficult, even under the best of circumstances, and trying to maintain one in the face of both his demanding career and the hundreds of miles between them was nothing short of crazy. He should shuttle this woman back home as quickly as possible, go about the business of putting her out of his mind.

That was something he usually excelled at. Compartmentalizing was an essential part of his job. To do what he needed to do, not think about the rest. If not, he would have driven himself crazy.

Kind of like right now.

He had to put Tate in some kind of off-limits category, because wanting her like this was going to kill him.

Tate was watching him, albeit surreptitiously, from under the heavy fringe of her lashes. This is the part where he should make some appropriate noises that conveyed non-committal acknowledgement of what she'd told him.

Of course, what he really wanted to say was "his loss, my gain."

But before he could say anything, Deputy Harding came skidding around the corner. He stopped short, flicked a glance at Tate, clearing his throat as he turned to Clay.

"Sorry to interrupt your lunch. But one of the search teams has just uncovered something. We think we might have a crime scene for you to look at."

CHAPTER TWELVE

THE body lay in a shallow grave, buried amidst a stand of loblolly pines just a couple of miles from the fairgrounds. A tattered, blood-spattered sneaker found nearby had caught the eye of a member of the search party, and after a brief survey of the area he'd discovered a young girl's partially exposed hand.

Thankfully, the man had the sense to leave the scene intact and call in the sheriff. Clay asked both the crime scene techs and the coroner to wait for his arrival to begin collecting evidence, as the way an offender left a scene revealed substantial information about his behavior. Outdoor crime scenes, particularly body dumps, were more difficult to process because both the elements and nature's clean-up crew – insects and small predators – conspired to erase the clues left behind.

But Clay gathered what information he could, like the fact that this must have been an unplanned attack, because the grave was inadequate. Clearly an afterthought, the girl's final resting spot was less than twenty-four inches deep. The perp hadn't brought along any tools to dig with, but instead had used a rock that Clay found tossed aside, and probably his hands. If he'd planned to kill the girl, he hadn't planned to do it here.

But Clay suspected that he hadn't planned to kill her at all. His action had most likely been brought on by a sudden, blind rage – maybe the girl resisted him, or said something to set him off – or he'd accidentally used more force than necessary when trying to subdue her.

Clay studied the scene, the proximity to the road, and the tread marks that suggested a heavy application of brakes.

Escape attempt, he mused, probably while the vehicle was moving. The perp slams on the brakes, exits the car, not going to let her get away. Already caused him enough trouble, he thinks, little bitch better step in line. Maybe he hits her in the face – the blood on the sneaker – and then proceeds to pound her into submission.

But he'd underestimated the force of his blows, and accidentally killed her.

The crime had occurred right here.

Clay believed that the offender panicked – killing her was not in his plan – and then sought to conceal the evidence of his misdoing. Not thinking entirely clearly, he left that sneaker above ground instead of tossing it into the grave. Then he dropped the rock, which probably wouldn't hold any fingerprints but may have managed to snag an epithelial, right next to the gravesite.

He'd have to wait for the autopsy to be able to say for sure, but he'd bet money the cause of death was blunt force trauma to the head.

The body had reached a point of decomp, aided by the rich, loamy soil beneath the pines, that made it impossible to reach a definitive hypothesis simply by doing a visual. But there were no other obvious injuries, such as a gunshot wound, that would suggest his theory was off base.

Intuition caused the little hairs on the back of his neck to stand up. This kind of rage could be attributed to a number of things, of course. One of them being 'roid rage.

Like, he suspected, the man who'd killed the girl in Kim's snuff film.

And possibly the same man who'd taken Casey.

Clay sighed as he looked over the remains of the young girl in the shallow grave. She was approximately early teens, light brown hair pulled into a matted ponytail. Eye color was difficult to tell – they'd turned milky due to decomposition. She'd been thin, possibly malnourished.

Her clothes looked to have been poor quality, stained and worn *before* they'd been covered with dirt. There was a small knapsack in the grave alongside her, and after the crime scene techs had photographed everything in situ, Clay used a gloved hand to examine the contents of the pink bag.

A tube of bubble-mint flavored toothpaste. A yellow Tweety-bird toothbrush. Some hair bands, a brush with rhinestones around the handle, a pair of white cotton underwear, three dollars, and a box of condoms.

A box of condoms.

Clay pushed his all too human reaction aside, continuing his search on autopilot. If he let emotion come into play, he'd never be able to do his job.

Even in the shelter of the trees, the afternoon sun was unbearably hot. The air was thicker here, the timber a natural windbreak. And death hung over this patch of earth like a sickly pall.

A cloud of insects droned in a low buzz, drawn from their lassitude by the smell of rotting flesh. They hovered impatiently and Clay swatted at them with his hand. Sweat dripped down the back of his neck, adding to the unmistakable aroma of violent death.

He himself was somewhat inured to the stench, as were the coroner and most of the crime scene techs. But he couldn't help but notice that one or two of the deputies on the scene looked a little green. Bentonville – in fact the whole county – was a relatively safe jurisdiction. Murdered, rotting corpses probably didn't turn up all that often.

He did a quick visual to see how Deputy Loverboy was holding up, and noticed him over by the road, talking to Tate.

Tate had insisted on coming along, rather than hanging back at the station or being dropped off at home, in case the body was Casey. Clay knew if that had indeed been the case, she would have wanted to also go to see Casey's mother, to offer what comfort she could. She was just that kind of person.

Guilt was going to rip her to shreds if they found Casey like this victim. Whether she should or not, Tate would wonder if she'd missed the opportunity to stop the man before he'd taken the girl from the carnival.

If she'd paid a little bit closer attention, would she have seen him lead her away?

If she'd been a little bit more observant, would Casey be safe in her mother's arms?

She didn't have the benefit of professional dispassion, of having been inundated with so much violence and pain and misery that she could let those questions roll off her shoulders. She'd be miserable as she tried to figure out what to do with her misplaced guilt.

Hell. Like he was one to talk.

He'd been miserable ever since that asshole in Topeka had fired his gun.

He needed… something to take the place of that emotion that was even now eating a hole in his gut.

He looked toward the road again, wiping the sweat from his brow as he straightened from the knapsack. The emotion that was sweeping through him currently was probably just as detrimental to his well-being as that misplaced guilt.

Deputy Harding had his hand on Tate's arm, and she was nodding, looking relieved. He was no doubt talking to her about the fact that the body wasn't Casey's. The physical description was all wrong, not to mention the fact that this girl had been buried in the woods for a good bit longer than a day. Tate had been waiting, very patiently, for the past hour. Hoping that it wasn't Casey. Fearing that it was.

Clay could tell from the way she was standing – shoulders slumped, arms limp – that she was now feeling the punch of released tension. The body language equivalent of *Thank God*. She was taking this entire thing very much to heart.

Deputy Harding moved his hand to her shoulder, then rubbed a comforting circle on her back.

The green-eyed monster reared its ugly head as Clay removed his gloves with a practiced *snap*. He was just about to move in that direction when he heard his name.

"Agent Copeland?"

Clay turned at the sound of the coroner's voice, looking toward where the older man was crouched as he examined the body. His bald head was covered with a fine sheen of sweat, giving it the appearance of a well-polished cue ball. He pushed his glasses up his nose, motioning abstractly to Clay.

"There's something I'd like you to see."

Right.

Clay carefully picked his way back toward the gravesite, and with one last glance toward the roadside, refocused his attention on doing his job.

CASEY Rodriguez stirred, trying to stretch her aching muscles. Her left arm seemed to float completely independent of her body, like a slab of flesh someone had stuck to her shoulder and forgotten to attach to her nerves. But as she shifted, pain lanced like a knife.

"Oh-oh-oh." She tried to jerk the limb back toward her side.

But her arm *was* attached, attached to something solid. Something that bit into her skin, rubbing it raw.

Turning her head on an achy wince, Casey blinked the arm into focus. A metal bracelet clamped her wrist, big and ugly and tight. A chain dangled from one end…

A handcuff. *She* was handcuffed.

To an old iron bed.

Rising up, muscles screaming, head pounding, Casey scrambled away as best she could. The bed was lumpy, the springs broken down, and her feet slipped on sheets gone clammy. The air in the room sat dense and heavy, the stink of her own sweat was like something spoiled. Dim light crept sulkily through the slats of yellowed blinds, serving only to illuminate the room's faded neglect.

So hot, she thought, looking around. Where the heck was she?

The clank of metal on metal had her eyes going wide, tears stinging as she looked back at the handcuffs. Panic didn't allow her to feel the pain of rent flesh when she yanked as hard as she could.

Gotta get away, she thought, desperately. *Gotta get out.*

But the blood seeping down her arm stopped her. It welled, then rolled, dripping off her elbow to stain the ratty white sheets.

Frightened, confused, Casey wiped at the blood which stung the burns on her forearm. The burns she'd gotten when grease had splattered from the frying funnel cakes.

The funnel cakes.

There'd been a man at her mother's trailer. Smiling at her even when her mother leaned over, offered up a serving of cleavage. Smiling at her as she walked by to throw away her sister's trash.

Smiling at her next to the Ferris wheel...

It was the last thing she could remember.

"Oh, God," Casey whispered, trembling.

Everything her mother told her had come true. She'd flirted with that man, shamefully encouraging him, even though he was old enough to be her dad. It had to be him who had her. Who'd chained her to the bed.

Was he going to kill her? Or merely... do things?

Tears mingling with sweat, Casey wiped her face, considering which fate was worse. To be kept alive as some sicko's toy, or maybe just shot through the head.

No. *Please.* She really didn't want to die. But at the thought of what that man could do if he kept her alive, she began to cry in earnest. And with sobs racking her slender body, didn't hear the heavy footsteps on the stairs.

When the door opened, fear turned her insides liquid.

"Oh good," the man said, acres of pale skin gleaming ghost-like in the dimness. "I was thinking it must be about time for you to wake up."

THE sun hovered just over the horizon by the time Clay drove his Four-Runner over the bridge, the pinks and oranges of impending sunset the final strokes on the day's canvas.

A day, he mused, that had turned singularly ugly.

He'd tried, several times, to talk Tate into allowing one of the deputies to see her home, but the damn fool woman had insisted on waiting for him. He saw the strain of that etched in the line between her eyes, but her determination hadn't faltered. Ridiculous as it was, he got the impression she was worried about him.

Like *he'd* never seen a teenage corpse.

And that concern, combined with the stench of senseless death and his own reservations about just what, exactly, he was doing, served to provide a fairly uncomfortable silence on the ride home.

He could tell Tate wanted to talk. But not about *her* feelings regarding what happened. Uh-uh. Oh no.

She wanted to talk about *him*. She'd been looking at him funny ever since he'd told her about Topeka.

Which one of them, exactly, held the degree in this relationship?

Relationship.

There was that freaking word again.

Somehow this entire thing had gone way off track.

When had he gone from pursuing this woman with the single-minded but reasonable goal of mutual pleasure, to worrying about her being offended if he didn't open up and spill his guts? He'd told her about what happened, game over, enough said. Being with Tate was supposed to be a no-strings-attached vacation from reality, and he damn well didn't need to be bringing along a luggage cart full of baggage.

And why the hell was she looking at him like that, all sweet and quietly supportive, when what she should have been doing was high-tailing it the other way?

He was *no good* for her; she deserved so much better. Better than a man who could maybe schedule a few days for her a couple of times a year.

She'd been right. There was no way they could do this. He'd end up hurting her, and Max, and ... hell, probably himself in the long run. He should make the break now, while it could still be clean and painless, and leave someone like Deputy Harding free to fill the vacancy he left behind.

Tate needed a good man, one who'd be there to hold her at night, and though Harding was a cop – not the easiest career for a relationship – he at least had the benefit of being local.

Shit.

Who the hell was he kidding? He'd sooner cut off his own hands than push her toward Josh Harding. And wasn't that just ridiculous? The desire to rip out the throat of any male who even sneezed in her direction?

Clay tried not to glance toward Tate as they drove past the old market, stopping to allow a group of tourists clutching sweetgrass baskets to shuffle across the street. "What's so funny?" she asked when he laughed.

"Life," he answered, knee-jerk. "I figure it's better to laugh than to cry."

It was the completely wrong thing to say. "I didn't mean –" he tried to backpedal, but she was already speaking over him.

"I've noticed that," she said. "You use humor as an anesthetic."

"Yes, well why do you think they call the stuff the dentist gives you laughing gas?"

He pulled into the parking lot behind the B&B, and left the engine idling.

"Do you want to come in?" Tate offered hesitantly, tucking a strand of hair behind her ear. "Grab some dinner? Talk?"

Well, well, well. Clay cocked a brow in her direction. Just what he'd been waiting to hear all day. Because underneath all of those polite dinner and conversation noises, Tate's body language suggested that wasn't all she had on her mind.

And for the past several hours, he hadn't even been *trying* to herd her in that direction.

After that attack of guilt at lunchtime, he'd simply been playing the whole thing straight.

And now that she was offering…

Well hell, he just couldn't do it.

He *liked* this woman too much to take her to bed.

Uncharted territory, to be sure.

And now came the tricky part. Did he fudge the truth, say that he had some calls to make, that he was tired, busy, or otherwise occupied in some legitimate way?

Past experience – both on the giving and the receiving end – led him to believe that such bullshit could be smelled from a mile away. And because he liked Tate too much to sleep with her, it should follow that he liked her too much to bullshit her. Therefore, he played the honesty card, laying it face up between them.

"I want to come in," he admitted, looking her squarely in the eye. "And while dinner sounds nice, it's secondary to the fact that I want to be inside you. Crude, but it's the truth. And while you've done the whole resistance thing very well, I'm sensing that that particular little wall might be crumbling."

He reached over, took her hand. "I'm not going to lie to you, Tate. I can't think of anything I'd rather do than spend the next, oh, say… twelve hours making love until neither one of us can walk. But crazy as it may seem, I think you were right in what you said last night. Taking this any further is too much like skating on thin ice – chances are one or both of us would end up falling through. You…" He looked out the window, sought the right words, "deserve a lot better than what I'd be able to give you. Not in bed," he clarified, lightening the moment with a wicked grin. "You and me together… well, let's just say we'd set a whole new standard for copulation."

Tate laughed, a small sound that faded quickly. "So what you're saying is that you're taking the high road and turning me down?"

Ignoring his penis as a navigational tool, Clay nodded, taking the high-road's first available on-ramp. "I like you, Tate. Very much. You're beautiful and special and good. And I don't want to be the next blond to let you down. Yeah, I remember what you said – I'm the latest in a line. You know, you might want to consider dating brunettes."

Tate's smile was both wry and a little sad. "At the risk of sounding trite, and turning this into a stereotypical 'I think we should just be friends' speech, I'd like to say that I would like that. You know, being friends. Because you're honestly the most amazing man I've ever met."

Clay winced, but she continued.

"I mean, I'd like you to call me, if you ever need to talk. Or *want* to talk. Or don't particularly feel like talking but are inclined to listen. Whatever. And whenever you're in town you'll always have a place to stay."

For some reason that made him feel worse.

"Thank you," he said, regardless. "And now, before I ruin this whole *amazing man* thing I have going by grabbing you and tossing you into the back seat, I think we'd better say good night."

Tate leaned toward him, hesitating, before planting a quick kiss on his cheek. For once, Clay didn't open her door, as that was just one step closer to following her inside. In fact, he moved his gearshift into drive and sat with his foot on the brake.

"You'll, uh, let me know how the case is going? If they find Casey. Either way?"

"I'll call you," Clay promised, taking the punch to the gut as she walked away.

When had he gotten so damn... pathetic?

This entire vacation was doing a number on his head.

He started to head back to Justin's, but as he passed Murphy's he pulled to the curb. If he wasn't going to spend the rest of the night with Tate, he saw no reason to spend the night sober.

HE hadn't raped her.

Casey repeated that to herself as she lay shivering in the middle of the bed. It was probably an easy ninety degrees inside, but she couldn't stop the chills that racked her. Turning, she pressed her chattering teeth against a pillow gone wet with tears.

But he hadn't raped her.

It was that thought alone that kept her from throwing up.

The man – he'd said his name was William – had actually been almost... nice.

Creepily, unbearably nice.

He'd put a bandage on her wrist to keep the handcuff from doing more damage, chiding her for hurting herself. He'd brought water, some food – which now sat uneasily in her stomach – and had un-cuffed her long enough for a desperately needed bathroom visit. Taking the opportunity to study the window over the tub, Casey had noted the layers of old paint with a sinking stomach. *Sealed shut,* she thought, and looked out for any neighbors, anyone who could help her.

But William – God help her, he looked like a fish's belly; he was so white – had known what she was up to. "There's no one around to hear you, Casey." And stood in the doorway, grinning.

Startled, Casey slipped from the bathtub ledge, where she'd been peering at an empty field.

"If you're a good girl," he held out one huge white hand "I'll make sure you don't get hurt."

Like that was supposed to make the whole thing better?

But figuring it best not to tick him off, Casey allowed herself to be led back to the bedroom.

Where he'd cuffed her, once more, to the bed.

Then stripped off the shorts he was wearing and laid, just laid, beside her.

But he hadn't raped her.

She reminded herself of that again.

He'd stroked her hair, touched her breasts – just once – and chatted as if they were friends. As if by *smiling,* simply smiling at him, she'd given the impression that's what she wanted.

Casey heard her mother's voice in her head, warning her not to encourage strange men.

Oh, Mama, she thought, throat constricting. *I'm so sorry I didn't listen.*

But the noise from downstairs had her eyes snapping open. The other man must be back.

The man who'd come into the room, seen William in the bed, and gone quietly, coldly ballistic. He'd told William that he couldn't mess with the merchandise, that the deal they had required a virgin. Somewhere in the midst of the men's argument, Casey'd come to realize they were talking about *her*.

And Casey knew enough to know that merchandise meant that they were actually planning to *sell* her.

Tears rolled again, hot this time, as anger mixed with fear. She'd find a way out. She *had* to find a way out. Before the creeps could make their first dollar.

CHAPTER THIRTEEN

ROGAN Murphy watched the FBI agent enter the bar, looking tired as hell and twice as grim. His blond hair bore channels from frustrated fingers, and dirt and sweat marred the shirt which had been virginal just that morning. He'd lost that freeze-dried Men in Black appearance, presumably shed while digging for God knows what in the dirt. The tie was gone, too, his sleeves pushed back above tanned forearms. All in all, the dude was definitely not looking his company best.

Whatever he and Tate had done today, it obviously hadn't been barrels of fun. The man appeared to be in dire need of a drink.

Rogan, with that sixth sense that seemed to come along with the liquor license, guessed that part of J. Edgar's problem came from a snafu with his lovely cousin.

So Tate had turned him down, eh?

The flag-planting expedition Rogan witnessed that morning apparently had been for naught.

Rogan topped off the pilsner he'd been filling, passing it and a tray full of shots to one of the waitresses. After drying his hands on a bar towel, he slapped it over his shoulder, watching Clay belly up to the bar. Declan took his order for Killian's in a bottle. But Rogan overrode the call, tapping his brother on the back.

"Let me get this one."

Declan cast a long glance over his shoulder. "Isn't that Tate's new man?"

"I believe he's applied for the position." Rogan poured a shot of whiskey, then dropped the glass in the middle of a highball, filling it with Guinness from the tap.

"You plan on blowing him up?" Declan motioned toward the Irish Car Bomb Rogan had prepared.

"Testing his mettle," Rogan clarified, smirking into identical blue eyes. "As should be expected of any man who wants a piece of this family."

Declan tipped his head toward Copeland. "And why might you be thinking he wants a piece of this family, might I ask?"

Rogan inspected the drink, satisfied with its contents. "He got all proprietary this morning, not only with Tate, but with Max. It would have been funny if it hadn't been so… refreshing. None of the losers Tate's dated before have been man enough to take on the kid." It was a sore point, as Rogan was devoted to them both. "This guy looked able, and willing."

Declan's brow shot skyward. "Yet here he sits, drinking alone."

"He and Tate were working on some kind of FBI thing today – missing girl, I think, but I didn't get the whole story. But I suspect that hang-dog expression has as much to do with our fair cousin as it does with his sucky job."

"Well, whatever. But just to clarify, I thought FBI was here for a limited time frame."

"Yeah. Tate said he was out of here at the end of the week."

"And so you're fretting about this because…?"

"I don't fret," Rogan protested. "I may, occasionally, express reservations, but I don't fret. That's physiologically impossible for a man."

Dec snorted. His brother, who could care less what their friends and relatives did in their private lives, claimed Rogan had the tendency to channel the Love Boat's Captain Steubing.

And Tate was his little Vicky.

"Have at it." Declan shrugged, moving off toward the opposite end of the bar. He sang low under his breath as he walked by, just loud enough for his brother to hear him.

"Set a course for adventure, your mind on a new romance –"

Rogan sent a well-placed elbow to Declan's ribs. Then he snagged Copeland's drink from the bar.

THE glass that was placed in front of him definitely contained alcohol, but it sure as hell wasn't what he'd ordered. Clay lifted his head from the hand he'd dropped it into to find Rogan Murphy staring back at him.

Perfect.

Exactly who he wanted to see. Maybe he should just call Josh Harding over, too, so that he could make this night a total suckfest. They could play The Good, The Bad, and The Ugly, challenge each other to a couple of duels. Or maybe Murphy could simply mediate while he and Harding shot each other, since his interest in Tate was platonic and the guy didn't carry a gun.

"What's this?" He was annoyed by the sullen tone of voice, but couldn't find *pleasant* in his current repertoire.

"Irish cure-all." Murphy nodded at the glass. "Looks like you could use one."

Clay studied the drink, studied the man. Tate's cousin had his hair tied back in a tail, and he'd decided to put on a shirt. Irritation spurted. Clay decided it had been a colossally poor decision to patronize this particular establishment.

Dozens of bars, he mused, sliding his hand toward the drink. And he plants his butt in the middle of the Irish Inquisition.

"Is this some sort of test, Murphy?"

Rogan offered a smile that was little more than a show of teeth. "I don't know, Agent Copeland. Should it be?"

Absurd to have to prove a point this way, but Clay figured when in Rome. And so figuring, downed the elaborate concoction in one fell swoop.

He turned it over, empty, on the bar.

About to make a comment regarding pissing contests and the like, the fire of that combination roared through him. Tears welled, flames licked, and his stomach exploded into a ball of burning embers. "Holy shit," he choked, relieved that his voice box hadn't been cremated. "What are you trying to do, man? Kill me?"

Rogan slapped a companionable hand on Clay's shoulder. "A moment or two of agony, and then you feel no pain."

Clay wiped at the moisture leaking from his eyes. "Well, I haven't quite reached the *no pain* part. Apparently that involves a side trip through Hell."

Rogan reached down, chuckling, and slid Clay a bottle of Killian's with practiced flourish. "So would you like to start a tab? Easier, all around, if you're planning to stay awhile."

Yet a little unsteady, Clay eyed the man to gauge his agenda. This was obviously a recon mission. Or maybe an all-out assault, complete with dirty bombs.

"I'd like to stay awhile." There was a double meaning there, and from the look on the other man's face, they both knew it. "But unfortunately my schedule doesn't allow for indulging in more than a couple drinks." And though his stomach rebelled, for principle's sake, he lifted the beer to his mouth.

Flipping the towel off his shoulder, Rogan wiped the ring from the bar. "It's always been my philosophy that if you have no intention of getting sotted, you're better off not visiting the bar."

Tongue tucked firmly in his cheek, Clay contemplated the analogy. Decided Murphy's position was admirable, in an utterly obnoxious way.

"You're close to Tate?" he asked, simply cutting through the crap. They could dance around this issue for the next three hours, but Clay had left his blue suede shoes in the car.

"Very." Murphy's arms crossed. "Tate's a sweetheart. The only time we've ever locked horns was over the situation with Max's father. I wanted to kill him. The man was a piece of shit."

"You'll get no argument from me." Clay tipped his bottle, pleased the contents went down easy. "And this is the part where you tell me that if I hurt her, you'll have to kill *me.*"

"I wouldn't have put it in so many words, because that might be construed as threatening a federal agent."

Clay smiled. "So do you go through this little dog and pony show with everybody who takes Tate out?"

Murphy's eyes went hard. "I saw how you were today, both of you, with each other. And the way Max went right to you, as well. Call it premature, but I'm good at reading situations. You're either going to be very good, or very bad, for Tate. Now I figure which way that goes depends upon whether or not you're a total asshole. If you're just hanging around her for kicks – a little side note to your vacation – then you make real sure you're clear about that up front. What she does with that is up to her, but at least she'll know where she stands. Goes the way you want it, you make damn sure your protection's reliable."

Clay almost choked on his beer. "You're kidding me, right? Because I'm pretty sure I'm older than you. That makes it biologically impossible for you to be my dad."

Rogan's glare only hardened.

Raising a conciliatory hand, Clay shook his head over the absurdity of the conversation. "Look, Fido. There's no need to bare the teeth. I appreciate the fact that you're trying to look out for Tate in a way that you weren't able to five years ago, but this is getting out of hand. Your cousin is… great, okay? I really, really like her. And I like the kid almost as much as I like his mom. But bottom lining it for you, man, I'm out of here in a few more days. And I have no intention of needing protection, reliable or otherwise."

"So you're not interested in her sexually?"

Jeez. Who was this guy, the procreation police? "I'm not dead, Murphy. Nor am I a saint. I *am* however, a good little Boy Scout. Tonight I'm working on my Leaving the Incredibly Hot Woman Alone Even Though I Really Want To Do Her merit badge. So bring me another beer and then shut the fuck up."

Thoughtful now, Rogan sucked a hollow into his cheek. "You're here because you're trying to keep your hands off Tate?"

"*Ding, ding, ding!* Give the man a bone. Apparently, you're the type that learns through repetition."

"You know, if you were really trying to stay away from Tate, you might have decided to tie one on in a bar that wasn't next door. Did you plan to get so drunk you couldn't drive, maybe take a room at the B&B? You're either stupid, or in complete and total denial."

Clay blinked, and then sighed in disgust.

"You're right, you know. I am stupid. In denial. And I apologize for coming into your bar and fouling up the air with my load of crap. It's been… a rough couple of weeks. Not that that's a justification. But you know, human nature dictates I have a ready excuse for my shitty behavior."

Rogan smiled. "Any of that crap you want to shovel out? Maybe clear the air a bit?"

"Bar psychology 101? I appreciate it, but…no. I'll just finish my beer and be on my merry way. There's a parade I need to rain on before I go home."

This time Rogan laughed. "Why don't you stay and have another drink," he suggested. "This one's on me. Have you had dinner yet? No? Well, I'll serve you right here at the bar. And leave it to me to see you get where you should be going at the end of the night."

Clay leaned back, considered, and figured what the hell.

Tate's guard dog surely wouldn't let him get near her.

TATE took a towel to her hair, grateful to have washed away the last vestiges of the day's filth. She'd soaped up twice because every time she closed her eyes she kept picturing that wooded gravesite.

The girl hadn't been Casey. Thank God, it hadn't been Casey. But it had been somebody – somebody's daughter, somebody's sister… *somebody*.

And a monster had taken her away.

Clay had been pretty close-mouthed about what was happening, and he made sure she was far enough away that she hadn't seen more than the cloud of flies. But that had been enough.

And the smell…

Even from a distance, it had been overwhelming.

How on earth did Clay do that sort of thing day in, day out? No wonder he was here, trying to pretend his real life didn't exist. What a depressing reality it was.

Slipping into the nightgown blooming with daisies that Max had given her for Mother's Day – along with a handmade card and a pretty rock – Tate flipped off the bathroom light and made her way into her bedroom. Max and her mother were both long asleep, the last of their overnight guests checked in and settled. But Tate was restless, edgy.

The air around her seemed expectant. Like the calm before a storm.

"Get a grip," she told herself, rolling her eyes as she turned down the covers. She'd become embroiled in a criminal investigation, all but witnessed the abduction of a young girl, and – ending a record drought – had met a man she liked well enough to take to bed. A man who mere hours ago had given her an unqualified *no, thanks*.

Of course she was edgy.

But feeling the pinch of tension, she wandered down to check on Max.

So innocent, she thought, watching him sleep, purple bear tucked beneath one arm. How could anyone ever look at a child, and want to strip that innocence away? But she knew that there were those who did – she'd seen it firsthand.

She hated to think what that poor girl had gone through to wind up in a shallow grave in the woods.

And given that particular train of thought, jumped when she heard the doorbell.

Likely one of Murphy's patrons, she mused as she headed down the back stairs and through the kitchen. She'd have to call a cab, because their guest rooms were totally booked.

It was only when she had her hand on the knob that she realized she'd neglected to put on a robe. Her nightgown was summer weight, and short. She was considering going back to retrieve something a little more modest when the bell chimed insistently again.

"Alright already." She swung the door open.

And came face to face with the last person she expected to see.

The man was gorgeous. Blond. Smelled an awful lot like a brewery.

And was clearly none too steady on his feet.

"I have no idea why I'm here," Clay admitted, taking pains to enunciate each word. "I told myself this wasn't going to happen, and I tried to stay away. I really did. And your cousin wasn't supposed to let me come over here. We had a deal."

Narrowing his eyes, he shot some irritation in the general direction of the bar. "But I suspect some kind of set-up."

Tate folded her arms across her chest. "You mean, like I *asked* one of the twins to get you drunk and send you over here?"

"I'm not drunk. Precisely."

Tate arched a single brow.

"You're wearing your nightgown," he pointed out, obviously figuring it was in his best interest to redirect the topic. "You shouldn't open the door to a stranger looking like that. Hell, you shouldn't open the door to *me* looking like that. And I meant that Rogan set me up, not you. Although to tell you the truth, it might have been Declan that sent me packing. They look an *awful* lot alike when one's been drinking. Are you going to let me in? Cause if not, I can just go sleep in my truck. Or call a cab. Because Justin's at the hospital. Poor guy needs to get a life. You know..."

He gestured grandly with his arm, and Tate pressed her fingers to her lips to keep from laughing.

"...that's really very unhealthy. It leads to burn out and all kinds of stress. I should know because I've recently lost my mind. God you're pretty. I just want to bury myself inside you until nothing else matters."

As propositions went, it was rambling and not all that cohesive. He looked like something a cat had mauled and then left on Tate's doorstep for inspection.

Still alive, but twitching and severely impaired.

And the really sad thing?

She *still* found the man absurdly appealing. She was either crazy about him, or more hard-up than she cared to admit.

"Come in." She sighed, pulling the door wider. A cloud of late night heat and bar fumes entered behind her guest. She'd have to get him cleaned up and then put him in her bed. She could always sleep with Max.

He scratched behind his ear, looked charmingly sheepish. "I'm sorry. I hope I didn't get you out of bed."

"I just got out of the shower. Bed was next on the agenda."

"You smell like peaches." He sniffed the air.

"I wish I could say the same."

Grimacing, Clay looked down at his clothes. "I, uh, bumped into something. There was spillage."

Amusement edging out irritation, she stroked a finger over a splotch on his chest. "Best get you out of your clothes, then." Too late, she realized what she'd said. "And boy, did that not come out right."

"Oh, I think it did." His eyes went hot, desire burning off the chagrin. His intention to kiss her was clear, and Tate took a step back.

Clay stalked slowly forward.

There were so many reasons not to do this. Hadn't he turned her down just a few hours ago? And now here he was in her entry, not precisely drunk.

But when his hand snapped forward, winding into her hair, she allowed herself to be drawn in.

"I need you." He breathed it, smelling of the mints he must have grabbed at the bar. The tempest she'd been expecting broke in a shower of electricity between them. "It scares the hell out of me, Tate, because I've never needed anyone so much."

And it was what she needed to hear.

Winding her own hands until they met at his nape, she pulled his head down to hers.

He licked his way into her mouth with way more hunger than finesse. She tasted mint, the mellow grain of beer, the tang of something spicy. And under, maybe through it all, the sweet punch of arousal. It had been so long since she'd felt like this.

Maybe she'd never felt like this.

When he lifted the edge of her gown, drew her closer, she gave herself up to the storm.

Hands streaking under the cotton, Clay groaned when he encountered skin. He plied the ins and outs of each of her curves, learning her with his fingers.

Tate's breath caught when he grazed the undersides of her breasts, brushed his callused palm over her nipples.

And when he eased a finger down, slipped inside, she was already slick with wanting.

"Ah, *Tate*." He said it reverently, like a prayer. And pushed another finger into her.

"Clay… we need…" The words stuttered out between searing kisses. The response he made was incoherent, and his muscles tightened beneath her hands when she grasped his arms. But she pushed him back with just enough force to let him know he needed to stop.

"Not here," she gasped when he lifted his head, the warm chocolate of his eyes unfocused. "I can't make love to you in the hall."

Clay pulled his hand from beneath the gown, slipped it around hers. Tate was startled by the wetness there, and even more surprised that it heightened her arousal.

She started to move toward the stairs, but Clay caught sight of the sofa in the front parlor.

"This is quicker." He pulled her with him.

"Clay, we can't—"

But he moved with single-minded determination, leading her toward the Victorian settee. It was an antique, hard and uncomfortable, and had been in Tate's family for years. Clay didn't seem too concerned. He closed the door behind them.

"Clay....mmmpf."

Tate found herself pressed against the smooth wood of the door, much as she had the night he'd fought the mugger in the alley. Only instead of his hand, his mouth covered hers, and instead of fear, her veins pulsed with excitement.

From somewhere beside her, she heard the lock turn with a soft snick.

His hand manacled her wrists, stretched her arms over her head so that she was well and truly pinned. Hot and hungry, he clamped his teeth against her neck.

"Oh God," she breathed, suspecting that if he wasn't holding her up, she'd just slide right down the wall. When his other hand, impatient, pushed inside her panties again, Tate marveled that she didn't simply dissolve.

"We... oh." Suddenly her feet were off the ground, her legs wrapped around his hips.

"We what?"

"Huh?" she said as his teeth found her ear, his tongue the sensitive spot just behind it.

"You said we need to do something."

She could feel him, the shockingly hard length of him, pressing against her center. "We need to hurry."

He made a noise, something guttural, then strode across the room. Shoving aside the toss pillows, he dumped her on the settee.

And muffled her gasp of surprise by closing his mouth over hers.

The kiss exploded into frenzy.

Open-mouthed, hot, wet – it wasn't the least bit polite. Tate felt the rasp of beard stubble against her chin, and shivered at the rough thrill. This was Clay, defenses down. No more cool-eyed agent or charming player.

He was raw. Open.

Hers.

For however long it lasted.

"Clothes," he breathed, when they had no choice but to come up for air. Grasping the edge of her gown, he pulled it over her head. "You're wearing entirely too many."

And at the sight of her bared breasts, feasted like a man starving.

Everything in Tate went hot, fluid and rushed toward the promise of more. She clasped his head, heart swelling as she gave herself over, because she knew that this was right. This night, this man, hell, even this sofa felt like the most natural thing in the world.

Until the elastic of her panties yielded to Clay's fingers with a resounding *rip*.

"You… tore my underwear." She twisted around, watched the ice blue nylon fall to the floor.

"I've lost the ability to be civilized."

When she looked back, she saw he was right. His tousled hair, the feral gleam in his eyes, gave the impression of something untamed.

And something a little wild, a little untamed in Tate knocked against the gate of her desire. "Guess I better go get my whip."

With a strangled sound, Clay practically ripped open his pants. She barely had time to appreciate the sight when he pressed forward with his hips, pushing the tip of his erection against the entrance to her body.

"Condom." He strained the word through gritted teeth. Fumbling his wallet from his back pocket, Clay tossed it aside, opened the foil wrapper with his teeth, then hastily covered himself.

Before she could touch him, kiss him, say his name, do something to add to the proceedings, he drove into her so fast and hard that she had to bite her lip to keep from screaming.

CLAY held himself still as Tate's liquid heat surrounded him, trying not to weep with gratitude.

The noise she'd made when he entered her nearly made him explode.

He wanted to take it slow, wanted to do everything exactly right, but she felt so good and he craved her like air, and he thought he might die if he didn't start moving.

So he pushed her legs wider and drove himself deeper, again and again, giving into his baser instincts.

It was so unbelievably erotic – her totally naked, still damp from her shower; him totally clothed and smelling vaguely of sweat. He couldn't slow down even if he'd wanted to. She was...

Light, and goodness, and beauty.

Everything that had been missing from his life.

It was... mind blowing.

With the certainty that he was only going to last maybe three seconds longer, he reached down between them to help her join him.

That was all it took – just his touch in the right spot – and she proceeded to shatter around him.

It triggered his own personal explosion.

He saw lights. Hell, he saw stars.

He saw Tate, head thrown back, damp hair spread like black silk against the brocade cushion, eyes closed tight against the surfeit of pleasure, and gathered her into his arms as he climaxed inside her.

He never – *never* – wanted to let her go.

Spent, he collapsed on top of her.

When he came to his senses, he was pretty well embarrassed, because he'd lasted all of about two minutes. It was a personal all-time low. Hell, he'd even performed better in Sara Carlson's bedroom closet when he was sixteen.

Way to make a first impression on the lady, Clay. Tie one on, ravage her in her living room, and then barely make it worth her while. He lifted his head, met her dancing eyes, and was relieved to see her smiling.

"Sorry," he said. Mortified. "I'm not entirely sure what happened."

Tate tilted her head to the side and ran her fingers through his hair. "I'm pretty sure we just had sex. You know – *tab A goes into slot B?*"

"No." Clay shook his head, loving what she was doing to his hair, loving the feeling of still being inside her. "That was more like spontaneous combustion. I'd like to blame it all on the alcohol, but I'm pretty sure it's actually your fault."

"My fault?" One perfect brow arched heavenward as a lazy smile curled those lips.

"Yep. Your fault entirely. You're just too damn sexy for your own good."

She laughed, and Clay found himself smiling. He could listen to her happiness forever.

"I'm also very, *very* naked. Dicey, when there's a houseful of paying guests upstairs. Speaking of which, you're fresh out of luck, Speedy. The only bed currently left unfilled is mine."

"Well now, it seems to me that that's actually quite convenient. You're naked *and* you have a bed. What more could an inebriated traveler ask for?"

"So you think you're going to just sweet talk your way into my bed, all drunk and smelly?"

"As a guest, I could offer to pay you for the pleasure, but you might find that offensive."

Tate shivered as he kissed her, made a little *mmmm* in the back of her throat, and Clay felt like a king.

"We should probably go upstairs," she whispered.

Looking around, Clay realized how very badly he'd behaved. Some king. This was the public parlor, for heaven's sake. He shifted his weight so that Tate could scoot out from beneath him.

Suddenly the smell of his own sweat didn't seem quite so erotic. "I could use a shower."

"No kidding." Casting her gaze around the floor for her nightgown, Tate scooted over to pick it up.

Clay divested himself of the condom, admiring the view of Tate's backside as she leaned over the couch.

When he considered taking her again, just like that, he could only shake his head. More like the court jester.

He put the condom in his pocket. It wouldn't do to have a guest find it tomorrow. Not to mention Tate's mother.

Or Max, God forbid.

"Clay?"

He looked up.

"I could use another shower. Unless…" she let the word drag out.

"Unless what?"

"Unless you're too *not precisely drunk* to try that standing up."

His crown had been reinstated. Clay decided it was good to be king.

CHAPTER FOURTEEN

"*OW*. Shit."

Bright morning light seared Clay's eyes, lids scraping like sandpaper as he dragged them open. He slammed them shut, hoping his other senses kicked in so that he could discover the source of the incessant buzzing. But when the bed revolved and his stomach dipped, he cautiously forced one back up.

And determined he'd gone colorblind overnight, because the room he was in was *pink*.

Fuchsia, he guessed you called it, screamed at him from the walls, while a lighter shade laughed amongst the white and yellow flowers rioting on the tangled sheets. Confused, cautious, he sat up gingerly and held a hand to his head.

Which pounded like the entire Marine Corps band was using his brain as a bass drum.

When the buzzing started again he vaguely recognized it as his cell phone, probably still lodged in the pocket of his pants.

His pants – as with the rest of his clothes – appeared to be MIA.

Swinging his legs over the side of the bed, which caused the whole room to spin a slow circle, he peered down toward the floor, locating a pile of discarded clothing. His pants were lying in a crumpled heap under a small pile of colored confetti. The kind of confetti that came lubricated and ribbed.

Bringing memory flooding back in a rush.

Well. At least he'd proven that he was capable of providing more than a scant minute's worth of entertainment.

And Rogan – damn him – should be pleased to note they'd used protection.

Memories, both hot and lovely, drifted in and out of focus like an old reel of film.

Tate, in the shower, laughing as he took her against the tile.

Tate, moving beneath him, whispering words he didn't deserve to hear.

Tate, warm against him, feeling like salvation in his arms, while the air went soft with dawn. Sometime very early this morning, he'd finally fallen asleep, and she must have slipped out to see to her responsibilities.

Speaking of which, he reached down to grab his phone.

"Copeland."

"I take it your lazy butt is still in bed?"

"It's in bed all right, but I can assure you it's been anything but lazy."

Spotting a glass of water on the nightstand, Clay snatched it up, trying to dispel the boll weevils that had knitted a fine new sweater for his tongue. Tate – bless her – obviously predicted how he'd be feeling. He popped the analgesics she'd left for him before attempting to read the clock.

There were several more digits than necessary, but he was pretty sure it read six forty-five. When Kim had said first thing in the morning, she apparently hadn't been kidding.

Through the silence on the other end of the line, Clay could practically hear the wheels turning. "Think a little bit louder, Kim. My supersonic auditory prowess is a little impaired this morning."

Kim laughed, and he knew it was because he'd finally gotten into the swing of his vacation. "Are you alone," she asked saucily, "or do you need to call me back in a few minutes?"

"I'm good to talk," he assured her, casting his gaze about in search of his shorts "as long as you do so in dulcet tones." Giving up on underwear, he pulled his pants up off the floor, wincing as the smell of alcohol hit him like a bare-knuckled punch. "Your people are evil," Clay informed her, thinking of Rogan and his insidious drink. "It's no wonder the Irish need so many patron saints."

"I'm guessing that sometime last night you ran afoul of a bottle of whiskey."

"At least." He pulled on his pants and tried to muster enough brain cells to focus on work. There was an investigation that needed his full attention. "But more to the point of your call, I'm thankful that you're here. We're still awaiting positive ID on the vic uncovered yesterday, but after comparing my visual against the descriptions in the missing persons files, I'm thinking that it was possibly a fourteen-year-old by the name of Janie Collier. I'll go over her file with you at the station, but she was reportedly seen with a man loosely matching our perp's description, aside from coloring – which we both know is easy to fake." He wandered into Tate's bathroom and checked himself out in the mirror.

Ouch. Not a pretty sight. Red-rimmed, scruffy, a little gray beneath his tan, and a victim of hit and run bed-head. He needed a shower, coffee, and a definite change of clothes before he could even think of meeting Kim at the station. "After I get a look at the footage, if it looks like there's a connection, you might want to talk to the agents at the Charleston RA and get them on board with the local investigation. That stack of files I went through yesterday stem from a number of jurisdictions, so this will definitely be a cooperative effort."

He pulled down one of his lower eyelids, studied the roadmap of crisscrossing blood vessels, and wondered absently if Tate owned any Visine. Feeling a little bit like a snooper, he opened up the medicine cabinet to check.

Toothpaste.

Face cream.

Mouthwash.

Kim yapped in his ear, and he made the appropriate noises to show he was listening. Something about a jerk at the local RA whom she'd had the displeasure of working with before.

He pushed aside a tube of hand lotion with his finger and found a bottle of Visine. Dropping the liquid in his eyes, he blinked heavily while Kim wound down her tirade. He swished a little mouthwash around, trying to dispel the Godzilla breath he had to be harboring, and winced as the potent liquid stung his lip.

He'd opened up that damn cut again, no doubt from overenthusiastically sucking Tate's various body parts last night.

A toe here. A breast there...

But, *damn,* it had sure as hell been worth it.

"So how long do you need before you can meet me at the sheriff's office?" she wanted to know. "It would probably be politic of me to let you make the introductions, since you're the invited party guest and I'm the crasher."

One thing that Clay had to give Kim, she never threw her federal weight around unless circumstances forced her to do so. "This is one party that I'm sure Sheriff Callahan doesn't mind you crashing, but if you'll give me an hour to, uh..." Say goodbye to Tate, run back to Justin's to shower and change, try to figure out what the hell he was going to say to Tate's mother this morning...

Morning, ma'am. Hope my shagging your daughter all through the night didn't disturb your sleep. God. What exactly was the protocol for this type of situation?

"... get ready, then I'll do you one better than meeting you. Tell me where you're staying, and I'll pick you up." She did, and Clay plugged the address into his phone. "Got it. We'll look the footage over with the locals, and then decide where to go from there."

Clay ended the call, splashed some water on his face and finger combed his hair. He looked exactly what he was – hungover, sleep deprived, and gluttonously sated – but as time was of the essence there wasn't much he could do.

He went back to Tate's room in search of the rest of his clothing.

He dressed – man he *really* couldn't believe he'd had any success with Tate last night, because his clothes smelled truly awful – and then steeled himself for facing whatever scene he was going to walk into downstairs.

Not only with regards to Tate's mother, and Max, but also with Tate herself. Things had been said and done and *implied* last night that he had no business saying or doing or implying. As crazy as he was about this woman – and facing facts honestly, he was pretty much totally gone – it still didn't change the fact that she lived here and he did not.

He'd do whatever it took to see her again, and work it out, but before everything was said and done he'd probably hurt her. Not so much by *commission* as by *omission*.

Such as *why haven't you bothered to come see me for the past six weeks?*

Yeah, he was pretty sure she might notice he was never around. And that the weekends they planned got cut short when he had to fly out of town, and that he was spending her birthday in Santa Monica with Ted Bundy Junior, instead of her.

Yup. He was prime relationship material, all right.

Grade A, USDA choice.

His presence in her life would be kind of like an F5 tornado: rare, and almost impossible to predict.

And it would probably do just as much damage.

He was chewing over that unhappy thought as he started down the stairs to the second floor.

And wouldn't you know it? He caught Mrs. H on the ascent.

She halted, mid-stride, but smiled before too much awkwardness ensued. "Good morning, Clay. I was actually on my way up to see if there was anything you needed."

Like fresh towels, Clay wondered. *Maybe a smack upside the head...*

"Uh..." Which was a brilliant comeback. And no less mortifying than when she'd seen him naked the other morning. "I'm, um, fine. Thanks." He glanced down at his soiled clothes. "I figured it would be easier if I showered when I got to Justin's. You know. Since my, um, clean clothes are there."

He was a highly respected FBI agent. A PhD, for God's sake. And yet in the presence of Tate's mother, he'd regressed to possibly seventh grade.

Maggie smiled. "You'll be working, then, again today?"

"Yes, ma'am. I've a colleague coming into town. I'll be assisting with the investigation until she no longer needs me."

"Very well, then. I'd better not keep you." She moved aside so he could pass. But when he drew even with her, she stopped him with a hand on the shoulder. "You're a fine man, Clay."

Well, hell. If that wasn't the strangest compliment he'd ever received. Not so much the sentiment, as the circumstances under which it was given.

He'd just been caught leaving her daughter's bedroom, and Mrs. Hennessy called him fine.

Why couldn't this kind of shit have happened to him when he was seventeen? Adulthood really did have its notable benefits.

"Thank you, ma'am." But how much longer would she feel that way? He found himself regretting things that hadn't even happened. "And just for the record, you've raised a really fine daughter. I... Well, she's really... very fine." He forced a smile. "It's important to me that you know that."

Maggie patted the shoulder under her hand. "I believe you're right. Now run along, dear, and grab a cup of coffee and a muffin on your way out the door. Tate can pack you something for the road, since you're in a hurry."

He was no stranger to hospitality – it was the southern way – but this humbled him. It had been a very long time since he'd been mothered. "I'll do that. Thank you." He watched Maggie go up the stairs.

And then continued down toward Tate.

She was in the kitchen, humming as she moved around, and he took a moment to simply appreciate that particular sight. There was something ridiculously pleasing to a man about finding the woman you'd spent the night loving glowing with satisfaction while she prepared food.

God save him if any women of his acquaintance heard that particular thought, but it didn't make it any less true.

Tate pulled a fresh batch of the most delicious smelling blueberry muffins he'd ever had the pleasure to encounter out of the oven, and he was glad, after the initial insult of waking up, that his hangover hadn't lent itself to nausea.

The noise of happily breakfasting guests drifted in from the dining area, and Tate glanced toward the door as if to listen for potential problems.

Then, sensing either his presence or his malodorous clothes, turned around as she set the muffins on a cooling rack. "You're awake." And her eyes were all smiles. "And not looking *too* worse for wear."

"You're either blind, or you're lying." Pulling himself away from the doorway, he moved close enough to stroke her hair.

"Maybe I have beer goggles – oh, wait! That was you last night."

He wrapped the sleek black strands around his fist, and pulling her close, kissed the teasing smile right off her lips. "I may have been a little drunk," he admitted, because there was no denying that fact. "But I'm stone cold sober this morning. And you're still the most beautiful thing I've ever seen."

"*WELL.*" Feeling her knees turn liquid, Tate struggled to stay upright. And just to keep things light, and maintain some perspective, patted his arm with an oven mitt. "I'm glad to see that your hangover hasn't made you grumpy. A little vision-impaired, maybe. But certainly pleasant."

"No." He kissed her throat, nipped her ear. "If I had more time, I'd prove to you how very desirable you are." He cupped her butt to draw her closer.

"I do believe you made that point quite a few times last night."

"Yeah. About that. It was some kind of fluke of nature. Like Haley's Comet. Or a blue moon. I wouldn't want you to get the impression that's what you'll have to put up with every time. I'm not sure whether you'll be disappointed or relieved."

Actually, Tate was more struck by the fact that he'd spoken as if that was something they'd be doing again in the future. She'd hoped, of course, but...

"Where's Max?" he asked, drawing her attention away from their sex life, and focusing it on her son. And she could tell that he wasn't asking out of mere courtesy. He looked around the kitchen, searching for signs of little boy life, and there was a flash of disappointment in his eyes when he found none.

"He's in the back parlor, watching cartoons." She'd shut the door to the family room earlier, because she wasn't sure of Clay's reaction this morning. So she'd tried to make his passage easier on both of them by distracting Max.

"Do you mind if I say good morning to him, or... do you not want him to know I spent the night?"

"He would love to see you," she said, pointing toward the door which led off the back hall. What had she done to deserve this turning out so well? "But just to warn you, you'll have to let him know up front that you have to run. Or else he'll be trying to talk you into another trip to the carnival."

Groaning, Clay backed toward the door. "Well, the carnival's out, but depending on what time I finish today, how about a little dinner? The three of us. My treat."

Tears pricked her eyes, but Tate blinked them back. "We'd love that." Then, because she wasn't sure she could keep the emotion from her face, turned away and started working on the muffins. "How about I fix you up some breakfast to go?"

"That would be great."

Tate thought the whole damn thing was great.

But unfortunately, the really great things in life were never easy.

"*I* thought you said the locals were friendly." Kim's blue eyes danced over him as she opened her hotel room door. "Was that before or after they busted your lip?"

"Ha, ha." Touching his finger against the flesh in question, Clay moved past her into the room, noting that Kim had made the bed. And actually used the closet. A row of neatly pressed business attire hung obediently along the rod, several pairs of shoes standing at attention beneath.

If she wasn't so much fun, he'd probably be obliged to hate her.

"What?" She turned from the mirror, tidying a deep auburn curl that had dared spring loose from her efficient twist.

"Nothing."

Clay moved from inspecting the closet to looking over Kim's shoulder into the mirror. He prodded his busted lip. Kim's hand flew to her nose. "Good God, Copeland. Tell me that's not you."

Clay stopped messing with his lip and sent her mirror image a grimace. "You can still smell it? I was hoping the Febreze would work. Apparently, I was overly optimistic."

He'd been seriously unhappy when he'd gotten back to Justin's only to discover that he'd packed no extra dress pants. He hadn't counted on needing even the one pair he'd brought. And he sure as hell hadn't anticipated sadistic bartenders and their lethal drinks.

"You smell like the barroom floor," she informed him, getting close enough to sniff his shirt. It was clean, nicely ironed, but his pants were another matter. Motioning for him to turn around, she gave his backside a considering glance. "You might want to consider emptying the whole bottle on your butt. What did you do, *sit* in a keg of beer?"

"These are the only pants I brought with me." Kim shooed him from the room, and as he looked down at the black trousers, he couldn't quite keep the defensiveness out of his voice. "It was either smelly pants or swim trunks, and I opted for malodorous as opposed to ridiculous. But after seeing your reaction, I'm questioning my decision."

Her room was on the fourth floor of the hotel, and by unspoken agreement they headed toward the stairs. The smell was bad enough out in the open, let alone closed up in a moving box.

On the landing of the second floor, she deployed the bottle of body spray she lifted from her purse.

He jumped back when she covered him in fine mist. "What the hell are you doing?"

Sniffing again, Kim nodded her approval before preceding him down the final flight and out the door. And spotting Clay's SUV in the relative shade of a palmetto, headed in that direction. "Making it tolerable for me to ride with you," she informed him over her shoulder. "Now stop acting like a baby and unlock the door."

He stood, arms akimbo, and plotted vile things as he hit his keyless entry. "At least the beer smell was something the folks at the sheriff's department could relate to. Now I smell like a freaking Gerbera daisy."

"I like daisies."

Clay grimaced as he took a tentative sniff, thinking of Josh Harding's expertly groomed face. The dude would probably laugh his ass off.

Ah, well. *He* hadn't spent the night in Tate's bed, now had he?

Fancy after-shave-smelling son of a bitch.

Feeling entirely more amenable, Clay climbed into the driver's seat and cranked the engine. The air conditioning blasted with a satisfying whirr. He caught the look on Kim's face as he backed out.

"What?" he asked, because she was definitely smiling. That smug little female smile that drove him nuts.

"Despite your aromatic contribution, you're giving off all kinds of interesting vibes. You fell into more last night than a bottle of whiskey."

It hadn't been phrased as a question, but she obviously expected an answer. So like any good game player, he executed evasive maneuvers. "Oh yeah? And what's that supposed to mean?"

I see your innuendo, and I raise you a question.

"Met any girls on your vacation? Seen any action? Gotten laid?"

He wasn't ready to talk about Tate, not yet, and definitely not that way. So he reached into his bag of tricks and pulled out a bald-faced lie.

"Like I've had the time?"

When the phone vibrated in his pocket, he held up a finger to indicate a conversational pause.

And ruined his bald-faced lie by pulling out a condom.

A used condom, stuffed into his pocket after the couch episode last night.

And currently stuck, like dried glue, to his actively vibrating cell phone.

Having no prayer that Kim hadn't seen it, he pried it off his phone's face. Then stuffed the damning prophylactic into the door's side pocket while he took the call.

"Copeland." Clay could feel the heat of embarrassment steam out of his pores. "Oh, hey Tate. No, you're not interrupting anything all that important. You found my badge under your bed?" Shit, it must have fallen out of his pocket. He did a quick pat, came up empty. "Oh no, that's okay sugar. I think I can get by without it. Luckily the officers I'm working with already know that I'm legit. But thank you. I'll pick it up tonight."

He sent a quick glance in Kim's direction, noted that she was watching him with unabashed glee. "Uh-huh. Tell Max that McDonald's is fine, if he really has his heart set on it. But if you can talk him into it, see if you might steer him in a different direction. Something with more emphasis on the 'food', as opposed to the 'fast.' I'm not sure my stomach can take another greasy hamburger… I know. It's my own fault for trying to outguess your cousin. I've learned never to trust an Irishman when it comes to whiskey or women."

He chuckled, a sound full of private meaning. "Uh-huh, I guess you're right. I'll have to thank him the next time I see him. Take care, sugar, and tell Max I'll see him later."

He hung up, rather slowly, making a production out of pocketing his phone. The longer he could draw out that simple task, the closer they got to the station. And the closer they got to the station, the less time Kim had to grill him.

When it became glaringly obvious what he was doing, Kim shocked the hell out of him by laying a hand on his arm. "Whatever it is, I think it's wonderful."

Luckily, he didn't have time to respond to that, because they'd arrived at the Bentonville sheriff's.

"*IT* could be him."

Clay leaned back in his chair, studying the image of the muscle-bound asshole beating the life out of a teenage girl. The balaclava hood he wore made facial recognition impossible, but the body was certainly similar to the man he'd seen at the carnival, and the behavioral profile fit.

Something had gotten away from his control during the assault, and he'd lashed out in blind fury. In the case of the girl on the screen, it was his own body that had defied him. With the victim they'd found in the woods it was the girl herself. Regardless, the man's obsessive need for control mixed with the predictable effects of the steroids served to form a potent combination which had turned deadly.

"Are you sure?" Sheriff Callahan asked from the edge of his desk.

"With his face covered that way, it's impossible to make a positive ID. You know that." Clay swiveled his chair toward the sheriff. Kim was seated in a chair to his right, and Deputies Jones and Harding stood behind him. Blinds closed tight against the sunlight, the only thing that stirred the air was an uncomfortable silence, as each of them processed the horror they'd seen. "But I *can* say, with absolute conviction, that the man who we just watched on this tape is more than capable of killing our second vic, and also of taking Casey Rodriguez. This is a business for him, but make no mistake, he likes doing things to the girls. He's what we call a power reassurance rapist, and hurting them isn't his usual agenda. Both from a financial standpoint – it's not good business to kill the merchandise – and regarding his psycho-sexual needs."

Clay looked around to make sure everyone was following. "In other words, he's not a sadist, nor could we classify him as a serial killer, despite the fact that we suspect he's killed at least twice. But he got no satisfaction from the killings. He probably views them as unfortunate accidents, and may even feel some remorse. But whatever remorse he feels is tempered by his justification that the girls somehow brought it on themselves. He can't admit to his own culpability, because that would mean that he wasn't in control. The control issues he's dealing with are long-standing, and probably derive from a power struggle in childhood."

"The classic garden variety psycho excuse: don't blame me, blame my mother?" Deputy Jones' dark features twisted, his disgust more than apparent.

"In this case, I wouldn't be so sure it was his mother," Clay clarified, "because he doesn't appear to exhibit hatred toward women."

Jones looked incredulous. "He beat the shit out of those girls, for God's sake."

"What Agent Copeland means," Kim interjected, "is that his behavior indicates no deep-seated need to punish women. Both times he killed, it was because the *situation* was beyond his control. We also have reason to believe that he treats his victims in what could be called a courteous manner. I know." She held up a hand, warding off the protests before they could get started. "That sounds crazy. But what I mean is that the power reassurance rapist often treats his victims as if they were dating, as if they really like what he's doing. He's convinced himself the rape is consensual. It gives him control over the outcome of the 'relationship' he's constructed in his mind."

She looked at Clay, who picked up the conversational baton.

"When we see this type of rape, it suggests that the perpetrator lacks control in his everyday life. He can't sustain a normal male/female relationship, most likely due to an image crisis suffered as the result of an overbearing parent, and some factor that leads to social awkwardness or unacceptability."

"But this guy was, you know, attractive," Jones pointed out, grimacing slightly when everyone looked at him. He glanced with some discomfort toward Kim. "Ms. Hennessey's words, not mine."

"Despite the fact that the man isn't obviously outwardly unattractive – we have both Agent Copeland's observations and the composite Ms. Hennessey helped with to back that up – *something* sets him apart from others. Something that he hides, that brings him shame and insecurity, and that he makes up for by exerting control over these young women. That's why we also believe that his business partner is dominant. It partially explains his continuing need for reassurance."

"So how does that help us?" Deputy Harding wanted to know. Clay flicked his eyes toward where the man was leaning against a file cabinet, and met his blue-eyed gaze. "I mean it's great that we understand that, but how does that help us catch him?"

"It helps, because if we can figure out what sets him apart, we'll have a better idea of how to find him." Clay flipped through his mental files for a pertinent example. "We once hypothesized that a serial killer we were profiling suffered from a speech impediment, and when that got out it made him that much easier to identify. We just keep narrowing the focus on these guys, getting more specific, and then eventually when you ask around you can say: *'hey, have you seen anybody around who's kind of a loner, not well-groomed, drives a van and has a speech impediment?* Well then, that's when the neighbors start to say *'hey, that sounds like John down the street.'* "

Of course it wasn't that easy. It was never that easy.

"Understood." Deputy Harding nodded at Clay. He looked like he slept, standing upright, in a vacuum. Nobody should wake up that perfect. "Do you have any theories on what it is that makes him different?"

Clay gave Harding points because he was unafraid to ask the right questions. And unlike other officers he'd worked with, wasn't skeptical about the answers. "Well, aside from his obvious physical attributes, I noticed something the other day that bothered me. It was hotter than hell at that carnival, but our boy wore a long sleeved shirt and jeans. Now, usually when people go to all that trouble to build their bodies, they're inclined to show them off. But this guy kept himself covered, which led me to notice him and wonder why. After looking at this video, I think I'm starting to have an idea."

They all turned to the TV screen, where a slightly grainy image of the masked man was frozen. Harding looked for identifying features which might have given the man away, thereby leading him to wish to conceal them. "No tattoos or easily identifiable markings."

"That's what I wondered about at first," Clay admitted. "But then I got to thinking about his behavior that day, and both times I observed him he was avoiding the sun."

"Not surprising," Sheriff Callahan said. "Since it was so hot."

"Yes," Clay agreed. "But it went beyond that. I'm thinking he stayed out of the sun so he wouldn't burn." He thought of the man on the beach the day he'd met Tate, the fair skinned man under the umbrella. The one who'd sparked their debate about sun protection. He reached over and pointed at the screen. "What do you notice about him here? Look at him in comparison to the girl."

"You mean aside from the fact that he's built like a tank?" Jones commented, then tilted his head as he studied the screen. "He's pretty pasty, even for a white dude. But maybe this was filmed during the winter."

"No," Kim countered, shifting in her chair to address the deputy. "The girl in this clip went missing last August. Her body wasn't found until this past spring, but by then she'd been dead for almost nine months."

Clay nodded, because that simply backed up his speculation. "Janie Collier went missing during the middle of the day – that service station attendant placed her in the back of his car mid-afternoon – and when I observed him at the carnival it was early evening. But he had been there all day. Lola Rodriguez said she served him a funnel cake around lunchtime. Meaning that he's out and about doing his scouting in the daytime, probably because his prey will have usually gone to ground at night. Unless they're real street walkers, and that's not the type he wants. He wants girls who have at least an air of innocence, for his own need and for the clients'. It feeds the pedophiles' fantasies, and makes him feel better about his own. So my guess is that's his usual pattern. And if his usual pattern is to be outside, but he's avoiding the sun so assiduously, he probably has to have a good reason."

"Do you think he's allergic to sunlight?" Josh asked.

"Good question," Clay admitted. And one that he had considered. "But I don't think it's that extreme. People with sun allergies usually can't risk even the kind of exposure I saw him getting. I think it's a little more mundane, but probably equally uncommon."

He waited to see who'd arrive at it first.

"He's an albino," Kim concluded. "How very Da Vinci Code."

"Well, that would certainly set him apart." Callahan shook his head. "And explain his feelings of inadequacy, because kids were almost certain to have teased him about *that*."

Clay agreed with the sheriff's assessment. "It explains his motivation, so to speak, and was probably a bone of contention with his parents. I'm theorizing, in this case, that his problem stemmed from his father, who probably didn't deal well with the fact that his son was somewhat of a freak. Almost like some men overreact when their boy shows an inclination toward effeminate behavior or another so-called undesirable characteristic. If the son is a reflection of the father, some men can't handle that kind of ego blow, so they take their frustration and disappointment out on the kid. That could explain the excessive weightlifting, which was either forced upon junior as a means of making him into an acceptable man, or was his own attempt to garner his father's favor."

"Not to sound like a broken record," Josh interjected, "but how does that assist the investigation?"

Again, Clay turned to address Harding. "If my speculation is correct, our offender's condition should still be something of a sore point. He covers it up with disguises out of a necessity to blend into a crowd, but at the same time he resents the disguises because they remind him that he's somehow inadequate. It would bring up the hurt and rage he felt over his father's disapproval, and he'd feel the periodic need to rebel. And by rebelling, I mean that there will be times when he goes into the public eye au natural. When he does, his hostility will be right under the surface, like he's almost daring anyone to make a comment. It's his way of asserting control, of thumbing his nose at his father, and reassuring himself that he's not really a freak. Of course, he's likely to encounter some curiosity or negative attention during these outings, which is really defeating his purpose. One, because that only serves to reinforce his subconscious fear that he's totally different from others; and two, because people are much more likely to remember a huge albino than a dark-skinned, attractive weightlifter."

"And when he encounters that curiosity," Josh surmised, "he's likely to react with hostility. Which would make him even more memorable to whoever saw him."

"Exactly." Clay began to feel a grudging respect for Harding. The man was a good cop.

"I should do another composite," he told Clay. "One that depicts our guy with his albino coloration. We can distribute the two together, and might be able to generate even more leads."

"We're talking about a pretty large area of distribution," Sheriff Callahan said. He slid off his desk to stroll over toward the map of Charleston and its surrounding counties which they'd taped to the wall of the office. Multicolored pins stuck out from various locations, indicating girls whose disappearances they were questioning. "Hit the lights, will you, Harding?"

Josh reached behind him to flip the switch, so that the office was bathed in florescence.

"These pins represent quite a number of jurisdictions. Janie Collier was reported missing here," Callahan pointed to a red pin on the map, just south of Charleston proper, "whereas Casey Rodriguez was abducted from here."

"Yes, but the fact that Janie's body – and I'm going to go out on a limb here and state for the record that I believe she's our vic – was located in your jurisdiction, only a few miles from where the Rodriguez girl was abducted, leads me to believe this area right around here," Clay stood up and crossed toward the map, motioning to a blocked-off area "is in the vicinity of our guy's home base."

"So he was bringing Janie Collier back here when she attempted to escape."

"It makes sense," Clay agreed with the sheriff. "These guys need to have a safe, quiet place where they can keep the girls until they deliver them to their clients. Something out of the way, so that nosy neighbors can't get all in their business."

Clay swung his gaze to Harding. "Deputy Harding, make sure you post both composites. This is our perp's temporary home base, his comfort zone, and this is where he'd most likely be seen in public as an albino."

"That's completely contrary to logic," Deputy Jones commented. "You would think this would be where he'd be most cautious about being recognized."

"If he were merely criminally minded, I'd be inclined to agree. But as I said, this guy has some serious psychological issues that drive him to be not always prudent in his behavior. Being seen in public in his most recognizable state is just another way that he's seeking control. It's his way of refusing to be held captive to his condition."

"So in other words, it's his hang-ups that will eventually hang him."

Clay's mouth tugged into a smile at Josh's observation. "It usually is. That's why profiling can be such a valuable tool. Deputy Harding, if you could put a rush on that new composite, I think that will be your *most* valuable tool in catching him. The sooner you can get those flyers out, the sooner someone who's seen him can come forward."

Josh nodded and shifted in his seat. "You, uh, don't feel the need to have Ms. Hennessey take a look at the new composite, or at the video for ID confirmation? I'd hate for her to have to see that." He nodded toward the image on the screen.

And elevated himself yet again in Clay's estimation. "I think we can spare her that discomfort," Clay assured him, "unless you don't trust *my* visual ID."

"I trust it."

"One question," Sheriff Callahan commented with a raised finger. "We've focused all of our attention on this one man, but you said you believe he operates with a partner. What, if anything, do you know about this other person?"

Clay turned to Kim for the answer, as she had a great deal more information than he did.

"What we know unfortunately isn't much." She looked at Clay. "I'd like you to take a look at what info we have, and see what you can put together."

"You can use the interview room," Sheriff Callahan offered. "Unless this guy wanders in here to ask directions, it should be free for most of the day."

"HE'S definitely dominant," Clay theorized as he and Kim went through what information she had. "The fact that you have almost no evidence on him leads me to believe as much. He's letting his partner get his fingers dirty, while he's content to stay behind the scenes. It suggests that he's organized and intelligent, and has no need to become intimately involved with the girls. I doubt that he ever touches them sexually."

"Because he has no interest or because he's cautious?"

Clay sighed and rubbed his hand across his neck. "If we had more to go on, I might be able to give you a better answer. There are several possibilities to consider. One – he's capable of what we would classify as normal adult interactions and therefore gets his kicks in a more traditional manner. In which case, he's probably a well-functioning male, dates or maybe even has a girlfriend, though I doubt he would let anything get serious. He's cautious and smart – not a risk taker, clearly – and looking at the situation from strictly a business standpoint, he would see the girls as a means to a financial end. Essentially nothing more than merchandise.

"Two – our man's a voyeur. He likes the girls' pain, their humiliation and subjugation, and he enjoys his role as director. His partner gets physical with the girls, but it happens under his instruction. Ironically, of the two of them *he's* probably the one with a deep-seated problem with women. He has his own need to control the situation, which would suggest his own childhood trauma. Maybe he was a victim, and this is how he reasserts domination. It's quite possible, given what we know about the other perp. Theirs would be a co-dependant relationship, with each feeding off the other's character disorder. Like some of the male/female partnerships we see in this kind of situation, there are elements of domination and submission. As long as the subordinate maintains his place, their interactions should proceed quite smoothly. That's tenuous, though, because offender number one – the albino – doesn't particularly like taking orders. His stepping out of line, making waves, might drive perp number two toward breaking."

He drummed his fingers on his knee and looked at Kim.

"I'm wondering," he admitted, "how seeing his partner's face plastered around town will affect him. The albino's obviously made a couple of errors in judgment – killing the girls is not part of the plan – and I'm speculating that our dominant perp will *not* be pleased with our composites. It may cause a fracture in their relationship, which could either prove beneficial for us or entirely disastrous. There's a very real possibility that the situation may incite him to violence, rather than risking us catching his partner and getting him talking. Once those wanted posters go up, the albino definitely falls from asset to liability."

"So if that happens," Kim surmised "and he knocks the guy off before we find him, we're essentially back to square one. Because almost all the information we have regards his partner. So our best way of catching one guy may make it almost impossible to catch the other."

"It's definitely a catch twenty-two," Clay agreed, leaning back in his chair and studying the ceiling. It was closing in on lunchtime, and he found himself wondering what Tate was doing.

"You know, that little smile thing you have working leads me to believe you're not entirely present beside me. Your body's here, sure, because I can see you as well as smell you. But your mind is clearly wherever your badge is."

Clay frowned, and then found himself laughing.

Kim leaned back in her seat, lashes fluttering.

"I have to compliment you on your control. It's been what, five hours, and this is the first time you've lowered the boom. You've shown an admirable level of restraint."

"Neither the time nor the place," she commented, sitting up straight and adjusting her jacket. "But I have to admit it's been killing me. Especially that thing with the condom."

Clay groaned, burying his face in his hand.

"I mean, how drunk *were* you, exactly, to stuff a *used* condom back in your pocket? Were there no trashcans in Hot Sex Land? Were you hoping to use it again? Because I have to tell you, that's highly ineffective. Not to mention a little gross. Of course, not quite as gross as seeing it stuck to your cell phone. Now I'll have *that* image in my head every time I call you, thanks very much. But just for the record, way to be bold and exciting. I had no idea you were the colored condom type."

He'd had no choice. They'd been the last available box at the drugstore.

Apparently the pharmacist had miscalculated demand, or there'd been a full moon when he wasn't looking. Maybe something in the water.

"Do they come in a rainbow assortment," Kim asked, "like, you know, today I'm in the mood for *Do Me Blue*? Or are they all that shockingly red? Were they flavored?"

The door, thank God, opened at that exact minute.

It was Josh Harding, bearing his composite, which he'd already transformed into a box full of flyers. "Sorry to interrupt." He jostled the box to get a better grip. "But we're a little short on manpower at the moment, and I was wondering if I could press you into service."

Clay looked at Kim, who nodded and shut down her computer. "We'll be happy to help." He stood, stretched his legs. "Do you have a list of addresses for the establishments you want us to visit?"

"Right here," Josh said, using his knee to balance the box while he procured the list. "A few post offices, several mail box places and a list of grocery stores and restaurants. I figured the guy has to eat."

"Right," Clay said, finally finding a companionable smile for the deputy. There was a busy brain behind the pretty face.

Then he took a sizable stack of flyers, and he and Kim went to work.

CHAPTER FIFTEEN

JOSH Harding carried a flyer into the Main Street Diner, sweating through his second uniform shirt of the day. It was ninety-two degrees, so humid the air was like syrup, and he was starting to smell almost as bad as Agent Copeland.

But at least *he* didn't reek of having had one too many the night before, and then somehow fallen into a field of pansies.

It was petty, he knew, because Copeland honestly seemed like a good guy. But Josh had overheard part of the two FBI agents' conversation, and the fact that the pansy field Copeland had fallen into the night before had involved Tate Hennessey and the use of a condom… well, it was okay to be bitterly pleased that the guy smelled bad.

Lucky bastard.

What kind of a name was *Clay,* anyway? It was like calling your kid Dirt.

Or… Sediment.

Mud.

Feeling marginally better, Josh scanned the restaurant, locating Sally Huggins – who'd worked at the diner since the dawn of time – and put on his cop face as he strode over. As Sally insisted on reminding him, she'd known him since he was in diapers, which meant she tended not to take him seriously.

His baby face was a definite liability in his line of work, but damn if he could help it. Unlike Copeland, who'd started to look ragged around the edges by twelve o'clock, Josh was cursed with appearing terminally clean shaven. And his hair – he didn't even have to arrange it. It just did that thing all on its own. And so what if he preferred to smell good? People thought he was obsessed with his appearance, and cultivated that teen idol image, but oh, if they only knew.

"Hello Mrs. Huggins," Josh said sternly, trying to set the stage for a serious discussion.

But apparently he'd only managed to look adorable, because Sally smiled and reached across the counter to pinch his cheek. "Joshua, honey, how are you? You want to sit down here and have a little pie? Lordy, baby, your cheeks are all red. Why don't I get you a glass of tea while you get out of this heat. Or would you rather have one of them grape sodas? They always were your favorite."

So much for Sally taking him seriously.

"Actually, I'm here in an official capacity." He placed the flyer on the counter.

A group of teens came in, momentarily distracting Sally, and she waved to them to let them know she'd seen them. They wandered down to the opposite end of the bar and took up residence on several stools, their cargo shorts dropping so low on their hips that they verged on indecent exposure.

"Be with you in a minute, boys," she called out. Then she turned to Josh with a frown. "Hooligans," she told him in an undertone. "These young ones nowadays don't know from respect."

Josh eyeballed the pack of young boys, thinking that they were probably more mischief than trouble. But if they were giving Sally a hard time, he wanted to know it. "Any problems I need to take care of?"

"Don't you worry yourself, honey." She patted his hand. "T'aint nothing old Sally can't handle. Just the usual shenanigans – loitering, stirring up the other customers, but there's no reason for you to be worried."

Josh shifted, placing his booted foot on the rail. "Well you just say the word, Mrs. Huggins."

"Thank you, baby. Now tell me your official business."

Josh handed her the flyer, the one showing their perp as Tate described him. This diner was right in the heart of the target area, which should fit Copeland's theory exactly. Of course that was assuming he wasn't too hung over to know what the hell he was talking about.

"I was just wondering if you might remember this man," he asked, "there's a chance he may have come in here."

Sally pulled her glasses up from the chain around her neck, perching them on the tip of her nose. "Not that I can recall. Unless it was one of my off days. What's he done, son? Robbed a bank or something?"

If only. "You know I'm not at liberty to say, Mrs. Huggins. Let's just call him a person of interest."

Sally gave the flyer another, more thorough, once over. "Sorry, Joshua. You know I've got a memory like an elephant, but I can't say as I recall this one."

Josh pulled out the second flyer, the one showing the man as an albino. "Do you by chance recall seeing this man?"

Glasses in place, Sally studied the flyer a moment. And a moment was all that it took before excitement had her hands fluttering. "I certainly do!" Her exclamation caused several customers to turn in their seats. "He was in here, oh, must have been a few days back. Almost got in a fight with those boys over yonder." She flicked a hand toward the teens.

Josh's boot slipped off the foot rail as he straightened in disbelief. Holy *crap*. Copeland had been on the money.

"They was calling him names, and snickering, being disrespectful, just like I said. Man can't help the face God gave him, I always say." She tapped her finger on the flyer. "Well this one, he was having none of that. He would have torn a strip off their hides, if not for his buddy."

Josh's heart beat double time. "His buddy?" he prompted.

"Yes'sum. A real swell-looking blond fellow. Bluest eyes I've ever seen. Well, exceptin' for yours, honey."

Josh ignored that and grabbed Sally's fingers. "If I came in here with my sketch pad, or you came down to the station, do you think you'd be able to describe what he looked like?" He knew the diner didn't have a security camera.

"I'm sure I could. But if you want another opinion, you should ask Ted." She gestured toward the long-haired teen currently demonstrating his spit-wad shooting prowess. "He got a real good look at that other man. Made Ted just about run right out the door."

CLAY'S cell phone jangled, and Kim smirked as he slid it from his pocket.

He supposed every time the phone rang from now on he'd have visions of red condoms dancing in his head like so many X-rated sugarplums.

Pausing under the meager shade of a large oleander, Clay wiped the trickle of sweat that slipped down his neck. "Copeland," he said on a sigh.

"You were right," an excited voice gushed. "Holy crap, you were totally right."

It took him a moment to place the voice as Harding's, another to translate what he meant. "You had some luck?" he hazarded a guess. *Damn,* but it was hot.

"The albino composite did it. I showed it at a local diner, and some people there remember seeing our perp. He almost got in a fight with a group of kids, just like you said he'd be inclined to. And the really spectacular part of this is that they also remember the man he was with. I've got at least two witnesses who can help with a composite. I thought you and Agent O'Connell might like to interview them, so they can tell you what they remember."

Well holy *crap,* Joshua. That was indeed exciting news. Clay hadn't expected it so soon.

"We might have a visual on the albino's partner," he told Kim, hand covering the phone's receiver.

Kim made the facial equivalent of *holy crap,* giving him two thumbs up.

"Okay," he told Josh. "Agent O'Connell and I are on our way to the station. Are you in route with the witnesses?"

"My ETA is about twenty minutes. I'll meet you there."

"Right. See you then. And Harding?" he said before hanging up. "Nice work."

IT was late when they finished the interviews, after factoring in waiting around for Spitball Ted's parents and sitting through an endless litany of Sally Huggins' stories.

Josh Harding had apparently been an adorable, well-mannered child.

Who would have guessed?

Clay dropped Kim at her hotel room, and felt like a shit as he considered dialing Tate for the umpteenth time.

He'd called once, at six o'clock, to say he was still working.

And again, at seven, to say the same.

He knew that Max couldn't wait forever to eat, so at eight he'd told her to go ahead and feed him. Twenty-four hours into their official relationship, and he was already destined to disappoint her. He should probably just head back to Justin's and spare them both the pain of facing that awkward truth. She'd tell him that it was really no problem, but there would be hurt and a little resentment in her eyes. She'd probably pout.

Withhold sex.

Send off all those behavioral clues women used to indicate you'd displeased them.

He'd apologize again – although he already had, profusely – and then feel defensive and slightly hunted that he'd been required to do so.

The whole situation was just a disaster waiting to happen.

Nevertheless, he pulled into the parking lot behind the B&B. Luckily, he'd had the foresight this time to bring a change of clothing, just in case Tate let him spend the night. And provided he decided to stay.

Who was he kidding?

The second she *blinked* at him he'd fall headfirst into her bed.

Disaster or not, he just couldn't seem to keep this from happening.

Gathering up his duffle, he locked his Glock in the glove box and set the alarm before heading inside, as curious little boys and weapons did not a good mix make.

He wondered if the little guy was sleeping. It had to be past his bedtime. Feeling a rush of disappointment for that missed fast food dinner, he climbed the step to the back stoop and knocked gently, hoping Tate would hear him.

A few moments later, the door swung open, and he was enveloped in sweet-smelling female. *Peaches,* he thought, unable to stop himself from burying his face in her hair. And when she took his hand, pulling him inside, he waited for the recriminations.

"You must be totally starving. And I know you have to be exhausted from working so late. I take it things went well today?"

"We had a good lead come in," he told her, listening for the other shoe to drop. For the hints that she'd grown tired of waiting, that she was upset with him for letting down Max.

"That's great," she told him instead, squeezing his fingers in her soft hand. "Any word yet on locating Casey?"

"Nothing positive. But we're a good bit closer to identifying her abductor. The composite really helped."

In fact, if it hadn't been for Tate, this entire investigation wouldn't be happening. If she hadn't seen that man talking to Casey, the girl's disappearance wouldn't have been given the attention it deserved, and he never would have put the observations he'd made earlier that day into use.

"I'm so glad," Tate said genuinely, "that I could help."

The smell hit him as they entered the kitchen – cookies, fresh-baked – and even as his mouth watered he caught sight of an obviously sleepy Max. The little boy glanced up from the truck book he'd been studying and smiled brilliantly when he discovered Clay.

"Mr. Clay!" And then suddenly he was around Clay's legs. "Mommy made you dinner, and I helped mash the potatoes, and I baked cookies for you *all by myself.* Well... Mommy took them out of the oven, but I got to scoop the dough onto the cookie sheet, and I didn't even drop any. And I saved the biggest one for you, 'cause you're the biggest, even though that one had the most chips. And I've just got to put my fingers over my nose because your pants *really* stink."

Laughing, charmed, utterly taken aback, Clay sank down to Max's level. Bright green eyes blinked at him over small fingers, and Max grinned from behind his hand.

If there was a man in the world who could resist that face, his name certainly wasn't Clay Copeland.

"Thank you for making me dinner. And for saving me the biggest cookie." He reached out, stroked Max's hair. "I'm sorry I got here so late. Maybe we can do McDonald's another time."

"That's okay," Max said diplomatically. Though he kept his hand in place. "Mommy said that we could have just as much fun making dinner at home, and she was right, 'cause I *love* making chocolate chip cookies. And it was even more fun making them for you."

Clay looked from the child to the mother. Felt love settle, just settle, more comfortably than he could have believed. This, he realized, was what it was all about. It was why people put forth every effort to make relationships stick.

It was why perfectly reasonable men did completely insane things like go and fall in love on their vacations.

Sighing, ridiculously content, he straightened and held out his hand. Max slapped it in their now customary manly exchange. "Do you think you could show me to the shower, my good man, so that I can get rid of these really stinky pants? I don't think your mama would appreciate it much if I came to the dinner table smelling like a brewery."

"Moms are funny that way," Max said philosophically, which had Clay fighting not to laugh. Then he took Clay's hand and headed toward the back stairs. "I'll show you where the shower is, so that she won't get mad and make you eat mushrooms."

So Clay showered, changed his clothes, and ate a delicious if reheated dinner that showed absolutely no trace of mushrooms.

Later, after he'd put Max to sleep with a story, and he and Tate shared a bedtime ritual of a different nature and lay tangled together beneath her sheets, Clay realized the other shoe was still on.

And about that, he felt they should talk.

"Tate," he whispered softly, stroking the arm draped over his chest.

"Hmm?" She stirred, shifted.

"I just thought that you should know… I mean, I'd like you to be aware… that what happened tonight is par for the course. My job is very demanding. It makes it difficult to have a life. Especially one with commitments."

Tate made the effort to open her eyes. "Are you saying that this is just about sex?"

"*No.*" Offended dignity made him stiffen. "If this was just about sex I wouldn't have..." Stopping that train of thought before it quickly derailed, he shook his head in consternation. "That's *not* what I was trying to say."

She waited a beat. "Are you setting up an out?"

"A what?" Clay's tone held suspicion.

"An out," she repeated. "You know, like when they put that little disclaimer on the packages of cigarettes portending that smoking may be hazardous to your health? Then they market the hell out of them anyway, and fall back on their disclaimer when the entire population comes down with lung cancer. *We told you these things were no good for you.* It's like a 'Get out of Morality Jail Free' card. They don't have to feel guilty when things go into the crapper, because they've already established their ready-made excuse."

She leaned up to study his face. "So I was wondering if that was what you were doing. Protecting yourself from future guilt by warning me ahead of time. *I didn't mean to hurt you, Tate. My job made me do it.*"

"I'm not..." He started to protest, but then blinked at her, looking chagrinned. "I know that's how it sounds, but I promise not to use my job as a fallback excuse for a lousy relationship."

"Good." Tate snuggled in again. "I know your job is demanding. Believe it or not, mine is, too. Not just running the inn, but being a mother. And I can't promise that I'll always be perfectly understanding, just as you can't promise you will be either. It's difficult, in a new relationship, when there are *three* people to consider instead of two. Any relationship is going to be work, and ours might present some bigger challenges than most. You might get irritated when Max comes down with the flu, and I have to cancel our dinner plans. Or worse yet, when *you* come down with the flu because Max sneezed all over your coffee. I might get irritated when you have to fly off to Nebraska instead of us going camping for the weekend. It will be hard as hell to only see you if and when your schedule allows. But unless I've read the situation wrong and have made a lot of erroneous assumptions, those are just some of the issues we'll have to deal with, as part of the regular program."

The hand stroking his chest went still. "I'm willing to deal with them as they come along. Are you?"

Blown away by her perspicacity, by her firm grasp on the situation, Clay lay there for another moment, too stunned to speak. She'd shocked the hell out of him tonight. Sweet as she was, Tate Hennessey was no man's fool – not any more. And he'd do well to remember that in the future.

A future, he realized, that they both saw happening together.

It was terrifying, and… terrifying, and yet comforting at the same time.

"I'm in," he said after a moment.

"Good." Then the hand on his chest began inching lower, and Clay groaned as it closed around his member.

This, he thought, rolling over to pin Tate beneath him, was a program he could definitely get used to.

CHAPTER SIXTEEN

JR Walker ambled into the Bentonville UPS store a mere ten minutes after it opened, stewing over the mess his idiot cousin had made. Probably, he mused, he should have stopped him from beating that girl. But a little sadism could foster sales in certain quarters, so he'd seen no reason to stop the filming.

Until Billy Wayne climbed off and she wasn't breathing.

JR had even done CPR – he still remembered how – but to no avail.

And now they had a murder on their heads.

How the hell had he managed to be related to such a fool? But then it shouldn't be that much of a surprise – JR's entire family had been worthless. From his junkie mother who more times than not forgot that he needed food, to his asshole of an uncle who'd been as free with his fists as he'd been with his gin.

Fury twisted inside him, quickly suppressed. That was something he hadn't allowed himself to think about in years.

"Hey, Rob."

JR blinked himself back to the present. He'd been standing in front of his mailbox. Staring into space.

Not acceptable behavior.

He turned, managed a smile, and put on some *aw, shucks*. He was Rob. It was something he couldn't forget.

"Hey, Julie." He exaggerated his drawl, scratched the deep brown hair of his wig. Just another tobacco-chewing local yokel – easy to recognize, easy to forget. "I didn't even see you," he told the woman whose acquaintanceship he'd been cultivating for the past couple months. Since it was impossible to remain anonymous in a small town, that left hiding in plain sight.

"No kidding," Julie chuckled, which did unflattering things to her jowls. But as her friendliness worked to his advantage, he kept his personal distaste in check. No way would she link "Rob" to anything, should it ever come to that. "You looked like your brain had been sucked out by aliens."

"I was having one of them, whaddaya call it, senior moments," he said as he opened his box, gathered his mail. And glancing at the small stack, made a face that said *more bills*.

"I think you have to be a little older to qualify for a senior moment."

"Tell that to my brain." And grinning, adjusted his pants under his padded gut.

Julie, stupid sow that she was, just kept talking as if he cared. Something about her decrepit mother, who *really* had senior moments, and *oh!* – some of the mirth-provoking situations that caused. As she was droning on, the WANTED poster behind her reached out like a fist to grab him.

Remarkable, actually, how well the artist had captured Billy Wayne.

"Hey," he interrupted Julie's nonsense, as absolutely casually as he could. "What's that poster over there all about?"

"Oh." Julie's eyes lit at the opportunity to pass on the latest gossip. "That man is wanted for questioning in some kind of abduction. Took a girl from that carnival they have goin' outside town."

"Is that so?" The fist tightened, and squeezed.

"Yep." Julie was utterly delighted. "*And* that's not all." She turned and lifted a stubby finger, which stilled in a flash of confusion. "Well huh. I wonder where the other one went." Moving to the table over which the sign hung, she peered under it, toward the floor. "Here it is!" Triumphant, she scooped another paper off the floor. Then ripping a piece of tape off the dispenser she wore clipped on her belt, affixed the second flyer to the wall.

And as she stood back to admire her handiwork, JR's vision began to gray.

"The FBI man who brought this in said that the guy might use a disguise, and that he could be one of those, what are they called? Albinos."

"Is that so?" he repeated weakly. Then clearing his throat, managed to look impressed. "FBI, you said?"

"Uh-huh." Then she lowered her voice. "But between you, me and the fencepost, he smelled like he'd been drinking."

If JR hadn't been going into free-fall, he might have found that amusing. But since his brain quickly calculated that Billy Wayne had to have been identified from that incident at the diner, where he'd simply refused to wear a disguise – and where JR, as usual, had gone along to make sure the imbecile stayed out of trouble…

As himself, he remembered, infuriated. Because he hadn't wanted to risk anyone seeing "Rob" with Billy Wayne.

But how the fuck had they managed to tie that incident to the missing girl?

Julie kept yammering away, mistaking speechless rage for fascination. "My cousin Jenny's boyfriend – do you know Jenny? No? – well anyway, Jenny's boyfriend works down at the sheriff's office as a dispatcher, and *he* said that the FBI man and his girlfriend saw this guy at the carnival, and that they were *this close* to stopping him from taking that girl. Because, you know, they saw them talking and stuff. Wild, huh? He abducted someone right in front of the FBI?"

But JR had stopped listening. He hadn't heard anything past the word *girlfriend*.

He knew who that girlfriend was.

Julie stopped blabbing. "Are you okay Rob? You got that alien look again."

Nausea roiled, but he smiled through it. "Just surprised about all this, I guess."

"I know what you mean. You don't think about that stuff happening around here. But that's not even the worst of it. They think he killed another girl."

"Really?"

"Uh-huh. Some run-away they found over by Piney Woods."

He had to fight to keep his hands from reaching. From squeezing her throat the way her words were squeezing him.

Piney Woods was just around the corner. A hop, skip and a jump from the old farm that had belonged to JR's grandmother.

And where Billy Wayne was staying.

Where they had the girl.

It was only a matter of time before the authorities came knocking.

And the arrogance of it all, the fact that Billy Wayne had killed a girl, left her in the woods, and then gone out and taken another, like no one would notice...

Rage bubbled inside and heated his veins, melting all the ice he'd cultivated for years.

People had messed with him – messed him up – for the last time.

And it was time the people who messed with him paid.

"*NICE* pants, by the way."

Clay shot Kim a look as they made their way down Bentonville's main thoroughfare – a palmetto-lined accumulation of shops and services that looked like a southern-fried version of Mayberry – heading toward the sheriff's office.

He'd run out this morning, in search of suitable attire, and the only store open at seven a.m. was the twenty-four hour Wal-Mart. His pants were serviceable, if not exactly the height of fashion. "Hardy har har. So I didn't come prepared for an investigation. Sue me."

Kim adjusted her own immaculate slacks, and gave him a thorough once over. "You probably could have found something nicer last night," she mused "if you hadn't been in such a hurry to get over to see your friend Justin. It *was* Justin that you kept calling every hour, wasn't it? So what – you had a front row ticket to an appendectomy? Maybe a triple by-pass that you just had to watch? Because he *was* working last night, right? You mentioned that, when I asked about him."

Clay briefly closed his eyes, because his grace period was apparently over.

"If I didn't know any better," she continued, immune to the fact that he was trying to ignore her. Like a mosquito buzzing in your ear.

A fly that you desperately wanted to swat...

"I'd think that my formerly commitment-phobic, changes-women-with-the-frequency-of-underwear, best friend Clay was in lo-o-o-ve." She did what could only be described as a happy dance in her seat. "So tell me, Lone Ranger – how the *hell* did you manage to do that?"

How the hell, precisely.

Clay had no frickin' clue.

He'd awakened quite early this morning, startled to find a small foot in his groin. At some point in the night Max had apparently snuck into Tate's bed and cuddled up between them, unbeknownst to the bed's occupants, who'd both thought the other one had locked the door.

Being a good mother, Tate had been equally freaked out to find him there, as the fact that they were sleeping together and there was a general lack of clothing made the situation uncomfortable for all. She'd started spouting off some sort of parental mumbo-jumbo about how when two adults really cared about each other they sometimes had "grown up sleepovers," which Max, perceptive kid that he was, clearly felt reeked of all kinds of bullshit, but he hadn't been the least perturbed. In fact, he'd told her with a fairly bored air that his friend Cole's mommy and daddy had sleepovers every night.

Then, with irrefutable five-year-old logic, he'd asked Clay if that meant he was going to be his new dad.

And okay. That had freaked him out a little.

Because as much as he cared about Tate and had gotten on board with this whole relationship program, despite previously discussed pitfalls and problems, the idea of marriage – of being someone's *daddy,* for God's sake – was just a little too much for his very recently *ex*-commitment phobic brain to take.

What did he know about being a good dad?

Sure, his own father had done a helluva job, raising him singlehandedly from the time Clay's mom died when he was eight.

But *jeez.*

What if he messed the kid up?

He'd been so worried about the stresses of his job on his and Tate's relationship, that he hadn't given nearly enough consideration to Max.

Like how would he feel when Clay missed his Little League games? Or parent-teacher conferences? Or those really embarrassing school plays that every self-respecting boy dreads because he has to dress up like an oak leaf?

So okay, maybe Max wouldn't be *too* sad if he missed that one. But still.

What exactly had he gone and done?

"Clay, *look out!*"

Kim's voice cut through his fugue, and Clay realized that he'd almost barreled through a crosswalk. An occupied crosswalk.

Slamming on the brakes, he thanked God for both Kim's ability to focus on what was really important – like *driving* – and also for seatbelts, because otherwise they'd both currently be getting intimate with his dashboard.

The man in the crosswalk – a slightly overweight brunette who'd obviously just conducted some business at the UPS store and was now making his way to his car – stopped like the proverbial deer in the headlights and stared at Clay's truck in horror.

Feeling like more than a little bit of an idiot, Clay rolled his window down and stuck out his head. "Sorry," he called. Totally mortified. Wouldn't *that* have been a headline to do the Bureau proud? "I'm afraid I wasn't paying enough attention."

A range of emotions crossed the other man's face, which finally settled into a scowl that read *asshole*.

Yeah. He'd arrived at that conclusion himself.

Clay watched the guy cross to an old blue pickup – one that Justin would have loved to have gotten hold of, because it was obviously in running condition but needed a serious bit of TLC. Out of habit, he looked at the license plate, while the man, after casting one last furious look in Clay's direction, climbed in as they pulled away.

"I'm sorry." Kim covered her surprise with humor. "I didn't realize that saying the 'L' word in the same sentence with your name would result in you mowing down pedestrians."

Shaken, Clay rubbed at the headache that was brewing steadily behind his eyes. "Let's just drop it, alright?"

"Sure," Kim agreed.

Clay took his foot off the brake and started driving.

JR sat in his truck, watching the SUV in his rearview mirror.

Damn, that had been close. He'd almost been taken out by the FBI, quite literally. It was that same agent he'd seen on TV. The one who was humping Tate Hennessey.

Good ole Julie had been a font of valuable information. Thank God for the small town grapevine, which made everybody's business public record. Tate Hennessy, who'd been the one to help construct the composite, was apparently hot and heavy with Mr. Visiting FBI, who, word had it, was some kind of profiler, just like on TV.

Blah, blah, blah, ad nauseam – the woman had droned on and on. But JR had discovered that the delectable Ms. Hennessey lived in Charleston proper and ran a bed and breakfast.

And was no doubt bedding and breakfasting Mr. FBI.

It gave JR a small burst of pleasure, however, to realize that the bastard had been so close to him and not even known it. It was dangerous thinking, he knew, because it was exactly that sort of arrogance that had led Billy Wayne to go and screw things up.

The son of a bitch.

Now *everything* was ruined.

He had to come up with a plan, and he had to make it quick – a way to complete this latest transaction, get the FBI off his tail, and spread around a little of his own personal misery in the process.

Vendetta was such an ugly word, but he had to admit it had a certain ring to it.

It was dangerous, and would mean extra risk, but hell – what exactly did he have to lose?

He'd lost everything that mattered, already.

So he'd pick up the pieces, just one last time, and then laugh his ass off as everyone else scrambled – the FBI, the local police.

Tate.

He studied his own reflection in the mirror, allowing a self-satisfied little wink.

Oh yeah. It was going to be a hot time in the old town tonight.

CHAPTER SEVENTEEN

CASEY trembled and tried not to cry as *William* climbed out of the bed.

Whatever they were doing with her, whatever they had planned, she hoped it would happen soon. Because whenever the blond man was away for the night William crept into her bed. Two nights ago he'd paid just a brief visit, chatting away as if she was interested.

Casey and William, long lost pals.

He'd touched her, but they'd both kept their clothes on, which she felt was due to the blond man's warning. Whoever he was, he seemed to be in charge, which worked out in her favor, because it made William keep his hands mostly to himself.

Mostly.

But last night...

A sob escaped before Casey could stop it. She'd learned that William didn't like for her to cry, and became agitated whenever she did so. So last night, after he came to her bed, she'd tried her best to appear calm and friendly. But it was so hard...

And it became harder before the night was over.

He'd stripped out of his clothes again.

The blond man apparently wasn't coming.

So he'd felt comfortable not only removing his shorts and his Gold's Gym T-shirt – folding them neatly, lying them beside the bed, while he smiled at her – but he'd also removed her clothes as well. Her shirt had been tricky for him, seeing as she was still handcuffed to the bed, so it had ended up dangling from her wrist like some sort of weird bracelet. And her pants…

Tears rolled down Casey's face in helpless currents as she remembered how very, *very* hard it had been not to cry. To not just break down and sob, sob, sob like a little baby. But William had put his fist through the wall – somehow, she'd always thought that was an expression, until she'd seen him actually do it – when she'd cried like that the other day. So she'd lain there, biting her bottom lip until it bled, so that she didn't cry while he undressed her. He'd skimmed his big, thick-fingered white hands over her hips, pulling down her shorts. Over her breasts…

He'd murmured endearments meant to charm but which turned her stomach. She kept her legs clenched together as tightly as she could, but he'd gently pried them apart and then knelt back on the bed, just… looking.

And touching himself while he looked.

But he hadn't raped her.

Pushing the reality of what he'd done out of her head, clearing her mind of that disgusting vision which made her feel dirty and shameful and used, she reminded herself of that fact.

But how much longer would she be able to comfort herself with that thought?

And how much longer before he actually did so?

Hearing the toilet flush, Casey turned her head into her pillow, wiping the tears away so that William wouldn't see. She was exhausted from keeping up the charade, and from getting no rest because William was sleeping beside her. He'd slept with his arm around her. And if she hadn't been so worried about what would happen if she tried to escape – about how easily he could put his hand through her as he had through that wall – she would have tried to kill him while he slept.

But she had been afraid, and she hadn't tried, so she was still lying in this bed.

Naked and terrified and desperately wanting someone to come save her.

As if on cue, the blond man stepped into the room. With her face pressed into the pillow she hadn't heard his footsteps on the stairs. But something in the air had given away his presence.

It made her shiver.

She looked up into his eyes – which were hazel now? – and he looked her over grimly. Then his attention shifted to the bathroom as William opened the door.

With a look that said *oh, shit.*

"Hey, cuz," he said casually, like he wasn't really standing there naked. Like the blond man hadn't just caught him in the act of doing exactly what he'd been warned not to do.

William, however, did his best to appear unconcerned. Like maybe if he ignored the great big pile of *oh, shit* he'd gotten himself into, the whole thing would just go away. He crossed the room with a nonchalant air and picked up his shorts from the floor. Pulling them on, he pretended the other man's stare didn't affect him.

When William finally looked up, the other man was waiting.

"Have fun last night?" he asked. And you didn't have to be a genius to be suspicious of his voice. It was way too pleasant, under the circumstances, to be anything but bad news.

Casey drew up her legs, trying to make herself as small as possible. Whatever was going down here, she didn't want to be an easy target.

"It's not what you think," William said calmly, his tone broadcasting *at ease*. Just a friendly little conversation between two twisted would-be molesters. "She's still a virgin," he said, pulling up his zipper with a practiced hand.

The blond man shifted, laughing a little as if this were all some funny joke.

But there was absolutely nothing funny about the gun he pulled from his pocket.

"That's good news, Billy Wayne. I'd hate to have to kill her, too."

And just like that, the man stepped into the room and raised the weapon to firing position. Before William could even wipe the shock from his face, a bullet pierced the side of his head.

Casey screamed; she couldn't help it. There was blood all over the bed. And blood and little pieces of... *something* livening up the faded paint on the wall.

Calmly, and with absolutely no emotion, the blond man stepped closer to William's body. While Casey screamed and dust motes danced, the blond man fitted the gun to William's hand and fired again.

Casey urinated all over her own legs.

Then he examined the dead man's hand, seemed satisfied by what he saw, and turned to look at Casey.

Bawling, blubbering, begging him frantically to spare her life – she'd do anything, *anything* he wanted – Casey scrambled across the bed until the handcuff snapped her back. She pulled as hard as she could, until blood seeped down from her wrist, but she couldn't work herself free.

Not fast enough to get away from the blond man.

She watched, horror making her shake uncontrollably, as he pulled a syringe out of his pocket.

Flicking it with a thumb and finger, he stepped over the body pouring blood and gore onto the floor and grabbed her by the wrist. "Don't worry," he said, plunging the needle into the fleshy part of her shoulder, where it burned and burned and burned.

The world tilted, got fuzzy. Finally faded toward black.

"Billy Wayne won't touch you anymore."

TATE scrambled toward the phone on her desk, grimacing as she remembered too late that there was finger-paint all over her hands. She'd been taking a fifteen minute break to do a little art project with Max, who was sitting on the floor of the office, head bent in concentration. Painting a picture of a Ferris wheel no doubt intended for Clay.

His *new daddy.*

Max's question had been like the exclamation point to their conversation of the night before, about this relationship being about three people instead of two. And she wasn't entirely sure Clay had been comfortable with such dramatic punctuation.

He seemed more the nice, conservative *period* type.

I want you – period.

I'd like to continue this relationship that we've started and see where it goes – period.

I like your kid, too, and am willing to accept him as part of the deal – period.

Not *Oh my God, Tate! I am so in love with you! And I just can't wait to marry you and have your baby call me Daddy!* Exclamation, exclamation, exclamation.

Yeah, she was pretty sure that had scared the screaming bejesus right out of him.

She'd be lucky if that wasn't him on the phone, calling from Botswana because he'd run for the hills.

"The Inn at Calhoun," she answered, wincing over the streaks of color decorating the receiver. "This is Tate speaking. How may I help you?"

"Oh, yes. Hello dear." The ancient voice crackled. "I'm calling to see if you by chance have any rooms available at your lovely inn tonight. I saw a brochure at the visitor's bureau and it looks positively to die for."

"Thank you." Tate's smile was warm as she sat down behind her desk and wheeled the chair in the direction of the computer. She made a mental note to tell her mother that the brochures – part of a new advertising program they'd implemented – had done the trick.

She punched a few keys, pulled up the screen she was looking for, and then spoke into the phone. "You're in luck, ma'am. We have one room left for tonight. It's a single, though, with only one king bed, so if that doesn't suit your needs you may want to consider other accommodations."

"Oh heavens." The old woman giggled. "A single will do just fine. I haven't traveled with a companion since I lost my husband back in eighty-nine."

"Excellent." Tate went about the process of taking down the woman's information, chatting a bit about local attractions, and clarifying any questions she might have as to directions. She also made certain that the woman wouldn't have any difficulty climbing a flight of stairs, as the first floor handicapped-accessible room was already booked.

"We'll see you this evening," Tate said after they'd concluded their conversation. "Thank you for choosing the Inn at Calhoun."

"Oh, the pleasure's mine, dearie. The pleasure's mine."

ON the other end of the line, JR dropped his spot-on imitation of his grandmother's voice, a talent which had served him well whenever he'd adopted the old bat's persona over the years. It came in almost as handy as her social security number, credit cards, banking account and the dilapidated farmhouse he was currently standing in.

Casting his gaze over the naked, unconscious girl on the bed, he once again sent a silent *thanks for nothing* to the old woman who'd made the mistake of tracking him down after an all too conspicuous absence from his childhood.

Where was she on the nights he'd gone to bed hungry? On the days when he'd ditched school, because he was embarrassed by his rainbow assortment of bruises? By the knowing looks the teachers sent his way but never did anything about?

Where was she, when that stupid outreach program for underprivileged kids had first sent him away to camp?

In short, the bitch had been AWOL.

And her misguided reconciliation attempt… well, he'd simply turned that to his advantage.

Striding toward the bed, he took one last look at the girl, making sure she was cuffed securely. With the drug he'd administered in her system, she should be out until this time tomorrow.

And he… he would be spending the night at the Inn.

Where the pleasure would definitely be his.

CHAPTER EIGHTEEN

THE commotion in the outer room brought Clay's head up from his notepad, where he'd been running through his notations from the interviews conducted that morning. Kim was out riding along with Deputy Jones, and Josh Harding was getting flyers printed with his newly completed composite. However, as one of the voices carrying on the stagnant, recycled government-building air definitely belonged to Harding, Clay gathered his little Tiger Beat buddy was back.

The other voice was more difficult to distinguish, as it was hysterical.

Curious, he pulled himself out of the chair which was in danger of becoming a permanent attachment to his ass, and moved closer to the open doorway.

"Surely you have to know *something,*" Lola Rodriguez all but sobbed, the strain she was under etched into lines of fatigue on her bare face. "It's been almost three days."

She had something – a T-shirt? – in her hands, which she was subconsciously stroking with her fingers.

Casey's shirt, Clay concluded with a frown.

Josh, encumbered by the box in his hands, did his best to clear the obstacle out of his way, shifting it to one hip, so that he could talk to Casey's mother without that barrier between them. It was the body language equivalent of saying that even though he was busy, whatever he'd been doing wasn't so important that he couldn't take the time to speak with her.

"We're doing everything we can," he said, his voice, his stance, his eyes sympathetic. "And we *are* making progress. You know I can't divulge too many details from an ongoing investigation – I'm sorry, I know how harsh that must seem – but suffice it to say that the composite we put out hit pay dirt. We're growing closer and closer to identifying the man who took your daughter, and that brings us that much closer to finding Casey. I hate to say it, because I know each minute without her must be agony, but you just have to give us time to do our job."

Lola nodded, tears threatening to break free from her already swollen eyes, and contemplated the shirt in her hand. Then she held it out to Harding.

"It's…" Her voice broke, and she struggled for composure, chest heaving mightily in her effort. Next to her, poor Josh looked ready to crack. "It's Casey's shirt. The one she sleeps in. I know you said that the dogs you brought in hadn't been able to follow her scent beyond the fairgrounds, but…" she hesitated, looking both embarrassed and hopeful. "I brought it in, you know, in case it might help you find her. I heard somewhere that personal possessions can be used as some kind of link, and since that FBI agent is still working with you…"

Her voice trailed off, and Clay pressed his thumb and index finger to the bridge of his nose.

Dear God. The woman thought he was some kind of psychic.

Josh, kind soul that he was, sat the box of flyers down on the floor beside his booted feet and accepted the T-shirt from the woman's trembling hands. "I'm not sure that's the way it works," he lied, with almost absolute believability. "But I'll be sure to get this to him, just in case."

Lola nodded her head again, pushed at her wild mane of hair. "Okay. Well, I..." At a loss, she looked around the station, and Clay realized that now that she'd completed that task she felt totally useless. Totally helpless to do anything to find her child.

As if her entire life as she'd known it was out of control, out of her hands.

Harding, once again proving himself to be more than just a pretty face, must have picked up on her emotions as well. Because as Clay watched, Josh seemed to flip through his mental file of things that might give her some sense of purpose. "You know," he said suddenly, snapping his fingers as if the idea had just dawned – add *acting* to the man's list of skills. "If you're not too busy, it would be great if you could help me pass out these flyers." He bent over and pulled one from the box. "This man was seen a couple of days ago with the man we believe took your daughter, and we'd like to bring him in for questioning."

Lola took the flyer, looked from it to Harding. "Do you think he might know where Casey is? That he might help?"

"We're not sure." That time, he'd fudged only slightly. They *weren't* sure if that man knew where Casey was, but it was pretty damn likely he did. And as for him helping...

Was Satan into ice sculpting?

"But the sooner we get these flyers out, the sooner we might find him so that we can ask him that ourselves. Do you think you'd be able to help?"

Good man, Clay thought. He'd given her a relatively simple task with the short term benefit of distracting her from her misery, and had given her a small sense of hope without filling her head with wishful thinking.

Too much hope could be just as detrimental as no hope at all.

"Okay." A solid sense of purpose eased some of the tension from her face. "Just tell me what you need me to –"

The door to Sheriff Callahan's office opened at that moment, and the older man leaned out, looking like he'd just endured a very uncomfortable dental procedure minus the Novocain.

When he spotted Lola Rodriguez, his level of discomfort seemed to ratchet up about a hundred degrees. His face actually twisted.

There were no poker championships foreseeable in this man's future.

"Deputy Harding?"

Uh-oh. His tone and stance indicated that this was not news he wanted Casey's mother to hear, and foreboding speared through Clay. *Damn.* He'd hoped for one, just one happy ending.

"Yes, Sir?" Josh excused himself from Lola's watchful presence, stepping toward his boss's office. The older man pulled him inside, and after several tense minutes Harding departed the office, slipped past Lola and headed toward Clay.

"Something's happened?" Clay prompted.

Josh exhaled on a pensive nod. "Another deputy, Purdy, just radioed in. He spotted a car parked along Greenwood Road – late model, dark blue BMW. He radioed for backup, as it fit the description of our man's transportation, and then proceeded to approach the car."

Okay. Harding was giving him the long, drawn out version of the story, which meant that he wasn't anxious to deliver the punch line. Clay's hopes for a happy ending dropped to nil. "And?"

"The driver of the car didn't respond to his requests to put his hands up where he could see him, and after Purdy drew even with the car, weapon drawn, he understood why."

This time Clay didn't prompt him. He simply waited for Josh to work his way to it.

"The man couldn't respond to any requests because half his head was missing. But his large, white, muscular body was intact."

Shit.

Clay uncrossed his arms and ran his fingers through his hair. He'd been afraid that something like this would happen. The other perp had been pushed past the point of breaking.

"Deputy Purdy said there appeared to be powder on his hands, from the weapon."

"Suicide?" Clay thought that highly unlikely.

"That's the big question. If you wouldn't mind, we need you at the crime scene. Agent O'Connell and Deputy Jones are on their way there, along with the coroner."

"Of course." Clay stepped over to Kim's laptop, which he'd temporarily requisitioned, to shut it down.

"What do you think this means?" Harding cleared his throat. "You know, for Casey?"

Nothing good, Clay thought, as he punched the final command into the computer.

Nothing good.

THE man was even more repulsive in death than he had been in life, all that pale, milky skin like molten wax in the brutal heat.

Despite the fact that the driver's side window had been lowered – a convenient way to make it more difficult to trace the bullet's trajectory – the car's interior felt like the inside of a crematory. And smelled worse.

What was left of their kidnapper, and Clay had no doubt this was their kidnapper, was slumped in the driver's seat, head lolling to the left.

Or rather, *half* a head lolling to the left.

Clay waved away the ever present flies, the tiny vultures of human carrion, and steeled himself against the smell as he climbed into the steel inferno.

The man wore loose fitting cargo shorts, and conversely, a blue, long-sleeved dress shirt. Buttoned wrong. Like he'd been in a hurry to run out the door so he could kill himself.

What was left of his head was bald as a cue ball, shaved razor close within the last day, maybe the last several hours. There was indeed powder on his right hand, and a twenty-two caliber weapon on the seat.

Kind of a wimpy little gun for such a big, macho man.

Of course, it was the kind of weapon that was easy to hide. And just as deadly as a forty caliber from a short distance.

Everything Clay saw backed up his supposition. This guy had *not* been the one to pull the trigger. Not the first time, anyway.

Clay intuited that the killer had fired a second shot, placing their man's finger on the trigger, in an attempt to feign suicide. He almost certainly killed the man from a short distance, close enough to do the job but far enough away to prevent him from fighting back. Because going up against a guy this size would be stupid.

And perp number two was not stupid.

He could have drugged him, or otherwise incapacitated him, and then used this man's own finger on the trigger for the fatal shot. But he almost certainly hadn't done that. He'd wanted to see the other man's expression – that *oh, shit* moment when he knew he was going to die – because his partner had failed him for the last time.

And he wanted him to know it, to feel his own folly. To accept his responsibility for his fate.

Passing blame. Like his accomplice, the remaining perp needed to pass blame to others.

The fact that the incident with the dead girl in Atlanta hadn't brought this about sooner suggested that he either needed this man, or this man meant something to him. Maybe both. He'd given him another chance, and he'd blown it. So *he'd* blown the guy away. More specifically, he'd blown the guy's *stupid* head off.

Poetic justice.

"What are you thinking?" Kim asked as she approached the grisly scene.

"No way he did this to himself."

She nodded her agreement, stepping back as Clay pulled himself from the car. "Some kind of decoy?" she mused, pushing one lose curl behind her ear.

"Some kind," Clay agreed. "The car we're looking for. The man we're looking for. The only thing missing is the silver platter. But our guy's smart enough to realize we wouldn't buy the suicide angle for long. There are too many things that just don't fit that tidy little scenario, including a notable lack of blood spatter inside the car."

"They won't rule it officially, you know, until the ME completes the autopsy. There's just enough physical evidence to make it look like suicide's possible, and the behavioral discrepancies don't hold as much water."

"I know it and you know it. And we're lucky that the locals trust our opinions enough that *they'll* know it, too. It will save us from having to wait out the autopsy to proceed with the investigation."

Kim looked around at the people milling about in various uniforms, the many individuals who were required to attend to a single, violent death. "At least we'll be able to get a good set of prints," she commented. "You think this guy's somewhere in AFIS?"

"I'll eat my new pants if he's not. This guy had way too much anger for that girl in Atlanta to have been his first violent outburst. I'll bet he's got a full rap sheet of assault and batteries, prior to starting his illustrious career as a rapist and human trafficker. But you'll probably find a rather abrupt stopping point. He's probably been clean as a whistle between then and now."

"Yeah. A real poster boy for anger management."

Clay motioned to Kim, moving a little farther away from the car, toward the shelter of the live oak which shaded the roadside. No point smelling that more than they had to.

"What's his motivation?" She chewed on her lip and followed. "This guy's bent over backwards to stay off the radar, and suddenly he's playing games. He obviously got wind that his partner's face was plastered all over town – no question that was the stressor that pushed him to pick up the gun – but why bother setting up this little dog and pony show? Wouldn't it have been much more in character for him to cut and run?"

Clay scratched the back of his neck as he played out the scenario. "The obvious answer is distraction. He's given us just enough crap to wade through to slow us down, which means he's concerned we're getting close to him."

"So what, he sets this up," she gestured toward the crime scene, "hoping to buy himself some time to get out of Dodge? It would have been a hell of a lot easier to just shoot the guy, hide the body, and hit the road."

"Exactly," Clay agreed. "So what does that tell us about his motive?"

Kim considered. "He obviously has something else on his agenda now, other than escaping detection. Maybe killing his partner wasn't enough for him in the way of punishment. Suicide is sort of the ultimate act of cowardice and personal failure. Maybe he wanted to humiliate this man in death. Put him down."

"I think you're right. This perp is definitely into retribution, of an almost eye-for-an-eye nature. His partner was stupid enough to get caught, so he blows his brains out. The man obviously had an ego – the weightlifting suggests as much – and suicide could be considered the ultimate destruction of ego. Only people who truly feel desperate or worthless take their own lives."

"Agreed," she said. "But how do we apply it to the investigation?"

Clay sighed, plucking at his damp shirt and cursing the heat. "For one thing, the remaining perp has suffered enough of a psychic stressor that he's now willing to take some risks. And we both know that risks often equal mistakes."

"Agents Copeland and O'Connell!"

Clay and Kim both turned to see Josh Harding striding their way, waving a piece of paper like a flag. "We ran the tags, and the car's registered to a William Wayne. Driver's license photo matches our vic, with the addition of blond hair, a mustache and a tan. Beaufort address. I just got off the phone with the Beaufort County Sheriff's Office, and they've executed a search of the apartment. No sign of Casey, but I figured you'd want to take a look. You want a ride?"

"We'll follow," Clay said, after getting a nod from Kim.

Harding walked off, and Clay pulled his keys from his pocket. "Okay, Tonto. Let's go see what kind of clues William Wayne left behind."

LAUGHTER chimed in the front hall, and Tate poked her head out of the office to find her mother chatting with an elderly woman. The white hair, long floral dress and no-nonsense, thick soled shoes said *grandma*. And despite the fact that she was stoop shouldered and pleasantly plump, it was obvious that she'd once been statuesque.

A small valise, looking like it dated back to the fifties, perched on top of a rather large Samsonite suitcase, forming a baggage mountain at the woman's feet.

Spying her daughter, Maggie waved her out to greet their guest.

"Tate, this is Alma Walker. You spoke to her on the phone this afternoon, when you took her reservation."

Smiling, Tate strode forward and extended her hand. The woman's grasp was firm and warm, roughened with calluses, which surprised Tate a bit until Alma spoke.

"Don't mind these old hands," she said, chuckling as she tucked them into the deep pockets of her dress. "I'm afraid I'm a bit of an overzealous gardener. It tends to... how do they say it these days? – do a number on the skin."

Afraid that she must have given something away from her expression, Tate covered her discomfort with a warm laugh. "It's a pleasure to meet you, Alma. Is this your first time in Charleston?"

"Oh, heavens no! I grew up over near Summerville, and lived around there most of my life. I've been living in Atlanta for a number of years, but when you get to be my age you just can't resist the urge to re-visit the old stomping grounds. Get back to your roots, so to speak."

"Tate and her sisters were raised, for the most part, just north of Atlanta," Maggie contributed. "A little town called Woodstock, up near Lake Allatoona."

"I've heard of it," Alma said, looking from Maggie to her daughter, blue eyes remarkably clear. "Nice place."

"It was a wonderful place to raise a family," Maggie agreed, and continued to chat with their elderly guest about the area.

The conversation began to recede into the background, as memories from her childhood flooded unbidden to Tate's brain. Casey's abduction had brought so many old feelings to the surface, and her mother's words seemed to release them from their dam. The shock of seeing a trusted adult defiling one of her peers. The fear, revulsion, and even guilt she'd felt during Donald Logan's trial. The nightmares she'd lived with for years afterward. And more recently, her struggle with over-protectiveness toward her own child.

Feeling unbalanced, Tate braced her hand against the wall.

"Are you alright?" Maggie asked, laying her hand on her daughter's shoulder.

"I'm fine," she lied, not wanting her mother to worry. And faintly embarrassed, turned her forced smile toward their guest. "Let's get you checked in, shall we?" She bent to grab the valise.

"Oh no, dear." Alma stepped forward, nudging Tate with her hip, and took the valise from her hand. "I'm not so old that I can't pull my own weight." And indeed, she hefted the large piece of Samsonite as if it weighed nothing at all.

"If you're sure –"

"I'm sure."

Okay then. "Well, why don't you follow me to the office? We'll get the paperwork taken care of and then I'll show you to your room."

As soon as the words left her mouth, Tate's cell phone rang in her pocket. She would have ignored it except for the fact that she hadn't heard from Clay since that morning. Considering the awkward circumstances, and the fact that he'd all but burned a hole in the floor in his hurry to leave, she couldn't help but feel the pinch of worry that he'd decided this gig wasn't for him. So quietly slipping the phone from her pocket, she couldn't stop the small smile when she saw his number.

Seeing her daughter's expression, Maggie grasped Alma's elbow. "Tate, why don't you take that call, and I'll go ahead and get Ms. Walker settled."

"Excuse me," Tate apologized to their guest, and moved toward the privacy of the parlor. "But this is a call I've been waiting for all day." And how pathetic was that? She felt worse than a lovesick teenager.

Closing the doors behind her, she walked over toward the settee, which seemed rather ironic as that was where she and Clay had first...

Okay. Not good. She chose a wingback chair instead.

"Hello?"

"Tate?" Clay's voice crackled.

"Where are you?" she asked automatically. "You're not getting very good reception."

"...Beaufort... storm knocked out... tower. I've been trying to call you... hours. This is the first... get through."

It was completely garbled, but she gathered that he'd gone to Beaufort, and a storm had knocked out a cell tower. And – hip, hip hooray! – he had a good reason for not calling. Not that she'd been worried, or anything.

"What are you doing in Beaufort?" she wondered, as that town was more than an hour south of Charleston.

"There's been… development. …going to be here awhile. It's going… late when I get in. …wondering if you'd prefer… to Justin's."

Tate held her breath. He was calling to tell her he was going to be late coming home. That was sweet. *God,* that was sweet. "You're welcome to stay here. No, scratch that. I would *like* for you to stay here. *Love* for you to stay here. I've gotten kind of used to you hogging all the covers."

His laughter was clear on the other end of the line. "I guess if you want the covers, you'll have to sleep on top of me."

Funny that *that* statement was the only one that came out intact.

"I'll be awake until about eleven, but if you get in past that I'll leave the alarm off and the back door key under the mat."

"No!" Their connection had grown stronger. And the note of censure in his voice was perfectly clear. "*Under the mat* is burglar code for *easy targets live here.* Engage the alarm, give me the code, and I'll let myself in. And remind me that we need to talk about security."

Rolling her eyes, Tate realized this was a downside she hadn't foreseen. "I guess you're going to use some of your FBI voodoo to open the door?"

"I never give away my secrets. I have to go, sugar, but I'll try to make it back before you're asleep. If not, I'll be the strange man climbing into your bed."

Tate laughed, a warm sound filled with happiness. "And I'll be the woman wallowing in the temporary luxury of covers. Anyway, take care and I'll see you tonight."

CLAY snapped his phone shut with a click, thinking that a little blanket tug-of-war sounded like a damn good idea.

Winner gets naked.

Or maybe the loser gets naked.

Hell, they should both get naked and forgo the blankets altogether. They'd been generating enough body heat the past couple of nights to incite some kind of nuclear reaction anyway, so nighttime chills shouldn't even be a factor.

Grinning, he realized that having Tate waiting for him in bed made the end of the work day a hundred times more appealing than it ever had been before.

He turned to find Kim, standing way too far inside his personal space. She grinned.

"So am I ever going to get to meet this woman who's put a smile on your ugly mug?"

"Now why would I want to scare her like that?" He slid his phone into his pocket. "Was there some specific reason you're hovering, or just your all-around need to be obnoxious?"

She pulled a handkerchief out of the inside pocket of her jacket – dear, sweet Lord, the woman actually carried a handkerchief – and wiped the delicate sheen of sweat that had dared to gather on her brow.

He, meanwhile, stood by looking like he'd run under somebody's sprinklers.

"They're getting ready to start bagging and tagging the evidence." She gestured over her shoulder toward the open apartment door behind her. "Is there anything else you wanted to look at again before they take it away?"

Clay shook his head. The evidence amounted to jack, because even though the weightlifting pills and powders, impressive collection of workout equipment, equally impressive but not so innocent collection of homemade pornography, fake ID's, professional level costuming equipment, bottles of Insta-Tan, etcetera, etcetera, told them a great deal about the sex offender known as William Wayne, the fact was that William Wayne was dead.

And Clay hadn't seen one shred of evidence which suggested the man had any type of association, professional or otherwise, with anyone else. Either the man they were searching for had come and swept the apartment prior to staging his accomplice's suicide, or their normal protocol involved living completely separate from one another.

Which was probably the case. The man who'd obviously engineered this enterprise was too smart to spend more time in the albino's presence than he had to, and he was probably adamant about circumspection in behavior.

Until today.

And now, joy of joys, Clay and the other law officers who'd drawn the short stick that was this case, got to sit through several hours of thoroughly stomach-turning porn, in the hopes that they might A.) Be able to identify some of the girls shown on the tapes, or B.) Find any clues which might help lead them to the dead man's partner.

"Tell 'em to go ahead with whatever they need to do. I've seen enough." And wasn't that the truth.

Kim disappeared through the door, and Clay leaned against the railing, watching the colors of impending sunset dance across the broad expanse of sky over Beaufort Bay. The apartment which William Wayne had inhabited for the past few months was one of four in an elegant old building, a shining example of antebellum architecture from the city's pre-Civil War heyday.

A graceful collection of curved balustrades, heavy masonry, tabby foundation and waved glass windows, the building was surrounded by both ancient oaks and towering palmettos, and offered stunning views of the water over which it stood watch.

Sailboats, wings unfurled, glided past other pleasure craft on the silent waters, which lapped gently along the seawall in undulating waves. A salt breeze blew in periodically, carrying the scents of diesel and brine, breaking the stillness of the air which hung thick and damp after the earlier storm. Lingering raindrops fell from the fronds of the nearby palmettos in a steady, rhythmic patter. A lone blue heron, unfurled wings more graceful than the sailboats', soared high and far into the heavy cover of dusk.

It was too beautiful a view for a degenerate.

Sighing, Clay loosened his tie from his sweat-dampened collar, trying to catch some of the cooling whisper of air as it sighed past. He was hot, tired and disgusted. More than ever, he'd like to pack it in and call it a day.

But there was a monster still out there somewhere, who saw dollar signs in a young girl's innocence.

And since he had to get into the forbidden corners in the mind of that monster, he, like evil, couldn't sleep.

CHAPTER NINETEEN

JR double-checked the contents of his grandmother's valise, making sure he had everything he needed. The chloroform would suffice until the stronger drug in the syringe could take effect, and he stuffed both into the deep pockets of his housecoat.

The padding he wore slicked his stomach with sweat, and the fake skin on his face and arms itched. But these were minor inconveniences, considering the end goal. He comforted himself with the fact that this was the last time he'd ever have to assume the old bitch's persona.

Of course, it was also the last time he'd be able to walk about publicly as JR Walker.

It wouldn't take long, after he'd done what he'd come to do, for the police to run everyone who'd stayed at the Inn tonight. And even though he'd done all that he could to eradicate his trail, eventually the fuzz would get around to putting two and two together. Then they'd show up at his grandmother's farm with a search warrant.

The place would be empty, but they'd find Billy Wayne's blood on the floor and the walls, and inevitably they'd start a search for sweet little Alma's grandson.

Of course, by that time he'd be long gone, with a completely new identity. Maybe this time he'd make his transformation a little more final with plastic surgery.

JR Walker, no more.

He'd move around for a while, lose himself in city after city. After the trail had gone cold and the search died off, he'd pick a nice spot and settle down.

Maybe get a dog.

Kids liked dogs.

He laughed lightly, thinking how perfect this whole thing had turned out. He'd jettisoned Billy Wayne, whom he'd been carrying like excess baggage for too many years, and he finally had the opportunity to mete out a little justice to Tate Hennessey.

He wondered how long it would take for her to figure it out.

She'd stood there, shaken his hand, and hadn't had an inkling of who he was.

He had to admit there was a little thrill in that.

He unlocked the latches on the old piece of Samsonite, and studied the size of the space within the hard walls. She'd come awfully damn close to picking up the suitcase, and then the little bitch might have realized it was empty. And wouldn't that have been an interesting situation? He could have played the crazy old lady card, but why make anyone suspicious before he had to?

He ran his hand around the inside of the case. It was solid, and air might be a problem after a while, but he wouldn't allow enough time to pass for suffocation. He'd only gotten one brief glimpse of the kid, as he was being shepherded upstairs for bedtime, because Tate hovered over him like a mother hen. Not encouraged to mingle with the guests. Blah, blah, blah. Paranoid bitch, wasn't she?

The boy looked like the mother, all dark hair and big green eyes.

And he was small enough to fit in the suitcase.

After milking the old lady – who was like most normal grandmas, and couldn't pass up a chance to talk about her progeny – he'd discovered the kid's name was Max.

Of course, it wouldn't be Max for long.

Like JR, he'd have to undergo an identity change. And while it might be tricky at first, after a while he'd have the kid believing whatever he wanted him to. Kids his age were malleable. Vulnerable.

Naïve.

Soon, his mother would be no more than a bad memory. Especially after he told the kid she'd wanted him to be taken.

Oh yeah, he was familiar with the tactics.

A little brainwashing, a little love, a nifty little system of reward and punishment. A few months, maybe less, and the kid would be totally his.

He laughed again, this time a little louder. Whoever said revenge was sweet didn't know the half of it.

CLAY fought a stomachache the entire way home.

It could have been the pound of grease he'd choked down several hours ago, in the form of a fried fish sandwich and homemade chips, dutifully chased by at least a gallon of sweet tea. It could have been the fact that Kim volunteered to drive, and her

Mario Andretti-blindfolded-and-hopped-up-on-speed style of piloting brought an entirely new dimension to motion sickness.

Of course, more likely, it was the fact that he'd just spent the past three or four hours watching tape after tape of scared, young girls being assaulted in the worst possible way.

It wasn't like he hadn't seen that kind of thing before. But for some reason, watching William Wayne on tape – knowing that he'd seen the man with his own eyes, suspected that he was a predator, and hadn't done a thing to stop Casey's abduction from happening – made him feel like throwing up.

Oh sure, he understood, logically, that there was almost nothing he could have done. He had no reason to approach the man, no evidence to suggest he was anything more than your run-of-the-mill pervert. No possible way to foretell that he was going to all but snatch a girl from under his nose.

Almost literally under his nose.

Clay had been on the Ferris wheel with Max when that girl was taken.

It was like compounding what had happened in Topeka.

What the hell good was his degree, his extensive Bureau training, if kids continued to be victimized virtually in front of him and he couldn't do a damn thing?

"You're beating yourself up."

Turning away from the darkened scenery flashing past his window, he slid a frown toward Kim.

"God, Clay, give yourself a break. You're a damn good agent, but contrary to popular belief, you're not exactly a psychic."

He winced. She'd obviously been talking to Deputy Harding.

"There's no way you could have known," she continued, "that the man you saw at that carnival was involved in what we just watched. You *did not fail*. In fact, we're damn lucky that you noticed his fishy behavior in the first place. If not, you wouldn't have placed so much importance on Casey Rodriguez's disappearance, and we wouldn't be where we are now."

"And where are we, exactly?" he asked mildly. "Our main suspect is dead, there's no sign of the girl, and I still don't have enough to go on to get a firm handle on his partner. I know he's undergone a psychic break, and is more prone to taking chances, but I can't say for sure whether he's already fled the area. Obviously, the area near the Collier crime scene needs to be canvassed, since Wayne was probably taking her to some sort of holding spot when he accidentally killed her. But even if we find that place, it will probably be too little, too late. He'll be gone, the girl will be gone – either sold or killed because she's been so much trouble. That's a very real possibility, you know. He's going to want to punish everyone he holds responsible. He's a big fan of passing the buck."

"So we take what evidence we can gather, and follow the bastard's trail."

"A lot of good that does Casey Rodriguez."

Kim's deep blue eyes shone hot in the darkness. "This is one of the main reasons I wanted to come down here. I shouldn't have to say this to you Clay, but you've been taking things way too personally. I know you feel bad about this girl, feel a certain amount of responsibility because you were *there*, but she's only part of the big picture. William Wayne is dead, which means he won't be hurting young girls any more. And I need you to stay in the game here, friend, because you're one of the best agents I've ever worked with. I thought, at first, that you'd benefit from time away, but now I wonder if this case isn't exactly what you needed. It's hard, and it sucks, but *you will get through it,* and you'll realize that life goes on. You'll do the best you can, help rid society of another lowlife, and accept that it's not up to you to singlehandedly save the world." She pulled into the parking lot of her hotel. "Now please go home to your woman. Remind yourself of what you've done right. And tomorrow morning put your game face on, because we're going to catch this bastard."

Clay turned away from her to stare out at the parking lot. Kim was right. He *knew* she was right, and there was no doubt he deserved the verbal face-slap. There was no room in his line of work for this useless, pitiful moping.

And like she said, he should just go home to Tate, and remind himself of the goodness life had to offer.

"So I'll pick you up same time tomorrow?" he asked, shifting back to face her.

"Sounds good." She dropped a quick kiss on his cheek, and slipped out the driver's side door. Tucking her jacket over her head to avoid the steadily increasing rain, she waggled her fingers and then disappeared into the hotel.

Clay played their conversation over in his mind as he drove through the rain-slicked streets. Kim had all but accused him of having a hero complex, which might have some basis in truth. He'd been a lifeguard through high school and on summer breaks during college, and had chosen both mental health and law enforcement as a profession.

And while helping one's fellow man was a noteworthy aspiration, striving for superhero status was both unrealistic and self-defeating. No one was perfect, and no one could do it all. He'd just have to do his job to the utmost of his abilities, and rely on a force greater than himself to handle the rest.

And boy, the Man Upstairs must be having quite a laugh right now, he thought as he pulled in beside Tate's car. He'd not only shown Clay a thing or two about humility and failure, but he'd also thrown love and hope into the mix. There was an old saying about doors closing and windows opening that pretty much summed up the situation. He felt like he was hitting an all-time professional low and an all-time personal high at exactly the same time.

Climbing out of his SUV, he started to run in out of the rain, but instead took a moment to look at the car seat strapped into the back of Tate's Honda.

He'd been having some pretty mixed up feelings about the scope of the situation he was taking on, but as he stood there, rain flattening his hair against his head, he realized that at least part of his pleasure in coming back here tonight had as much to do with Max as with Max's mama. He looked toward his own vehicle. Tried to picture that car seat there.

Thought it might look pretty nice.

Maybe even with another one beside it.

And when *that* thought didn't make him turn and run, he knew that as Kim said, this was something he'd done right. He might not be a perfect father figure to this little boy, but he'd damn sure try to do his best. Just do his best with the hand he'd been given, and let the cards fall where they may.

Right now, his deck was firmly stacked right here at the Inn at Calhoun.

So slipping his handy-dandy lock pick out of his pocket, he trotted up the steps to the back door, pulling up short when he saw Tate's note.

Please don't get any chicken blood on the door

For a moment, he thought the woman he loved had gone crazy, until he made the association to her earlier comment about voodoo. And then couldn't stop the laugh that ripped out of his throat. You had to love a woman with a good sense of humor.

Especially when it came packaged with such a killer set of legs.

And speaking of legs, he hoped she wasn't sleeping, because he sure wouldn't take exception if she wanted to wrap them around his waist.

He slipped the lock, dealt with the alarm, and considered the myriad ways he could improve the Inn's security. It was a difficult balance, wanting to secure your home and yet opening it up to paying guests. Overall, it wasn't a choice he would have made, but he guessed he'd have to learn to live with it. Worry about it, but live with it. Which was going to make all the time spent away just that much more difficult to handle.

Shaking the water from his hair like a dog, Clay headed toward the back set of stairs, ascended two at a time, and coming out on the second floor landing, discovered he wasn't alone in the hall.

Watery light from an antique sconce illuminated an elderly woman several doors down, hovering near the stairs leading to the third floor and the owner's bedrooms. As Clay watched she put her hand on the doorknob, and began twisting it open.

"Ma'am?"

The woman stiffened, seemed to tense, then turned slightly toward the sound of his voice. Cautious smile in place, Clay moved forward, doing his best to appear nonthreatening. No need to give the old lady a heart attack, since she seemed to be pretty confused. Drawing closer he watched her eyes dart around, her hands stab into her pockets.

"Are you having trouble finding your room?" he asked, using his most honeyed Boy Scout inflection. "That door leads to the third floor, and there are no guest rooms on that level."

She was tall, very tall, though bent as an old oak. Clay guessed that before osteoporosis struck she'd been only a couple inches shorter than him.

She wore soft-soled shoes, rather than slippers.

"Oh. I'm sorry." She eased back into the shadows. "I'm afraid these eyes aren't what they used to be."

"That's no problem, ma'am. Can I offer you some assistance?"

"Oh, goodness no." She laughed, but her blue eyes narrowed. "I'll be fine. You run along to bed. You've done more than enough for one night."

As Clay watched, she turned and shuffled off.

Two doors down, she slipped her hand into her pocket, pulled out a key and attempted to turn it in the lock. On the third try, her hand stopped shaking enough to make it work. Then she disappeared into her room and shut the door.

Clay stood there for a moment, waiting for what he wasn't entirely sure. But there was something…

He shook it off, wanting to set everything to do with work or profiling or his all-around general professional paranoia aside. So he opened the door, turned the lock, and tiptoed up the stairs. He found himself drawn to Max's room, where a weak stream of light filtered out from beneath his door.

And pushing it open with only the lightest squeak of hinges, peeked his head in to find the little guy sprawled with one arm and leg off the bed, blankets bunched at his feet, and that goofy purple bear tucked beside him.

Something inside Clay moved.

Whether his heart, his soul, his latent paternal instincts – he couldn't decide and it really didn't matter. In every way other than the strictest biological sense, he had the overwhelming feeling that this child was his.

It was one of the most powerful emotions he'd ever felt.

Negotiating the toy-strewn floor, he lifted Max away from the edge of the bed, tucking the sheet in, nice and tight, around his pajama-covered bottom. Then lingered long enough to drop a kiss on one sweet-smelling cheek before backing from the room.

And very nearly bumped into Tate.

"Hey," he whispered, surprised. "I didn't see you there."

He had just enough time to catch the sheen of tears before she launched herself into his arms. "Hey now." He squeezed her tight, then gently pushed her back so he could cup her face. And rubbing his thumb across her cheek, caught the first tear as it spilled over. "What's this all about?"

"You," she admitted, smiling as she swiped at her other cheek. "If I hadn't already fallen for you that certainly would have done it."

Whatever had moved inside Clay began to shimmy. Do a happy little tango inside his chest. "I love you, Tate." And he said it without stuttering. "I never believed it when people said it happened like this, but I think I was gone the moment I saw you. In that yellow bikini, on the beach. Trying to burn all this beautiful skin to a crisp."

She laughed. Cried some more. And then took his hand to draw him with her.

"Come on," she said, pulling him toward her bedroom. "Let's get you out of these wet clothes so that I can cry all over your manly chest." And stopping at the door, stretched up to kiss his cheek.

"And in case you haven't figured it out yet, I love you too."

CHAPTER TWENTY

CLAY considered that next morning at breakfast that he was happier than he'd ever been in his life.

Not content, merely. But actually *happy*.

Goofy happy. The kind of happy that made other people reach for the Pepto Bismol, because they got indigestion just looking at you.

He'd found himself singing in the shower. Of course, the fact that Tate had slipped into that steamy little enclosure with him and given him something to sing about could very well have had something to do with it.

Oh yeah. He'd definitely gone off the deep end. A big ole' fat belly flop into love.

And yet here he sat, grinning like an idiot.

Max, who was firmly ensconced on his lap while they debated the merits of having syrup versus powdered sugar on their waffles, twisted around to peek over Clay's shoulder when he heard the squeaky hinges on the door.

Rogan Murphy – looking more disreputable than ever with his shoulder length brown hair all loose and wet around his face; a face heavily shadowed by at least three days worth of stubble – made an appearance at the doorway to the dining room. The man's jeans looked like they'd been through a shredder, and his T-shirt today recommended *Peace, Love and Beer*.

Clay, resplendent in his newly dry-cleaned suit, frowned.

Max, sporting bed-head and Sponge Bob Squarepants pajamas, was a little more gracious with his greeting. "Cousin Rogan!"

"Hey squirt." Rogan snagged a muffin and an apple from the sideboard, pulling a chair right up to their table. And crunching noisily into the fruit, flashed a grin at Clay. "Copeland. Fancy meeting you here."

Clay's frown twisted into a rueful grimace. He had no doubt that Rogan had known exactly what he was doing the other night. Clay'd made a crack about bar psychology, but the joke seemed to be on him. "You know, if you ever get sick of pulling pints, I might be able to get you a pretty good gig."

Rogan snorted, and then laughed outright. "Why, so I can dress like Ward Cleaver? No thanks. But, you know," he crunched another bite of apple, "it was nice of you to offer."

"Cousin Rogan's taking me to the aquarium today," Max piped up, and reached for the powdered sugar. He hit the bottom of the canister hard enough to send a cloud of white all over his waffles, Rogan's wet hair, and Clay's black suit.

"So you said," Clay coughed, waved the powder away, and looked at Murphy through the haze. "Max says these Thursday outings are something of a tradition."

"Yep." Having finished with the apple, Rogan pulled the wrapper away from his chocolate muffin, sinking a row of white teeth into the side. "It goes back to when the little guy was a baby. We were all pitching in so that Tate could finish up her degree, and

Thursday sort of fell to me. I figure since he's off to the School of Hard Knocks this year when he gets locked down in kindergarten, I better snatch my Thursdays while I can." He chewed, pointed the muffin at Clay. "That's not going to interfere with any plans you might have made now, is it?"

"No." It was absolutely stupid to feel jealous. As a reasonable adult he should be happy for this man who was a pretty solid fixture in Max's life.

Even if he *was* teaching the kid to cuss.

But damn it, this whole male role model thing was new and he was kind of enjoying it.

"I'll be working, pretty long hours, probably for the next several days."

"You gonna stick around after that?" Rogan came right out and asked.

"Since I've ended up working this case while I was supposed to be on vacation, I'll have a week or so coming to me when my part's through. And after that," he reached around Max's shoulders and began cutting the waffle into neat little pieces. "I'll be here as often as I can."

Seemingly satisfied, Rogan nodded and worked on his muffin. "That's good to hear. I got the impression you were a stand-up kind of guy."

Clay dug into his own waffles. "In all honesty, Murphy, I used to be the guy that trips and falls down while trying to run away."

"That happens to me," Max agreed "when I forget to tie my shoelaces."

Clay and Rogan both stopped, mid bite, and looked at the child between them. Then burst out in shared laughter.

THE son of a bitch was laughing.

Just sitting over there at that table, like he owned the damn place, stuffing his face with waffles.

Holding the kid on his lap.

He'd been so close – *so damn close* – to snatching the boy last night.

He'd waited, well past a reasonable hour, for the friggin' FBI agent to show up.

When midnight had rolled around, JR thought he was in the clear. He'd tucked the chloroform, the syringe, and a lock-pick into his pockets. And his pistol. Just in case somebody tried to get in his way.

Except the friggin' *FBI agent* had gotten in his way.

Killing a federal cop was just asking for some serious shit. A bullet with his name on it, discharged with "necessary force." Or worse yet, a massive manhunt that would result in his arrest, and then he'd spend the next fifty or so years as some lifer's girlfriend.

No.

He was not going to go to prison. There was no way he'd end up dead on some shower floor, bleeding to death from the shank that had been shoved up his rectum.

Like Logan.

His tea cup slipped in his hand. The china dropped to the table with a clatter, spilling the stupid-ass tea that crazy old ladies were required to like all over his ugly dress and friggin' support hose.

The hot liquid scalded his hand, threatening to dissolve the latex skin which covered it, and seeped into the layers of padding filling the dress.

He stifled the string of curses trembling on the edge of his lips, because *yes,* the FBI agent, his long-haired hippy-looking friend, the kid, the old lady and everyone else in the dining room were now looking at him with concern.

The FBI agent actually started to move the kid off of his lap and rise from his chair, but – *surprise, surprise* – Tate friggin' Do-Gooder Hennessey put her hand on his shoulder to keep him down, and then hurried over with a bunch of napkins.

Concern marred her pretty face.

"Are you alright, Mrs. Walker?" She took a napkin and patted it on his lap.

Thank God for layers of padding, or else there might be some pretty interesting questions coming up. He wanted to snatch the napkin away, and take care of the problem himself. But hey, since the little whore was here, he might as well sit back and enjoy it.

"Thank you dear." He entertained visions of doing the mother in front of the kid. Of doing the kid in front of the mother.

"I apologize for making a mess. It seems the cup slipped right out of my hand."

"That's okay." Tate smiled at him as she blotted. Leaning over as she was, JR could see down her shirt, and thought she'd filled out much nicer than expected.

She'd been such a gangly little thing.

Looking at him with those big green eyes, all but begging him to throw her a little action.

He should have just gone ahead and done the bitch back then, and then she wouldn't have come to the boys' camp that night. Probably looking for him. Wanting to crawl into her favorite lifeguard's bunk for a little mouth-to-mouth resuscitation.

And Logan wouldn't have landed in jail. Wouldn't have bled to death in that shower.

His hand fisted beneath the folds of his dress.

But he couldn't get greedy, or careless, or he'd end up dead as Logan and Billy Wayne. So as much as he'd like to do otherwise, he'd have to leave the little blabbermouth alone. If he so much as blinked wrong in her direction, she'd run over and tattle to her boyfriend.

JR looked over, and sure enough, FBI was watching.

Making sure his little bed-warmer was safe.

He probably kept his tie on while he screwed her.

He briefly entertained a new, exciting fantasy, about pulling Tate's head into his lap. Blowing her head off while the FBI man watched.

But that was neither prudent, nor smart, so he reached up to pat her cheek instead.

She smiled, and then hurried off to fetch more tea.

From across the dining room, JR felt the agent's stare.

JOSH Harding wasn't a real big fan of autopsies.

He tried to approach the whole process from an entirely objective standpoint, looking at the corpse on the stainless steel table as no more than one of the anatomical dummies he'd used in his life drawing classes, but the smell made it rather difficult.

Was there anything more nauseating than the aroma of bone dust as the medical examiner used his electric saw – which seemed *much* more appropriate at one of those Home Depot *You Can Build A Tree House* type things – to cut through what was left of a man's cranium?

That *whirr, whirr, whirr* was almost as stomach-turning as the smell.

Josh looked up, caught Copeland's glance from across the room, and managed a weak nod for the other man's benefit. No doubt the FBI agent had witnessed dozens of autopsies, and this was business as usual for him.

He probably had a bottle of *Eau de Bone Dust* that he spritzed around just for the hell of it.

Behind Josh, a door opened, and he gratefully turned toward the distraction. Agent O'Connell entered the room, looking as cool and put together as always, though he could tell from the set of her mouth that she hadn't enjoyed her conversation with the local Bureau honcho. Apparently he was one of those people who didn't believe in interdepartmental task forces, cooperation, democracy or anyone or anything that otherwise challenged his self-appointed position as God.

So far, he seemed content to let her handle the situation out in East Podunk, which was no doubt how he felt about their little town. But when the results of this autopsy came back as homicide – a given, as far as those present were concerned – there was every chance he would try to throw his weight into the investigation. Murder, as such, was not necessarily a federal crime, but the murder of one of the main suspects in an interstate human trafficking ring had media coverage written all over it.

And there wasn't much that was more appealing to a glory-seeking bureaucrat than positive media coverage.

Finally, after what seemed like eons – mountain ranges eroded to plains before that damn autopsy was over – the ME pronounced that the man on the table had died from gunshot trauma to the head.

Inflicted from a distance of at least eight feet.

In short, he hadn't pulled the trigger.

A secondary shot, fired at point blank range, was responsible for the powder residue on the man's fingers.

And speaking of fingers – boy wasn't this fun? – it turned out that the dead man's fingerprints had been removed with a razor. All except for a partial thumbprint. The thumbprint might give them just enough to be able to run the man through AFIS, but it would make the search both longer and less conclusive.

"Do you think the partial print was an oversight or left intentionally?" Josh asked Clay as he and the agents left the morgue.

Clay sighed and pushed his sunglasses onto his nose, squinting against the bright noonday heat. "The perp is in a state of flux right now, which unfortunately makes either possibility viable. He's been pushed to a point where he's lost some control, which could definitely make him prone to sloppy mistakes. However, the way he set up his accomplice yesterday also leads me to believe he may have reached a stage where he's become much more interested in game playing. His relationship with the albino, his business with the girls, fed a need in him to assert his own dominance. Now that the other man is dead and his business has been threatened, that need may have been transferred to this new battle with the authorities. He's no longer content to escape and evade, but might challenge and attempt to outwit. It'll make him more dangerous, because he'll be less careful in his behavior, but it will also make him easier to draw out. We get proactive, possibly challenge his competence or intelligence, and he'll be bound and determined to prove us wrong."

"So you don't think he's already bought a one way ticket to South America?"

"Gut instinct – I'd have to say no. If he left that print on purpose, then logic would dictate that he knows his accomplice's fingerprints are on record, and he's going to want to be here to see us scramble around, trying to match it. He wants us to figure out his accomplice's identity, but he doesn't want it to happen too soon. So he's probably planning on being in the area for at least the next little while."

"So we get to work on this print."

"And organize a canvass of the area near the Collier crime scene," Kim reminded him.

"There are a lot of farms near those woods," Josh said. "Several abandoned farm houses."

"Which would make a perfect, out-of-the-way location to hold the girls until they deliver them." Kim took her own sunglasses out of her pocket. Then she made a small noise of disgust. "Given the limited size of your force, Deputy Harding, we may want to consider calling in a couple of local agents. We can't risk any of your untrained volunteers stumbling across an armed, dangerous and mentally unstable felon."

"Okay." Josh knew she was loath to have a truckload of feds coming in here, steamrolling his department's investigation. But at this point, with other lives at risk, jurisdictional issues were of little importance. "Make whatever calls you think you need to. But most of the farmers out that way will be much more free and easy with information if it's a local doing the asking."

"Understood. Let's head back to the station and pull up a map of the area, mark it off into quadrants. The areas that seem the most feasible for our man's hideout, we'll pair local and federal agents. Then we'll work our way out from there."

"Well, boys and girls." Clay hit the remote to unlock his vehicle. "Let's get this show on the road."

THE Goliath bird-eating spider was a hit.

Rogan calculated that this was his and Max's third or fourth trip to the aquarium, so the fish, alligators, and various indigenous Lowcountry wildlife were pretty much old hat. But the visiting *Creatures of the Amazon* exhibit held Max's enrapt attention for over an hour.

They'd seen piranhas, an anaconda, a couple funky looking birds, and some kind of blind rodent.

And a *really* huge spider.

With hair on all of its eight dinner-plate width legs.

And way too many eyes. All of them looking at him.

Rogan wasn't particularly a fan.

In fact, after seeing the arachnid that was big enough to take down a parrot, he decided to cross *Amazon* off his list of Fun Places to Visit.

"So," he said to Max, hoping to ease the kid toward the exit. "How 'bout taking another look at those jellyfish? Or maybe see if we can work our way into a spot at the Touch Pool? Those nurse sharks looked pretty cool."

"Okay."

Rogan tried not to go limp with relief.

Opting for the touch pool, which was really no big surprise, Rogan took hold of Max's hand and they began to make their way toward the escalator. They weaved around sunburned children and harried parents, chatting along the way.

"So," he said again, very casually, because Max was a perceptive kid. "Your mom seems to like that FBI agent."

"His name is Clay."

"Right," Rogan agreed. "Clay. Your mom seems to really like him."

"I guess so." Max shrugged, in the way of five-year-olds. "They kiss and stuff, when they think I'm not looking."

"And how do you feel about that? Clay kissing your mom?"

Max stopped to check out a flounder. "He asked me, and I said it was okay. Why do you think he has two eyes on one side of his head?"

"Uh..."

It took Rogan a moment to realize they were now discussing the fish, rather than the man.

"I don't know," he admitted, leaning closer to the glass. "I guess that's just the way nature designed him." The flounder, tired of the speculation, swam off toward the other side of the tank. "Um, *Clay* said he's going to be hanging around some. Are you feeling okay with that?"

Max stopped watching the fish, and looked up at his cousin. He had that worried, lip-biting expression that suggested he was about to impart Something Bad.

"Will you get mad if I tell you something?"

Uh-oh, Rogan thought dismally. Maybe the kid didn't like Copeland. He'd seemed to well enough, sure. But who knew what went through a little kid's mind? "I'd never be mad at you for telling the truth."

"I'll still be your friend," Max said gravely. "But I think Mr. Clay might be a better daddy. I used to want Mommy to marry you, but she said cousins can't marry each other. I hope you're not too awful disappointed."

Rogan laughed, a short burst of surprise. The kid had actually thought…?

He bent down to Max's level. "I think I'll be able to manage." Then he tweaked the little rug-rat on the nose. And wondered if either Tate or Clay suspected the grand plans he'd hatched for the three of them. "Now how about you and I go touch ourselves a couple of sharks?"

They pushed their way through the throng near the escalator, and Rogan noticed the stairs weren't as crowded. Grabbing Max's hand, he started that way, and felt a prick on his ass from behind. What the hell? It felt like someone had stuck him with the business end of an upholstery needle.

He turned around to gauge the situation, thinking some kid was playing a none-too-funny joke.

But his vision tunneled, went blurry at the edges, and the hand holding Max's went limp.

He found himself going boneless, as if he were just melting right into the floor. The stairs were there, right under his feet, and the next moment just slipped away.

Max's little face, filled up by frightened green eyes, was the last thing he saw before he fell.

CLAY turned away from the computer, which was doing its thing to narrow down the possibilities regarding the owner of that partial thumbprint, when his cell phone began to dance in his pocket.

He slipped it out, checked the caller ID, and noted an incoming from Justin. The guy probably wanted him to clear the rest of his crap out of the guest room since it was beyond obvious he was no longer staying there.

"Justin," he said with a hint of sheepishness, "you calling to kick me out?"

"Clay, I need you to get to the hospital." There was absolutely no humor in the other man's voice. "I don't have long to talk, because I'm needed in surgery, but Tate's here, and you need to be with her. She's not hurt," he assured him, before Clay could ask "but the situation is pretty critical. Someone hit her cousin, or pushed him down the stairs – I'm not entirely clear on that part – and… it appears they've kidnapped her son."

Clay's heart stopped beating. Just *bam!* – gave up thumping inside of his chest.

"I guess it happened when they were at the aquarium," Justin continued, unaware that Clay couldn't hear him over the roar of denial in his head. "Anyway, she would have called herself, but I had no choice but to give her a sedative. Her cousin Kathleen – have you met her? She's a Charleston PD detective – well, she's here, and she's asked me to call you." He paused, just a moment, to listen. "Dude, you need to say something so that I know whether or not you're still there."

"I'm on my way."

Clay was amazed he could speak, with his heart lodged so firmly in his throat. Now that it had started pumping again, it was trying to push its way out of his body. He stood, legs like rubber, and had to catch himself on the back of the chair. From across the room, Kim saw his face, and immediately hustled over.

"Did Rogan," Oh God, "say anything? Do you have any idea how this happened?"

Kim reached him, and helped him get moving. He was as wobbly as a three day drunk.

"The guy was unconscious when they brought him in. He's banged up pretty badly from his fall. But Kathleen's partner's down at the scene, interviewing witnesses. She might have something more to tell you when you get here. I'm sorry, man, but I have to go. I'll try to catch up with you later."

When the line went dead, something inside Clay clicked. He saw the life he wanted – a life with Tate and Max – hanging in the balance before him.

"We're going to MUSC Hospital," he told Kim, as he handed her the keys to his truck. "Drive like a bat out of hell, sweetheart, because we need to go find my son."

CHAPTER TWENTY-ONE

JR laughed as he pulled off the wig.

It had been so easy. Ridiculously, pitifully easy. He'd lingered around the dining room that morning just long enough to hear all their plans. He'd even finagled an introduction to the boy, courtesy of his over-proud grandma. All the better to get the kid to trust him. Make getting him out of the aquarium that much easier. What's not to trust about a sweet little grandma, and especially one that you met just that morning?

God, kids really were gullible. Even easier than teenage girls. Offer 'em some candy and a few soothing words, and they'll go wherever you want.

By the time their parents' warnings about accepting candy from strangers kick into gear, you've already got them tucked right next to you in the front of your truck.

And telling them that the cops would see them if they tried to get out of their seatbelt, probably send their mama to jail – no threat could perform more effectively.

Little kids, they sure loved their mamas.

Even when they were hateful, falling-down drunks.

And hey, thinking about falling down, that hippy sure took a digger! He had to have cracked a few bones. Maybe even broken his neck.

Then all those Good Samaritans, rushing to his aid, creating a diversion that JR couldn't have paid for.

And he – helpful old lady that he was – had led the little boy away from the commotion. Right out the door and into his truck.

Of course, the kid hadn't taken the candy – apparently he'd been paying attention to those warnings – so he'd resorted to the syringe. And now the boy lay, peaceful as a little lamb, with his head resting on JR's lap.

He reached down, stroked the dark hair.

Then looked out the windshield, wondering what Max's mother was doing. Crying all over her FBI lover? Clutching her poor, distraught cousin's broken hand?

He laughed again, pulling the truck into his grandmother's barn, next to the minivan registered to Sean Roberts. The car that would drive him into the next phase of his life.

His life as a responsible, upstanding father. Just him and the kid, day in, day out. They could fish, or toss a ball. Watch movies.

Maybe he could show him a thing or two he'd learned at camp.

Overjoyed, JR couldn't contain his laughter. He had no idea this would be so much fun.

CLAY strode through the waiting room, which seemed to be filled to capacity, and gripped the edge of the registration desk.

"Excuse me, I'm here to see Tate Hennessey. I need to know what room she's been taken to."

The woman at the desk used wildly manicured fingers to tap some information into the computer before frowning up at Clay. "Are you family?"

Clay pulled his badge out and flipped it open. He didn't have time to play games. "What room is she in?"

The woman harrumphed and went back to her computer. "Emergency suite 121. Go left and around the corner. Then through the swinging doors on the right. Push the button on the wall and I'll buzz you in."

"Thanks."

He and Kim took off at a trot. Clay found the button, shoved it in, and waited for the doors to swing open. When they did, he ran into Justin.

"Oh, hey," his friend said, pulling a mask off his face. "Wow, that was quick. You must have set a new land-speed record." He stepped aside and extended his hand. "Justin Wellington," he said to Kim, even as he moved to walk with them.

"Kim O'Connell. Under any other circumstances, I would say it's a pleasure to meet you."

Justin smiled briefly and then turned his attention to Clay. "I'll take you to her room. She's pretty out of it, but conscious. Unfortunately I can't stick around, because I need to get back to the OR. It's a zoo around here today. My last patient got up off the gurney and walked out – with a bullet wound to the leg – before I could get to him."

Justin paused outside the door to Room 121, laying his hand on Clay's shoulder. "I'm really sorry about all of this. My prayers will be with you and that little boy."

"Thanks." Clay's voice was scratchy with unshed tears. He took a deep breath, glanced at Kim, and rapped his knuckles on the door before entering. A pretty redhead in a linen suit sat in a chair beside the bed. No doubt Kathleen, Tate's cousin.

And on the bed…

Oh, holy God in Heaven.

"You're here." Tate's face crumpled. And he was beside her in an instant. "Oh, thank God, you're here. They t…t…took Max. Somebody took m… m…my baby."

"We'll get him back." It was foolish to make that promise. The reasonable, federally-trained part of his brain *tsk*ed at the fact that he'd done so. All sorts of statistics and case files and remembered tragedies flew around in his head.

Most stranger abducted children were killed within twenty-four hours…

No. He refused to let that happen. He couldn't have found happiness only to have it so cruelly snatched away.

"I promise you." And he meant every bloody word. Stroking her hair, Clay lifted his head away from Tate's, turning his gaze on the room's other occupant. "You must be Tate's cousin."

"Kathleen Murphy." The two of them shook. "I'm glad you're here."

"This is Kim O'Connell," he introduced the two women. Like Clay, they seemed ramped up with adrenaline, and he guessed that sitting here and waiting had been hell on Kathleen. Against his chest, Clay felt Tate's sobs begin to ease. And her steady, rhythmic breathing told him the sedative had taken effect. "Tell me what you know," he requested.

"About one-fifteen several 911 calls started pouring into the system, indicating there'd been some kind of accident at the aquarium. A man had fallen down the stairs, knocked into a couple of other people, there were injuries, an ambulance was requested, yada, yada, yada. Well, one of the first responders pulled Rogan's ID, realized it was my brother, and gave me a call. I said *hell,* and *take care of Max until I get there.* He says *who's Max?*"

"Shit."

"Yeah." She ran her fingers through her chin length hair. "No sign of Max anywhere near Rogan. I bust my ass to get there, have the aquarium put in lockdown in the meantime, and we scour every inch of that place with a fine tooth comb. No Max. Rogan's hauled off to the hospital by ambulance, totally unconscious and unable to tell us what the hell happened, and so we start interviewing witnesses who saw him fall. A couple of people saw Max being led away from the crowd by the stairs by his grandma."

"*What?*" Confusion muddled. "I thought Maggie was going down to St. Simons Island today to visit one of Tate's sisters."

"She did. I spoke with her about thirty minutes ago. She and Kelly – Tate's sister – are on their way back here now."

What the hell was going on? "You get a description on the *grandma?*"

"Gray hair, wrinkles, ugly shoes. Like every other grandma in the world. Either tall or stooped, depending on who you talk to. People see what they expect to see, you know what I mean?"

Did he ever. Society's fringes – the elderly, the homeless, illegal immigrants, and many other marginal classes – were almost like non-people to a large portion of the American public. Just shades that drifted along at the periphery of their vision, not worth the time or discomfort it took to actually take a good look.

"So I go to the Inn to tell Tate what's happened because that's just not the kind of news you impart over the phone, and my partner and about every other available officer in the department is busting their ass looking for Max."

"Did anyone see him leaving the building?" Kim asked.

"No, but we have people reviewing footage from the aquarium's outside cameras, as well as the parking garage which services that area. As soon as we can get a better description on the woman, and an idea whether or not he was taken from the scene in a vehicle, we'll issue an Amber alert."

Clay nodded his head. The sooner they could get that information out over the radio, the TV, and traffic monitors along the highway, the better chance they stood of locating Max. "We're here to offer whatever resources the Bureau has that you might need. Just say the word."

Tears, quickly dispatched, shimmered in her blue eyes. "Since y'all are here with Tate, I'd like to get back to the aquarium. Just sitting here's making me crazy. And when my brother wakes up – he was drugged by the way. *Damn,* I forgot to mention that. They found a puncture mark on his right buttocks and GHB in his system."

"GHB?" Clay repeated.

"Yeah. Gamma-... uh, what's it called, Hydroxybutyric acid. The date rape drug?"

"Yeah, I know what it is." He tightened his arms on Tate. The fact that Rogan was drugged meant that the abduction had been planned, not simply a crime of opportunity. "Did they say how long it would take for Rogan to come out of it?" He really needed to question the man.

"From what I understand, it could normally take hours, considering the dose he was given. But I think they were working to try to find a way to counteract the drug and get it out of his system. Something about a stimulant, but I think it involves some risks. I've been in here with Tate, so I don't have the whole story. But he's down the hall in the recovery room, with my father and my brother. My sister's taking care of things at the Inn, and one of the managers is handling Murphy's. If you want to walk down and talk to either Dec or my dad, they might be able to tell you more."

Clay nodded and Kathleen moved to leave.

"Keep us updated," he asked plaintively.

"You can count on it."

Kim shook the taller woman's hand as she walked past, and then turned to look at Clay. "I know you're going crazy, and need to do something, but why don't you let me go see about the cousin. Just hold your lady for a little while. You need each other right now."

"Alright. But if Murphy's awake, come get me."

"Agreed."

KIM left Clay in the ER and asked an orderly for the location of the recovery room, where a muffled "come in" followed her knock.

"Mr. Murphy?" An older man lifted his wet face from large hands. "I'm Kim O'Connell, with the FBI. I'm a friend of Clay's. Is it okay if I come in?"

After wiping one hand across his ruddy face, the man stood and extended the other. "Ms. O'Connell. Or rather *Agent* O'Connell. Sorry. I'm not all together."

The hand she shook trembled. "In your place, I'd be in pieces also." Then she turned her attention to the bed.

Whoa.

The man was beaten up. A broken ankle, a broken arm from what she could tell. Bruises all over one of his cheeks.

His really attractive cheeks.

And okay, that was *so* not appropriate.

"How's your son?" *Hot.* She looked at his left hand. *Single.* Shit, she really had to stop this.

"Holding on," his father said, gaze settling with concern on the bed. "That drug in him, it's bad news. Convulsions, vomiting – even when he's out of it. I have to watch him to make sure he doesn't swallow his own tongue."

"Your daughter mentioned something about a stimulant to counteract the effects of lost consciousness?"

"Yeah. They tried something, but it doesn't appear to have worked. The one that really works is apparently too risky, because it lowers the convulsion threshold. So he still hasn't regained consciousness. Which, uh, might not be such a bad thing, I guess, because he's gonna blame himself when he wakes up. You know. For Max." Choked up, he looked her way. "You'll be able to find him, right? I mean, between Katie and the FBI, the bastards that took him don't stand a chance."

Katie was obviously his nickname for his daughter. And if sheer force of will and desire could bring that little boy home, then yeah, the kid would be back by dinnertime. "We'll do everything we can."

And as soon as she left this room, she was going to be on the phone with the local RA, pulling out every stop she could to suit action to words.

Behind her, the door opened, and…

She was pretty much struck dumb.

There were *two* of them, these gorgeous creatures, right here in the very same room. One in front of her, one behind, like really nifty bookends.

"Oh, hey. I didn't realize we had company," said bookend number two. He jostled the drinks he was holding into the crook of his arm and flashed a hint of dimple her way. His hair was shorter than his brother's but it was obvious they were twins. "I'm Declan."

"Kim O'Connell."

"She's with the FBI," said his father.

One masculine eyebrow arched skyward. "Is that so?"

"I'm a friend of Clay's."

For a moment, the bookend looked blank. But then comprehension dawned. "Agent Copeland. Got it. I didn't realize he was still around."

Something about his attitude – a certain… nonchalance – turned Kim off. She started to say something about Clay being right down the hall, holding his traumatized cousin, but a terrible noise erupted from the bed behind her, and she jumped and whirled around.

The man on the bed, face twisted in pain, stretched his good arm toward his father and brother. "Max," he cried, through gritted teeth. "Ah *God,* that woman took Max!"

IT wasn't very pleasant to watch.

Because of the other drugs in his system, Rogan's doctor had to be stingy with the painkillers. And since he needed to be conscious to answer Clay's questions, putting him under again was definitely out. So he lay there, jaw clenched, sweat rolling off him in waves, trying to concentrate on being as accurate as he could over the pain of three broken bones.

Whoever had dubbed the drug he'd been given *ecstasy* was guilty of a very serious misnomer.

"White hair. Pulled back in, you know…in a bun."

"Okay," Clay continued from his position beside the bed. "Anything else you can tell me? Anything that really stood out?"

Pain squeezed Rogan's eyes shut, determination forced them back open. "A lot of it's… fuzzy."

"It's a side effect of the GHB," Clay assured him. "We're actually lucky that you can remember anything at all."

His lips formed a grim smile. "Yeah. Lucky."

From somewhere behind Clay, Declan snorted.

"I remember her shoes," Rogan continued. "I saw them as I was going down. They were… big. Almost as big as mine." He stiffened as a wave of pain washed through him, fisting his hands in the sheets.

"Do we really have to do this?" Declan pushed his way to his brother's side, repressed frustration vibrating. "I mean, come on. Big shoes? It's obvious he didn't see anything important, and he's half out of his head with pain. Instead of wasting your time grilling him, why not go out there and look for Max?"

Patrick Murphy laid a hand on his son's arm, started to pull him away. But Clay gave a conciliatory wave because he understood the outburst. "I know it seems like I'm pushing him unfairly, but the first few hours after an abduction are critical. Our best chance to find Max, and bring him home unharmed, will rely on what information we can gather about his abductor. And while *big shoes* might not seem all that important, there are a few things you have to consider. Any information like that, any distinguishing characteristics, helps narrow our suspect pool. We narrow it down far enough, and it leads us to Max that much sooner."

"Familiar," Rogan claimed from the bed. "Something about her... familiar."

Clay forgot all about Declan. "Familiar how? Like she reminded you of someone or she's someone you've seen before?"

"Not sure." Rogan turned an unhealthy shade of gray. "Sort of like... the old lady that spilled the tea."

"What?" Oh, shit, shit, *shit*.

"You know what he's talking about?" Declan asked.

"The woman at the Inn this morning." Clay leaned closer to the bed. "Is that who you mean, Rogan?"

The man nodded, and Clay got to his feet. Why hadn't he thought of this sooner? He was paid to notice behavior, pick up patterns. And he'd realized the abduction was premeditated.

He'd seen *that* woman, the old lady with the big shoes and the nervous hands, in the hallway just last night. With her hand on the door that led to the third floor, and the bed where Max slept.

Damn. She'd been trying to take him then.

If he hadn't come home when he did, Max might have been whisked off into the night.

Of course if he'd been paying closer attention, Max might not have been taken at all.

Kim came into the room, after having excused herself to take a call from Deputy Harding, and caught the look on Clay's face. "Something's up?"

"We need to get into the Inn's computer and find the name of the person who took Max."

CHAPTER TWENTY-TWO

JOSH Harding pulled his cruiser into the long, tree-lined drive which led back to the old Walker place.

He'd just gotten off the phone with Agent O'Connell, who'd instructed him to continue canvassing without her. Seemed she was going to be wrapped up with Agent Copeland in the search for Tate Hennessey's son.

And hadn't *that* been a piece of crappy news. As if the case they were working weren't foul enough.

A pothole in the neglected drive had Josh prying his teeth out of his bottom lip, and after examining the overgrown vegetation, chalking this up as a waste of time. Old lady Walker had gone to live with her grandson in Atlanta a while back, and the farm was in disrepair. Where once corn and tobacco had marched in well-tended and orderly rows, undergrowth snarled and sapling pines bumped together like boisterous children.

Around the bend the farmhouse rose, half obscured by a cloud of dust. When the debris settled in the heavy air, Josh decided the place was a pit.

It had been white – once – with neatly painted blue trim. But the blue had long since faded to gray, the white peeling like cosmetic leprosy. Weeds sprouted two feet high from inch-wide crevices in the broken sidewalk.

"Crap." Josh eyed the sagging front porch, wondering if worker's comp would cover him falling through. But he had to search every dwelling, barn and outbuilding in his particular quadrant. Exiting the car, feeling the slap of heat, he donned his hat and started to sweat.

Then adjusting his weapon to within easy reach, set off toward the house.

AFTER seeing to it that a member of Tate's family would be with her on the off chance that she awoke, Clay tried to reason things out while Kim drove. His brain – which he definitely needed in good working order – was suffering the profiler's equivalent of writer's block.

He just couldn't put himself in the mind frame of an elderly woman using a date rape drug to facilitate kidnapping. It was a weird combination of daring and non-confrontational, the way she'd gone about it.

When Clay thwarted the apparent initial attempt, she'd backed off and gotten nervous. Her hand had shaken as she'd turned the key in the lock, giving her unsteady nerves away.

At first, Clay had attributed the tremors to age or a possible neurological disorder. But given the fact that he'd surprised her in the act, it made sense that she succumbed to nerves. Unless, of course, she wasn't nervous at all, and had used the shaking to make herself appear feeble.

And if *that* was the case, then the woman was much more clearheaded than he thought. And also very determined. When Plan A had crumbled like dust at her feet, she'd regrouped rather quickly.

By waiting out the night, paying attention at breakfast, and following Rogan and Max to the aquarium, she'd been able to facilitate Rogan's fall.

An excellent distraction.

And leading Max away, through all the confusion, played the helpful old lady card to perfection. Who was to question an elderly woman walking off with a little kid?

Nothing suspicious there.

In fact, the whole abduction had been so well thought out and smoothly executed that Clay suspected she'd done this sort of thing before.

But why? A pedophiliac Grandma?

The chances of that were pretty slim.

And most women who kidnapped children to fulfill a maternal need were younger, and selected younger children. Not to mention that that particular scenario played in a negligible amount of abductions.

So why specifically target Max? There had to be easier children to take. Did he remind her of a lost child? Was he the latest in a string of replacements?

He'd obviously been targeted before she ever made the reservation at the Inn. Tate didn't allow Max to mingle with guests, except on a very limited basis. And the woman had come prepared with the drug and a plan for taking Max.

He wished the sheer, nauseating terror he felt would stop messing with his ability to think. Because the more he tried to fit the pieces together the more confusing the puzzle became. There was a reason cops didn't investigate cases dealing with loved ones, because it shot your objectivity to hell.

"Figure anything out?" Kim asked as she pulled up behind the Inn.

"I'm an embarrassment to the Investigative Support Unit right now, because I can't figure out shit."

"Give yourself a break," she advised as they got out. "You're under a lot of stress. And please remember that as important as this is – and I know what this little boy means to you – this is not up to you alone. You have the Charleston PD and several federal agents working to get Max back. So whatever happens," she stopped him just outside the door to the Inn with a hand laid in friendship on his arm, "you can*not* hold yourself responsible."

Her meaning was clear. If Max died, that was just the way things went.

"Thanks for that vote of confidence." Clay shook off her hand, pinching his fingers against the bridge of his nose. Visions of Max, terrified and alone, made the words a ragged lance of pain. "I'm sorry."

"Don't be."

Clay took the key Tate had given him to let them in the back door, and headed straight for the office. A feminine voice drifted out, engaged in one-sided conversation.

A shorter, rounder version of Kathleen Murphy sat behind the desk, cell phone to her ear. She tapped away at the computer keyboard while leaving a message asking Maggie for help.

Tate's cousin, Maureen. The pharmacist looked up from the computer as they entered, and though a smile attempted to flutter at the corners of her mouth, the eyes behind her glasses were worried.

She shook their hands as introductions were made, then quickly got down to business. "I was having some trouble getting into the file that keeps the records of the Inn's guests so I called Maggie to see if she could help. Or better yet remember the name of the woman you mentioned. Her cell phone's apparently in a dead zone because I can't get through."

Hell, Clay thought. They didn't have time for this. And while he was competent with computers he was no technical guru. He turned a hopeful look toward Kim.

"I'm not much better than you. But why don't I give somebody in tech support a call and see if they can walk me through it?"

"Excellent idea."

Kim moved to take the chair behind the desk, and Maureen hustled out of her way. "If this doesn't work, should somebody wake Tate?"

"If this doesn't work, we might have to. In the meantime, I'm going to go up to the room where our mystery guest spent the night."

The door was unlocked, and Clay pulled a latex glove – an occupational staple – out of his pocket so as not to disturb any prints. From the unmade state of the ornately carved bed, he determined that the daily cleaning hadn't yet taken place, and thanked whatever stars had determined that at least one thing go their way.

He wasn't sure what, if anything, he might find, especially since this woman seemed careful. But at the moment any clue, however small, was better than none.

He checked the closet, under the bed. In the drawers of the bureau to see if anything may have fallen out of a pocket and been left behind. Unsurprisingly, the place was clean.

Flipping back the covers on the barely disturbed bed, he noted that not one single hair or detectable fiber was visible to the naked eye. No creases or drool marks on the pillow or residue from that night cream old ladies tended to wear.

In fact, it looked like no actual human skin had touched the sheets. Bending to sniff the bedding, he found no tell-tale odor of mothballs. Or rose water. Or sweat. Or anything other than Bounce.

Finding absolutely nothing even remotely useful in the bedroom, Clay flipped on the lights in the adjoining bath. The shower/tub combo was perfectly dry, the complimentary toiletries undisturbed, and neither the bathmat nor any of the large towels appeared to have been used.

Okay. So the woman hadn't bothered to bathe. Not totally strange, considering his own grandmother had done so only every other day, and had positively refused to use the facilities whenever she'd stayed in a hotel. Germophobic, maybe, but not conclusive proof of wrongdoing.

The sink area also seemed in pretty much perfect condition. No watermarks from overzealous hand-washing, or toothpaste spit on the mirror. Which didn't exactly fit if she was a germophobe.

So why hadn't she wanted to bathe?

The ripped end of the roll of toilet paper suggested that at least she had normal bodily functions, as the end would have been folded into a neat little triangle if it hadn't been used.

Then Clay squatted down, pulled out the wastebasket for an inspection, and was somewhat surprised to see that she'd actually generated some trash. One lone tissue lay crumpled on the bottom of the small bag. He fished it out, opened it gently, trying to disturb it as little as possible. It seemed stuck together with something resembling chewed bubblegum. Or half-dried latex paint. As he sorted through his mental files of what the hell this could possibly be, his phone jangled in his pocket.

And at the same moment, he heard muffled yelling from downstairs, followed quickly by the echo of footsteps.

Clutching the tissue, he prioritized the chaos, and chose phone-answering over dealing with whatever was happening downstairs. Computer glitches could probably wait, but a phone call might be vitally important.

Spying Kathleen's number on his caller ID, he hoped she was calling with good news. He pressed the phone to his ear as he went toward the door. "What do you have for me, Kathleen?"

There was a rush of noise – phones ringing, people talking – and he figured she was calling from her desk.

"We have a positive shot of Max on a surveillance video," she told him, words tumbling out in a rush "leaving the aquarium with an elderly woman. She kept her face averted, and put on a wide brimmed hat as soon as they stepped outside, so ID is going to be sketchy. But at least we have positive proof of abduction, and it's enough to issue the Amber alert."

"That's great."

"And another thing of interest, she had a bandage on her hand, which backs up your theory on the old lady at the Inn."

Clay sighed. It was both wonderful and terrible to be right.

"She certainly was cool about the burn this morning. She just sat there and let Tate bring her more tea."

"Maybe she didn't want to call more attention to herself."

Before Clay could respond, Maureen burst through the door, harried and out of breath. "You need to come downstairs," she gasped. "Some kind of virus is eating the computer!"

CLAY stood by, totally helpless, and watched the information on the Inn's computer disappear.

Apparently, someone had attached a virus to one of the files – make that *the* file, actually – which had activated when Kim finally opened it.

Whoever took Max was damn clever with computers.

A clever, computer savvy, non-bathing, burn tolerant, GHB-packing, large shoe-wearing, non-rose water-smelling granny.

Right.

No wonder it didn't add up. As he listened to Kim deal with the computer crisis, he opened up the tissue again and examined it. He'd have to get it to a lab to say for sure, but he'd stake his life on the fact that he was looking at liquid skin. Liquid skin that had been partially melted by hot tea.

Little old lady, his ass.

He flipped open his phone and hit redial, knowing Kathleen needed to correct the erroneous info on the Amber alert.

Clay was very nearly certain Max had been abducted by a *man*.

And he was going to tear the bastard limb from limb.

Kathleen answered on the first ring, asking about the computer, but Clay quickly cut her off. "The computer virus is the least of our problems." Anger laced his words. He'd been *three feet* away from Max's abductor. "I have some very strong reasons to suspect that our infamous little old lady is in reality a very clever man."

"*What?* Damn, that is not good news."

"Tell me about it." Clay watched the computer die, Kim giving up CPR on a string of curses. And Maureen, pacing a hole in the Oriental rug, stopped and gaped at him in horror. "We're dealing with a cool, experienced offender. And since there's been no demand for ransom, you know what's left."

"Oh God."

"If you have His ear, you might want to bend it. But otherwise, give me everything you have. I don't think I need to tell you that time is the enemy."

"Okay. The parking garage came up empty because their surveillance camera apparently malfunctioned this morning, and the slacker who was working the gate forgot to report it. In the better news department, there's a bank across the street, and we have a very *distant* and *grainy* photo of the suspected get-away vehicle, which, after our imaging guru did his hocus pocus, appears to be a dark-colored pickup truck. Maybe blue, maybe green – it doesn't look to be totally one solid color. Like it has some rusted parts, or maybe some spots of primer. Unfortunately that's the best we can do with black and white."

"Do I dare hope that any part of the license plate might have been visible?"

"The guru's still working on it. But at least the truck itself is pretty distinct."

"In what way?" Kim and Maureen were both watching him now. Apparently the words *man* and *experienced offender* had caught their attention. Yes ladies, this situation was even shittier than they'd previously imagined.

"Well, it's one of those old-fashioned Ford pickups. You know the kind that you see at classic car shows after people've restored them?"

Something inside Clay clicked. And his mind began reeling. "Kathleen, tell your guru we need that license plate number *now.*"

JR caught the movement out of the corner of his eye.

He was in the process of changing the sheets because the girl had soiled them during the night, and it wouldn't do to have his prize virgin delivered covered in her own vomit and urine. Technically, he guessed he should be thankful that she hadn't asphyxiated while she was drugged. But with Billy Wayne out of the picture it was simply a chance he'd been forced to take.

He'd taken a lot of chances lately, but look how they'd paid off.

The girl huddled near the window, dressed in the clothes she'd been wearing when Billy Wayne abducted her, handcuffed to the old radiator. It was difficult to say whether her hollow, half-there look was due to the GHB or the situation. He'd seen it before in the girls they'd taken, but usually not until after they made the video with Billy Wayne.

This one didn't know how lucky she was to have avoided that particular fate.

Of course, there was no guarantee that she was headed to anything better. In fact, it could very well be worse.

Not that it really mattered.

He was just the broker. What happened to the commodity after he'd provided it wasn't up to him.

As he looked at the girl, and at the unconscious boy lying next to her, he saw the flash of tan outside of the window.

Cautiously approaching from the side, he moved one slat of the blinds.

"What the hell?" Outside the house, about to go snooping in the barn, was that stupid, pretty-boy deputy. The one who'd used his fancy art skills to draw the composite of Billy Wayne. As if he hadn't already been a big enough pain in the ass, he was about to discover the vehicles.

JR leaned close to the girl. "If you so much as breathe the wrong way, I'll blow your pretty little head off." He tipped her chin with the barrel of the pistol. "Understand?"

Her brown eyes, still hazy with the drug, widened into pools of terror. No doubt she recalled, vividly, what had happened to Billy Wayne.

JR eased up and unlocked the window. It was a little farther shot than he would have liked, but he really had no choice. He had to take the deputy out before he could radio in to the station. And since it was almost certain that others knew he was here, they'd come looking for him after a bit.

Which meant he would have to move quickly.

Releasing the safety on his nine mil, he aimed for the deputy's chest. One shot to take the man down and another to finish him off.

He'd have to hide the body. And get rid of the car.

Then he remembered the old fishing hole down the road, and thought *two birds with one stone*. Just lock the deputy's body in his trunk, and let him and his cruiser commune with the fishes.

JR smiled as he squeezed the trigger.

Laughed as the deputy went down.

And just because he was having so much fun, fired off two more rounds.

CHAPTER TWENTY-THREE

CLAY couldn't simply stand around with his head up his ass, waiting for something to happen. Despite the fact that Kathleen's computer guy couldn't yet offer anything conclusive, he had a hunch that he'd seen that truck before.

And that yet again, he'd been only a matter of feet from Max's abductor.

Just let him near the guy once more. The third time would definitely be a charm.

"Call Josh Harding," he told Kim after he'd gotten off the phone with Kathleen. "Tell him to drop what he's doing, and go over to the UPS store on Main Street. We need to know the identity of that man I almost hit yesterday morning, ASAP. The vehicle used to abduct Max was a classic Ford pickup, circa 1940's, with rust deterioration and two-tone paint."

"Well crap," Kim said, even as she flipped her phone open and dialed. "You think this has something to do with that man? What are the chances? I mean, that is either one hell of a weird coincidence, or this guy's carried road rage to a whole new level."

"No," Clay said as she waited for Harding to answer. "There's a bigger picture here that we're missing. This is just one pine out of the forest, and I think we need to step back and try to bring the whole thing into view." But the hell of it was that he was too damn close to the case to do anything other than stare blankly at the tree in front of him.

"Harding's not answering," she told Clay after a moment, looking up from her position behind Tate's desk. "He was going out to canvass one of the quadrants near the Collier crime scene, and he might be tangled up in that. I'll try Sheriff Callahan and see if he can send someone else."

From across the room, Maureen held up her cell phone and waggled it back and forth. "Do you want me to see if I have any luck getting hold of Aunt Maggie? She's bound to remember the woman's name."

"Sure. That'd be great." Although he wasn't sure how much it would help. Obviously, the woman's name was a pseudonym. But at least it gave Tate's cousin something positive to do, so that she didn't just stand around feeling useless.

Like he was doing right now.

He walked over and looked out the window, finding it entirely too sunny and blue-sky gorgeous to suit how he felt inside. The cheerful array of rainbow colors decorating the buildings across the street made him want to scream.

"Callahan's down in Beaufort," Kim informed him after she concluded her brief conversation. "Wrapping up some of the loose ends from the William Wayne murder. Deputy Jones is busy tracking down some of the records for the offenders that came up as possible matches for that partial print, and the other deputies are otherwise engaged. Apparently, even the dispatcher called in sick. We want to talk to the lady at the UPS Store, we're going to have to do it ourselves. Did she strike you as the kind of woman who'd be willing to dole out that information over the phone?"

"As long as she can call ten friends and tell them all about it, she'll tell us anything we want to know."

"All hail the small town gossip."

Clay got the store's number from information, and tried to remember the woman's name as it connected. Something with a "J", he thought. Like Jenny or Jane or…

"Julie?" It rolled off his tongue when she answered, scoring, no doubt, big brownie points for him. "This is Special Agent Clay Copeland, with the FBI. I spoke with you the other day? That's right." He rolled his eyes at Kim. "The profiler."

He went through the whole little chit-chat routine, sensing that this woman would respond better to honey than to vinegar, although he had to strain the meaningless pleasantries through his teeth. Then he got around to the point of the conversation, asking about the dark-haired man and his truck.

"Rob Johns, you say?" He gestured for Kim to grab a piece of paper and write it down. "No, he's not in any trouble," yet, "but we think he might have some information that we need. I don't guess you'd happen to have his address?"

He waited a beat while she answered. "No, I understand all about your privacy policy regarding customers, and I certainly wouldn't ask you to violate it." And he couldn't demand it, without the proper court order. "But listen, Julie, just in case Rob comes in, I need you to do me a favor. Don't say anything about our conversation to him, but give me a call at this number."

He looked over at Kim, who was already on her own phone with the local RA. Hopefully, within a few minutes they'd know everything there was to know about Rob Johns.

Snapping his phone shut, he started to walk away from the window, but something under the desk caught his eye and stopped him cold.

He bent down, pulled it out, in all its ugly glory.

And very nearly wept over a stupid purple bear.

IT was the vibrations on his hip that woke Josh up.

Actually, the vibrations were technically *under* his hip, as he was lying face down in the dirt. The hard rectangle that was his phone dug deep into his flesh, and in reality should have been uncomfortable. But given the fact that both his shoulder and thigh were on fire, he figured the cell phone problem was pretty minor.

And when he said *on fire,* he meant ON FIRE. Like someone had gored him with a poker dipped in molten lead.

"*Ugh.*" Even his eyelids hurt. *Way* too much for him to attempt to pry them open. But *shit,* something was very wrong with this picture, and he knew he had to check things out.

Mustering every bit of energy, Josh willed himself to ignore the pain, concentrating on the facial muscles involved in operating his eyelids. He twitched and pulled and got the left one open a crack, but the right remained caked together.

What exactly had he done? Bathed in honey and fallen into a mound of fire ants?

No. *Shit.* This was far worse than that. Maybe he'd crashed his car.

He tried, really tried, to remember where he was and what he was doing. And to facilitate that goal, he needed to get his face out of the dirt.

He lifted his head – very slightly – and spat the dust away from his lips, but when he tried to turn it the right side nearly exploded.

"Ah, *hell.*" He dropped his face again, because in the grand scheme of things he figured dirt-eating amnesia was better than exploding. Then stuck his tongue out, very tentatively, and tasted the stickiness on the right side of his face.

Which tasted nothing at all like honey, but an awful lot like blood.

His head ached, his leg throbbed, his shoulder redefined pain. And he'd definitely just established that he was bleeding. Profusely. Like a stuck pig.

Or more specifically, like someone who'd just been shot.

Ah, *hell,* he thought again, because it hurt too much to say it. And because he was now absolutely, positively certain that was what had happened.

Apparently, the saggy front porch had been the least of his worries.

The fact that he'd been shot meant he needed to be able to move his arm, so that he could both radio in for backup and reach his sidearm.

Of course the real *ah, hell* moment here was that his arm was attached to his shoulder, which was quickly progressing from hell's seventh to eighth level. *Damn,* it hurt. His hot poker analogy hadn't been far off, because he'd definitely been pumped full of molten lead.

Prying his right eyelid open through sheer force of will, he realized the sticky substance caking it was blood, and came to the equally unsettling conclusion that he'd been shot in the head. Or rather, *grazed,* more than likely. He'd been grazed by a damn bullet.

After, of course, two others had torn through his shoulder and leg.

And because he was still bleeding profusely and was at serious risk of dying in the dirt, he knew that he had to make his arm work without help from his shoulder.

If he could just get to his radio…

But his cell phone was closer to his hand. And at this point, closer seemed like a good plan.

Sliding fingers slick with his own blood toward the phone clipped onto his belt, Josh cursed, quite baldly, as the ripping pain nearly destroyed him. Grinding his teeth together, he called up every reserve of strength he could manage to push a button.

He thought it was redial – hoped, prayed – but given the blood in his eyes and the pain waving his vision, he could have hit nothing at all. But he hit it again, hoping against hope that it would go through. Given his incapacitation and the spotty coverage in the area, he figured his chances were fifty/fifty.

He also figured that his chances of whoever shot him coming out from the house and adding a nice little tap to the head for insurance were considerably higher.

Super.

He could have the ignominious distinction of being the only deputy in the history of the Bentonville sheriff's department to ever be killed in the line of duty. Maybe they could build a monument to that absurdity in the form of a nice bronze statue in the town square.

Distantly, through a haze of pain, Josh heard his phone make the connection. Hope bloomed, even as he gave into the darkness once more.

CLAY was on the phone with Sheriff Callahan, asking him what, if anything, he knew about Rob Johns, when his phone alerted him to a call waiting. A quick glance determined it came from Kathleen, and he excused himself to take it. "You have a license plate number?" he asked in lieu of a greeting.

"We have a partial. There was dirt or something obscuring the last two digits on the plate, but the rest of it looks to be South Carolina tag 801-D…"

"CK," Clay completed for her, running his fingers through his hair as he paced. "I remember it because… well, for obvious and juvenile reasons, it caught my attention. Shit. I didn't want to send you off on a wild goose chase in case I was wrong, but I saw that truck in Bentonville. In fact, I almost ran over the driver as he crossed the street. His name is Rob Johns, and I just got an address on him from the sheriff." He rattled it off to Kathleen. "The entire Bentonville sheriff's department is currently unaccounted for or unavailable, so we need to get somebody over there quick. If you want to issue a BOLO, the man's about six foot, dark brown hair, overweight… although I wouldn't put much stock in that description. He's obviously proficient with disguises. *Shit.*"

Across the room, Kim's cell phone jangled, and she pounced on it and looked at the number. "It's Harding."

"Kathleen, I'll call you right back." Clay hung up on Tate's cousin, because he really wanted to talk with Josh.

"Hello," Kim said for the second time. "Deputy Harding, are you there?" A beat passed, and then another, and then she looked at the message window on her phone to see whether the call had been dropped. "The line's still open," she told Clay, looking up from her position at the desk. "But he's not answering."

Clay held out his hand and she passed him the phone. There was the distinct, slightly fuzzy sound of an open connection, but no human noises to be detected.

Until Clay heard a soft moan.

He tossed his own phone to Kim. "See if you can get them to triangulate Harding's location through his phone. Whatever happened, I'm pretty sure he's hurt." And wasn't that just great? This day was definitely going down in the record books as the shittiest ever.

Then he pressed his mouth back to the receiver. "Harding, this is Clay Copeland. Can you hear me? Are you able to tell us where you are and what your status is?"

Silence followed again, and Clay listened to it echo as Kim placed the call he'd asked her to make. Then he looked at Maureen and quickly crossed the room. "Listen to this," he handed her Kim's cell, "and let me know if you hear anything." Then he asked to borrow her phone, dialing Kathleen's number at the station.

"Maureen?" she answered it as a question.

"Nope. Clay. We're playing pass the cell phone. A call came in on Agent O'Connell's cell from one of the deputies over in Bentonville, and it looks like he might be in some kind of distress. Did you get anything on the plates?"

"Yes, but it didn't match either the name or the address you gave. It came back as registered to one Alma W. Walker, Bentonville address. Could be either the vehicle or the plates were stolen."

Something about that just didn't fit. "Our man's too careful to be driving around with stolen anything. Alma Walker might be the pseudonym for his old lady identity. Although if he was out around town as Rob Johns, being seen driving that truck, he had to have a plausible explanation for it in case he was ever pulled over. Sheriff Callahan said that he was some kind of property manager or caretaker, so that might be it."

"So which address do we raid first, the one for Rob Johns or Alma Walker?"

Clay considered a moment. If the identity the man used for snatching Max was the old lady's, then it was more plausible that he would have taken Max to Rob Johns' residence, thinking it would take the authorities a while to make any sort of connection between the two. Which it would have, if Clay hadn't seen the man get into that vehicle. Of course it was also entirely possible that the man had another identity, another residence, and another vehicle which they knew nothing about.

"Start with –"

"Walker!" Maureen burst out, surprising Clay out of what he'd been about to say. "The man on the phone just said the name *Walker!*"

CHAOS reigned.

Between the Charleston PD, what Bentonville sheriff's department deputies they'd managed to locate, and the contingent of federal agents, three different law enforcement agencies were now rushing to the Walker farm. Clay was on the phone with Kathleen, telling her to make sure the officers on her end didn't come in with sirens blaring, because this was obviously not the kind of man who was going to give up peaceably when cornered. In fact, Clay believed that type of situation would only make him more dangerous.

Kim, who was driving at something approximating the speed of light, talked to the Special Agent in Charge of the local RA, updating him on the situation, and on the phone he held to his other ear, Clay listened for sounds of life from Josh Harding. He'd roused himself enough to tell them he'd been shot and was lying in front of a barn on the Walker property, but for the past ten minutes Clay'd heard nothing. No talking, no moaning, no hint of breath.

If the man was still alive, it was just barely.

After concluding her conversation, Kim waited for Clay to finish his, and then risked taking her eyes from the road to glance his way. "You think this guy – the one who abducted Max – is the other perp we've been looking for."

"Has to be. It's the only thing that makes sense, even though – holy *God* – I never would have predicted he'd do something like this."

"So you think this is part of his revenge and retribution thing? He took out his accomplice, who was stupid enough to allow himself to be made, took out the deputy who did the composite, and went after the son of the woman who ID'd the partner?"

Clay laid the open phone – their link to Harding – on his lap so that he could rake both hands through his hair. At this rate, he'd be bald before morning. But he needed to think, needed to figure this whole thing out. He had to get inside this asshole's head so that he knew best how to help Max.

"Yes," he admitted to Kim as he watched the outside scenery fly by, "that's essentially what I think. Although to be quite honest, it's more extreme than I would have imagined. Josh Harding – well, I think he just happened to be at the wrong place at the wrong time, so the guy shot him. But with Max…" Clay shook his head, looked at Kim. "It's like he didn't just want to strike back at Tate, but he wanted to do it in the most painful way possible. And he went to a lot of trouble to do so, at the risk of getting caught. We're talking about the sort of man who up to this point has avoided risky behavior, so that begs the question *why is he willing to do so now?* That sort of thing reeks of some sort of personal connection, of prior knowledge of his victim. It's too extreme an act of retribution against a perfect stranger who's pissed you off."

Kim seemed to swallow that piece of information like something akin to spoiled milk. "So you think this man is someone who knows Tate? Someone she has some kind of history with?"

"I don't know." Clay rubbed his eyes, went with his gut. "Yes, that's what I think. Kathleen's running everything they can on the old lady who owns the farm, to see if they can turn anything up from that quarter. But I'm afraid if we can't approach the situation at that farm stealthily – if it becomes a hostage situation – someone's going to have to wake Tate and show her the second composite, to see if she recognizes the blond man from the diner." He remembered something she'd said to him once, about him being the latest in a string of gorgeous blonds that she'd fallen for. He prayed to God that this man wasn't one of them. "We'll need to know everything we can about this guy and what makes him tick if we have any hope of getting Max back unharmed."

Clay's phone rang, and he flipped it open to continue his dialogue with Kathleen.

"We're here," she informed him, just slightly out of breath. "We have our snipers moving into position. No sign of life so far, but two members of the SWAT team just cleared the barn and made a positive ID on the blue pickup. There's also a late model minivan parked beside it."

A minivan? Interesting choice. It was excellent cover for a man traveling with a young child.

"Kathleen, find out if there's a car seat in the back of the second vehicle."

Clay could hear her muffled voice as she turned away to make the inquiry. "Affirmative," she told him after a moment. "I guess that means he was planning to take Max out of here alive?"

"Not only that, but it means they're both probably still there. He'd want to move quickly, after shooting Harding, so our best bet might be to wait him out, have one of the snipers take him down when he heads out toward the car." But it was going to take nerves of steel for him to wait, knowing that Max was probably in that house. Kathleen must have felt the same way.

"I want to bust that door down right now."

"I do, too. But that might endanger Max. We need to be sure that the guy isn't in there, holding a gun to Max's head before we go alerting him to our presence." Clay listened to the silence coming from the phone on his lap and asked her another tough question. "Any word on Deputy Harding?"

Kathleen sighed, and Clay could hear her tension. "His position is such that he's in full view of the house, and if we get near him we'll give ourselves away. I had to take a hard line with a couple of his fellow deputies, who wanted to run to his aid. We can't risk it, as you said, until we know what we're dealing with inside. But in all honesty, I'm not sure the guy's alive. There's an awful lot of blood under him."

Clay swallowed and looked at the phone on his lap, feeling a real pang of loss for the other man. In the short time Clay had known him, Josh had managed to earn his respect.

But then suddenly, noise erupted from that phone, and Kathleen began *oh, shit*ting in the other.

"Kathleen? What the hell's going on?"

There was a barrage of voices, most raised in angry shouts, and then a very definite gunshot.

Two. Three shots.

Between the two phones it was like hearing the situation in some kind of weird stereo. "Please tell me that was one of the snipers."

"Another of the Bentonville deputies is down." Panic pitched Kathleen's words. "He ignored orders and went after Harding. The first two shots came from an upstairs window, the third from one of our snipers, to get the gunman to back off." She made a noise that sounded an awful lot like a sob. "I'd say our perp definitely knows we're here."

THE situation had gone to hell in a hand-basket by the time Clay and Kim made the scene. Federal agents descended in a flurry of dark-tinted vehicles while a mixture of sheriff's deputies and Charleston PD tried to maintain some kind of perimeter. Gossip in small towns traveled faster than wildfire, and the curious were already flocking. A hostage negotiator with the Charleston PD was trying to find out if there was a land line so that he could establish communication, as the name of the game was to keep the offender as calm as possible, and bullhorns were not the way to go.

Nor, of course, was busting down the door, which was what the remaining sheriff's deputies were advocating. They had two men down – one badly wounded, one maybe dead – and were on an adrenaline rush of anger and retribution. Tempers were heated, emotions close to the surface, the whole situation a ticking bomb. The man inside the house had created an incredibly dangerous situation for himself, because now he was not only a child abductor but a cop killer.

Every law enforcement official present wanted him dead.

None of them more than Clay.

But first they had to get Max out safely.

He and Kim parked alongside the road, arriving in time to see several members of the SWAT team gearing up to pull the downed deputies out. Aside from body armor and riot shields, they had the backup support of their snipers. So far Rob Johns, or whoever the hell he was, had made no further attempts to fire his weapon. There was speculation that he had a limited amount of ammo, but everyone knew it was foolish to make assumptions.

Well, almost everyone. Apparently the deputy who'd gone after Harding hadn't thought the whole thing through.

Locating Kathleen in the throng, Clay pushed past some Charleston PD officers who asked him for ID, leaving Kim to flash her badge and smooth things over. He simply didn't have the wherewithal to tolerate needless distractions.

A short man – early forties, with ruthlessly tamed dark hair and an FBI raid jacket over a very expensively tailored suit – looked up at Kathleen, exuding irritation.

"Your opinion is of no consequence. You should not be on this case, let alone part of the decision making process," Clay heard the man say. "There's no way for you to maintain your objectivity, Detective."

"Look," Kathleen was going toe to toe, refusing to back down at all. She obviously had her Irish up, a condition that Clay recognized from working with Kim. "My cousin's little boy is in that house –"

"Exactly my point." The agent talked right over her protests. "You *assume* you have a family member in imminent peril, which makes your judgment questionable at best. I'd like to remind you that we have no viable proof the child is in there, and yet you've created an atmosphere of extreme urgency which has caused a local uniform to get himself shot."

Kathleen's fair skin turned red at the unjustified accusation. Clay knew this man's type, knew exactly what he was up to, and given the asshole factor concluded he was the man Kim had spoken of earlier. The fact that an officer had been shot – two officers, in fact – meant that the ugliness quotient had ratcheted up to damaging levels. Anytime a law enforcement official or innocent bystander was wounded or killed in the course of a tactical situation, everyone's first and immediate question was *who screwed up?*

Clearly, this man – Special Agent in Charge Beall – was already pointing fingers to pass the blame.

"Detective Murphy hasn't done anything in her handling of the situation that wasn't carried out with the utmost professionalism, and she has proceeded as both her lieutenant and I have instructed."

The older man frowned at Clay as he spoke. "And who the hell are you?"

"Agent Clay Copeland. I'm with the Investigative Support Unit." He reached into his pocket, produced ID. "I've been working with the Bentonville sheriff's department on their investigation, which has spilled over into Detective Murphy's kidnapping."

No way was he going to give this guy any indication that he had a personal interest in the case. He was just the kind of man to use that against Clay, to ignore every piece of advice he had to offer. And technically, the man was the highest ranking official on the scene, so like it or not that put him in charge.

"So you believe Detective Murphy's assertion that the boy's in there and still alive? That we need to approach this as if it were a hostage situation?"

"Yes, I do."

Beall motioned to the van behind him, which held a boatload of taxpayer dollars in the form of expensive equipment. "We have a parabolic microphone that suggests otherwise. Other than the sound of our gunman moving around, we've been unable to detect any signs of a hostage. How do we know this isn't simply some old farmer who thinks he's defending his property? It would have been prudent to follow protocol and make your presence known from the outset. This situation might have turned out peacefully."

Clay took a breath and tried to hold onto his patience. "You haven't heard any sounds of anyone else in the house, because in all likelihood he has the child drugged. And I believe Agent O'Connell already filled you in on the situation, and the fact that Deputy Harding was shot during a routine canvass as part of his department's investigation. This residence is supposed to be empty. Both the farm and the truck that we positively identified as the getaway vehicle for the abduction – and which is currently parked in the barn, I might add – are the property of an elderly woman who supposedly now resides in Atlanta."

"With a grandson," Kathleen interjected. "Who we're currently checking out."

Beall sent the detective a glare, and Clay continued as if he hadn't noticed. "We have reason to believe that the man inside the house assumed the elderly woman – Alma Walker's – identity as part of his plan to kidnap the child. We have reason to believe that this is a dangerous, unstable individual who is part of a long-standing human trafficking operation. We have reason to believe that just yesterday he killed his partner in cold blood. So no, sir, this isn't some farmer defending his property."

"Okay." A little of the bite had gone out of the older man's attitude at the calm authority in Clay's voice. "So I guess we need to try to establish some kind of dialogue. Any idea what kind of demands we'll be looking at to make this end the way we want it to?"

Clay shook his head and stuffed his hands into his pockets, afraid Agent Beall would notice them shaking. "Aside from retribution and a free ticket out of here, I'm afraid I don't have enough information about our abductor to make any viable comments at this time." Once Clay heard some of the negotiator's dialogue with the man – *if* he was willing to talk – he might have a better idea. "I do know, however, that this is a man who's on the edge. And the fact that we showed up when we did, essentially trapping him, is going to make that edge he's on even slipperier. Most hostage-takers go into their situation expecting the police to show up. It gives them a forum to air their grievances. We took this guy by surprise, and he's not going to like it. I think that we should approach the situation with as little show of force as possible, because he's likely to strike back, hard and fast."

Agent Beall nodded. "Okay, Agent Copeland. You just earned a spot next to the negotiator. He's going to need backup if this thing drags out."

Clay hesitated. Because he knew that wasn't a good idea. Not only was he completely biased and in fact wanted nothing more than for that son of a bitch to die and die hard – and that sort of emotion was completely contrary to setting up a productive dialogue with a hostage-taker – but also because the bastard clearly knew who he was and what Max meant to him.

But how to broach that subject without Beall ordering him off the scene?

Clay cleared his throat, sweat trickling down his back. It ran cold, despite the relentless heat.

"With all due respect, sir, that's a position I'd rather not take. The last time I tried to negotiate a little boy died. I'll be happy to advise, but I can't talk to the offender."

Beall's raised eyebrows suggested his opinion of Clay had just tanked. But he was prevented from commenting on that fact by the appearance of a member of the Charleston PD's SWAT team.

"Our men are ready to move in," he said, staring at Beall as if he dared him to stop them. "Webster, the negotiator, hasn't been able to pull up a land line, and so far the HT seems either unwilling or unable to call the cell number we posted to get him to communicate. He's going to use the bullhorn to tell him we're only moving in to get the deputies some medical attention."

Clay tensed. It was a horrible situation. They needed to get those deputies out of there, but he felt that anything they did to upset this man's perceived balance of power was going to put Max in further danger. "Offer him a trade," he said suddenly, surprising the others into looking his direction. Surprising himself. "Right now, those injured deputies are his leverage. You go in there and take them out, however peaceably, and he might perceive that as loss of control. We need to offer him something in return."

"How do we know what to offer," Kathleen asked, "when he won't even talk to us?"

"Offer me."

A chorus of shocked protests erupted, as Clay had known it would. But dammit he had to try *something*. Him walking into that house as a voluntary hostage would not only give him a chance to assess the situation from the inside, but also create a heightened sense of power for Rob Johns. He'd have a federal agent in the doubly vulnerable position of hostage and man who wanted to protect his child. Johns' need for control would be safely unassailed, and Clay would have a better chance of influencing him.

Beall held up a hand to silence everyone's comments. "You're not seriously suggesting that I allow an unarmed federal agent to walk into a crisis situation with an unstable offender, who has already shown no compunction about shooting cops."

Clay held the other man's gaze. "Yes sir. I am."

Beall expelled a short burst of disbelieving air. "You just said you didn't want to negotiate with the man, but you're willing to let him hold a gun on you?"

Clay tried to get Beall to see the logic of his suggestion. Or maybe it wasn't logical. Hell, he didn't know. And he was too desperate right now to figure it out. "As a negotiator and a hostage-taker, Johns and I are on relatively equal footing. However, put me in the position of hostage and Johns suddenly becomes the one in control. He's the type personality who'll be less dangerous if he feels less threatened. He'll feel less threatened if he has both me and the child as leverage."

And Clay could get close enough to him to snap the other man's neck.

"Do you have any idea what kind of precedent that would set, Agent Copeland? Word gets out that I let something like that go down, and every hostage-taking psychotic in the country would be demanding a federal agent for every civilian they release."

"Sir. You realize that every situation is different. If you would just –"

Beall shook his head, body language dismissive, and turned his attention to the SWAT team member at his side. "Get your men ready to get those deputies out of there. Tell your negotiator to get on the bull horn and let the HT know you're coming, and that he'd better hold his fire."

Frustrated, Clay stepped forward and got large, looming directly over the other agent. "Sir, I really think this would go much more smoothly if we offer the exchange I suggested."

"Duly noted," Beall said dryly. "Now why don't you and Detective Murphy step behind that line over there, and I'll let you know if I need your opinion again."

CHAPTER TWENTY-FOUR

INSIDE the farmhouse that had become her own personal hell, Casey listened to the sound of the bullhorn. She couldn't make out most of the words – something about *deputies* and *fire* – but what the man said didn't really matter.

What mattered was that he was *here*.

Someone had finally come for her.

Or maybe he'd come for the little boy who was currently lying across her lap.

Whatever. It didn't matter. As long as he – they, whoever the heck was out there – got her *out*.

She was so giddy that she started to weep.

Shifting the kid's head off her thigh until it lay on the cool bathroom tile, she shimmied out from under him. She couldn't stand fully, because she was handcuffed to an old, rusty pipe under the sink, but she twisted and strained and almost wrenched her shoulder from its socket in an attempt to see through the narrow window.

There were trees – not up next to the house, but close enough to distinguish their leaves – and she knew from the time she'd stood on the edge of the tub that there was a roof almost directly beneath the window. It wasn't large, maybe five feet wide at most, and she guessed it covered some kind of stoop.

Very quietly, Casey pulled on the handcuff to test its hold. The blond man had told her that if he heard her make one sound he'd shoot her in the head. And she had no doubt that he would actually do it. After all, he'd already…

No. Don't think about that now. Right now she just had to think about getting out of there. About sleeping in her own bed. Playing Chutes and Ladders with her sister.

She even wanted to smell those stupid funnel cakes.

Shaking, tears streaming down her face from so much hope, Casey sat back down on the floor next to the boy. He was a cute little guy – all freckles and shaggy dark hair – and she bet he had a mom and dad somewhere who were really worried.

She lifted his head again, settling his soft cheek against her lap.

"Don't worry," she whispered, stroking an unruly lock of hair off his forehead. "The good guys are out there now, and they're going to help us."

CLAY was losing it.

Losing. It.

In typical SNAFU fashion, someone had let it slip that he had a personal involvement with the child inside, and now Beall was even *less* inclined to listen to anything he had to say. In the field, the behavioral side of the Bureau lacked the authority to dictate how tactical situations were handled, serving only in an advisory capacity. They could suggest, and recommend, but in the end it was out of their hands. And when they had a personal stake in the case that could be construed as clouding their judgment – well, they might as well not even bother.

And that was exactly how Agent Beall was acting toward Clay. Like things would be so much easier if he and his psychobabble opinions weren't around.

"I'm a damn agent with the damn Bureau, just like him – although on second thought, *he* doesn't have a PhD – and yet he's treating me like the village idiot."

Kim reached out to grab Clay's arm. He was pacing so fast and furiously in one small patch of dirt that he'd worn a groove under his feet.

It had been over thirty minutes since Beall had dismissed his suggestion that he trade himself for the deputies and there was still no sign of communication from the house.

On the up side, the SWAT team had pulled the two Bentonville deputies out, without an exchange of gunfire, and miraculously, Josh Harding was still alive. He'd lost a tremendous amount of blood, but none of the three bullet wounds were in themselves life threatening. There was a strong chance that he would pull through his ordeal in one piece.

On the down side, Rob Johns was refusing to communicate, and they'd still been unable to determine whether or not Max was faring okay. Patience was running low, nerves were running high, and Clay knew they were running out of time.

"We have to find out more about him," he said to Kim when she finally managed to force him to stand still. "I'm afraid someone's going to have to wake Tate and show her that composite. If she recognizes him, she might be able to offer us some insight as to his background. There has to be something there – some personal connection – and if we find out what it is I might be able to reach him." He blew out a breath of frustration. "This isn't your run-of-the-mill child abduction, so I'm not sure what buttons to push."

Kim nodded and squeezed the hard arm under her hand. "I know you were holding that out as a kind of last resort because you wanted to spare her from having to go through this, but I think that's a good idea. Why don't I fax a copy of the composite over to the hospital? Maybe get her uncle or her cousin to look at it first. If they recognize him, Tate sleeps through this. If not, they can wake her up."

"Okay." Clay scrubbed a hand down his sweat-streaked face, watching Beall and a handful of others confer over how long to wait before they breached the interior. He knew that unless Johns opened up a dialogue, or unless one of the snipers got a chance to take him out through a window, that eventually that's what would happen. The reactive stage of the situation would give way to a proactive operational strategy.

But something in Clay's gut told him that if they pushed Johns that way, he'd push back. He was probably *planning* to push back. His lack of willingness to negotiate up to this point suggested that he had no interest in playing give and take. Some personality types – like, dear God, the man they'd cornered in

Topeka – refused to accept any part in a production over which they didn't exert absolute control. Left with no options or meaningful choices, he'd be desperate to end this on his own terms.

And Clay feared that was what they were dealing with.

This man would probably prefer to go down in a design of his own making than allow himself to be taken by the authorities.

Most likely taking Max with him.

Unless Clay could find that one significant factor that would somehow tip the balance in their favor. But what then? Could he persuade Beall to even listen?

Clay breathed, a ragged intake of humid air.

Thought of that purple bear.

And prayed to God Max lived to call him *Daddy*.

JR went about his business as quietly as he could. He was sure those assholes had listening devices aimed in his direction. He'd studied up on enough law enforcement techniques to know that was SOP. And he also knew exactly what they were hoping to accomplish with that piece of shit negotiator and his bullhorn.

Just talk to me, the idiot said. *Let me know what you need. I want to help you resolve this.*

What a bunch of crap. What that cop wanted was for him to spend the rest of his life looking at the world through a set of iron bars.

He was *not* going to end up in prison.

He wrenched the old-fashioned stove sideways, turning the valve so that gas leaked into the air. JR figured he had maybe thirty minutes before the goons out there got antsy enough to come after him. Now if he were *negotiating,* that could go on for hours. But by refusing to talk, he'd speed this farce up and get it over with.

He pulled himself out from his awkward crouch behind the stove, rubbed the dirt and grease he'd accumulated onto his pants. Thirty minutes was plenty to turn this place into a time bomb. Enough gas would build up that one spark – one shot from a weapon – would send the entire place up in flames, taking everyone nearby with it.

It wasn't exactly the way he'd planned for things to turn out, but he figured it would do in a pinch. He'd lose the girl and he'd lose the kid, but hey, watching Tate and her FBI prick pick pieces of the kid off the surrounding vegetation had to be good for a laugh or two.

He wondered where Tate was right now.

He'd tried to catch a glimpse of her from one of the upstairs windows, but he knew there were snipers around and hanging out where they could pick him off was not such a hot idea. Still, he really hoped she was here to see this. Her boyfriend probably had her stashed somewhere, sitting safe and comfortable in an air conditioned police car, waiting to tell her that he'd saved her precious son.

Hah. He'd like to be a fly on the wall for *that* little conversation, after good old grandma Alma's farmhouse went sky high.

But he knew better than to risk sticking around. If nothing else, this little fiasco had reminded him that it didn't pay to get cocky and take chances. A smart man knew when to cut his losses and walk away.

And JR was nothing if not smart.

Satisfied with his handiwork, he turned to leave the kitchen, heading toward the door to the cellar. Good thing he'd gone exploring during that one summer he'd actually been invited to visit. If he hadn't, he never would have known about the old tunnel that ran under the house. Some kind of leftover hidey hole from Prohibition, his grandma had informed him. After she'd whooped his hide for getting into places he didn't belong.

He paused at the head of the stairs, reconsidering his decision about leaving the boy. He'd actually been looking forward to the idea of keeping him…

But no. That was a liability he didn't need. It was going to be challenging enough to get out of here himself, to disappear and fade into the background, without trying to drag a kid with him.

Dismissing all that he was leaving behind, JR turned and headed toward freedom.

CASEY was growing tired of waiting. It had been a long while since the blond man locked them in, and she hadn't seen or heard him since.

Was he waiting outside the door, listening for her to make a noise?

Was he downstairs, hiding from the police?

She knew he wasn't talking to them because she could hear bits and pieces of what the man with the bullhorn was saying. But what was taking so *long*? Why didn't they just come in and get her?

She shivered, despite the heat that filled the small bathroom in steamy waves. With the door closed, no air moved in the tight space, and Casey was beginning to feel both light-headed and nauseous. There was a funny smell to the stagnant air.

Something tightened in her gut. She felt herself sliding into panic.

She had to get out. *Had* to. Maybe the policemen outside didn't even know she was here. Maybe the blond man would just give up, go with them, and then they'd all go away, never realizing she'd been left.

Maybe the blond man would shoot her and the little boy before he gave himself up.

Oh *God,* she had to get out of here.

Casey used her free hand to push her sweat-dampened hair off her face, shifting the little boy back onto the floor. Poor kid. She guessed he was lucky that he was drugged.

He didn't have to worry about the fact that he was probably going to die.

No. Casey refused to let that happen. She refused to be *this* close to ending this nightmare and then just sit here, waiting.

She pulled on the handcuff attached to the pipe – really *yanked,* with all the strength she had left – and bit back the cry that threatened to erupt when the hard metal bit into her flesh. Oh it *hurt.*

Biting down to distract herself from the pain, Casey kept yanking until blood ran. Its slick metallic warmth brought bile rushing into her throat, but she choked it down and pulled and pulled and pulled.

Chunks of flesh scraped off the bone, but Casey stifled her sobs. This agony was nothing compared to a bullet. Like an animal desperate enough to gnaw its paw off to escape a trap, she would do whatever it took to get out of there.

Finally, tears streaming down her sweaty face, dizzy from a combination of pain and drugs and hunger, she managed to yank her mangled hand free, collapsing in a ball of anguish.

Oh God, oh God, oh God. It hurt so bad she thought she might pass out.

But she just knew that if she did, she might never awaken.

Mustering every bit of will that she had left, Casey lifted her head and looked toward the bathroom window.

CHAPTER TWENTY-FIVE

THE hand on her shoulder gently shook Tate into waking.

Webs of confusion clouded her brain, making it difficult to get her bearings. Something told her to just slip back into unconsciousness and let it all fade away.

But something even stronger drew her forward. Some reason that she needed to be up and functioning.

"Max." She sat up suddenly, rubbed the grit from her swollen eyes. Oh God, her baby was *missing,* and she'd actually allowed herself to sleep.

When she opened her eyes her uncle was there. The look on his face made hope bloom, then just as quickly shrivel up and die. He knew something, and she didn't think it was good.

"Max?" she said again, fear turning his name into a question.

Patrick Murphy laid an awkward hand on his niece's arm. "They found him," he said, and Tate's heart turned over in her chest. "Your, uh... friend, Agent Copeland, *Clay*...he, um, did whatever it is that he does and they figured out where to find Max. It's pretty amazing, really, when you think about it."

"Uncle Patrick," Tate's voice was tremulous, as she laid her own hand over his. "Is Max..."

She couldn't bring herself to say it. She simply couldn't put *Max* and *dead* into the same sentence without imploding.

Patrick's eyes widened and he blew out a nervous burst of air. "Oh *no,* honey. Lord, I'm so sorry. I should have just come right out and said it. Max is alive, Tate. They're sure that he's alive.

But the problem is that the man who took him is holding him hostage."

Oh, the *joy*. The joy that crashed into her took her breath. If her baby wasn't dead then there was hope. Tears of relief streaked down her face. She'd been so afraid of what her uncle would say.

"Okay." She used the heel of her hand to dry her cheeks. The rush of relief gave way to worry. "And so he wants what… money?" Like she had big piles of it lying around. She wondered if someone had taken Max by mistake. But then her frazzled mind processed some of what Patrick said. "I thought Kathleen said that he'd been abducted by an old woman."

Patrick sighed, admitting his own confusion. "Apparently it was a man in disguise. Your boyfriend could probably explain the whole thing better, but the woman who called – Agent O'Connell – said that Clay thinks you might know the man." He pulled the composite from his shirt pocket. "She asked me to show you this."

Tate took the paper, unrolling it quickly, beside herself that someone she knew would have done something this… unthinkable. But as she looked at the composite – noticing it was almost certainly Josh Harding's work – she tried to reconcile the image of the light-haired, light-eyed man with someone she should recognize. After several tense moments, she admitted she couldn't do it.

"I don't know him," she told her uncle, wondering if that was good or bad. "*Should* I know him?" She looked at the composite again. "I mean if this man took Max, and I'm supposed to know why…" She shook her head, because that made no kind of sense. "Can I borrow your cell phone?"

She needed to call Clay, to understand what was happening. But then she looked out the window, out at the pure cerulean of the sky. The sky under which a man she didn't recognize was holding her son hostage. "On second thought," she threw back the covers and climbed shakily from the bed, "I think that maybe I'd better borrow your car."

"HEY." Clay answered his phone almost casually, but Tate could hear the tremor in his voice. It made her own nerves fray even further. "I'm sorry we had to wake you up."

Working against the clog in her throat, Tate made a noise of despair. "Don't be," she said fiercely. If I'd held it together better, Justin wouldn't have had to give me that sedative, and I wouldn't have been sleeping at all. Sleeping, when Max needs me." Her breath caught on a sob. "What kind of mother am I?"

"You can't be beating yourself up about that, Tate. And we'll talk about that later. I guess your uncle and your cousin struck out, or else you wouldn't be calling. Did you, uh, have a chance to look at that composite?"

"I did. Oh, Clay, you think that this is the man who has Max?"

"We're pretty certain." He cleared his throat, and his voice emerged stronger. "You don't recognize him, sugar? He's not someone you know?"

In her uncle's car, Tate used her free hand to hold the composite against the steering wheel as she drove. He was handsome, blond… and totally didn't ring any bells.

"Not that I can recall," she told Clay, raising her eyes to gage her distance from the car in front of her. The last thing she needed was to rear-end somebody and have yet another delay keeping her from her son. "*Should* I know him, Clay? Did you have some reason to think I would?"

"Behaviorally speaking, it makes sense." He hesitated, and Tate knew that what was coming would be bad. Her stomach clenched. *Max.*

Her baby.

"I'm not sure how much your uncle or cousin was able to tell you, but we believe this man is the perp we've been looking for. His partner is the one who abducted Casey."

"*No.*" Heart leaping like a wild thing, Tate almost sideswiped the next car. The man driving laid his hand on the horn, sending her a dirty look that she was blind to.

"Tate? Where are you?"

"I'm driving," she admitted, trying to keep her shaky hands on the wheel. "I'm on my way to Bentonville."

"*No.* No. Sweetheart, I don't think that's such a good idea."

"What do you mean it's not a good idea?" And the words were pure anger. All the helpless rage she was feeling boiled up to spill over Clay. "You just told me that some perverted child molester has my son, and you're telling me to… what? Go home and wait? Do nothing while he violates my b-baby?"

Her voice broke. She couldn't help it. "This is like… my worst nightmare come to life."

"Believe me, I know. It's unthinkable for any parent, but given what you experienced as a child…"

His words trailed off, and Tate couldn't stand it. She shoved the images from all those years ago out of her head.

"Tate." The renewed energy in Clay's voice cut through her misery. "I know this is unbelievably difficult, but I need you to listen to me for a moment. Can you think of any reason, any reason at all, for the man in that composite to know what happened to you at camp?"

"What? Why would he? And what does that have to do with Max? *Why* did that man take Max?"

"I don't have time to go into the full psychological explanation, but I believe he's seeking revenge on everyone he construes as having screwed things up for him. You saw his partner with Casey, you started this whole ball rolling, so to speak, and he decided to make you pay. However, the means he used – abducting Max – and the risks he took to go about it, suggest some kind of more personal connection to you. It's too out of character for him to take those risks for this to be just some passing irritation. He… despises you, wants to punish you in the worst possible way. I believe he knows you, and has some knowledge of the summer you saw the camp director molesting that boy."

Tate blinked, thinking that was absurd. How could *anyone* she knew be capable of this? "It's not something I go around discussing."

"Then could it be someone who had a personal connection to what happened? I'm assuming the camp director went to prison. Did he have a son? Or how about the boy you saw with him?"

Tate blew out a frustrated puff of air. "Donald Logan wasn't married and didn't have any children as far as I know. And the boy he molested... his name was Timothy Russell. But surely you don't think it could be him. Why on earth would he hate me for putting a stop to what was happening?" She nearly missed the exit to Bentonville, and jerked the steering wheel to the right.

"The psychology that goes along with child abuse – particularly sexual abuse – is complicated stuff. The abuser can twist the situation until the child believes that what has been done is an act of love. But because the child knows that it's inherently wrong, his confliction over the situation results in a whole stockpile of anger just looking for a suitable outlet. If the victim isn't counseled, they might misplace their anger by turning into abusers themselves."

"So you think that this man might be one of the boys Logan abused, he turned to a life of crime, and somehow found out that I had been the one to see his accomplice? And he remembered me?" She laughed, completely without mirth. "I don't mean to question that you know what you're doing, but that just seems so far-fetched."

"Truth's stranger than fiction, sugar. Can you think of anyone, anyone at all, who might fit the bill? The more I know about the man inside that house with Max, the better chance I have of knowing what needs to be done to get Max out."

Tate looked at the composite again, wondering how she was supposed to recognize anyone after all these years. And how did they even know for sure that this was what he really looked like? Her uncle had said that this man used disguises. That he had in fact checked into the Inn, dressed like an old lady. Tate shuddered, thinking about the fact that she'd been so close, and hadn't even realized. She'd felt so bad when Mrs. Walker spilled the tea on her hand...

"Oh my God." Her stomach turned, and she studied the drawing closely, pulling off to the side of the road to give it her full attention. Gravel crunched beneath the tires as she slammed the car into park.

The eyes, she thought. Something about the set of the mouth...

"What is it? You remember something?"

Tate's hand shook as she straightened out the paper. "I could be wrong," she said, heart sinking at the possibility. "But there's a chance this could be Lifeguard John."

KIM was on the phone with one of the Bureau's information specialists, who was turning up everything they could possibly get on Jonathan Robert Walker.

Clay had no doubt that was the man inside with Max. The pieces of the puzzle fit.

From what he could piece together, Clay determined that Walker was probably a classic case of a neglected child falling victim to an opportunistic child molester – in this case a revered camp director who worked with several churches to create a program for underprivileged youth. In reality, a pool of needy, vulnerable children for him to systematically abuse. At Donald Logan's trial, it had been determined that the man had been molesting boys from the church program for years.

From the information he'd been able to glean from Tate, Clay determined that Walker had started out attending the camp around the age of ten, and had returned every summer thereafter, eventually moving into a position of counselor by the time he reached his late teens. That was several long years during which his abuser twisted their relationship into something that approximated caring. To a child who probably had virtually no adult attention or interest in his life, that relationship – however wrong – became a critical part of his identity.

When Tate witnessed Logan molesting Timothy Russell, a major thread of Walker's sense of self began to unravel. When Logan was convicted and sent to prison – publically accused and punished for his criminal behavior – it forced Walker to face that what had happened between them was wrong. Psychologically, however, he couldn't handle it. So instead of feeling anger toward the perpetrator of the crimes committed against him, he embarked on a life of using the repeated and systematic abuse of others in the most clinical way possible – as a means of gaining wealth. It both gave him an outlet for his abnormal and aggressive sexual tendencies, and yet at the same time allowed him to believe that he was firmly in control of them.

Until another thread began to unravel.

Almost a decade ago, Logan was murdered in prison.

Then just last year, another thread.

His accomplice – and though they didn't yet have positive identification, Clay felt certain that the other man was either a friend or relative from those early days, possibly someone who'd shared similar abuse – had begun a series of mistakes which led them to flee Atlanta and take up their business in Charleston. Where, ironically enough, they'd run into Tate. Who'd driven a significant nail into their business coffin by witnessing Casey Rodriguez talking to her abductor. By drawing in himself, and the FBI.

By completely unraveling Walker's life.

Hence, he'd gone after Tate in the worst way imaginable – by abducting her son.

And Clay had no doubt now that the man had intended to take Max out of here alive, because in his mind – even if Tate had no idea what was happening – he would be hurting her every time he abused Max. Killing Max would have been too simple, not fitting enough punishment for what he saw as her crime. By taking Max and forcing him into the same kind of twisted relationship he himself had had with Logan, he was both punishing Tate and creating a new sense of purpose for himself. And in some ways, attempting to justify his feelings for Logan.

But now, with his latest plan being thwarted after he'd gone through so much trouble to set it into motion, Clay strongly suspected that Jonathan Walker was going to come unglued. He felt there was very little chance of them using negotiation to talk the man down.

He was not going to let Max out of there alive.

Realizing this, feeling sure of his conclusion, Clay trotted over to the van near which Agent Beall was standing. Heart racing, he stepped into the other man's line of sight. "He's not going to negotiate," he told him baldly. "We're wasting our breath trying to get him to talk."

Beall looked him up and down. "Thanks for that newsflash." Then he turned to study some information the computer had spit out.

Clay grabbed the older agent's arm. "Look, what I mean to say is that he will not let Max go. He will not be talked down. The longer we wait, the more time it gives him to hatch whatever plan he's in there hatching. He's going to… kill Max, and look for a means of ending this on his own terms."

Beall squinted as he digested that opinion. "You think he's suicidal?"

"No," Clay disagreed. "I don't. But I *do* feel that if that were the only option left available to him in order to stay on top of the situation, he would take it. My guess is that given no other choice, he'd choose death over going to prison. And he'd be sure to take Max with him."

"So what are you suggesting we do?"

Clay took a deep breath, and just said it. "I know how this is going to sound, but I need to go in there." Beall started making negative noises, but Clay talked over him and forged ahead. "I know about his background, and I have a personal connection to Max. I'm also Max's mother's lover. He has a need to wreak vengeance on her, and if he has me, there's a real chance that I can provide at least enough of a distraction that one of the snipers can move in and take him out."

Disbelief radiated. "I'm pretty sure I've already given you the answer to that proposition, Agent Copeland. Look, I can appreciate what you're going through –"

"No," Clay said. "You really can't."

"But," it was Beall's turn to bulldoze Clay. "This is precisely why you shouldn't be part of this. Your judgment simply cannot be trusted."

"What other choice do we have?" Clay shouted, in a rare display of losing his cool. "Just sit out here and wait for him to kill him?"

"I'm not," Beall said evenly "going to give the okay for allowing a federal agent to sign his own death warrant."

"Better me than that little boy! How is it going to look, sir, when they show Max's body being carried out of that house in a black bag, right alongside your face on the five o'clock news?" Clay gestured toward the news vans which were being held back at the end of the driveway. "You know how that's going to play? A whole hell of a lot worse than an agent being killed in the line of duty."

Clay could tell that he'd struck a chord with the older man, and lowering his voice, stepped closer. "I'll make it look like I didn't have your approval. I'll stomp off right now, you can climb into the van, and when your back's turned I'll approach the house. You can make all kinds of angry noises and no one will be the wiser. It will help make the situation tenable for you, and may even play well with our HT. If he believes I'm that desperate," which he was, truth be told. Totally desperate. "It will add to his feeling of control. Come on, sir." Emotion stripped Clay's voice bare enough to break. "What do you have to lose?"

Beall's eyes narrowed as they assessed Clay's, and he gave a brief nod before moving back. "The answer is still *no,* Agent Copeland." He said it loud enough for others to hear. "Now don't come to me with this nonsense again."

Beall struck off toward the back of the van, and Clay hung his head, defeated.

Then affixing an angry mask to his face, tried not to smile as he stormed off.

JR emerged from the tunnel's back entrance at the edge of the field. Sapling pines and saw palmettos grew thick, affording cover as he crept out. Moving closer, on hands and knees, toward the tree line that meant salvation, he pulled out his binoculars and studied the scene.

Cops and federal agents were scurrying about like rats in a lab, and as he shifted the field glasses higher he picked out one, two…three snipers positioned in trees near the house, waiting for him to actually be dumb enough to pass in front of one of the windows. Or perhaps step out onto the porch to offer them all some iced tea.

Scanning toward the driveway, he saw several news crews gathered like vultures, waiting for some flesh to pluck.

Ha! Weren't they going to be happy when that damn house blew all to hell?

JR lifted his head briefly, pulling his bottom lip between his teeth as he considered a slight problem. How could he be sure that one of the pigs actually fired off a shot toward the house?

Damn. Why hadn't he considered that before? He would have, if he hadn't been penned in, the surprise of it all making him sloppy. How the hell had they found him so quickly, anyway? Was it that damn pretty boy he'd shot? He probably should have gone outside and given him an insurance tap to the head, but the guy had looked like a goner.

And he'd been in a hurry to get out, so…

He lifted the binoculars again, trying to gage what the Feebs were going to do. Lo and behold, if it wasn't Agent Copeland, little Tate's screw buddy, getting all fired up and causing a scene.

Maybe he should call that damn number the negotiator kept repeating, and tell them that he was going to kill the kid. Once Copeland got word of that, he'd go racing into the place, gun blasting.

Then, *boom*.

Just as he was trying to work out the angles for making that a viable plan, he caught sight of a commotion near the driveway. Somebody was causing a ruckus, yelling at some cops, and a couple of reporters were scrambling.

Then the crowd parted and he saw...

Tate.

JR smiled with something approaching giddiness. She'd made it to see the show after all.

He swung the binoculars around, and saw Copeland getting ready to... walk up to the door?

Damn, the asshole had balls.

And just as he was getting ready to slip his phone from his pocket, he heard a noise in one of the trees several yards away.

"What the hell is that idiot doing?"

Startled, JR quietly lifted his binoculars, and saw that the question had been uttered by sniper number *four*, who was perched in a tree not thirty feet in front of him.

Damn, that had been close. If the sniper hadn't been keeping his full attention on the house through the scope of his rifle, he probably would have spotted JR.

Sweating from the heat, and from his own frayed nerves, JR started to slink away.

But then another thought occurred, and had him reaching for his weapon.

CLAY focused on the farmhouse door, absolutely ignoring the fact that he could be shot down at any second. He'd removed his sidearm and kept his hands raised high to show Walker he wasn't carrying.

Behind him, Beall was indeed going through the motions of outrage, and he heard both Kim and Kathleen's anxious voices.

He blocked it all out.

All he saw right now was the door to that house, and a vision of the child who was behind it. Holding his hand, laying his head on his shoulder in that sleepy, trusting way kids had... asking if he was going to be his daddy.

Yes, he wanted to tell Max right now, wished in fact that he'd said so yesterday morning. If Max and Tate would have him, he was utterly prepared to step into that role.

"*Clay!*"

He heard the voice, frantic and filled with pain.

"*Clay!*"

He turned, halfway to the front porch, and met Tate's eyes across the dirt and scrabble of the front yard. She stood next to Kathleen, who'd wrapped an arm around Tate's shoulders, helping to keep her on her feet.

"I love you."

Willing away the tears that stung the back of his eyes, Clay briefly put his hand over his heart before turning back toward the house. If he tried to speak now, he'd probably lose it.

Then Kim called to him again, urgently, Beall's voice ringing along with hers.

Clay ignored them both.

He'd just taken another step toward that front door when it blew off its hinges and splintered toward him.

CHAPTER TWENTY-SIX

NO.

Every cell in Clay's body screamed the protest, reacting to the shock. The house had freakin'... blown up.

"No." This time he managed to mutter it aloud, despite the fact that something sat like an anvil atop his chest. Blocked the sun from his face. Prevented air from reaching his lungs.

He lifted one arm in a feeble bid for freedom, but pain propelled through it like a rocket. *"Shit."*

"Clay!"

The voice rang familiar, frantic and female. What sounded like boards clattered, followed by the peal of sirens and the whoosh of water. Around him, fire cackled and roared. He wondered how close he was to the flames.

"I think he's over here!"

Kim. That was definitely Kim.

"I need a hand with this!"

More clattering, then light speared his eyes. Until a cloud of black smoke roiled to obscure the sun, its acrid scent falling like dirty rain.

"Oh, thank God." Kim's worried frown hovered. She touched his cheek, brought her fingers away bloody. He wondered if she knew that her face was smudged. "Just hang on a minute, Clay, and we'll get this off of you."

With the admission of daylight, Clay could see that he'd been pinned by a chunk of door. The door that had been connected to the house. The house that had just blown up.

With Max in it.

"On three…"

Clay cried out as the heavy piece of wood was lifted, oxygen filling his lungs in a painful rush. Two men he didn't recognize carried the door off to the side, and tears flooded his eyes as he attempted to lever himself onto his good arm. "*Max.*"

"Shh," Kim cajoled, closing in, easing him down. Concerned blue eyes darted over him, visibly widening at the sight of his arm. "Don't try to move yet. Max is fine."

Yeah, right. Like he was going to believe that. Kim was just trying to pacify him to keep him from moving – as if he cared if he'd broken a few bones. "Don't lie to me, dammit." And heaving his weight, pushed her off. "Where's Tate?" Jesus God, he had to see her. "*Tate!*"

"Is he okay?" he heard her voice, wrecked from grief, but he couldn't see her. Then Kim moved back, calling for an EMT, and there she was, dropping to her knees. "Oh Clay. Your arm." She visibly paled, touched his cheek. "I thought you were dead." And her sob was pitiful. "You just… flew into the air…"

Unable to speak, she leaned over, tears dripping onto his cheeks to mingle with his own. "I'm sorry," he whispered, lips a hair's breadth from her ear. "I'm so, so sorry. God, Tate. I… I loved him, too."

Leaning back, Tate blinked at him, and unbelievably, started to smile. It dawned slow at first, hesitant, but burst forth into a blinding grin. "Max is fine," she echoed Kim's earlier declaration. "Well, maybe not fine, but he will be. In all the panic and chaos, I forgot that you couldn't have…" She shook her head, and pointed toward a nearby ambulance. "He's drugged, still, and we're getting ready to head to the hospital. But his vital signs are all good. He'll be sick, some, they said, but he's alive, Clay. He's…" she lifted her shoulders and then relaxed them in a heartfelt sigh. "Alive."

The rush of emotion was like nothing he'd ever known. Relief. Awe. Love…

Confusion.

"How –" he started, but then Kim appeared, medical technician in tow, two others following with a stretcher. The EMT knelt next to him, asking Tate if she could please move back.

"Casey Rodriguez," she explained, reluctantly leaving his side. "She was in the house. She went through the bathroom window and climbed out onto the porch roof, carrying Max. One of the snipers saw her, and radioed that they were out. That's what your friend Kim was trying to tell you. Casey jumped, holding onto Max, and, I think, twisted her ankle, but she managed to get clear of the house." She pushed her fingers to lips that trembled. "They're going to be okay."

"Sir," the EMT interrupted as Clay tried to sort through what Tate was saying. Casey Rodriguez had saved Max? What about

Walker? "We're going to need to get you into an ambulance," the man continued his professional buzzing in Clay's ear. "Your arm's busted up pretty good."

Yeah, Clay was beginning to get that picture.

"Can he ride in the ambulance with Max?" Tate wanted to know, watching the proceedings with anxious eyes.

"That's not standard procedure." The man braced Clay's neck, stabilized his arm so that they could lift him onto the stretcher. Clay felt little right now, but knew the shock would wear off and it was going to hurt like a bitch.

"Please," he said, grabbing the man's arm with his good hand. "He's... mine."

The EMT blew out a breath, glanced at the nods from his colleagues. "Okay. But anybody asks, we went by the book."

THE IV Clay was hooked to contained some pretty awesome drugs.

He was feeling no pain, that was for sure, as Tate ran her fingers through his hair while they waited for the EMTs to wrap things up. He groggily looked over at Max, noticed Tate's other hand clutching her son's. Other than a few scrapes, bruises and a good bit of dirt, the boy didn't look too worse for wear. There was the drug to worry about, of course, but if his respiration was good...

It could have been so much worse.

Frowning, he glanced toward the open ambulance doors.

"Do you see Kim anywhere out there?" He wanted to know if they'd found any sign of Walker.

"Um..." Tate shifted beside him, straining her neck so that she could see around the doors. "She's over by that van. Do you want me to go get her?"

"If you wouldn't mind. Once they get me into surgery, it will be a while before I can talk to her."

After dropping a kiss onto both his and Max's cheeks, Tate reluctantly climbed out from beside them. "Be right back."

Clay closed his eyes, feeling his body float, as if the laws of gravity could hold him no longer. And though the sensation wasn't entirely unpleasant, he wanted to stay alert until he spoke with Kim.

The click of the doors closing startled Clay's eyes open, and then one of the EMTs climbed into the driver's seat. He engaged the ignition, threw the gearshift into drive, and started to pull away.

"Hey," Clay called, thankful that the man hadn't turned on the siren, because otherwise he probably couldn't have heard him. "Could you hold off there, just a minute? We need to wait for our other passenger."

"Sorry pal," the EMT called back, "I've waited too long already." He laughed softly, and Clay craned his neck in the brace, trying to get a look at the man. He couldn't see more from his position than a glimpse of dark uniform and hat.

"Seriously." He tried to keep his words from slurring, because those awesome drugs worked pretty damn fast. "You need to wait for the child's mother. She's had a pretty rough day, and she really needs to be with her son."

The EMT ignored him as the crunch of dirt and gravel gave way to the smooth hum of the pavement. "Buddy," Clay said again, more forcefully. "Stop the ambulance. Now."

"Yeah, I don't think so, Agent Copeland."

Fear rushed, icy cold, and just like that, he knew.

Jonathan Walker was driving the ambulance.

The relentless son of a bitch. The explosion must have been a distraction…

Clay fumbled around as unobtrusively as possible, slipping the IV needle from the back of his hand with a decided lack of finesse. He had to stop the steady flow of narcotic into his veins or he'd be out cold in a matter of minutes. Fighting to keep his breathing even, his fogged brain from slipping into panic, Clay scanned the interior of the ambulance for a readily available weapon. It probably should have galled him that he wasn't even considering reasoning with the man, but he wanted Walker dead as quickly as possible, and to hell with any repercussions.

His eyes lit on the various medical paraphernalia: stethoscopes, IV tubing and bags, blood pressure cuffs. Maybe he could get something around the guy's neck, strangle him, except that his dominant arm was totally useless.

"Whatever you're thinking about attempting," Walker went on, his voice decidedly friendly. It was easy to be happy-go-lucky, after all, when the situation was utterly in your control. And it was definitely in Walker's control, alright, because discombobulated as Clay was, there was no mistaking the man's gun. "I'd advise you against it. I don't want to hurt the boy, Agent, but I can't seem to feel the same compunction about you."

Fury erupted, hot and bright, but Clay fought it under control. If he miscalculated and got himself killed, then Max would be alone with this monster. He figured he had maybe five minutes before Kim and the others figured out what had happened. But five minutes was more than enough time for Walker to shoot them both.

Except that he didn't want to hurt Max.

Clay seized that comment with both hands, trying to remember to think like a professional. His initial instinct to say Walker sure as hell had a funny way of showing it wasn't likely to win him any points. Nor could he point out the fact that taking Max away from his mother was definitely hurting him, because a stable family life wasn't something Walker could relate to. He needed to open the man's emotional and psychological baggage, unfold the subconscious reasons he wanted to take Max. If he could throw him off his game, shake his confidence, just a little, he might be able to distract him enough to gain control of the gun.

"You want to use him to recreate what you had with Donald Logan."

The hand holding the gun wavered slightly, but Walker laughed, a short burst of irritation.

Clay pressed the advantage. "He was the only one who ever offered you caring of any sort, and you were bereft when he was sent to prison. However unhealthy your relationship, you miss that feeling of intimacy, of belonging to someone or something. That's why you went to all the trouble to get Max. You want to experience that feeling again. Only this time you'd be in control."

"Well congratulations, *Doctor* Copeland." The hostility underlying the amusement in his voice suggested Clay was right on target. "You've clearly been doing your homework. But you can spare us both the head-shrinking bullshit because you obviously don't know *shit.*"

Okay. Direct hit. Clay looked around again, weighing each object's value as a weapon. If he just landed one solid blow on the wrist he could loosen Walker's grip on the gun. But one blow was all that he was going to get, so he had to make sure it counted.

"I know that Logan molested you. You were physically and emotionally vulnerable, and he convinced you that what he was doing to you was love. But it wasn't love, Jonathan. He violated you, plain and simple."

The gun crashing down on his broken arm ripped a scream of pain from Clay's throat. Even the drug coursing through him couldn't dull the full impact of the blow. Ambulance swerving wildly, Walker's breathing ragged intakes of fury, he hissed at Clay before using both hands to regain control of the vehicle.

"You stupid sonofabitch. I was going to shoot you before I sent the ambulance in, but now I think I'll let you drown. It'll be slower and a lot more painful."

The meaning behind Walker's words sank in just as the vehicle pulled off the pavement. He stopped the ambulance, threw the gearshift into park, and Clay knew that he had to act fast. Struggling to release the straps holding him as Walker opened the driver's side door, he figured the man was probably looking for a stick he could lodge between the seat and the gas pedal. And sure enough, Clay heard him thrashing around outside just as he managed to get out of the restraints. He swung his unsteady legs to the side, finally managed to locate a weapon. Reaching over Max, pulling it out of its compartment, Clay fumbled to do what he needed to with his left hand before lying back down on his stretcher. Walker would shoot him in a heartbeat if he had any idea that Clay was mobile.

So when Walker came back to the vehicle, messed around with the gas pedal until Clay heard it revving, he lay perfectly still and pretended to be the next thing to catatonic.

Walker crawled into the back, and Clay could sense him looking at him, no doubt assessing to make certain he was out.

But the bastard hit his arm again, just for good measure.

It took everything Clay had not to react.

Grunting in apparent satisfaction, the man turned away and began to remove the restraints holding Max. He obviously planned on taking him with him.

Clay didn't waste any time. He reached beside him, pulled the portable defibrillator from where he'd stashed it, ignored the screaming agony in his arm and delivered what he hoped were a billion volts.

Walker yelled hoarsely, his body jumping with the shock, and fell backwards almost on top of Clay. The gun he'd been holding clattered to the metal floor beneath Max's stretcher.

Pushing the stunned man aside, Clay scrambled toward the weapon, pitching forward when Walker landed heavily against his back. They went down hard, knocking into Max's stretcher, which tilted but held onto Max. Luckily Walker hadn't managed to undo the straps before Clay hit him.

Clay's left hand snaked toward the weapon as his kidney seemed to explode from a short-armed punch. Gasping, he threw his left elbow back until it connected with Walker's ribcage. Shifting his weight to his right forearm, he felt the snapped bone poke through his skin, and gritted his teeth against the liquid rush of pain that threatened to pull him under. Gray dots swimming at the edges of his vision, he groped blindly along the floor for the gun, stretching his abused fingers until he felt the familiar shape. He'd just managed to wrap his hand around it when Walker's right arm formed a noose around his neck.

Max, Clay could only think as his vision blurred, his head pounded. And feeling that rush of primal fear, slammed his head into Walker's nose. Blood spurted, thick and warm, but the chokehold didn't lessen. And when Walker fell backward toward the ambulance's front, he managed to drag Clay with him.

Twisting, striving to get the gun aimed, Clay's knee hit the gearshift and the ambulance started to roll. Somewhere in his adrenaline-fueled brain, he realized that was definitely not good. Using every bit of the strength he had left, Clay heaved his body until they were face to face. The gun went off in his hand just as the ambulance hit the pond.

Through the rush of dirty water came the still-distant wailing of sirens.

CHAPTER TWENTY-SEVEN

THE touch of soft lips on his cheek stirred Clay, and he was conscious of the purple bear being tucked into the crook of his good arm.

Again.

"*Max.*" Tate's voice softly scolded, although it was still too soon after their hellish ordeal for her to work up any real irritation with her son. Still, she'd told him several times to stay out of her room when Clay was sleeping, but the child usually weaseled his way up here whenever she turned her back. With the absence of guests at the usually busy inn, Clay guessed Max was a little bit bored.

Thank God.

Thank God he was here, safe and sound, enduring nothing more traumatic than a healthy case of childish doldrums, rather than blown to pieces, subjected to Walker's twisted sense of father/son bonding, or lying on the bottom of a cow pasture's pond.

All three outcomes had been so close…

"It's okay," Clay reassured Tate, waking enough to give Max a conspiratorial smile. Men folk had to stick together. He held his left hand out, palm up, and Max walloped him with a low five. Despite the fact that Clay was recuperating from complicated surgery to repair the compound fracture in his arm, not to mention almost drowning, Max didn't hold off on the heat. He grinned at Clay in a *what do you think about THEM apples* kind of way, and

Clay laughed his heartfelt approval. The kid was unbelievably adorable.

Then he shifted his gaze toward the end of the bed, where Tate was no doubt about to remonstrate Max for not being careful enough of Clay's condition.

Well, screw that.

He was tired of feeling like an invalid, and heartily sick of her treating him like spun glass. They hadn't had sex in over a week. His *arm* wasn't working, for God's sake. Not his...

The snarky look on her face told him that she had guessed what he was thinking.

He gave her his best *I'm innocent* grin.

From her answering *yeah, right* expression it was obvious she didn't believe him.

"Tonight," she promised softly as she hustled Max from the room, leaving Clay wondering not for the first time over how quickly they'd established that telepathy. "If you behave yourself now."

And he guessed he deserved that one. Yesterday, against doctor's orders (what did Justin know, anyway?) he'd been determined to take a real shower. Not that he hadn't enjoyed the sponge bath Tate had given him – in fact he'd enjoyed it a little *too* much – but a man needed a little independence. If he'd waited until today, when he was supposedly going to be steadier on his feet, he probably wouldn't have slipped and bruised his ass.

Tate's smirk – showing that once again, she knew where his thoughts had drifted – probably should have been offensive, but he was too damn happy with that bait she'd dangled in front of him to worry about a little thing like pride. He blasted her with a full eyebrow wiggle/hip thrust and she laughed as she closed the door behind her.

Dear God, he loved that woman.

Yep, he was happy as a damn clam.

Despite the fact that not everything had gone quite as planned.

Walker was still alive.

The bastard was in a coma, true, but he was still sucking up oxygen. And Clay suspected it wasn't very humanitarian of him to wish that wasn't the case. The bullet discharged from the weapon they'd struggled over hit Walker in the chest, doing extensive damage, but apparently not enough. What kind of tenacious asshole survives being shot at point blank range, anyway? In retrospect, maybe he should have left that gear shift alone and let the ambulance keep rolling into the pond. Of course, there was always the fact that he and Max might have drowned to consider. So yeah, he guessed he'd made the right move.

But Walker's continued presence on earth still grated. When he woke up – *if* he woke up – they'd all have to go through the misery of a trial. There was no question of the man being convicted; the evidence was too overwhelming – including the fact that he'd killed one of the Charleston PD snipers in order to get the man's rifle and fire off that igniting shot into the farmhouse. Then left the man lying mortally wounded while he stripped him bare for his uniform, so that he could blend in with the chaotic crowd.

Murder, attempted murder, kidnapping, racketeering, arson... the charges Walker faced were too numerous to list. If he ever regained consciousness, he'd face either the death penalty or a life in prison.

On second thought, given the way Clay suspected the man felt about prison, maybe things had worked out for the best after all.

Josh Harding was going to make it. He faced a long, hard recovery given the severity of his injuries, but at least the younger man was alive.

And Casey Rodriguez – Clay was so proud of her. Of her spirit in the face of what she'd endured. He'd stopped in to see her before he left the hospital the other day, and was humbled by her amazing resilience. She, also, would have a lengthy path to full physical recovery, and her emotional scars would probably last forever. No amount of therapy could ever fully make the memory of what happened to her go away. But with the right treatment, the right support, she'd learn to live with the scars and the memories. In fact, Clay had already seen to it that she'd have regular access to one of his colleagues. And to help ease her stay in the hospital, he'd gotten her that iPhone she'd wanted for her birthday.

He owed her so damn much.

He strongly suspected that Walker's initial plan was to blow up the house with both of the kids in it. When he'd spotted Casey and Max through the scope of the rifle, he'd probably resorted to plan B.

And Rogan was on the road to recovery. Like Clay he'd suffered a broken arm, and several other injuries to boot, not to mention the blow to his soul. Sympathetic to his plight, Kim had spent an inordinate amount of time "debriefing" Tate's cousin in his hospital room.

Yeah, like Clay was falling for that.

Who would have guessed his anal-retentive, freakishly neat friend would go for a pirate? But then Rogan was pretty damn anal about some things himself, so maybe there was something to the attraction.

And speaking of attraction...

He smiled as Tate came back into the room.

She was looking incredibly lovely this morning, carrying a tray loaded with mouth-watering breakfast items, wearing her cute little shorty pajamas and casually mussed hair.

He could stand waking up to that every day.

For the next fifty or so years.

"Hi."

Tate smiled at Clay's expression, giving him a warm hello with her eyes. He still looked a little battered, a little less than robust, but his appetite seemed to be coming back. Of course it probably wasn't the food he was eyeing so hungrily. She set the tray on the nightstand and sat down.

"Sorry about Max waking you up again. I'm afraid he's a little bit... restless."

Clay wiped his *I want to have sex* expression off his face and took her hand into his good one.

"It's going to be tough for him, for a little while, to adjust to all that's going on. Even though he doesn't remember anything, he knows something happened, and that it was bad. Telling him truthfully about some of the dangers he faced was the right decision to make."

Tate had agonized over that one. When he'd awakened in the hospital, Max had so many questions, that she didn't know how to answer. How do you tell a little boy that there really are monsters in the world? But Clay had encouraged her to be mostly honest. It would give Max a greater sense of well-being if he understood a basic outline of what happened. The truth usually wasn't quite as fear-inspiring as what could fester in the imagination.

And given his own injuries, and those of both Clay and Rogan, it had been impossible to keep him from the truth. When she'd connected what happened to him with the girl who'd gone missing from the carnival, it had allowed him a degree of understanding. And when she'd told him how very, very hard Kathleen and Clay and the others had worked to find him, it helped restore his sense of security. There might be monsters in the world, but there were good guys who helped put the monsters away.

One of the only things Tate hadn't told him was about the "old lady" who'd stayed at the Inn. He couldn't remember anything about that, thank God, and she wasn't about to tell him. This was his home, after all. She didn't want him to feel it wasn't safe.

But she couldn't help feeling that way herself.

It was the reason the inn remained closed.

"I know you don't want to hear this, but he'll heal faster the quicker things seem normal." Clay stroked her fingers. "Have you given any more thought to what you're going to do? When you might reopen?"

Tate sighed, feeling utterly defeated. She and her mother had gone over this last night. Maggie, horrified by what happened, by what they'd inadvertently brought into their home, was ready to shut the inn's doors. But there was no way she could afford to keep the house without the income, and it had been in her family for generations. Tate could move out, find an apartment somewhere, but it would be difficult to make ends meet while shelling out rent. It was pretty much a lose/lose situation.

"I don't know what we're going to do," she admitted. "Neither Mom nor I feel comfortable with the current arrangement, given what almost happened. It's either sell out or move out, and frankly, neither option holds appeal."

Clay knew that money was an issue. By living here together, sharing the income from the inn, they were both in a fairly comfortable position. But if Tate had to move out…

"How about the carriage house?" he inquired, referring to the old structure behind the inn's garden. It had once been used, not surprisingly, to house carriages, and later functioned as a store-all and garage. It was roomy enough to hold three cars, and boasted an attic of sorts with stairs, but lacked plumbing and all but the most rudimentary electrical wiring.

"It's a nice thought," she said wistfully, "but it would take an unbelievable amount of work to make it livable. Unfortunately, I don't have that sort of cash lying around, nor am I given to carpentry."

"How much do you think it would take," Clay asked, "to make it workable?"

Tate shrugged her shoulders in a futile gesture. "I honestly don't know. Probably at least a hundred thousand."

Clay did a few rapid calculations. The real estate market around the DC area had taken a hit recently, but he'd purchased his house several years ago, and had accrued a tidy little bit of equity. If he sold out, his cash profit would probably just about cover it. Maybe even allow for a little bit of room. This close to the water, he'd want a boat.

"What if I told you I was good for it?"

Tate blinked, and looked at him in confusion. "You mean, like a loan?" She shook her head before he could even answer. "That's awfully generous of you, Clay, but..." She gave a short burst of surprised laughter. "There are enough complications to our relationship already without adding financial obligations to the mix."

"Are you sure?" he asked, toying with her fingers, enjoying the anticipation of the moment. He should have been pee-in-his-pants nervous, but maybe it was the drugs or an undiscovered brain tumor or something because he was feeling totally jazzed. He'd given this thing a lot of consideration over the past few days, and was completely at ease with his decision. "Because, I was thinking that we could work out a really creative reimbursement plan. Like you could marry me and give me more children. I mean, Max is great, but he could probably stand a brother or a sister. Help keep him in line."

Her hand jerked beneath his. The faint blush which tinted her cheeks disappeared. And she looked at him with such a wide-eyed gape, that he realized he should have been nervous. What the hell would he do if she said no?

No way was he going to let her say no.

He regrouped, and changed his tactic. Maybe the casual, dropping-the-bomb-as-a-joke approach was not the way to go. Tate was a romantic. Okay. He could do romantic.

He levered himself off his pillow, stifling his unromantic urge to shout out an obscenity over the stab of pain, and swung his legs over the edge of the bed.

"What are you doing?" Tate demanded, finally finding her voice. "Get back in bed!"

"No." He shook her off, because he was going to do this right. He probably could have made a better impression dressed in something other than pink – yes, he'd mixed his whites with his colors – boxers, but hell, he'd just have to work with what he had.

He lowered himself to one knee.

"Tate." He took her hand, kissed her palm as his gaze never wavered. "You are everything I've ever needed, and never knew that I was missing. And Max is the son I never realized I already had. When I look at you – at both of you – I see my life stretching out before me. And it's filled with happiness, and love, and a sense of… accomplishment and contentment that I never even knew existed. You're goodness and light and beauty." He remembered thinking that the first time they'd made love. "And if you'll have me, I'll love and treasure you and our family for the rest of my days. Marry me?"

And Tate thought she was speechless before. She hadn't been prepared, hadn't known how to respond to that half-joking proposal out of nowhere. But this…

The look in Clay's eyes took her breath away.

And she saw her future, there, too.

"Your work?" It was a question that needed answering. She wasn't sure what he was offering, or sacrificing.

Clay held her penetrating look with his own. "I can't give it up entirely, sugar. It's… what I do, and I'm not ready, yet, to stop."

"I didn't mean –"

He held up a hand. "Let me finish. However, there is no way that I would have asked you to share your life with me if I felt that mine would be going along as it had before. I've made some inquiries, and there's a position that could be made available to me at the local RA, as a profiling coordinator. I'd still work consults when invited, but primarily I'd function as a bridge between local law enforcement and the resources at Quantico. I'd run a lot of workshops, that sort of thing. There'd be some travel involved, but not a lot. Bottom line, I'd be home most nights. And I want to be home. With you."

"But that Agent in charge, Beall. You hate him. Are you sure you want to work with him?"

Clay huffed out an abrupt laugh, feeling that flutter of nerves again. "Are you *trying* to talk me out of this, sugar? Beall's an ass, but it's not something I can't handle. And there's talk that he'll be rotating up and out fairly soon." He gave her a dry look. "Any more points you want to needle to death before you answer the most important question I've ever asked in my life?"

Tate laughed, then let the tears fall that she'd been holding. "I just wanted to be sure," she admitted, "that you knew what you were saying. You just had a near death experience, you know. And you're on pain meds."

Clay smiled, lopsidedly, because he thought those were good tears. Happy tears. He damn near cried himself.

"Is that a yes?"

"Yes." She launched herself toward him.

"Easy there," he smiled over the zinging in his arm, and the steady pounding of his swollen heart. "No killing the groom-to-be before the wedding."

"Oh no, I'm sorry." Tate laughed and tried to pull away, suddenly conscious of his injury, but he held her tight against him. Even one-armed, his grip was like steel. He was solid and steady and perfect.

And he was hers.

For the rest of their lives.

"I love you, you know." She pressed her lips against his neck. "Pink boxers and all."

"Smart ass." Clay laughed softly, and pressed his own lips into her hair.

By his way of thinking, he figured he had a good forty or fifty years to get even.

Thanks for reading! Connect with me online at:

http://www.lisaclarkoneill.com/

Facebook:https://www.facebook.com/pages/Lisa-Clark-ONeill-Novelist/287773574604107

Twitter: https://twitter.com/LisaClarkONeill

And here's a sneak peek at DECEPTION, book three in the series, featuring forensic artist Josh Harding...

CHAPTER ONE

SAMANTHA Martin pulled her car over on the side of Highway 17 for the sole purpose of throwing up. And once she'd communed with the scraggly weeds and scattered litter and a strip of rubber from an eighteen wheeler's blowout, she felt... no better at all.

She absolutely, positively could not believe that she was doing this.

She, who loathed the idea of being valued solely on the basis of her physical attributes – of any woman being judged by the way she filled out her shirt – was going to take off her clothes in order to turn a profit. She was actually going to strip – as in naked – and somebody was going to pay her good money to do so.

Well... technically she wouldn't be naked. She'd eventually wind up in pasties and a G-string. With little pink sequins decorating her crotch. And tassels hanging off her nipples.

"Oh, God." Upchuck, take two. And after she'd seen the very, very last of the chocolate milkshake she'd mistakenly assumed would calm her stomach, she still didn't feel any better. Clutching her middle, Sam stumbled around the front of her car. Right at that moment another car blew by, and wouldn't you know it? It was filled with teenage boys. The heat from their exhaust stirred the air, fluttering the edges of her trench coat. The old London Fog concealed the worst of her get-up, but the go-go boots were decidedly visible. The bright red wig was an eye-catcher, too.

Sure enough, as she made her way weakly to the door, the geniuses in the souped-up GTO hit the brakes. And if that didn't qualify as a sure-fire way to ensure they didn't make it to their respective twenty-first birthdays, she wasn't really certain what did. What were the idiots thinking? That the next car that came barreling up behind them was going to automatically stop for their stupidity?

Luckily for their parents' sakes, the driver had the wherewithal to steer his teen dream machine over to the berm.

Unluckily for Sam, they decided to roll down the windows.

"Hey baby!" The front passenger hanged himself out the window. Scrawny arms dangled from a ratty wife-beater, but Sam knew that scrawny didn't always equal weak. "Why don't you come on over here a minute and we'll have ourselves a little party."

How to resist the temptation? She should simply ignore the little turds, but letting men get away with bad behavior was a practice she'd abandoned long ago.

"I'm guessing *little* is the operative word," she called over her shoulder as she yanked on her door handle. But the darn thing stuck and she couldn't get it to budge. From behind her she heard a burst of sophomoric laughter, followed by a barked order to "shut up!" She wasn't sure whether the kid was talking to her or to his friends, and really didn't give a damn either way.

Pulling on the handle and swearing under her breath, Sam almost didn't hear his approach. But the scent of Obsession for men drifted in on the night breeze like a bad department store fog, and she rolled her eyes with impatience. She didn't have time for this shit.

She turned and – no big surprise – the kid walked toward her, backlit from his friend's brake lights, cupping himself in some kind of challenge. It was difficult to distinguish his features as he had a camouflage boonie hat pulled low over his head, but his swagger practically radiated testosterone-charged contention, a walking billboard of up-to-no-good. As he moved even closer she caught the unmistakable scent of booze. Great. This kid was probably sixteen, seventeen at the outside, and walking along the dark highway half-cocked. If the Halfwit of the Month Club was looking for October's poster child, they needed to search no further.

"Look, son." Yeah, he didn't like her calling him that, but she wasn't in the mood to placate his fragile ego. "I understand that at your age your social acceptability is directly proportional to your ability to exercise poor judgment, but I'm telling you right now that you need to turn around and walk away. I'm running late, I'm cranky, and this is a very busy highway. If you're not careful someone acting even more irresponsibly than you are is going to come along and run over your ass. So do us both a favor and pretend you have some sense."

Junior laughed, as she'd feared he would, and swaggered even closer. Sam squeezed her eyes shut briefly, wondering why she seemed to draw assholes like flies to sticky paper. Maybe there was a jerk-magnet buried under her skin. "Why don't you put that mouth to better use, sweet thing, and then we'll see who you're calling little. I got money." He reached into the back pocket of his baggy jeans. "Ten bucks should cover it."

What the... was he serious? Just because she was wearing a trench coat and go-go boots the little punk had the right to assume? "Okay, kiddo." She barely resisted the urge to slap him. "I'm going to offer you a piece of advice. You and your friends need to go home and sober up before you do something truly stupid."

He reached out and grabbed for her breast. "The only stupid thing I'm looking to do tonight is you."

Sam's hand snapped out so fast that the kid had no idea what hit him. Blood spurted – the heel of her palm had connected pretty solidly with his nose – as he stumbled back with a shriek. His bloodshot eyes registered surprise even as they went watery from the force of the impact. Before that surprise could morph into humiliation and anger – a dangerous combination in a teenaged male – Sam had her hand on her cell phone.

She held it up so the kid could make an informed decision as to what he should do next. "Unless you'd like to explain to your parents how you ended up in jail, drunk off your ass, booked on charges for underage drinking and attempted assault, I suggest you think twice about attempting to touch me. I don't take lightly to unsolicited groping, and here's a hint – no means no. Always. No exceptions. Now unless you'd like me to have a chat with the 911 operator who's standing by, you need to turn around and get out of my sight."

Using the edge of his shirt to mop the blood which still trickled from his nose, the kid glared and weighed the options. Sam swallowed the bitter taste of fear – there were three other boys in that car, and no amount of self-defense training would even those odds – but another car passed by, slowing to survey the scene, and thankfully Junior had the smarts to check his pride in favor of avoiding a trip to the pokey.

"Bitch," he hissed, stooping to retrieve the hat which had been knocked from his head when she hit him.

"Sticks and stones, pal."

As he stalked off toward his friends, Sam's breath whooshed out in a rush, legs trembling beneath her coat. No matter how many times she'd been in that kind of situation, it never got any easier.

But she hadn't let him see her fear.

Watching the kid climb into the car amid the cackling laughter of his friends, she hoped he'd at least learned a lesson. "Hell," she said out loud, as the GTO peeled away. "I could seriously use a drink." And because the thought of a drink reminded her that she was supposed to have been at Murphy's Pub as of – she glanced at her watch – ten minutes ago, Sam turned toward her car and gave another violent tug on the handle. The stupid thing decided to cooperate, and she yanked the door open in frustration.

Settling her long legs, which with the addition of the three-inch platforms on the boots had become ridiculously unwieldy, into the cramped area between the bucket seat and the gas pedal, Sam wrapped her arms around the steering wheel and leaned her head down with a shaky sigh. The vomiting and then the fun little tango with that shining example of teenage stupidity had played havoc with her already frazzled nerves.

Lifting her head, she flipped down her visor so that she could check her makeup in the little lighted mirror. Most of the war paint was still in place, but she'd worn off all of her lipstick. Pulling a tube of Kiss-Me Red from the cup-holder between the seats, she hastily performed a repair job.

Although really, she might as well not have bothered. No one ever looked at her face.

Without the multiple layers of make-up and the shockingly red wig, her face wasn't much to speak of. Plain hazel eyes surrounded by stubby lashes topped off a button nose and nondescript lips. Her cheeks were too full, her face too round, and though she was spared the ignominy of freckles, her features were so aw-shucks bland and uninteresting that she could only be described as average. She'd heard cute a few times, and more often, wholesome.

Which was why it was some kind of great, cosmic joke that that face was attached to her body. Because her body was blatant sin.

Double-D breasts, a narrow waist and legs that seemed to go on forever. True, her hips might show the evidence of a few too many candy bars here lately, but there was no question that overall Sam was built like one of Hugh Hefner's wet dreams.

Trying not to resent the fact that she was going to have to use that body in a way that made her sick, Sam put the key in the ignition of her ancient Ford, and listened as the engine turned over.

How the hell she was going to take off her clothes in front of a room full of men, she honestly had no idea.